7

My God is a
Woman

My God is a Woman

Noor Zaheer

Vitasta Publishing Pvt. Ltd.
New Delhi

Published by
Renu Kaul Verma for
Vitasta Publishing Pvt. Ltd.
2/15 Ansari Road, Daryaganj,
New Delhi - 110 002

ISBN 81-89766-52-X

Typeset by Vitasta Publishing Pvt. Ltd.
Printed at Saurabh Printers Pvt. Ltd., New Delhi
Cover design by Prabha Singh

To

Ammi
in gratitude
for bringing me up human

Preface

This book has been written exactly twenty-one years after the introduction of the Bill for the Protection of Muslim Women. More than two decades after the Supreme Court's historic verdict upholding the high court's judgment of granting maintenance to a Muslim woman, Shah Bano. The manner in which the decision of the apex judicial body had been quashed had provoked many progressive women to question various organizations concerned with women. The answer they received had been the same—it is up to the Muslims to make any changes in their laws. Twenty-one years we have waited for an initiative from a democratic set up, which professes equality for all its citizens, towards giving a section of women the right to live with dignity. Had it been taken, this book would have become unnecessary. As the noose of the fundamentalists tightens, the target remain constant—the woman. It is time to shake off lethargy and complacency. It is time to fight back. It is time to speak and call a spade a spade because that is what it is.

As a journalist, in the early nineties, I had held three long discussions with Danial Latifi, Shah Bano's lawyer. These discussions surpassed the parameters of the newspaper interviews they were meant to be and led me towards studying the religious law for women and those existing in the constitutions of the major democratic states. In a way, these discussions have formed the background for this book.

For the facts about the Shah Bano case and the quotes in the interlude, I gratefully acknowledge the help drawn from the book *Shah Bano* by Janak Raj Jai. It is perhaps the most precise documentation of the proceeding of the case and its aftermath. A word of thanks is due to Aastha Sharma for the pain she took in editing the book and the patience she maintained during my spells of possessive zeal for each word.

I am grateful to Renu Kaul Verma, Managing Director, Vitasta Publishing Pvt. Ltd., for deciding to publish the book after reading the first two chapters but more so for standing by me whenever I had cold feet about the subject and for persuading me to give her the completed version in spite of the way freedom of speech and writing have been sidelined in the recent times.

Noor Zaheer

ONE

It was a long and arduous journey. A journey from the scorching Thar Desert to the lush greenery of the Gangetic plains. Safia had not been able to sleep the whole night. Who could, wearing eleven *seers* of brocades and jewellery? The First Class carriage was adorned with flowers and shimmers, inviting curious glances at every station. Safia was considered born with a silver spoon, getting married into a family that boasted of two Knights, five Khan Bahadurs and nine Barristers. Her own husband was a Barrister and his father a judge in the Oudh High Court. He had been recently knighted by the British Government. This combination was enough to raise many eyebrows as her father was a mere Inspector of schools. The excitement and the joy the proposal brought with it had been infectious, so that even Safia, who should have been downcast, went round correcting anyone who cared to listen that it was 'bar-ris-ter' and not 'ballishter' as the rural Muslims pronounced it.

She had been confined to purdah from the age of nine when she had committed the crime of writing a short story for *Ghuncha* a magazine for children. The editor had published the story and had also written a note of encouragement. This was enough for her grandfather to order purdah because she was receiving letters from unknown men.

The train journey was the second one in her short life of seventeen years. For the first time she was enjoying the tremors of the unknown world, the world of the rich. She stole a glance at her husband. He already had one book published which had generated a lot of controversy. The book was not mentioned in respectable Muslim households and she had learnt about it quite by chance.

Her father Syed Murtuza Mehdi had been discussing the proposal with Mirza Ashfaque Barni, his long time friend and confidante. Mirza *Saheb* was treated as one of the family and Safia was allowed to serve him tea. Carrying a loaded tray, Safia heard Mirza *Saheb*'s loud exclamation at the mention of Abbas Jafri's name. She quickly stepped behind the curtain to hear the rest.

"You are planning to give our daughter to Abbas Jafri? That infidel, that heathen! The man who has written *Fireworks*! Don't you know that book is not allowed in any respectable Muslim household? The *Dar-ul-ulum* is appealing to the Crown that it should be banned." Safia gripped the tray tight, willing the crockery not to make a tinkle, her body taut, waiting for her father's reply which took rather long in coming.

"You don't know my Safia. She is mature and sensible. More than that, her knowledge and understanding of the Holy Scriptures is perfect. She shall bring him back to God's true faith." Safia's eyes misted at the confidence shown by her father. "After all, the Holy Book says that it is the duty of every good Muslim to reclaim the lost souls and bring them back to the true faith—Islam. I am sure my daughter will be able to do just that."

The argument was solid; it quoted the Holy Book and reminded one of their Islamic duties. Mirza *Saheb* kept quiet. Safia heaved a sigh and stepped out. Putting down the tray, she addressed a low *salaam* to Mirza *Saheb* and poured the tea, diplomatically reminding herself to put four spoons of sugar in his cup. Gathering his blessings and catching her father's eye, she turned to leave, just as Mirza *Saheb* began his advice: "It would still be a good idea to fix a high *meher*, say around fifty thousand *asharfis*. Just in case."

Syed Murtuza Mehdi apparently agreed with this and when the bridegroom's family came to finalize the contract of marriage, and he was politely asked to name the amount for the *meher*, as was the custom, he put forward his request. All hell broke lose in the *Deewankhana* of the Islamia College guesthouse where the guest were staying. Without saying it in so many words, the elder brother of the bridegroom and the leader of the delegation reminded him that he was asking for something which was far beyond his own status. Not to be cowed down, Syed Mehdi got up saying that the boy's family was at a liberty to give it some thought but there would be no bargaining or settlement regarding the same from his side.

"Please sit down Syed *Saheb*. Sons in our family do not divorce their wives. Women are respected and honoured in clans like ours.

However, since you have expressed a doubt, it is only honourable that we set your apprehensions to rest. Your proposal for the *meher* is accepted and will be formally agreed upon at the time of *nikaah* and to be paid at the time of *talaaq*."

The cold metallic voice sent a chill down Mehdi *Saheb*'s spine. "Our mother, Lady Zeenat Jafri," said the bridegroom's brother. Mehdi *Saheb* stood up to *salaam* the green satin curtain. "I am sorry; I did not know that you too had come all the way from Lucknow."

"You didn't think that I would leave such an important settlement to a mere boy." The voice held a studied sneer and the boy it referred to was a strapping thirty-five. The chill in Mehdi *Saheb*'s spine dropped to a sub-zero and for the first time, he wondered if he was doing the right thing in marrying his only daughter into this family. A whiff of saffron and ground cardamoms brought him back from his thoughts. A beautiful hand with one *aqueek* and three diamond rings was waving a dish of choicest *kalakand* under his nose. "Now if you are satisfied and all fears have been allayed, please sweeten your mouth." The speed of events left Mehdi *Saheb* nonplussed. The rest of his questions about the boy's religious inclinations were forgotten. He nervously popped a piece of the sweet meat and mumbled his thanks, blessings and begged for forgiveness in the same breath.

The train rumbled into the Sandila station and Safia peeped out lifting the heavy brocade *dupatta*, bordered with a six-inch *champa kiran*. Her father often came to Sandila on inspection and would take back earthen pots full of the famed *laddoos* of this town. How she loved the small mud pots tied at the neck with a piece of red cloth, like a group of Arabs who had decided to let their hair down. The *laddoos* laden with *kewra* and the fragrance of damp earth just melted in the mouth. God! She was hungry. Last night she had been too frightened to eat anything of the sumptuous dinner provided by her maternal uncles. She might as well have eaten, because her husband stayed away from her. He did not even speak to her.

Safia watched him get up and suddenly the spacious first class coupe turned into a suffocating six by six cell. Tall, frightening and silent. Heart in mouth, she watched him step down on the platform, with visions of his being left on the station as the train moved away clouding her mind. What would be her fate then? She'd be left like the heroine of Asghari Memon's novel *The Lost Bride*!

The train let out a sharp whistle giving Safia such a start that she screamed. Her husband entered the coupe, balancing two cups of tea and a pot of *laddoos*.

"Why did you scream? In any case, it was too mild a sound to get you anywhere. If you have to draw attention scream like this—"yaaaaaaaa". Safia jumped out of her skin. "Eat. In another half an hour we will be in Lucknow and you shall have to put on the act of the shy bride. Isn't all that very heavy?" He pointed at the heavy dress and jewels.

"Eleven *seers*," Safia mumbled. She restrained from adding that the weight had fallen short of half a seer creating a hullabaloo amongst the women. Luckily, her paternal aunt had arrived in time to add a silver *jhanjhar* of the right weight. Each piece was weighed and handed over to one of the happily married women—the *suhagan*—specially pressed into service for dressing the bride, while a woman good at addition jotted down the weight in a register and kept adding up. All this could very well have been done the day before the wedding. But then what would happen to the chaos, yelling and screaming, the accusations and the vulgar jokes that constituted such an important part of the Indian wedding?

Safia's *mamujan*, who was a rich zamindar, had ordered a Swiss alarm clock for his favourite niece. This alarm clock had become the centre of attention, drawing exclamations of wonder and surprise from everyone. All hell broke lose when the clock went missing. Safia's mother promptly squatted herself on the floor and started howling—something which she was accustomed of in such situations of crisis. Feverish search began overturning all the neatly packed trousseau trunks, even rolling up the white sheets and carpet but it yielded no result. The volume of the howling increased as more contributors decided to join in, when suddenly the sharp whirring of the alarm was heard above all the brouhaha. The howling stopped in mid-blast and all eyes of the gathering roved to focus on the seat of a middle-aged aunt. She too had been howling and had the quick wit to turn it into a giggle. "Now how could this have got inside my pyjamas? I must have sat on it."

Remembering the incident, Safia smiled to herself.

"Good. I was beginning to think you were one of the moron kinds." Abbas smiled, his serious and determined face lighting up.

Safia jerked up as if she had been hit. She a moron? She was the joke store of the family. "What do you mean? I am a matric with a second division and no moron can achieve that."

"God! A matriculate with spunk! This is getting better and better." He was laughing at her. Safia subsided, marvelling at the way his light brown eyes threw green sparks before vanishing into slits as his smile progressed to laughter. "Eat, you didn't have dinner."

So he had noticed. Safia glanced at him gratefully, gobbling four *laddoos* one after another.

Poor child! He was still angry with his elder sister and brother-in-law for leaving them alone in the coupe, smirking on the joys of the first night. With any luck, this girl would not understand any of their vulgar jokes. What did they think—that he would want to perform in the train with a girl twelve years his junior? Disgusting! He shook open the morning papers he had bought at the station. "Good God!" His exclamation was superimposed with "*Hai Allah*". Abbas jerked his head up and caught Safia staring at the headlines. 'Ali brothers under house arrest,' screamed the black print.

"So you are aware of the Ali brothers and the Khilafat Movement?" Safia's heart turned cold. She should not be talking about the freedom struggle. After all, he had been educated in England and who wants a Miss Know-It-All for a wife.

"No, just heard about the Ali brothers," she stammered.

"Then you should catch up. The Nationalist Movements are not something that we can just hear about anymore. They are a part of our lives. Why are you so nervous? Awareness is not punishable, it is ignorance which is a crime." Then as if it suddenly dawned on him, "You read English?"

"Well I am a matric...."

"With a high second division, how could I forget." Seeing her face, he burst out laughing and she joined him in the sheer joy of having made him laugh.

"Our first laugh together," he murmured. "Look you can see the minarets of the Charbagh Station from here. They are laid out like a chessboard. It took six years to build and cost twenty-two lakh. It covers an area of more than forty acres." He said all this with pride, for Lucknow, its living culture, its grand buildings, its musical alleys and homogeneity of Hindu-Shia culture. This Lucknow was to be Safia's home from today.

A High Court judge's daughter-in-law has to be received in proper style. A uniformed band struck the notes of 'Here comes the bride' as the train crawled into the platform. By a special contraption of planks and bamboo poles, the family Dodge that had replaced the traditional *palki* was standing near the door of the railway carriage. Hidden inside the safety of three red sheets, Safia was bundled into the rear seat of the car. She was gathering her extra eleven *seers* when her ears caught a whispered altercation.

"But you can't do this? You cannot stop here and leave her alone. This is preposterous." It was her elder sister-in-law Sajida, who was ten years Abbas' senior and the second in command in the family.

Abbas' reply was mild but firm. "So many people have come to receive us, is it polite to leave without saying a word of thanks? I will speak to Safia." The door opened, "Safia I am sorry, I have to meet all my friends who have come to receive us. Would you like to go ahead or would you rather wait?"

"Wait," she mumbled from behind the heavy red and gold veil.

Abbas returned after an hour amidst calls of "See you at Safdar Manzil!"

"As if this was not enough, you had to invite everyone home," Sajida grumbled.

As the car wove its way through the crowded station area, Safia yearned to get a glimpse of Lucknow, but the heavy velvet curtains of the window were tightly drawn and Safia was left to her own imagination to interpret the sounds and allocate them to the venues. The car gave a loud honk and swerved, its wheels crunching on rough gravel.

"We have just entered the main gate of Safdar Manzil. From here it is another half a mile to the house." Sajida's proud voice was recounting the years it had taken to build Safdar Manzil, the money spent on laying the gardens, the fountains and the five feet high seat of the main building so that damp from the nearby Gomti river would not seep into the walls. If she had intended to make Safia nervous, she had succeeded.

"You shall manage," whispered Abbas and Safia smiled as the car came to a stop.

Abbas unwound himself carefully, letting out his full six feet two inches. Amidst the sounds of the *Tasha*, several women lined themselves holding long sheets to form a corridor from the car to the main entrance.

"We won't need this Bubu."

Zeenat Begum who was bending towards the car to welcome the new daughter-in-law stopped as if stung.

"What is that you said Abbas?"

"I said we won't need this purdah."

"But I thought a *burqa* would be too cumbersome."

"That won't be needed either."

Zeenat Begum straightened up. "What do you mean?"

"I mean Safia is going to give up purdah from today."

"Shameless boy, parading the woman you own like a nautch girl." Begum Zeenat had lost her cool.

"I don't own Safia. She is my life partner and has to act like one."

Safia was reciting the '*Sura-e-yasin*'. She had been taught to do this every time she was afraid and dear God was she afraid! These blue-blooded mother and son. The more their arguments heated up, the icier became their tones.

Begum Zeenat smiled. "Your wife has been brought up in the finest Syed Muslim traditions. She shall never agree to give up her religion and her God."

"I have always believed that every individual is entitled to freedom. Given the choice and a little support, no woman in her right mind would want to wear the *burqa*."

"Ask her then. Ask her if she would give up her honour, her shame and follow you." There was a smugness of righteous assurance in Zeenat Begum's voice.

"Alright. Safia listen, this is your world. How do you hope to survive in it without its recognition? Come down, you are a woman and that is nothing to be ashamed of."

That face, as her eyes raked it, did not have a drop of arrogance or pride. The light brown eyes were forthright with a quiet faith in his belief.

It was a moment of negation, of all that had been systematically inculcated in her. It was a moment of shame. Shame as has been defined for women by men for centuries. It was also a moment of decision, to remain with yesterday or reach out towards the tomorrow. Holding her fourteen-yard *kalidar gharara*, Safia stepped out, feeling strangely naked in-spite of the mounds of brocades enveloping her. It was also a moment that sealed her bond with Abbas.

Keeping her head down, she moved towards the twenty alabaster steps when she suddenly jerked back in fright and would have fallen if Abbas had not caught her elbow in time.

"Don't be frightened, it is only a lotus." Laughed the hefty grey haired man. "This is a blue lotus. Its original habitat is China but it has been successfully cultivated in our Sikander Bagh Botanical Gardens. Be to our son what a lotus is to a shimmering lake." It was the first moment that marked the beginning of a long friendship with her father-in-law, Justice Sir Safdar Ali Jafri.

It was also the moment that marked the beginning of an unending cold war with Zeenat Begum.

* * * * *

TWO

"Safia could you please go down and see what has happened to the evening tea." Abbas was pouring over the dummy of new Marxist Party's mouthpiece. Safia smiled to herself. She had still not got used to the formal 'please' and 'thank you' of her husband every time he addressed her. In the beginning, she had thought it was a mere put on. But then she noticed that everyone in Lucknow spoke with a formality that sounded almost cynical. While formality was dropped as acquaintance developed into friendship, politeness would stay on like the lingering fragrance of the Akbar Ali Mohammad Ali's *attar*. No Lucknowite worth his salt would be caught without either of them.

For the last six days, Abbas had confined himself to his room, pouring over the galleys of the articles that would go into the first edition of the Urdu weekly tabloid *Kaumi Morcha*. These six days had opened a gateway to the fascinating world of journalism and publishing for Safia. She had shown a knack for proof reading and Abbas had gratefully passed on that work to her. As she read and argued over the Quit India Movement and the call given by Mahatma Gandhi to give up government jobs, Abbas observed with profound pleasure that she argued with logic and reason rather than with tears and tantrums. Seven years in England had taught him to respect the English woman's self-possessed attitude. He analysed that it had come after years of hard labour, grooming and self-discipline. It did not mean a lack of emotions, rather disciplined emotions and a strong belief that vulgar display of one's feelings not only meant lack of control, but it often gave the opponent—usually male in most cases—an upper hand. When he compared what the women from his kind of households achieved through tears and quarrels with what the women in the west had accomplished by sheer grit, he felt ashamed and strangely humiliated. As if in a way, he was responsible. But then if he considered himself to be a part of this society, he had to shoulder that responsibility to some extent. It was the men after all who had taught women to treat themselves as a non-entity. Confronted with reason, men always placate logic with jewellery, questions with clothes and their wish for some private space for mental growth with the kitchen and trowel full of children. He had seen the look of yearning in Safia's eyes as she had looked longingly at the bookshelves of his personal library. He did not miss the way her eyes shone with delight when he told her to read whatever she wanted. The innocent joy had made him curse his society. He could not imagine one of the girls at Oxford waiting for permission to read a book. What did the society achieve by carefully cultivating imbeciles, who could think of nothing beyond personal comfort, who measured happiness with the number of dishes on the dinner tables, pride themselves by the number of sons they produced and possessions by the gold buried under their bed? Whose brains received exercise in the form of petty connivances woven to trap women, as helpless as themselves, whose hearts swelled with victory in seeing them squirm? It was like the silly game of 'pass it on without return' played by Anglo-Indian boys in the English medium school he attended for two years to prepare for Oxford.

The purebred Indians regarded the half-breds with superficial disdain, secretly admiring their muscular bodies, their open frankness and total disregard for their future. The Anglo-Indians, who were sure of a secured job in the railways and nothing beyond, hated the purebreds who managed to make it to foreign universities and went on to join the Indian Civil Services. One way of expressing their hatred was through this game. A half-bred would give a stinging slap on the back of the purebred yelling 'pass it on without return.' Afraid of the passionate unity exhibited by their opponents, the purebreds would not dare to defy their orders and ended up slapping each other, pretending to enjoy the game while the Anglos hooted with laughter.

The Indian woman was in a similar position. Humiliation, abuse and torture was heaped on her. Silently, not even daring to question the right of her tormentors, she accepted this treatment, carefully collecting and chronologically cataloguing each one of them, waiting tirelessly to hand them over as family heirlooms to the women of the next generation. Each generation tortured the next, who bided their time, waiting for the pleasure of torturing their successor. This arrangement had gone on comfortably for centuries.

Abbas glanced at Safia who was correcting a galley, a deep frown furrowing her broad forehead. She was not reading aloud which meant that she did not understand what she read. He had come to understand that whenever Safia read something that she did not fully comprehend, she became silent. Otherwise, reading was a noisy affair with Safia which reminded him of the Qur'an lessons, where maintaining a steady rumble with sudden highs was the only way to keep *Maulvi Saheb* awake. Would Safia have the guts to stand by him? Or would she rather flow with the stream to its undefined but familiar end.

"What was that you said?" Safia looked up.

"Please see what has happened to our tea."

Safia got up from the *divan* and walked down. The family got together for the three meals at the eighteen feet long teak wood dining table, but evening tea was served in separate trays in each room. This was mainly to provide a peaceful evening to Justice Jafri who did not come home for the mid-day meal and enjoyed a quiet cup before leaving for a game of bridge at the Gymkhana in the evening.

Justice *Saheb* was sitting on a swing chair sipping the strong Darjeeling brew, specially prepared for him, while his wife filled him with the day's events. Safia hesitated at the door. Zeenat Begum stopped in mid-sentence and raised an inquiring brow.

"Come in child, what do you want?" Safia blushed at the warmth in her father-in-law's voice.

"I came for the tea."

"Then say so. What are you gaping at? The tray is ready on the sideboard. Take it and go," said Zeenat Begum brusquely.

Picking up the tray, stung by the curt dismissal she added apologetically, "Has something happened to Vaseem?" She had become particularly fond of the adolescent boy who was the odd job hand for the family.

"Why? Is the tray very heavy?" Her mother-in-law asked sarcastically.

"No harm in the girl's asking, is there?" Justice *Saheb*'s parting shot as he left to change for the club did not thaw the coldness in his wife's eyes.

Turning towards the door, Safia added as an explanation, "It's just that he asked and….."

"Who Abbi? Why didn't you say so? Tell him there is a famine in Bengal."

Upstairs, Abbas was reclining on an easy chair; his feet propped on a stool, a lap pillow balanced on his knee, tilting the sheaf of papers to eye level. "Oh good, tea at last." He thrust away the papers. "Why did you have to carry it up?"

Safia smiled to herself. For all his socialist beliefs, Abbas disdained any kind of physical labour and took pride in the pink softness of his hands.

"I have just finished reading *Discovery of India* and Pandit Jawaharlal Nehru thinks that anyone who doesn't work has no rights on the benefits. I am simply earning my keep."

Discovery of India was one of the first three books Abbas had presented her and the first one she had read in her new house. Discussions on each chapter had consolidated the bond of friendship between the seventeen-year-old girl and the twenty eight-year-old scholar. As Safia slowly absorbed the difference between the written, the said and the meant, Abbas saw that her mind was like a bubbling cauldron of molasses. The scum had to be frothed every now and then under stable heat and constant fuelling so that it does not solidify before clarity was attained and also does not turn sour due to over boiling.

"I am glad you have understood the book well enough to absorb it in your life."

"I would say I have superficially understood the book, but there are still so many concepts that go over my head, just like so many things in this house."

"Like what?" Abbas sipped the warm liquid.

"Well, I asked Bubu what happened to Vaseem and she said there was a famine in Bengal. But Vaseem is from Gonda, so how does a famine in Bengal……What is the matter, what have I done, where are you going…..? Listen…….," Safia watched in horror at the spilt tea and the pieces of the expensive china Abbas had just knocked down. Her arm instinctively covered her head in a sudden surge of fear expecting his anger to break over her. However, few seconds later, she heard him taking two steps at a time. Realizing that she was not the target of his anger but was still somehow related, she ran after him, her heart thudding an ominous outcome.

Begum Zeenat looked up from the betel leaf she was preparing. It was one chore she did not leave to the servants. Preparing a betel leaf required delicacy; a slightly heavy hand in applying the varied bouquets and the betel leaf would be ruined. The large silver *paandaan* weighing four kilograms with twenty-two small pots and cavities was one of her pride possessions. She opened it twice a day to prepare paans for the day, laid them on the bed of damp *khas* and covered the dish with a shining *ganga jamni* dome.

Abbas was her youngest and best-looking offspring. Like all women, she had a weakness for good-looking men. Added to the fact that this man was her product, Begum Zeenat softened like a cake of soap left in the sun, every time Abbas came to her. The rigid regime of her household always developed some loopholes to meet any demand of his. That he knew no corruption and had lived a celibate life corroborated her value as producer.

When his turn had come for going to England, Begum Zeenat had in her anxiety called the *Imam* of Juma Masjid who had proclaimed that if Abbas swore to something he would stick to it. Pleased with this public acceptance of the value of her son's word, she had called Abbas and in *Imam Saheb*'s presence asked him to swear not to touch pork, wine or woman in England. Abbas had very innocently asked, "Then why go to England?" The *Imam* had left proclaiming that Abbas was Satan in an excellent disguise. Zeenat Begum had seen his honesty and had decided to keep her religion and his conscience in two very separate compartments. To date she had never let one judge the other. Seeing his expression, she had a foreboding that this might be the day when she might not be able to keep things so tidily segregated.

"Why are you doing this Bubu?" It was a straight question and Begum Zeenat had, over the years, learnt that straight questions are best countered by straight answers.

"If I don't, somebody else will."

"That is not the point. This is a crime."

"I have a house to run. Your elder sister's daughter is to be married. Your Baba retires in less than two years."

"And *bade bhaiyya* has become tired of his wife and has been wasting a lot of money in '*Dal ki Mandi*' on Jigaran Bai."

"Keep quiet! How dare you talk like this about your elders?"

"I will not stand by and see you purchasing girls little more than children for a few rupees."

"What will you do?" It was an open challenge. A challenge to his lack of income, the fastidious demands of his soft body, the new burden of a wife and more than that the safety of a judge's house, which protected him from being arrested in the numerous demonstrations and public meetings he organized and attended.

Yes, the house was a shield. In the recent months, it had also become a claustrophobic demon, throttling the being it was supposed to protect. He was never arrested while his comrades spent months in jail for participating in non-violent picketing. The fact made him ashamed and his friends wary. The depths of doubts increased everyday. He knew that the rigours of prison would be hard on his body. Yet his heart yearned for the sharp hit of the baton that rained on fellow demonstrators but stopped in mid-air for him. This could be the day that might iron out these differences and make him an equal among his fellow *satyagrahis*. Abbas turned and walked out quickly, almost colliding with Safia who was standing behind the door.

"Don't eavesdrop. It shows your lack of courage to openly ask and checks your right to know," said Abbas shortly.

A week had gone by since this incident. Other servants, the cook, the *khansama*, the old man who dusted and cleaned, and the woman who helped the ladies of the house in their toilet and dressing had all been slowly done away with. Safia helped in the kitchen, that was now manned only by the chef who claimed to be French, cooked only for Justice *Saheb* and walked out every time something Indian was cooked, claiming that his sensitive nostrils could not stand the strong odours of Indian tempering. The quality of food remained the same because Begum Zeenat was an ordinary cook and a miserly administrator. Coldness remained between the mother and son but for all practical purposes, the incident had been put to rest.

One afternoon, Safia came down to find her mother-in-law interviewing a dirty middle aged man, dressed in pyjamas not quite reaching his ankles, a colour that must have been blue once but now hovered between dirty grey and slimy green and a short kurta. His unkempt beard with no mustache proclaimed him a religious man and the green checkered neck scarf was a sign of being part of the many undefined layers of clergy.

In the corner were half a dozen emaciated girls, dressed in what was supposed to be a sari but acted more like a loincloth. What arrested Safia's attention, were the dead eyes of the girls, the total lack of expression which spoke not of subjugation, hunger or pain, but just of nothingness. The man strutted about like a fighter cock whose cumbersome feathers had been plucked to give him more agility. He pulled each girl from the bunch while Zeenat Begum examined each one with the eyes of an experienced buyer.

Safia decided to go upstairs and stay there until whatever was happening downstairs was over. She met Abbas coming out of their room.

"Do you cook? I mean cook independently without help?"

"Of course. Why?"

"We have to leave."

"Leave? For where?" The question reverberated in the empty room. Abbas had walked inside the dressing room and was digging out his khadi kurta pyjamas from the huge piles of silks and satins. Seeing the situation getting out of hand, Safia stood before the dressing table blocking his exit. "What is going on? You must explain things to me."

Probably the fear of the unknown, resonating in her voice communicated itself to Abbas who stopped his excavation and turned.

"Do you know what is Bubu doing? She is buying some slaves." The cold tone of his voice did not match the stark pain in his eyes. The pain made Safia yearn to hold his head to her breast.

"I am terribly suffocated here. Don't you think we should leave?" Doubt at one's own decision and the desire for confirmation and support.

"At once. Bring down the trunk from the loft and we will begin packing." Practical as always, Safia was turning towards the shelves when two hands gripped her shoulders and she turned, a question forming on her lips to meet the warm golden glow of the green brown eyes.

"Abbas?" Justice *Saheb* cleared his throat—an indication to his daughter-in-law to cover her head. "I understand and I have a solution. Leave this house but don't leave the premises."

"I don't understand Baba."

"I know you don't. I also know your financial position. You think you can run a household on the twenty rupees that a Marxist Party whole timer gets."

"So I swallow this degradation of humanity?" Abbas rummaged in his shirt pocket for a cigarette. He never smoked in his father's presence. Just holding it would sooth his strained nerves.

"No. You move to the outhouse," came the calm reply.

"The outhouse!" All of Abbas' sensibilities were outraged at the mere suggestion of inhabiting the damp, ill-planned hovels, which alternatively became the shelter for poor relatives, buffaloes, goats and the servants whose marriages Bubu connived to get the work of two for the salary of one.

"I don't think it is a bad proposition," Safia interposed hurriedly. "The rooms are not bad at all and we shall be able to move immediately."

"But the damp and the smell of the cow urine." Abbas turned up his aristocratic nose. Safia hid her smile. It was a people's war and Abbas was proud to be one of its soldiers but it had to be fought from long dinner tables covered with Venetian lace, laden with the choicest dishes of the best meat, served in Dresden china and Czech cut glass.

"What about furnishing it?" Abbas' first practical utterance gave Justice *Saheb* an opportunity to elaborate on his suggestion.

"Exactly. So much easier to move chairs and beds from here. You can even eat here. I mean at festivals and family get-togethers," he added lamely.

Packing progressed and Justice *Saheb* himself selected each piece and supervised its shifting. News spread that Abbas *bhai* was leaving Safdar Manzil. Friends, relatives and spectators converged to the palatial house, some to get juicy titbits and others to howl and curse the cycle of fate.

The small outhouse had very little flat space and now with so many people, there was hardly any room to stand. To the sweaty heat of the month of May was added the stench of decaying wood and cow dung. Flabbergasted by the crowd and their umpteen questions, Safia was at her wits end trying to locate the beginning of the Herculean task before her—of making this place habitable.

Help came from an unexpected quarter when Irfan entering the main room, gauged the situation in a glance and declared that those with strong arms should accompany him to fill buckets of water at the solitary tap while the rest should arm themselves with brooms and brushes to wash the house. The crowd was reduced in size as a moulded jelly loses its shape under a hot blast. Soon there were just six of them left and Irfan organized them into going to the bazaar for bottles of acid, phenyl and lumps of camphor. The rest were dry sweeping the house before the water arrived. Smiling proudly at his handiwork, he fished out a crumpled packet of Charminar cigarettes from his pocket.

Irfan—the vagabond who was not allowed into the inner chambers of respectable households; a poet with a promising future who had been banned from All India Radio because he had had the audacity of reading one of his banned poems in a live programme; who was regularly hunted down in the disreputable quarters of the city, usually sleeping off a hangover in the bedroom of one of the well-known nautch girls and who laughingly admitted that in spite of all this, there were still takers of his poetry in the cultural capital of the country. Irfan, Safia's senior by eight years but who had attached himself to her like an adolescent brother. Irfan who had lost his heart somewhere in the Aligarh University and instead of rueing his loss had now decided to write with his head. The unreliable, characterless, crass, insolent Irfan had become the most reliable member of her household.

"Why are you smiling? I would have thought you would be too tired," Abbas asked Safia. "I myself could do with some rest."

"Oh yes, I know how wonderful it is to rest after having done nothing," teased Safia.

"Especially with a cup of tea in hand. However, why the smile? I am still curious."

"I was thinking of this as my household, my establishment with Irfan and other friends as members of this family."

The smile vanished from Abbas' lips, his serious eyes gazed deep into hers, reaching the depth of her soul. "We have to do it. This house from today shall be centre of all writing movements and nationalist activities and anyone making even the smallest contribution shall have a home here. In your heart is the resonance of my emotions. We two are together, the rest shall follow."

That night many mats were laid on the floor of the main hall of the outhouse. The air was heavy with the smoke of incense, cigarettes and the fragrance of the kebabs from the well-known Tunde Wala and Kashmiri tea. As many as fifty writers and poets came with small gifts, ranging from a kerchief full of Jasmine flowers to an incomplete porcelain dinner set being sold for a few rupees by an impoverished Nawab. None of the family came to see how they settled down in the hovel that was to be their home. The impromptu *mushaira* lasted until midnight and the small lamps of the outhouse continued to burn even hours after the chandeliers of Safdar Manzil had been turned off.

Three girls were bought that day. Two for rupees seventy each and the third, because she was fair, with long black hair and almond shaped eyes, came for a hundred. The debate over the price had been long drawn, beginning at four hundred for three and slowly working itself down to two hundred and forty. Begum Zeenat congratulated herself on the bargain. She had expected to shelve out at least three hundred. The girls who stood for three lingering hours while their fate was being decided were taken for purification. God knows what they had eaten on the way and if they really were Muslims or were simply trying to pass themselves as one to get into respectable households. The *Maulana* pocketed the money, begged for a pair of kurta pyjama which was firmly refused. Instead was given half a seer of polished rice, with a stiff reminder that this generosity was being shown to him because he was a holy man. He was asked to have dinner, which he quickly refused seeing the gooey brown rice and the dirty green watery dal being served to the girls. He calculated that he had made more than two hundred per cent profit in the transaction and was impatient to get on his clanky bicycle and share his good luck with his two wives and five children.

The girls, in the meanwhile, had fallen on the leftovers served in chipped enamel plates, had thrown up, their stomachs revolting to solid food after weeks of starvation or because most of the food was well on its way to rotting. They were then made to wash up the filth they had vomited and given three gunny bags to sleep on. Such was the misery that the outside glitter hid.

As Begum Zeenat often pointed out, she had to do one to get the other. She was fond of reciting the ballad of a girl from a rich and generous family who was married into a rich but miserly clan. One day, the girl saw a fly fall into the tin of butter. Her mother-in-law took out the fly, squeezing it out before throwing away the carcass. The girl was disgusted at this miserliness. Next day she feigned a severe headache, claiming that a balm of ground pearls was the only cure. The mother-in-law quickly opened her box of jewels and taking a fistful of pearls picked up the mortar to grind them. The girl caught her hand and asked for an explanation for yesterday's act and today's extravagance. The mother-in-law laughed and explained that had she not squeezed flies all her life, she would not have had the pearls to grind at the end of it.

That night, before going to bed, Begum Zeenat calculated that if the girls stayed for even four years, she would manage to save more than six thousand on the servants' salaries and keep. Training them would of course be hard work. So would making them wear respectable clothes instead of the round, knee high saris, as if they were expecting to wade through a paddy field. Usually these Bengali girls created more trouble getting used to the *salwars* and *churidar* pyjamas than to the horrible conditions they were kept in. The freedom of a round sari worn without a petticoat or a blouse was difficult to give up. But one could not have them parading semi-nude in a respectable household. Often the obstinacy of the girls had to be dealt with long periods of 'all work, no food, and frequent beatings'. Hunger, Begum *Sahib* had learnt, with a few beatings thrown in would sublimate even the toughest ones. She opened her cupboard and put her hand behind the pile of clothes. Allah! The neem cane had become stiff. It was now time to open the store, oil the stick and soak it in water. A woman's work is never done. Well, what has to be done, has to be done. What use is a dry cane? It has neither flexibility nor strength. She would also have to give them new names. The one with big eyes and fair skin would be called Ladli.

Oiling and soaking the neem stick was the last thing done at Safdar Manzil. Abbas' arrest was the first thing that happened next morning at the outhouse.

* * * * *

THREE

Dinner at Sheldon Palace was always a sumptuous affair. Lord Sheldon was one Englishman who openly served the Oudh cuisine in porcelain crockery accompanied by excellent wines. He was a bachelor, yet banquets at his house were intricately planned down to the fashionable style of folding the serviette. Governors were not yet at the mercy of the politicians and once appointed, they stayed put until ready to pack up and leave for the good old English countryside. In the first year of his appointment, a good four decades back, Lord Sheldon had bought a large piece of land, at the cost of the British *Sarkar*, at a safe distance from the river Gomti, but with a panoramic view of the lush banks, sprinkled with dense green clusters of mango and guava groves. The palace that had come up was a tribute to the Lucknowi—not to be confused with Moghal—architecture and the superb use of space of the British. A team of scavengers set out at regular intervals, returning with invaluable pieces of artifacts bought in *Nakkhas* where impoverished Nawabs discreetly disposed of their household goods to eat two square meals a day. Rarest *kandiels* and chandeliers of Belgian glass came to adorn the ceiling of Sheldon Palace, where the owner did not have the same qualms as an Indian would have about scavenging on a down and out Nawab.

It was at Lord Sheldon's insistence that Sir Safdar Ali Jafri had moved permanent residence from the centre of the town to Safdar Manzil, built like a pleasure countryseat by his grandfather Nisar Hasan Jafri. The Lord himself had designed the garden fondly called the *chaman* in reverence to the Chaman near Kabul. Muslims, whatever their origin, continued to build associations with the other side of the Hindukush. Lord Sheldon believed that the Indian habit of flattening down any piece of land before growing anything was agrarian and can never make a beautiful garden for the natural beauty is lost. He had left the *chaman* with uneven slopes and mounds. So beautiful was the effect from monsoon to spring that even Lord Sheldon could not help envying it. The proximity of residence allowed for quick get-togethers and the two could often be seen in one buggy, trotting towards the upper class quarters of '*Dal ki Mandi*', where famed courtesans preserved the legacy of ancient musical *gharanas*.

However, where was Sir Jafri today? The large walnut table that could seat thirty-two was groaning under the weight of the succulent partridge and quail, the lord had himself shot in the Barabanki jungles that morning. The candle butts, lighted to keep the dishes deliciously warm were burning low. Discreetly, Lord Sheldon drew the heavy gold watch out of his pocket. Anyone who was anyone knew that the Governor dined at nine. It would never do to change the rules for a nigger—even if a knighted one. A few seconds to nine and a horse trotted to a stop, followed by an urgent whine of wheels coming to a halt. Sir Jafri jumped the steps two at a time, then steadied himself and entered the hall with dignity. Acknowledging his greetings, Lord Sheldon added, "So Indian Standard Time eh?"

Sir Safdar Jafri blushed to the tips of his ears. Some of the guest had been his clients in the practice days. "But I have a good cause."

"Oh really! Lady *Sahib* has thrown out the French chef again?"

The crowd tittered. Lady *Sahib*'s open war with the French chef, Sir Jafri insisted on employing, was a joke among the Lucknow upper circles. Sometimes the chef spent days without cooking, at others he had his mood swings and a vile temper. Lady *Sahib* could never understand his lack of output and the amount of salary he was being paid.

"No," the knight smiled. "I have a better reason. My eldest one has just returned from Jaipur with a casket of *Aasha*. I have brought it as a humble gift."

"Mellow an angry Englishman with wine." The Governor had once made a passing remark that had scorched itself in Jafri's mind.

"What are we waiting for then?" Lord Sheldon was all animated. "Let's get it warmed."

"Relax, it is warm. That is what took time. It has been transferred into earthen pitchers and covered with hay."

"Voila." If there is one thing the English language lacks, it is exclamations. A reflection of their character, trained never to show that they have lost control of their emotions. Those who have lived in the east and come to terms with the handicap, borrow shamelessly from across the channel. "Remove the table wines. Let's have *Aasha* all the way from stuffed quails to *shahi tukra*."

"I hope it will be enough," Sir Jafri added humbly.

"The bounties of friendship never run dry." An Urdu proverb spoken in an unfamiliar accent. Safdar Ali turned, with a look of enquiry at the audacity of the female who dared to interrupt a Lord and a Knight. Two whiskey brown eyes stared back at him. Was the smile in the eyes or the red lips that parted so seductively?

"This is Sylvia Robinson. She will sit with you." The introduction over, Lord Sheldon was ushering everyone to the dining hall.

"Sylvia," murmured Safari Ali. "It is my favourite flower."

"And...?"

"It likes shade, doesn't it?"

"Not a very heavy one and not all the time. But it does like a tree to be handy."

"To provide some shade?"

"To provide some care."

"She is in Lucknow to claim a legacy from her father's side. Does not stand a chance though. Her mother was of mixed blood and her father was a Eurasian. No definite proof of any English blood."

Sir Jafri was being handed all this information over cigar and brandy.

"Doesn't she know?"

"No harm in trying, is there?"

"Are you interested?"

Lord Sheldon grimaced. "Don't come so sudden. It is undignified and un-Lucknow like. Why can't you beat about the bush for a good half an hour like the rest of them? No, I am not interested. You know my taste. I go for the dusky classical ones. Take her for a walk to the Eucalyptus clump. The aroma of the trees helps digest the rich spices."

Lord Sheldon was grateful to Justice Jafri and it was not for the *Aasha*. It was for understanding that he, Lord Sheldon, was not the top boss and those who were, refused to understand why he arrested a bunch of slogan-shouting boys and let go of the main speaker. He knew that Sir Jafri loved his youngest son. Abbas' political activities were cause for an unspoken awkwardness between the two good friends. It must have been difficult coming to terms with the fact that his career and British goodwill towards him could only be saved by getting Abbas arrested. Yet, Sir Jafri saved his friend from the embarrassment of arresting his son from his house. Even though Sir Jafri would have understood this extreme step, decorum and society would have expected him to practice coldness towards his friend for having invaded the privacy of his home. The way in which he had used a stray incident that had presented itself in the form of three starving girls was not hidden from Lord Sheldon. He appreciated a man who could make use of opportunities but he admired one who could milk his problems. Abbas' political linkage was out of his house but he as a person was not far away. Lady *Sahib* had been placated without any direct interference in her administration. Abbas had been able to uphold his ideals but not forced into setting up house. Most importantly, their friendship was provided room to survive. While acknowledging his astuteness in successfully straightening a complex tangle, Sir Sheldon knew that one good turn deserves another. Maybe several. Sylvia was the beginning.

Down the Eucalyptus lined paths, Jafri discovered the warm feeling a man derives in talking to a well-informed and well-read woman. If the information she holds is about him, he is flattered. Talking to her gave him an opportunity to know of her knowledge regarding all the important cases he had defended or judged, the arguments he had given, the judgments passed, the acclaim that had come, the knighthood bestowed. Sylvia enjoyed talking and spoke Urdu with just a mild accent, like a dash of cloves adding that extra zing to an otherwise well cooked *Yakhni*. Sir Jafri tried to bring the conversation to the immediate problem of her reason for being in Lucknow, but she skillfully steered it away and he felt a surge of admiration. She was not seeking any favours from a judge of the Oudh High Court. A word from him would have carried weight.

"She is bright today, even though it is two days to a full one."

"A beautiful observation, but why 'she'? I thought the moon was a 'he' for Indians." A lovely smile, engaging without being inviting.

"Depends who addresses her." The dry Eucalyptus leaves rustled and something slithered over them. "Sounds like a snake, doesn't it?"

Sylvia raised an eyebrow. "If you are trying to frighten me, let me tell you that I am not English enough to be frightened of a snake and not Indian enough to feign fright. I am an Anglo-Indian and life has made me unafraid."

"Unafraid and frank—two unforgivable sins in a woman. In a moonlit night, when in the company of a beautiful woman, it is a sin not to drink from the goblet of her lips, because she expects it. So says Omar Khayyam."

"I don't remember reading that one." Her eyes twinkled and her lips became inviting.

"Oh this is the latest version of the old rascal. He gets naughtier with every new translation."

She kissed with her whole body and Sir Jafri knew with that first touch that he was hooked.

Lady *Sahib* had cultivated the style with care. She had studied, observed, thought and planned to develop the stance of apathy, the capacity of ignoring Justice Safdar Ali's waywardness. Between her and Justice *Saheb* was an unwritten deal. Do not bring another woman to the house and I shall not interfere with what you do outside it. In her heart, she treated the nautch girls of '*Dal ki Mandi*' as unavoidable. The money spent on them was always accounted separately and then discreetly divided under the other heads of expenses. However, in the recent months, the figure had become too big to be discreetly divisible. Lady *Sahib* had reason to react. For otherwise, didn't the prostitutes have to eat? But God forbid, did they have to bite into her share? It was time to make enquiries about this newcomer in Lucknow. There had to be a new one. Sir Jafri was not one to go bonkers over an old flame.

Lady *Sahib* never made direct enquiries. Her network of spies was so strong that a casual grumble about the way money was turning to water these days set the train of information into motion. What it brought back struck like a slap across her face. While singers and nautch girls were a necessary evil and to some extent showed a class, an Anglo-Indian keep was a discredit. A mixture, whose mother and hers before her had had no qualms about going to bed with a *firangi*! To think all this was happening at Sheldon Palace and the man had the cheek to send a basket of strawberries only the other day!! She should have judged by the lushness of the red fruits that something was amiss. Well, it was time to do something about it. She glanced down, the closed buggy was waiting in the portico. In spite of having acquired a Dodge almost six years back, Justice *Saheb* could not give up the romance of the traditional buggy for his evening gallivants. But why a closed one? It was the beginning of June and the evening air was hot and dry. So the coachman was right. The woman accompanies him to the banks of the Gomti. How shameless! Well, if he could break the rules of the game, she would follow suit.

Sir Jafri grimaced as Lady *Sahib* entered without knocking. Try as he might, he had not been able to teach her good manners. "*Vilayati teem-taam*" as she termed it, was not for her. How beautiful she was. Even at this age, she was more attractive than both her daughters put together. Beautiful and cold—steel cold that had driven Sir Jafri to hunt recklessly for warmth elsewhere. He straightened the black bow and glanced at her in the full-length of the Belgian mirror.

"I have no objection but she is proving too expensive."

Sir Jafri's hand unwittingly travelled to the left breast pocket where a turquoise and diamond pendant was nestling in its velvet bed. Lady *Sahib* smiled, "It is also becoming too open—in spite of the closed buggy."

"I shall retire in six months and will begin practice. There will be no shortage of money then."

"Provided you are permitted to practice. In the meantime, will it not be advisable for you to observe some restrain? In money and otherwise?"

The lines on Sir Jafri's forehead deepened. It was true. Just half a year left and no sign from the Imperial Government. Lord Sheldon had written three times, recommending that he be allowed to practice in Lucknow after retirement but there had been no reply. His future was as bleak as that of a peasant's after a flood. She was right—he had to be careful.

"Oh by the way, I bought this for you." Nimble fingers opened the velvet-lined box.

"Allah, how exquisite! However, you should not spend money like this. I can hardly be seen wearing new jewellery at my age."

"You can still do justice to it. I had better be going and I will not dine at home."

This was the seventh time in the month that he was dining out. Her fist closed over the trinket. It was a victory, a small one, but a victory nevertheless. She would fight on.

So deep were his thoughts that the coachman had to announce the arrival twice before he realized that the buggy had reached Sheldon Palace. Sylvia was waiting for him as always and came down the steps only to stop midway.

"What is the matter, has something happened?"

"Nothing that should concern you my dear."

"But everything about you concerns me. Let me guess. A tiff with Lady *Sahib*? No that would put you in a bad mood but not get you worried."

"You know me too well."

"Not well enough to know what is eating you. Tell me my love, maybe I can help."

"Hardly Sylvia."

"Still, two heads are better than one. Sometimes it helps to talk, clears the picture and a solution trickles out from where none seemed possible."

"It's nothing much really. I am not mentally ready to retire but officially, I am of age. I would like to practice again, but the Bar Council has appealed that as an advocate I would be able to influence the judges who have worked with me and justice would not be impartial."

"Well, they do have a point."

"Whose side are you?"

"Oh my dear knight, the case has not reached the stage where one is obliged to take sides. That you are really a judge through and through is proved by this question of yours."

"So I have to learn the law from you?"

"No. However, a judge is bound to the law and his approach is rigid. It is up to the lawyer to have a flexible approach and to show the judge the space available within those laws. You, my dear, are behaving like a rigid judge."

"And what exactly do you suggest I should do?"

"Provide the Government with an alternative."

"What do you mean?"

"Why can't you practice in Allahabad? It is a High Court. You have never worked there. It is not far from Lucknow and most importantly, Lady *Sahib* need not accompany you."

"Why of all the......How did I not think of this? So simple a solution. I would have been quite afraid of you, had you been a man, my dear."

"Well since you have been spared that worry, how would like me for an accomplice? I could even keep house for you."

* * * * *

FOUR

Lucknow was at its hottest and driest best. Scorching sun and blistering winds, a typical reminder of the month of June. However, the temperature in the heavily curtained Dodge was chilled. Not the fluid cold, that allows for freshness, but the damp chill of an unused mosque—frightening in its stillness and silence.

Begum Zeenat had refused to take Safia to meet Abbas at the Lucknow Central Jail. Justice Jafri had been equally firm.

"How can I? She doesn't wear a veil, the shameless hussy," fumed Begum Zeenat.

"Those are your son's orders, her lord and master, remember? You have always maintained that a woman must obey her master."

"Pah! You always say that Islam puts too many restrictions on the women."

Justice *Saheb* smiled. "Well, I am switching over to your side now. Like a devout Muslim, I think a woman should blindly do what her husband says. You have two alternatives now. Either switch to my earlier view so that we can maintain the status quo of having different opinions about everything under the sun or stick to your earlier beliefs and agree with me now."

"There is no use arguing with you."

"None," agreed Justice *Saheb* sympathetically.

"You had agreed never to interfere in household matters."

"You are the one who is interfering in matters which concern the court." Justice *Saheb*'s tone was considerably dry now. She knew the tone. She also knew she was fighting a losing battle. But perversely she continued, obsessed with her dominant role inside the house, drunk in her own power, like Kali trampling on everything till she bangs headlong into Shiva.

"What do you mean? How does this concern your precious court?"

"Well you asked permission for two and you have been granted it."

"I never did.... So that's the trick. She added her name on the sly."

"Shhh. Not so loud. I have tried to persuade you to learn reading and writing beyond the Holy Qur'an, but you insisted on remaining barely literate. See what happens."

Safia remembered the smarting in her eyes as she tried to fight back the tears of humiliation, writing the application her mother-in-law dictated. She was not even asked if she wanted to see her husband. She had carried the paper to her father-in-law's study and the solution had come so easily that she had gone into a fit of giggles.

"Not so much mirth, your husband is in jail, remember."

The driver went inside to announce Lady *Sahib*'s arrival and the jailer stepped out of his office to receive them. The long trek to the 'A' class cells, the acrid smell of carbolic acid and parchment paper, the smile on her caged man's lips and the high wails emitting from the black shuttlecock. She would have had no chance to talk to Abbas had it not been for the policeman who stopped the driver entering with his arms full of the *khas* mats, white bedsheets and dry sweet meats and snacks. Begum Zeenat had marched to the jailer's office demanding that her son, whose soft skin could not bear the scorching heat of the summer months, must be allowed the use of *khas* mats and special arrangements should be made that they are watered every hour. The respectful jailer had been equally firm that he would not discriminate between the prisoners. An intense argument followed, giving Safia precious minutes with Abbas. However, if Safia had been expecting a loving exchange, she was cured for good. Abbas knew about the meeting and had plans for her.

"Don't waste your time. Try to educate yourself. You have completed Intermediate, why don't you join the university and complete graduation."

"But how and where?"

"Baba shall be leaving Lucknow. Go with him."

"Will he agree?"

"He'll have to, once Bubu gets down to it."

Time flew by and Safia had no chance to counter Abbas. Nor did she really want to. It was enough for the moment that he was helping her formulate dreams that might never materialize. Nevertheless, just dreaming them sent waves of pleasure down to her toes. Soon, Begum Zeenat was back. She had been defeated and was loudly abusing the poor jailer for being Yazid in the guise of an Englishman. She looked Safia up and down and hissed, "Still here. Can't I have a minute alone with my boy?"

"Yes Safia, I have something important to discuss with Bubu."

As Safia backed out with a goodbye, she heard a curt instruction, "Don't stop in the waiting room, sit outside in the car." Her back bristling Safia turned back to smile at Abbas, trying to capture his face without the jail bars cutting across it.

Once alone with her son, Begum Zeenat searched his face trying to gauge which side he was. Abbas let her, waiting for her to draw her own conclusions. Getting no clue, she sighed and whispered, "Why my house?"

"Bubu you have to see this from Baba's point of view. You have never tried to be a partner, a support or even a beloved to him. He yearns for warmth and you have none to give."

"I am what I am. I couldn't have been any different."

"You did not even try. You refused to see any other person's point of view, his expectations, and his desires from life. You wanted to rule, to command. The house became your castle with you as its reigning queen and all of us your poor subjects."

"I only tried to keep everyone together."

"No. You only tried to subjugate us and ended up destroying the family. Had we been united, we would have been a force, but because of the mistrust you sowed amongst us, there is no real relationship between us. We are forever looking for motives in each other's actions. Baba is the first one to break away. The rest of us shall follow."

"She is a troubled soul, don't you think you should be kind to her?" said Abbas' manservant. Strange how the upper class, even those who subscribe to socialism believe that servants were deaf and dumb. Being an "A" class prisoner, Abbas was entitled to an attendant from the "C" class. An old, white haired Muslim, serving life sentence for killing his entire family to save them from dying of hunger, had been assigned to Abbas and had in the months become his shadow, literally, because he often did not register his presence. He had been present throughout the conversation, standing unobtrusively in one corner.

"She is your mother Syed *Saheb*," he continued. The matter-of-fact reminder of the relationship that existed between the woman and the man brought a strange reaction in Zeenat Begum—a flood of silent tears. Abbas who could never remember his mother crying, melting like a lump of salt in water. "Don't Bubu. Tell me why you have come to me. I am in jail. Of what use can I be to you? Why not speak to Wali *bhai* or Hyder *bhai* or to one of your sons-in-law?"

"They are family; you are my son and friend."

"I have an idea but I am afraid you will not agree to it."

"Anything, so long at it saves a scandal."

"Oh Bubu! Speak for yourself, why bring in social stigmas."

"Well if you want a humiliating admission, I cannot bear the thought of becoming the laughing stock of Lucknow."

"It is good to be honest."

"Remember you once told me that society is the integrated form of individuals."

Abbas guffawed. "This is just what I needed. To have Lenin thrown on my face in the meeting room of Lucknow Central Jail. So it is agreed, we shall take Safia's help."

"What's that? You want to degrade me to such an extent that I have to ask for your wife's help. Let my house burn, I shall never stoop so low."

"Bubu, you have got to understand," the urgency in Abbas' voice quietened Lady *Sahib*'s angry burst. "Baba does not want you in Allahabad. He has other plans. Most probably, he wants that woman to keep house for him. Don't try to keep up pretences. Lucknow is abuzz with rumors so thick that even jail walls cannot stop them. You cannot leave Lucknow and the Estate. You need Safia at this moment. Suggest to Baba that Safia should go with him. She is alone, she is educated and can take care of things."

"And what else can she do there?"

"Educate herself. She has completed her inter-mediate, now she can do her graduation and assist Baba. That way he can save some money."

Abbas got his way. Lady *Sahib* was astute enough to see the logic of his arguments. On the way back, her mind was already planning the next course of action. Sir Jafri would not quietly let her topple his plans. Her arguments had to be sound, logical and with a touch of concern for the poor child who had two years of waiting before her.

"But you are the one who disliked her so much. You wanted her out of the house. You couldn't tolerate her independent spirit."

"True, but all that when her husband was beside her. Today her husband is in jail. You and me, we have a duty towards her."

"Well bring her back to this house then."

"And insult my son. Even if I were to do it, she would still be wasting her time. Look, I am worried for you and for her. She wants to continue her education and join a proper university. Imagine the scandal here, especially with you and her husband absent from the scene. If she was in Allahabad, I would know that she was safe and you are well looked after. In Allahabad, who would dare to raise a finger against your will?"

The matter was left undecided. Safia was at tenterhooks, her heart yearning to begin organized education. It took two hours of a lonely wait at the makeshift bamboo gate of the outhouse to finalize the matter. The coachman had been nonplussed seeing the daughter-in-law of the house waving madly at him. As the buggy stopped, Safia walked behind to the dark cavity. "No Baba, no need to get down. I have only one thing to say. My presence in Allahabad will not hamper you in anyway and will considerably decrease the number of Bubu's visits. I shall never be a spy for her but I might be your much needed shield."

Unpacking Sir Jafri's glassware, Safia received her first lecture on crystal glass. Feigning confusion and lack of knowledge, Safia innocently asked him why they could not solicit the help of Sylvia Robinson. "I have never really conversed in English and if nothing else, her presence would improve my vocabulary."

Sir Jafri had gratefully accepted the reasoning and Sylvia's afternoon visits became a regular feature. The two women lunched together and then gossiped or read the classics. Sir Jafri returned around four and the three had tea together. Safia then retired to her room to catch up with her reading or writing long letters to her parents, friends and of course, to Abbas. She also wrote regularly to Bubu. In fact, she was so regular that it raised doubts. Little did she understand that her mundane regularity would vibrate Zeenat Begum's antennas?

"One is so regular in providing unnecessary information only when one has something to hide," was the first comment she made when she was alone with Safia.

"You are right," Safia had admitted with unexpected ease.

"Your letters give me no information about that woman."

"My responsibility is to look after Baba, not to spy for you."

Zeenat Begum clamped up. The ice between the two, which had just begun to thaw, froze and it was cold war again.

"What exactly are you trying to do?" Zeenat Begum looked up from the latest edition of *Dosheeza*, the women's monthly magazine catering to embroidery and stitching, to the corner of the courtyard where, Safia was unsuccessfully trying to maneuver the seat of the new bicycle under her buttocks.

"Trying to get up on the bicycle Bubu. But somehow I cannot synchronize the pedal, the seat and myself."

"And why pray are you trying to get on the bicycle?"

"I would have thought it was self explanatory. She wants to ride it," Justice *Saheb* intervened. "Now don't ask why she wants to ride it. Haven't you understood that your cross-stitch kind of questioning doesn't fluster the girl?"

Safia smiled gratefully at her father-in-law and looked down to see where the problem was. She found her *dupatta* entangled in the spokes of the back wheel, making the wobbly contraption completely static.

"By the way, I have asked Dr Zahida for tea this evening. She said she would be here at five. She is very punctual."

"Oh Baba, how kind of you. I had better go and change. What would she think of my grease covered clothes?"

"That you have been trying to clean a bicycle." In later years, Safia would get used to Zahida's way of entering unannounced and speaking out of turn.

"So this is Dr Zahida. Do sit down my dear." Lady *Sahib* was all sugar for the only daughter of Khan Bahadur Shohaib Ansari.

"I shall, after I have helped Safia release herself from the cycle. Now hold on to the bicycle while I rotate the wheel. Move when the wheel rotates silly. There, it is out now. Not much of a *dupatta* though. Looks more like a dish cloth to handle blackened *deghchis*."

"I am glad you have come. I so much wanted to meet you." Safia shyly eyed the robust, shorthaired woman, the first Muslim woman doctor, who wore her Leucoderma patches with nonchalance, even arrogance.

"Well you could have stepped up to the Civil Hospital. I am always there. You are not queasy about hospitals are you?"

"No, but how could I without a proper introduction?"

"Stand on ceremony and you shall be left standing." Ignoring Lady *Sahib*'s scandalized stare, Zahida brought out a packet of cheap cigarettes. "May I borrow your lighter, Justice *Saheb*?"

"Women should not smoke," Lady *Sahib* intervened determinedly.

"Oh come Lady *Sahib*, our miniature paintings are full of groups of women sharing a hookah."

"Well not in the presence of men and elders."

"Hypocrisy! By the way, Safia, I had come with a purpose. Not in a million years are you going to be able to ride a bicycle. I would like to have it for the party office. Comrades have to run errands for organizational work. The rickshaw is too expensive and walking too slow."

"But *Bibi*, isn't it our class that your party wants to destroy. Fancy taking help from us to build a classless society." Lady *Sahib* sniggered and looked Zahida straight in the eye.

"Oh never fear, Lady *Sahib*, we will take the bicycle for now. Later we shall have your head."

Sir Jafri guffawed and Safia joined in, while Zahida sat with her serious I-didn't-really-make-a-joke expression.

Later in Safia's room, Zahida coolly offered her a smoke. "You are a strong one, no coughing at the first drag. I almost collapsed the first time Razak made me smoke."

"How long is Razak *bhai* to remain underground?"

"Who knows? Till the British leave, I suppose."

"But that is a long way off." Safia could have bitten her tongue.

"That is why one needs to smoke. It brings relief to overwrought nerves, but doesn't deaden the senses like alcohol."

"True. It does seem to ease tension and give calmness."

"But you should smoke openly. The first one is okay in a closed room, because one doesn't know how one's body is going to react."

Safia began to smoke, at first furtively, then openly. She enjoyed the stares. With time, she conquered her shyness and brazenness, smoking with mundane ease. But somehow, somewhere her mind came across a block every time she wanted to smoke in front of Prof Ram Sharan Srivastava. The ugly, pockmarked professor of English always overawed her and even the mention of his name was enough to make her stub out her cigarette.

* * * * *

FIVE

Zahida had insisted that Safia should go alone to fill up the form and the fee at the Allahabad University. "Why do you want a man tagging along? Nature has given the female more courage and strength. When are we going to start using it?" So here she was, standing in a queue of thirty men. Incredibly the queue melted, all of them offering her their place after the first curious glance. Her job was done in a few minutes and she decided to use the hour to stroll the campus known as the 'Oxford of the East'. It was in one of the corridors that she met Prof Ram Sharan Srivastava. Dressed in a milk white dhoti and starched kurta, he looked Safia up and down. Then, as if not fully comprehending, he took out a thick pair of spectacles that he carefully wiped with the corner of his kurta and placing them on his nose, he openly stared at Safia who remained rooted to the spot. Later on, she was never able to understand what it was that nailed her to the spot. Was it the open frankness of the stare, or the serene glow of knowledge that seemed to surround the broad, ugly face?

"A student, guardian or a casual visitor?" The volume of the query and its tone told Safia that it had been repeated.

"A student, Sir."

"Name?"

"Safia Hasan."

"I don't know anyone of this name." He said making it sound like an accusation.

"No. I mean, I am in BA previous. I have just paid the fee." As proof, she extended the receipt.

"I never doubted that. What combination?"

"Urdu, History, English."

"Good. But wrong sequence. It is English, Urdu, and History. Ram Sharan Srivastava, I teach English." He had walked away. When recognition dawned, Safia ran after him.

"You are the great poet Ram Sharan '*Fikr*'!"

"I am glad you are well read in Urdu. However, your admiration for me as a poet will not help in the English tutorials."

During the session, Safia learnt that Srivastava *Saheb* had a great admiration for girls who wanted to study, but he made no concessions for them. Gayatri was the only other girl besides Safia and she had no inkling whatsoever of English grammar. She would often be in tears after Srivastava *Saheb* had finished with her. He was fond of repeating, "Education is education—the amount of grey matter is equal, no reason why it's output should be different."

With the first lecture, Safia got a taste of community study. She was introduced to the pleasure of reading together, discussions, preparing and comparing notes rather than mugging up notes prepared by others. The joy of moving between musty shelves full of books, getting the library card, making timeless surveys of the innumerable wads of knowledge was something that Safia had for long been kept away from. Why did society deny its one-half this pleasure, she asked herself for the nth time.

"Women should not study. What use is education for them?" Right on dot, almost in answer to her chain of thoughts. It was Sadaqat Rehmani, holding an impromptu meeting of five or six classmates. "Which respectable household would allow its daughters to work? They would end up cooking and keeping house. Women do not possess the capacity to channelize education to proper use. It only spoils their brains that become an easy prey of Satan. Imagine women from respectable Muslim households have given up purdah!"

"So what is your problem? You are not Safia's caretaker." Gayatri rarely spoke but when she did, it was always to the point and usually drove the nail not into the head but right through it.

"Oh let him be Gayatri! Surely you have better things to do than argue with a man who gets half our grades." Safia and Gayatri were amongst the best in the batch of twenty-eight students and they never failed to drive home this point. Even the boys tittered at Sadaqat. "My dear Sadaqat, our absence is not going to get you better marks. But if you like, we could coach you—just correct your tenses and verbs." War of words was an ongoing process with Sadaqat. While he held one front, Gayatri and Safia the other, rest of the class was what Abbas would have called 'floating population', siding with the victorious of the moment.

It was the dry dusty month of October. The afternoons were congenial to flying sparks—that things should boil over for Sadaqat, and Safia was an expected outcome. Dr Inteshaar Hussain, Professor of Urdu Literature organized a National Seminar of the Progressive Writers. Typically, the women of the university were given the charge of serving tea. Safia could not contain her excitement. Justice *Saheb* had given her permission to stay out late to help in the arrangements. She would be rubbing shoulders with writers from Bengal, Punjab, Kerela and Maharashtra. One room in the Urdu Department had been converted into an office. Safia and Gayatri were now sitting hunched on a *divan*, preparing a long list ranging from the number of cups to be arranged, packets of tea and biscuits to be bought, tablecloths to be borrowed and milk powder sachets to be collected from the army canteen.

"Look how diligently these girls work," Sadaqat rolled in with his group of friends. The addition of an electric heater and teapot to the office had made many students interested in the seminar. The girls took no notice of the intruders. "My my! Such labour. Too busy to offer a fellow a cup of tea, I suppose."

"This is an office not a tea shop. If you want tea, you have to work for it." Gayatri was irritable. Her family did not allow her late evenings and sharp at 4.30 in the afternoon, her younger brother came on a bicycle and collected her. She knew she would not be able to attend the evening sessions or the late night *mushaira*.

"Oh come Gayatri, don't be such a miser. How much time would a cup of tea take."

"Suppose you make it and while you are at it, make a cup for me and Safia also."

"Safia is too busy with her work. See how good she is at these household chores. I have to make an admission. One reason why women should be educated is to manage the economics of the kitchen."

"Stop baiting Safia. She is working harder than any of us."

"Thank you Gayatri, but I would rather not be discussed. Anyway my work is almost done and I too will need tea, so I will make it in a few minutes."

Having poured tea, Safia sat back and lighted a cigarette. She knew this was one way to get under Sadaqat's skin. Expectedly, Sadaqat started a long lecture of how Islam restricts the fundamental concept of enjoyment in the case of a woman. A woman is there to give pleasure, she has no right to demand or expect pleasure. Safia smiled and pointed to the watch on Sadaqat's wrist. "What about my watch?"

"Nothing. Just that times are changing. Sooner than later you will find most women doing what they want to."

"Oh no I won't! I will see Gayatri leaving this room in twenty minutes obediently following her father's instructions." Gayatri swung round to face Sadaqat but before she could say anything, Prof Ram Sharan Srivastava and Prof Inteshaar Hussain entered the room.

"No seminar." Prof Srivastava never did dress up his words.

"What! But we have prepared everything. Even the letters of invitation have been sent. What has happened?"

"We have run short of money. I had hoped the Vice Chancellor would help. He had verbally agreed to give us a thousand. But has backed out now."

"We don't really need that money for the seminar. It would have gone for hiring the chairs and tables."

"But why is the Vice Chancellor backing out now, after all the arrangements have been made?"

"Someone told him that all the writers attending the seminar are communists. So being a *pucca* brown *saheb*, he will not support a cause that is even mildly red."

"Does he have any objection to our using the auditorium for the conference?"

"No, he dare not do that. He is well aware that half the faculty identifies with the cause of the Progressive Writers."

"Then let's make arrangements on the floor. I am coming, stop ringing the bell." Gayatri was not going to be defeated and she was not leaving until a solution was found.

"It will be clumsy. Everyone taking off shoes and losing them. We might as well have a *Sanathan Dharam Pravachan*." Professor Srivastava made a face.

"Or a *Qur'an Khani*," Inteshaar *Saheb* smirked.

"Sir, why can't we use the classroom chairs? Then we shall only need to hire a few cushioned chairs for the speakers." Safia was nervous for the hidden cigarette and her worry threw up ideas.

"There will be a terrible mess up when we have to return the chairs."

"We can mark them. Each classroom will have a different number."

"The girl has brains inside her pretty head. But who will carry the chairs, back and forth?"

"We are eight students in the welcome committee and we can get more volunteers."

"Count me out of this." Sadaqat was quick to extract himself from any situation that demanded physical labour.

"Dear Sadaqat, whatever the degree of need we would never count you amongst us," Safia smiled sweetly.

Ram Sharan Srivastava sniffed the air. "Something is burning."

"Stop talking in satires, Srivastava."

"I am not Inteshaar. Something really is burning, something like silk."

It was. Unable to stub out the cigarette in time, Safia had slipped it into the black *shervani* pocket that was now sending up blue grey clouds.

"My dear boy, if smoking is such a compulsive habit with you, we would be grateful if you added an ashtray to this office."

"But I never did, it was….."

"Never mind. So this is settled. We shall mark four hundred chairs for this seminar and carry them to the hall. Come Inteshaar, leave the youngsters to smoke in peace."

Once the masters were outside, Sadaqat turned on the girls. "I know who did this and I am going to wait for an opportunity. Let the culprit not think that I am going to let her go just because she is a woman. This was the best *shervani* I had. Whatever will I do now?" Sadaqat would have rushed out, but Safia barred her way.

"I am sorry Sadaqat, I didn't want this to happen. I was flustered, I am sorry. Please forgive me. If you like, I can apologize to you before the professors or even the Vice Chancellor. I really am grateful you did not expose me to our masters. Please give me your *shervani* tomorrow, I shall repair it."

Sadaqat looked at her straight in the eye, and then quickly looked away. "Don't apologize so much, it is only a pocket," Sadaqat mumbled gruffly. "Now please let me pass." Sadaqat and his friends trouped out.

"Gosh, you really laid it thick."

"Well, it was my fault. I don't think that Sadaqat has completely forgiven me."

"He cannot do anything else. He is in love with you."

"How dare you hint at such a thing? It is insulting."

"Maybe. However, it is still the truth. You and Sadaqat have been at loggerheads from day one. He is angry with himself for loving a married woman and angry with you for being married."

"My dear Gayatri, why are you rotting your talents in literature? Psychology would have been more your cup of tea. Only a psychologist could have found such colourful logic for common quarrels. You would be telling next that Prof Srivastava who cuts up Sadaqat into bits every time the poor boy submits a tutorial, actually has homosexual designs on him."

"Not a bad analysis. I had better rush. See you tomorrow."

The seminar being over, Safia concentrated on the finals. She became the ghost who haunted the library and her hard work began to bear fruit. Her teachers approved of her style of analysis and started giving her more time and help. Prof Inteshaar was a fine speaker and he tried to turn Safia's analytical powers and fine sense of humor towards public speaking. Eighteen months had flown by and though Safia loved each minute of it and a part of her willed time to stop, another part wanted to hurry up so that she could move on with a University degree. Move back to Lucknow, to the outhouse that was home. Safia was in the library for one last time before she confined herself to her room for the next ten weeks preparing for the finals.

For the last hour or so, Sadaqat too had been around. Glancing round, she had caught him staring straight at her. Catching her eye, he fumbled with the books he was holding, dropping one to invite 'please be careful' from the librarian.

"Don't stare so hard Sadaqat. I am not the library catalogue," Safia joked to ease the flustered man. Sadaqat turned red up to his ears and quickly turned his back to her. Safia frowned. Sadaqat had been acting strangely since the day she had put the lighted cigarette in his pocket. Gayatri's analysis had only increased the discomfort between them. The days of quarrelling and bickering were over and an awkward truce existed between them. Safia smiled, registering her thoughts. Abbas would have hated those scenes, but then he hated all kinds of showdowns in personal life. Hers was a strange man. He could handle a crowd of peasants and labourers shouting at the top of their voices. But raised voices in personal relationships would have him locking himself in the furthest room. In his analysis, all scenes within the family or friend circle were a form of play-acting. The same things could have been said quietly and with dignity. Major upheavals that change the course of history stem from household frictions that are carried beyond and vented on outsiders, setting a series of chain reactions. A chain that grows longer till it becomes an insatiable dragon, devouring away relationships and degrading characters till one doesn't recognize one's own actions and gestures. So righteous are those who indulge in these frictions that they do not realize the crevice they are creating, until the day they stand alone surrounded by these crevices for company.

How well Abbas could analyse everything! Had he been in her place, it would have taken him a few days to handle Sadaqat and here she was without a clue on how to address Sadaqat directly. Only two months more and Abbas would be a free man. She would have graduated and both of them would begin their life struggle again. Struggle for an independent, progressive India.

She was in the midst of her reveries when someone dropped a heavy book on her foot. She turned with strong words of admonition on the tip of her tongue. "Oh, It's you. Why are you dropping books at my feet? I almost jumped out of my skin."

"Why do you always use that scolding tone with me?"

"Why do you always censure me? You don't own me, you know."

"I know, but I would like to."

"Fat chance of anyone like....what do you mean?"

"Be mine Safia. Come away with me as my wife. Pakistan comes into existence in a little more than a year. Let us migrate to our home-land. Let us contribute in building it, a new land, a shining star that would be an example before the world—this is what a country can be like when true Muslims get down to building it—a pure land…a land for the pure."

Safia stared unblinkingly at the young man, fired by the pictures of the shining kaleidoscopic future. A ripple of laughter rose from her inner depths, followed by another and another, the soundless mirth shook her entire frame so that she had to hold the iron frame of the bookcase for support.

"I shall keep you like a queen. What has Abbas given you? No comfort, no pleasure, no peace. He is always going to be on the wrong side of the establishment. Tied to your neck like a sack of sand, he will weigh you down into the abyss of pain and sorrow, where misfortune shall be your only companion. Wipe all this out like a bad dream and come away with me to the future that welcomes us with open arms."

"And what shall I live on?"

"I have enough to begin with. I shall earn more."

"Oh I wasn't talking about you, how shall I live?"

"The same as me. I will………"

"You don't understand. Perhaps I loved Abbas in the first few months of our marriage."

"But this makes things easier doesn't it? If you have fallen out of love, all the better."

"It is not so simple. Instead of the man, I fell in love with his cause. Today I live for that cause and I love Abbas all the more for giving me a cause to live for. Oh yes, Abbas is still very important to me but what is meaningful is my cause. I do not care for material comforts, never will. As far as your pure land is concerned, if it really does come into existence, you are welcome to it. I was born an Indian and God willing, I shall die as one and be buried here. I had better be going now. It is time for Baba's tea. I have only one request to make. I do not wish to bring your shameful conduct to the notice of our professors. Kindly do not give me the opportunity to do so."

"But why? Why let that swine go scot free." Being a confidante was not enough for Zahida. She wanted to take decisions and implement them.

"I don't know. Somehow, I feel everyone has a right to love."

"Oooooh."

"What was that for?" Safia enquired.

"Perhaps you too do not mind a few scalps on your belt. If nothing else, it is an ego booster. The reassurance that one is still part of the race, that one has not been completely discarded."

"I don't think I was thinking about myself, though now that you point out, the whole episode does probably have this silver lining. However, I do think that society has been rather unjust to man. It is he who has to overcome his doubts, make the first approach, make the proposal, face the rejection, bear the humiliation that comes with it, grit his teeth, rejuvenate till he can again fortify himself to approach another and perhaps face the same humiliation again."

"Oh, don't you pity the uglier sex so much. They thrive on our pity only to trample on us. Since you want the chapter to be closed, we shall not open it again. How about a smoke?"

Safia and Zahida had been having a quiet smoke when Abbas walked in. "Good! I am now sure of a constant supply at home." Then seeing her flustered, Abbas added soothingly, "Either don't take a decision without your master's permission or else learn to shrug your shoulders and say 'So what?'"

Zahida clapped in appreciation. "Abbi, I would give you eight out of ten on the Women's liberation front."

"Really Zahida, doesn't anyone ever get full marks from you?"

"Not men—because they are men. Anyway what are you doing here instead of the Lucknow Central Jail?"

"Two months less for good behaviour. I am always at my best with the authorities."

Safia was standing in a corner when two arms engulfed her. Burying his lips in her abundant black hair, Abbas looked up at Zahida.

"Any news of Razak?"

"Still underground," Zahida mumbled before turning away to hide the lonely yearning in her eyes.

"I'll be meeting him soon."

"I have no message to send. Tell him to be safe, not that it is in his hands."

"True. Soon we shall be a free country. The ban on the Marxist Party shall be lifted and he shall be able to surface."

Much as she loved Zahida, Safia did not want to share these moments with anyone. Zahida must have felt that she was the crowd because a mere glimmer of pain crossed her face, covering it quickly with a warm smile. "I must be going. I am on night duty and I don't want to be late."

"Night duty! From five in the evening? I thought you took over a night shift from eight," Abbas looked at her enquiringly.

"True but I have just......"

"Realized that you are the third in the company. I am the one who has made you feel this way. However, is that enough reason to leave and give me a guilty conscience forever? Stay, I'll get some tea."

As Safia walked towards the kitchen, Abbas said incredulously, "She has matured!"

"No, only learnt to be natural and honesty is the natural way with her, not the cultivated way."

"I am glad she has persuaded you to stay. I have something to discuss with her and with Baba. I want you to be present."

"As a witness?"

"As an impersonal friend."

"You are not sure he would agree to what you have to say?"

"I am certain he would agree. But I am not sure I am right. Safia, is the tea served?"

"No. Baba has just come in. He wants us to join him in his room."

"Good. I want to get this over with."

"What is he talking about?" Safia asked Zahida.

"You shall know presently, just as I will."

"Well! The black sheep is back." Sir Jafri opened his arms to his youngest son.

"Don't be so welcoming Sir," intervened Zahida. "He has not reformed at all."

"I'll accept him as he is," smiled Sir Jafri.

"Would you?" Abbas' eyes raked his father's face and then as if satisfied by the honesty, he said, "Then I am left with no choice but to accept you as you are." Their eyes held for a moment and then looked away.

Sir Jafri coughed and said, "You have something to tell me."

"First things first Baba. Have you talked to Bubu?"

"She knows."

"Getting to know something is not the same thing as being told about it. Her knowing it means that she has found out from her own sources. Your telling her would mean you have nothing to hide."

"It might not be serious. It might just fizzle out."

"It has not in more than two years. Maybe it is the real thing."

"In any case, I shall be moving back to Lucknow in about six months. I shall decide what to do. Tell me what you want to talk about?"

"Baba, our country shall be free soon. My party would no longer be underground. I would be expected to play a more definite role from the Pakhtoons to the Bengali Muslims. Me and the other Muslim comrades shall have to work hard to bring the Muslims to our beliefs—a free and fair state with equal opportunities for all."

"If you want my blessings, you won't get them. I don't agree with the Reds."

"I want more than your blessings. Baba, Safia would often have to be alone and it would be safer if she had a permanent place in Safdar Manzil."

"But you are my son. You shall always have equal right to my property as your other two brothers. Safia is my daughter-in-law. Of course she will stay at Safdar Manzil."

"No Baba. I want no share in your vast inheritance. My ideology does not allow it. But could I have your word that Safia would always have the outhouse—even if I am dead."

"God forbid!" Sir Jafri and Safia exclaimed together. "You shall have the outhouse or rather Safia shall have it. I shall will it to her. Knowing you, perhaps it is the safer way. However son, do not give up everything for an ideology. If it lets you down, you shall be left with nothing, but you shall still have to continue to live."

"An ideology does not let its believer down. It is men who forsake the ideology. It is they who are either strong or weak-kneed and spineless."

"Then you should also realize that men are human. They have desires and ambitions, greed and lust. An ideology has to be implemented by men. They can make mistakes even blunders. Sometimes these mistakes can destroy individuals."

"I have accepted it as my life. I have made my choice. There is no looking back now."

"I am not trying to dissuade you from following your beliefs. Nevertheless, let me make you a bit more secure. Let me leave Safia what I want to."

"We shall only have to refuse it and that would hurt you Baba," Safia spoke for the first time.

"Dr Zahida, why don't you say something. I expected you to take my side, but you are silent like the sphinx."

"I am marveling."

"At us, the filthy rich?" Joked Sir Jafri.

"No. When Abbas agreed to an arranged marriage, I hated him for being party to this system of legal prostitution. How could he have known that he would find his soul mate in this renegade way?"

"Alas! I am left in the minority. I cannot but agree with you."

* * * * *

SIX

It was a clear November night. Winter had still not quite set in, but Diwali was over and nights brought a mild chill which was ideal for making love—the reason for most Lucknowites celebrating their birthdays in the monsoon. In Lucknow, there are many ways to differentiate between the original inhabitants and the new migrants. One of them is through the use of winter bedcover. A Lucknowite would never take the heavy quilt. *Balaposh* or *dulai* made with a few ounces of soft cotton, mildly scented with cloves and henna, is the winter cover. As the mercury drops, the number of *dulais* would increase and the cold would be measured in terms of *dulais*—'cold enough for three *dulais*.'

Mujtaba Hussain *Saheb* loved these nights and was one of the few Lucknowites who had learnt the pleasure of walking through them. For years, he had walked for the pleasure of it. But now, for the last decade or so, he walked with a definite aim. This was the time he paid his 'collection visits' or 'collection raids' as some liked to call them. Impeccably dressed in broad white pyjamas and bottle green *shervani*, his long silver hair waving in the mild breeze, his thinning head covered with a *duppalli topi*. A silver headed rosewood cane in his right hand and a silver box of betel leaf in his left, feet encased in thick leather shoes, he was an inseparable part of the evening sights of Lucknow. As he turned on the Monkey Bridge, a good half mile trek, several buggies stopped for him, heads popped out to ask him if he was planning to cross the bridge. Mujtaba Hussain *Saheb* smiled and replied, "Well I'm in no mood for suicide and the water is far too shallow. Its three months past monsoon."

It was typical of a Lucknowite not to come to the point directly but to ask politely about all and sundry before reaching the question that might be answered with a simple yes or no and make further dallying impossible. How else could one pass the evenings in Lucknow, which from any end to end measured four miles? However, Mujtaba *Saheb* did not have anyone about whom one could inquire. His wife had died young. His only child, a daughter, had been returned to him by his English educated son-in-law with the *fatmahi meher* of five rupees that he had himself fixed with pride at being a Syed. Not able to bear the humiliation, the girl had committed suicide and was buried next to her mother in the graveyard which was religiously visited by Mujtaba *Saheb* every Thursday.

The enquiring head enquired if he would like a lift across. Blessing the generous gesture, Mujtaba *Saheb* refused and walked on. It was difficult to explain that walking helped him formulate his thoughts for the coming meeting, plan the next day, sought out his accounts and dig his memories.

In the last decade, Mujtaba *Saheb* had become something of a legend. People said his daughter's premature death had done it. He possessed a large estate across Gomti. The first obvious proof he gave, of not being all there, was selling off his ancestral *haveli* in Lucknow Chowk and moving to this estate. Whoever heard of any respectable person shifting across the Gomti where the Gujjars roamed with their herds of cattle? Next, he got a few rooms on the estate vacated using persuasion, threats and small amounts of money. This was the second proof. Then he put all his money to construct a six-foot high wall all round the estate, enough to set Lucknow on fire, which crackled with gossip about a secret harem to a chemistry laboratory for producing gold to cultivation of poppy for mass scale production of opium. Not bothered by the gossip, he put up a green coloured board on the main gate that announced in bold white alphabets the opening of the 'Sajeda Hussain Muslim Girls School'. The crackling fire roared up. 'What! A school for Muslim girls. The man was raving mad. Even madness should have its limits; imagine reaching out to our family pride and self-respect! The man deserved a good beating.'

The day after this, Mujtaba *Saheb* was seen entering the shop of the famous jeweller Jhun Jhunji. But why the shop? He and Jhun Jhunji were childhood friends and normally he went straight to his house from where a boy would run to the shop to inform Jhun Jhunji. The jeweller was equally surprised and presuming that it was an emergency, took his friend to the inner chamber. Mujtaba *Saheb* took out a small bundle from his pocket and handed it to his friend. "These are your sister-in-law's and daughter's jewels. I want to sell them."

"But why?"

"There is no one to wear them and I need the cash."

"If you are in need, perhaps I could…..."

"No personal need. I want to buy a bus that will safely ferry girls from respectable homes to my school and back."

"Mujtaba, are you sure? This is not some wild goose chase. After all, which Muslim family is going to educate its daughter in a modern kind of school?"

"Those who do not want their England returned sons-in-law to summarily divorce their daughter because she cannot read and write English."

Jhun Jhunji understood it was time to shut up. Mujtaba *Saheb* seldom spoke about the dead daughter and when he did, it was to end a conversation. Quietly he began to weigh the ornaments, most of which had been fashioned at his shop. "It is all of fifty five *tolas*. I shall give you five thousand for them."

Mujtaba *Saheb* inclined his head. Jhun Jhunji counted the big notes and handed the bundle to him. Mumbling a quiet thank you, Mujtaba *Saheb* pocketed the money and got up to leave. His friend's familiar *taab* made him turn back. "Can I be the first one to make a contribution?" Jhun Jhunji enquired hesitatingly. "I know I am not a Muslim but….." He could not complete the sentence. Mujtaba *Saheb* had clasped his hand holding the hundred-rupee note in both hands and touched it to his forehead. The man who had not shed a tear on his daughter's suicide wept inconsolably.

Jhun Jhunji, blinking back his own tears, said, "You are a sly fox; nothing short of a gold theft can make a goldsmith weep. You will see it shall be a great school, a landmark in Lucknow."

When Mujtaba *Saheb* emerged from Jhun Jhunji's shop, a small crowd of onlookers had collected outside on the street. This is one of the specialties of Lucknow. Events are difficult to come, by but spectators are no problem. Even something as mundane as the open-ing of a manhole attracts curious inquiries, turning a daily wage labourer into a performer, who at length and in detail describes the reason for opening of the manhole. Jhun Jhunji himself announced, "Mujtaba *Saheb* had come to sell his late wife's and daughter's jewels."

There was an audible gasp from the audience. People often came to dispose off their family heirlooms to jewellers but they always tried to hide the fact. "He is going to open a school for girls. He wants to buy a bus to deliver the girls safely to the school. Though the name of the school is 'Sajeda Hussain Muslim Girls School', it shall also admit Hindu girls. This school shall give free education to the poor girls so that they can come up in society and be at par with their more fortunate sisters." The whole concept was too novel to get a ready-made reaction and as the crowd remunerated on how to react, a middle-aged man stepped out.

"You shall then need a driver. I have driven the *Chhota Laat's* Austin for twelve years. I retired yesterday because a new man with two eyes intact has been found. Name is Rasheed."

The crowd tittered at the honest admission of the one-eyed Rasheed, but Mujtaba *Saheb* stepped up and patted his shoulder. "Come along then Rasheed, there is a lot of work to be done."

Mujtaba *Saheb* walked briskly as the gaping crowd parted to make way for him. In the years to come, Rasheed became the bus driver, cleaner, cook and gardener. He cleaned out the nine built-up rooms, insisted on reserving two for Mujtaba *Saheb* when he would have had only one, cleared the ground and planted vegetables enough for the two of them.

And so began the tirade of the two friends on the rich and the poor of Lucknow. Who could celebrate a wedding or a festival without a visit to Jhun Jhunji's? The goldsmith, a businessman through and through, kept a record of the clients who had been treated to his 'fish in and out of water' treatment. He usually started by providing a long list of Mujtaba Hussain's virtues, his education, his mesmerizing rendering of the *Marsiya*, the description of Imam Hussein's martyrdom and of course, his immaculate family background. These were unquestionable qualities and the poor fish had no choice but to agree. Next, Jhun Jhunji elaborated on his wish to educate everyone, particularly women. If this was contradicted violently, he would change the topic to *karanphools* and *jhumkas*. Later in the day, he would write the client's name in a register and add three zeroes after it. He would then tick the first, cross the second and pit an arrow on the third. This was to remind him that he should begin the conversation from the second round next time.

If rarely, the fish acquiesced the second zero, Jhun Jhunji would immediately get down to the third and final round. This was a tricky one because it demanded dual strategy for the Hindus and Muslims. If the fish were Muslim, the strategy would be based on flattery, complimenting the far-sightedness of the community. Jhun Jhunji would humbly accept that they were, after all, the leaders. So why shouldn't they be leaders in education? The fish would usually swell up with pride and twirling his mustache, walk an inch taller. A discussion with his wife or mother would usually deflate him a bit but he would make enquiries about the school. For the Hindu fish, it was taunt and satire. It is true that Muslims are ahead; they are the lawyers, doctors, and civil servants. They have no qualms about crossing the sea to gain knowledge. However, it is really, because we let them. If we would also educate our girls, what is to stop our sons from becoming top rankers? The world was moving towards modernization. Could India afford to be left behind? It is time we asserted our capabilities and increased our assets. The Hindus who were smarting from the second grade position under British Imperial rule, were often quick to swallow the bait.

Mujtaba *Saheb*'s approach was more direct. He went personally to each house and requested that girls be sent to the school that was planning to shape itself on the line of modern education. Had he used the phrase Muslim education, he might have met with some success but he refused to distort facts.

And so it was that between the two friends and an old cousin of Mujtaba *Saheb*, Ustaaniji, who taught basic arithmetic and the Holy Scriptures, a one-eyed driver, honest intentions and very little fanfare, Sajeda Hussain Muslim Girls School was opened with eight Muslim and two Hindu girls. Every morning, except on Fridays, the brown bus with green curtains clanked through Lucknow, with Rasheed firmly encased in the driver's seat, squeezing the brass horn to meet the deadline of the 9 am morning assembly.

The evenings were different. While Rasheed prepared dinner, vegetable curry and chapattis, Mujtaba *Saheb* carefully brushed one of his three *shervanis*, mildly scented with seasonal *attar*. Waving the family heirloom—the silver-headed stick—he walked out of the gates of the school, the only imposing fixture of the building, turned left towards the Gomti and crossed the Monkey Bridge to reach Lucknow city. His destination was always one of the well-to-do houses. His aim was some donation for the school, which was quick to come, and persuasion to allow the girls of the family to join the school that was always met with a discrete silence.

The school was now ten years old. Mujtaba *Saheb* still walked to Lucknow city. This time too he was aiming for a rich and respectable household. However, the goal was different. Crossing the bridge, he turned towards Bhainsakund cremation ground. It was twilight with the stars appearing one by one on the clean post monsoon sky. Far away on the banks of the river, a lonely pyre was burning brightly—life shedding its last light. "*Inna illahe, Inna-illahee rajaun,*" he mumbled, 'from Him we come and to Him we shall return'.

The inner courtyard was pleasantly moist. On a *divan* were the last blooms of *bela* and the first ones of *moulsari*. Mujtaba *Saheb* gazed at the pensively strange mixture. A polite cough brought him back to the present. He turned round to see Abbas. "Do be seated Sir. It is an honour to have you here."

"Dispel with the politeness young man, everyone knows the reason of my evening jaunts. Let us get down to the point."

Mujtaba *Saheb*'s bluntness produced a smile on Abbas's lips. "Then your evening walk has been in vain. We are broke."

"An evening walk is never in vain. At the least, it gives one a good appetite. Ah! I hear tea coming."

Safia brought the tea reluctantly. There were no eats to go with it. But she could not forgo the chance to meet Mujtaba Hussain, who was trying to give modern education to Muslim and Hindu girls under the same roof, who was telling people that organized education was important right from childhood and who believed that poor girls had as much right to it as the rich ones. She had been educated at home and though she was grateful for it, she had yearned for the fun and company that the school provided her brothers. She lapped up the crumbs of school life and when she was alone, she visualized herself on the scene.

Accepting the cup of tea, Mujtaba *Saheb* looked at her long and straight. So long that Safia began to feel uncomfortable. "There is an Old Persian saying that goes something like 'forgo wealth for health, give up health for knowledge and distribute knowledge for true faith.'"

"How beautiful!" Safia forgot her embarrassment and meeting his unblinking gaze added, "But how remote. Who gets the opportunity to distribute knowledge?"

"The girls of the community need you my child. Will you answer the need of the hour?"

Safia was dumbstruck. She was being offered a job.

"Service." Her elder sister-in-law turned up her diamond-studded nose. "Are you so down and out?"

Safia blushed, however, before she could say anything, Abbas was agreeing with his brother's wife. "How very astute of you *bhabhi*! My politics leaves me no time and gets me no money. Safia will use her time and her degree to earn some money."

"We had thought that an educated wife would be able to bring you round to practice law. But it seems she is quite incompetent." Begum Zeenat was at her acid best.

"Yes, isn't she? Unable to persuade me to distort, exaggerate, lie and be dishonest. Since such is her incapability, let her pay the price." Abbas might never have practiced law but he was a Barrister all right, turning every argument in his favour. Safia marvelled at his levelheaded quick wit.

"If it is money, perhaps we could……."

"I have not come to ask for alms," Safia butted in for the first time, "and neither for advice or permission."

"Pray why have you come then?" *Bhabhi* enquired.

"To inform you all *bhabhi*. Wish Safia good luck." Abbas got up without ceremony. Somewhere, he knew that this coldness would one day envelope his relationship with his family. He belonged to a different wavelength where honesty and forthrightness were the key strikers. Then were his people not honest? Perhaps they were, in a hypocritical way. Not because it was the only way, but because it was the social way. One had to seem honest and at all cost never become the pepper-provider in the society gossip. Let society be jealous, nasty or curious about you but never let them discover one of the skeletons in your cupboard, lest they reach out and make fun of you. Were they both then in the process of becoming one such skeleton? Were they giving people an opportunity to laugh at the Jafri family?

* * * * *

SEVEN

"Why do so many girls cough in the class? God bless them, most come from reasonably well off families, yet they have an emaciated look and are a bundle of nerves."

"Consumption," mumbled Abbas, speaking through the cigarette he perpetually held between his lips.

"What are you saying?" Countered Safia passing him the ashtray. "At such a young age! Why, most of them are in their teens."

"So?" Abbas was holding the ashtray but the ash at the end of his cigarette continued to grow longer. "What has consumption got to do with age? Most of them live in small unlighted rooms of *Nakkhas*, wear dirty black veils when they come out. Ideal situation for bacilli to multiply. One third of them would die before they reach twenty, another third during childbirth."

"How can you be so cool about it?" His reasoning agitated Safia.

"Don't confuse helplessness with lack of concern, though often both taper to the same end—inaction. But this is not the case with you. You can take action, albeit a small one. Discuss this with Mujtaba *Saheb*. Keep the girls in the open for at least an hour everyday and get them to exercise. When I was in Switzerland, long walks across hills was an important part of any sanatorium's schedule. Apparently the panting pumps fresh air in and out of the lungs, giving them a chance to fight the bacilli."

Getting permission from Mujtaba *Saheb* had been easier than she had imagined. Strangely though, most of the girls had taken initial interest in outdoor games but the group soon petered down to a mere handful. Cross-questioning yielded no result and insistence brought polite notes from guardians requesting that their daughters be excused from physical exercise. Reading one such note to Ustaniji, Safia sighed in exasperation. Ustaniji taught the Holy Book, the alphabet and basic arithmetic, in that order. Seventy year old Ustaniji who wore bright yellow through *phagun* and lush greens in *sawan*, whose curly white mass of hair, slightly bent back and sharp black eyes saw not with sight but with experience; eyes that warmed to Safia because of her devotion to her job and now filled with mirth at her childish display of disgust.

"Perhaps you are neglecting something very basic."

"Like what?" Safia queried.

"I don't know. There are things that people enjoy doing but they don't like being watched while doing them."

Safia turned a bright red. Really! She had noticed that the older women grew, the more vulgar and obscene they became.

"Oh I don't mean that," Ustaniji added following Safia's track. "Though the same rules apply on that too. What I meant was, perhaps the girls feel that they are on display."

It was the summer of 1946. Safia had been correcting papers of Class IX the whole night. Abbas had gone to make rounds of the nearby villages. These villages were around the Gomti and invariably flooded every year during monsoon. The loss of human life, cattle and crop was substantial. Government's inaction and the constant fear of being swept away made them the right pocket for Marxist activity. He was expected back sometime tomorrow. At four in the morning, Safia called it a night. As Abbas would jokingly say to his friends, when it came to hard work, Safia could work him under the table. She could sleep for a couple of hours before the daily help turned up around six and then she would be free to complete the examination papers.

She was being shaken almost at once and waking up with a jerk, she saw it was bright morning and the sun that touched the outer wall at six was down to the ground. It must be half past six. Where was the daily help and why had she woken up like this?

"*Aapa,*" a soft voice behind her bed made her jump.

"Good God Nigar! What are you doing here?"

"I came to see you."

"I can understand that but at this time? And how did you get in?"

"I climbed the wall."

"What! The seven feet straight wall! You must be desperate."

Nigar gave a watery smile that suddenly turned into a deluge of tears.

"Oh Nigar, don't! Not on my best sheets." Nigar smiled through her tears and made an effort to control herself. "Now first things first, let's make a cup of tea." Lighting the primus stove, she quickly made two cups of tea. Meanwhile, Nigar folded the sheets and spread the bedcover. Indian girls never wait to be asked.

Safia put down her cup of tea and wiped her tears. She never could control them, much to Begum Zeenat's satisfaction who kept her own emotions in an iron grip and enjoyed others breaking down. Nigar's story had been heart-rending but more than the story, it was the uncertain appeal for help and the quiet, firm acceptance that none would come. Her fate was sealed. It was an acceptance that struggle would get her nowhere, the surety of the failure, the faith in the strength of the powerful, the knowledge of the outcome of such efforts, the placidness of knowing and the helplessness in reaching for the unknown. Safia wondered if all this did not amount to death that takes away the pleasures of living, the lust for life, for beauty, for warmth. A yearning to fill one's inner emptiness, to empty one's heart so that the inner vacuum is filled with endless rivers that surge down from the mountains of emotions to the endless sea of the soul. Death! Because the major part, the meaningful half is dead inside a woman. The lesser half, the pigmy, exerts itself, surging and distorting her personality, giving it the course of self-destruction, the greed to be superficial, the lust for possession. Not for the beauty of art but the weight of gold, its resale value—the rising gluttony that surpasses all greed for food. Why don't women ever try to think differently? Why have all the prophets been men? Why is the God forever male? To be remote, at an unreachable and safe distance? Why did scholars like Maitreyi and Gargi follow their husbands in the search for knowledge? Why did they not reach out in the opposite direction? Perhaps they would have found a different God? A more human God, a God who was neither man nor woman, neither father nor mother; A God who made no demands to be worshipped; A God who walked with her, sometimes behind and sometimes beyond. Or maybe they would have been able to dispel with God, accept that life was there and there was really no need to find its meaning, to know it's beginning or end. Just understand and float between the known and the undiscovered, until tired out by the cold-shouldering, the unknown would be forced to show its face.

Ali and Khadija were the first two people to come to the true faith, who recited the first *namaaz* and who stood by the Prophet when the entire Arab world thirsted for his blood. Why and how did Ali become an *Imam* and Khadija remained just Mrs Prophet? Yes, women chose to live dead and were treated like living dead. Washed, cleaned, balmed, anointed, wrapped in the finest clothes, seen a few times and then buried somewhere unknown. When they did come out, they emerged with someone else's identification and were not recognized as their true selves.

"I was expecting a loving wife waiting for me. Why this long face? And why didn't I know that I had become a father." Abbas smiled at the flustered Nigar who blushed a deep beetroot. Safia's heart warmed towards her man and his simple way of putting people at ease.

Nigar gave her no time. From the high chair, she jumped and grabbed Abbas' feet, almost toppling the tall frame. "Save me. Save me, my benefactor, save me."

Grabbing her by armpits, Abbas pulled her up and shook her like a rag, so hard that her teeth chattered. "You are not a thing to be pitied. Get up and stop pitying yourself. What is the matter, getting married?"

"How did you know?" Nigar and Safia asked together.

"Nothing else seems to shake you women out of your feeling of well being. So, he is old enough to be your father?"

"Grandfather," hissed Safia.

"My! Men seem to get better and better at this," smirked Abbas.

"He has buried two wives, has one living and wants another one." Safia broke eggs for Abbas' omelette with vengeance. The shell crumbled, spilling the egg all over the table.

"This is an old story. Give me something new, something to remove the fatigue of the inter-class passenger coach, something distinguishingly horrible, to turn my insides into over-cooked macaroni." Abbas yawned and stretched, his fingers almost touching the old clanging ceiling fan. Safia glanced at Nigar. Poor girl, she would be completely depleted by this nonchalant attitude. How was she to know that it was Abbas' way of getting people to talk about their problems?

Nigar had been looking down at her toes, her big nail drawing invisible patterns on the hard floor. She looked up and very quietly but clearly said, "I love his son."

Abbas' stretch stopped in mid-air. "Does the old man know this?"

"Know? He had come with the formal proposal—the *paigham*. He saw me and......"

"The filthy lecher," Abbas swore under his breath.

"Please save me."

Abbas sat down near Nigar. "Look girl, you save yourself. Stop asking for help like a trained beggar. Learn to help yourself."

"You mean run away with Zain? He also suggested this. But where and for how long? We will be followed, found and handed back to our parents. Even if we succeed, how will we live, what will we eat?"

"Everything boils down to economics, even love," mumbled Abbas.

"We are not afraid of hard work. Zain would be a graduate next year. We want only one year."

Abbas sat quietly for a minute. Safia knew this minute was crucial. She took off the omelette, lest even its sizzle might disturb Abbas' plan. It would turn solid but it was not important to eat a fluffy omelette. It was crucial that the plan Abbas made was flawless.

"Listen Nigar and listen well, because there shall be no chance of my repeating it and you will have to act on what you can remember of it. Islam gives women some rights. Those rights are few and there is a lot of noise about having granted them. Still, they are there and let us thank the lawmakers for small mercies. Make use of these rights and we shall take care of the rest."

The sky was not really overcast. The few thin clouds made a half-hearted effort and dropped a few unnecessary raindrops. Drops that had been quickly absorbed by the thirsty earth and had doubled its thirst for a proper shower. Drops that spelt good omen for the newly weds, drops that were warm and lucid like the tears of a new bride, drops that foretold the futility of those tears, drops that made barren a fertile womb. All water, a few untimely drops, the deluge that broke the banks of Gomti. Both useless, both effortless, both wasted.

When Safia got down from the rickshaw, there was an audible murmur from the gathering. Abbas paid the rickshaw and turned.

The bride's father was already at the door. The arrival of a member of Sir Safdar Jafri's family was as important as the arrival of the *baraat*. Safia was ushered into the *zenana*, while Abbas walked into the male crowd accepting sherbet and declining paan. Abbas turned to smile at the bride's father, who was thanking him for coming. "But we had to come. Nigar is one of Safia's favourite students. If you allow me, I would like to be one of the witnesses to the *nikaah*." The poor man was floored. His seven generations would remember that a member from such a great Syed family was witness to one of their weddings. Abbas smiled again. "Well I am not going to be there and I suppose neither will you to check if their memory is as good as you claim."

"You will have your joke, Syed *Saheb*," Simpered the bride's ef-feminate uncle.

"Certainly. Are not weddings meant for jokes and laughter? Tell me, what does the boy do?"

The bride's father drew himself up with pride. "He owns seven shops in Shahganj."

"Oh! Then he doesn't need to work."

"Thank God no! The rent itself is enough to live comfortably."

After all the trouble the last Prophet went in to provide dignity to labour, why did the urban Muslim dislike work? Why was the man who did not have to work for a living considered lucky? Why good honest labour was looked down upon? Why did pink soft palms invite so much admiration? The rural Muslim worked as hard as his Hindu counterpart, sang the same songs, ate the same frugal meals and was like his Hindu neighbour, denied an honest share in the produce. Why did the urban Muslims deprive themselves of the joy of creating? Why was sex the only creative activity? Why did they not want to contribute to the earth, the country, the society, and the community; Contribute to the united effort of celebrating life?

Abbas kept quiet for a few moments and then tried a different course. "I have heard that the bridegroom has been married before." The bride's father looked a little sheepish but the effeminate uncle was quick to rise to the occasion. "Yes he is, poor man. Lost his first two wives in childbirth. Luckily, the children survived. So he had to marry a third time, after all someone has to look after the children. However, this third wife has turned out barren. So unfair. But these are God's ways of finding bridegrooms for girls from poor families."

"So he is marrying our Nigar to have more children and he has two children from his earlier marriages."

"No, five. Two elder daughters are married and the eldest son is a student of the Lucknow University."

There was a sudden noise from the *zenana*. However deep inside the house it might be, the women in the *zenana* were always the first to know of the arrival of the *baraat*. As the women crowded the doorway, Abbas' eyes met Safia and an unnoticeable nod was exchanged between them—all was well, everything under control.

The bridegroom had arrived and was being welcomed by the *mirasins*. Dressed in gold brocade, surrounded by five *naushe* in silver brocade, mounted on a blinkered white horse, led by the gaudy red band of musicians, oily cheeked and thick lipped, with beady eyes and henna dyed mustaches, a gold and black turban sitting on his balding head, skin tight pyjamas that ended in golden *saleem shahi* slippers. He grinned foolishly as he was introduced to Abbas. With the girls, he was in his elements. Nigar's younger sister, a seven-year-old girl with large black eyes and a red determined mouth flatly refused to hide his shoes. However, the bridegroom was not offended and gave her ten rupees. He joked with the older women and *mirasins*, throwing money left and right.

It is strange how all Indian customs and festivals rotate round money. Even love among siblings is based on money. A newborn child is given money even before he has learnt to breathe rhythmically, just to teach him that money is more important than the breath it is struggling to maintain. Why don't Indians make an effort to buy gifts? Why shake away the responsibility of showing that we care, that a person is important enough for us to spend quality time buying gifts for them. Giving dead money, we expect love—the life's source. The equation remains lopsided and never balances itself. The result is more inputs of money, more demand for money, more loss of love.

The bridegroom sat down in the centre of the main *divan*. Abbas sat on his left and the *Maulvi* on his right. The *mirasins* began the songs of marriage, their droning voices and the rhythmic drum making the shortest marriage ceremony in the world the longest and the most boring one. The Qur'an was brought out and the questioning began. "Do you, so and so, son of so and so, accept in marriage so and so, daughter of so and so for the amount of *meher* this and this to be paid at the time of *talaaq*?" The groom quickly said yes and the whole troupe minus the bridegroom, moved to the inner room. The *Maulvi* stood beside the bamboo screen, and repeated the question. No reply came from behind the screen. The *Maulvi* was old and experienced. He nodded his head—it happens as a part of decorum and good upbringing. It was only dignified that the girl did not show that she was in a hurry to be married. Repeated again, the question again met with silence. The *Maulvi* coughed. This was the third and the last time. The question was again followed by a stony silence in which an angry voice repeated, 'Say yes you wretched girl.'

Then a firm voice said, "No, the proposal is not acceptable to me." There was an audible gasp from inside, followed by a scuffle and a sharp twang of a tough hand meeting a soft cheek. This was followed by a sharp interaction.

"You can't do that."

"What do you mean? I am her mother."

"Even so, you don't have the right."

"Oh, why was this girl born in my house? Curse is on my womb."

"It is her right, the Holy Book says so."

"Oh, shut up. You and your modern ideas."

Amidst the din, Abbas' voice rang out sharp and clear. "What is it Safia? Come out and tell us."

This was her queue and Safia stepped out. "Thing is *Maulvi Saheb*, the girl is not willing to marry this man."

Maulvi Saheb was nonplussed. He gathered his scattered wits and said, "Perhaps the women folk of the family should persuade her."

"What do you mean? No persuasion, threat or blackmail can be used to make a girl marry against her wishes. The Holy Book is very clear on this point. Let me show it to you." Abbas held out his hand for the Qur'an and *Maulvi Saheb* held on to it for his dear life.

"No, no. No need for that. But why stop a union? The girl would be happy. After all the man is rich and ..."

"Are you out of your mind? You want to rewrite the Qur'an, you want to interfere with His dictates, want to be a Prophet yourself?"

"God forbid!" *Maulvi Saheb* was visibly trembling.

"Then stop a marriage where the Qur'an is being insulted. Your work is to see that the word of Allah is maintained and that no distortions are committed in the Holy Scriptures."

Safdar Manzil was still a good half-mile away when Abbas asked the rickshaw to stop. There were only two lamp-posts at each end of the road. The vague yellow circle of the streetlight was soon behind them and they were walking in the warm pitch-black night. Most of the hedges had varieties of strong scented flowers and the fragrance of *champa* and *bela* wafted down with sudden spurts of *raat ki rani* and *mongra*. In a few henna bushes, there were the last blooms braving the wilting heat and their acrid smell made definite passage, bringing with it memories of preparations of anointing the bride for the flower bed.

It is only in Lucknow that the genteel changes perfume with the weather. It is *khas* for the hot dry season, *gulab* and *motia* during rains, henna in the mild months of fall and *shamama-tul-ambar* in severe winter. During spring, the orange and white blossoms of *har shringhar* are carefully collected at dawn and soaked in a vessel of boiling water. Sashes and *dupattas* are dipped in this water to give the wearer a mild, doubtful bouquet of the blooms. Sensuous. Everything about Lucknow's culture is sensuous. The play with the senses, the seen, mingling with the unseen. The melodious lyricism of the *thumri* and *dadra* that played with the *taal*, tentatively mingling, sensuously drawing towards the *samn* but not quite banging on it, only lightly flirting with it, a reminder that both exist. Food here is not cooked to fill stomachs but to aggravate and placate, excite and sooth the senses. Lucknow, where beauty is not worshipped, but is created. Where life flows at the placid pace of the Gomti, where no *attar* is allowed when the *dussheri* mango blooms. So delicate is the flower that it takes offence at the presence of another fragrance. Lucknow, where everything, natural and the other, man-made and God gifted, is a male or a female and thus hangs on the most delicate balance, complimentary to each other, incomplete without one another.

Entering the dark zone, Abbas held out his hand. Safia quickly glanced up and down the street. There was not a soul in sight. "Precaution, my love," Abbas teased.

"Sensible to be careful," but she reached for his broad hand.

"Mission successful?"

"A hundred and ten per cent," replied Abbas.

"What is the extra ten per cent?"

"I didn't expect Zain to rise to the occasion. That little mouse of a boy has more guts than his whole size."

"It was mainly your presence."

"No Safia. One must always give credit where it is due. It takes a lot of courage to fire a shot like this one. I didn't expect him to get up and offer to marry Nigar and then to publicly tell the whole story."

"Well, I am glad she is happily married to the man she loves. Her father disowning her almost made my heart stop."

"Uh huh. But this Zain is a man to watch. I must get him to come to the party meetings. We need people like him. Look at that one, the one right in the centre. It looks like an angel trying to weigh down its strings to get a better view of us earthling. Poor fellow, strapped up so high, with two wings and a wand, allowed only the swing possible on its limited string watching us banished earthlings who can do so much more. Poor lonely star angel."

Safia gave a sigh of well-being. Contentment at possessing a man who could talk of a revolution and the crystal stars in the same breath.

Then Abbas began to hum.

"I have never heard this one. Is it a new poem?"

"It is Irfan's. He sent a copy."

'The night of city lights
Sky covered with a net of stars
Like the vision of a sage, like the imagery of a poet
Oh, my heart's desire, tell me what shall I do?'

* * * * *

EIGHT

"Perhaps the girls feel that they are on display," Ustaniji's words kept ringing in her ears. Late for school, she struggled separating the starched folds of the *chikan* sari, willing it to fall in neat pleats. For the sake of convenience, she had given up the *gharara* and the six yard *dupatta* and had switched to sari, however the six yards curse remained just as the fate of the landless tribesman is tied to the cycle of 99, '*ninanve ka pher*' and no amount of *bhudaan* can change that—the omnipotent ring of the moneylender. So is the freedom of the Indian women, encased in the six yards of cloth irrespective of the religion or sect they belong to. Last week, she had met an American couple who called sari 'a sexy dress'. She had giggled recalling Abbas' irritation as he invariably unwound it the wrong way.

She tried to walk faster, praying that the gates of the railway crossing would not be closed. As if on cue, the signalman with cracked heels, swung one of the huge gates, while the chugging of the train reverberated the surroundings. Cyclists, *Ikkas*, rickshaw pullers and pedestrians made a last minute rush to get across. A rickshaw puller urged her on, "It is still faraway Begum *Sahib*." Safia smiled and shook her head.

The signalman looked at her approvingly. "You are right. Accidents are never far away." Pushing the three feet long bolt into the deep hole, he ran to the gate on the other side.

Well, she might as well relax. It was going to be a good ten minutes wait. She looked around. The early morning roadside market was clearing up. The vendors were picking up their straw baskets and jute mats. The cows, goats and an occasional buffalo were gorging themselves on the leftovers. Half an hour later, the cattle—having eaten their fill—would make way for the fat sweeper woman with a big broom and perpetual chanting, "*Hato hato, bacho bacho, Bhangi* comes." She would clean the pavement for the regular shops to open. Adjustment—the pivot of Indian society. The human beings waited for the cattle to fill their stomachs, the lower castes accepted the humiliation of shouting "*Bacho bacho*" so that the upper castes were spared the danger of their shadows falling on their bodies, or else the poor upper castes would have to bathe again. Her glance travelled further to the *nanbai*. Nishat Ganj was a typical Muslim area and what Muslim locality could even think of existing without a *nanbai*? It is he who would make huge *kofta* balls of pounded meat dripping oily juice, red with finely ground chillies and spewing the fragrance of *garam masala*, prepared by grinding hundred and thirteen spices. All women look down on cooking and the Muslim women of Lucknow go a step further—they detest it. The routine of cleaning the *chulha*, trimming the pieces of wood, selecting the dry ones, piling cow dung cakes, wood shavings and covering them with long pieces of wood and then the blowing through the long iron pipe for hours. It was enough once a day and that is where the *nanbai* came in. No man in his right senses could complain about the *korma* or the *paye*, accompanied by the fluffy *sheermal* or the *abi roti*. Just now having taken off the *nehari* from last night's oven and tested it for the three finger deep grease topping, he was busy pummeling the proven dough, breaking it into equal mounds and banging it on the large wooden board. A young boy dressed in a knee length kurta and nothing else, a dirty lace skullcap adorning his tousled head, was running back and forth, trying to light the double-mouthed hearth. His agile movements shook his almost transparent kurta seductively showing the shape of his rounded buttocks.

Above the *nanbai* was a small eating-place. Eating here was more respectable than near the hearth where the joints of the low benches and stools would pinch the bottom, causing sudden squirms and grimaces. Upstairs sat the clientele who could order a glass of tea and sit through the whole morning nursing it and the *nanbai*, who would announce the bill after the first roti of the lower ones, would smile and welcome these upper storey customers and become worried if they left early. Safia would often see Irfan sitting here, but he always chose to ignore her. She too was not in a hurry to show her familiarity here. Sometimes she also saw Katayanji, the well-known scholar of Sanskrit, Prakrit and Pali revelling in being termed a *malaich* by the Hindu upper castes. He took pleasure in shocking them by eating at a Muslim *nanbai*. She had also seen the dark thin man who had helped to retrieve her Burmese *chappal* from the railway track.

Hurrying to cross the railway track after a super fast had passed, she had unwittingly stepped on the hot rail and her foot had come away without the *chappal*. How was she to know that a running train could make a rail hot enough to melt a cheap rubber sole! A small crowd gathered smirking and tittering at her discomfiture while she stood there like a misplaced exclamation mark.

"Quite useless, but I suppose you would have to manage somehow till the school. What is the *tamasha*?" The crowd melted away at his smooth enquiry. "Do you think this would be of any help?" A green checkered handkerchief was extended towards her. Safia tied her foot to the two pieces of the Burmese *chappal* and started limping towards the school. Remembering her manners, she turned to thank him only to find him entering the *nanbai* and disappearing up the wooden staircase, his wide pyjamas flapping over the hard leather *nagra* shoes.

"I have to open the gate Begum *Sahib*." Safia jumped back and apologized profusely to the coal black grin of the signalman. The grin shrank to a stiff line as a look of disbelief appeared in the eyes. No genteel lady ever apologized to a worker. Remembering to jump over the hot rails, Safia crossed over to the other side. Holding up her sari, she maneuvered the few steps of the uneven climb to the road. Heaving a sigh, she dropped the sari. She had missed the assembly but was in time for the drill. Should she manipulate the henna hedge like the girls? There was space in between but it was rather undignified and Mrs Yusuf Zai would never forgive her. Nevertheless, it would save a clean ten minutes walk. Deciding to risk the general disapproval, she walked towards the gap. Why did the gap seem filled up today? Had Rasheed planted some new saplings in the last few days? But the green did not seem like the struggling green of the newly planted saplings. It was also more solid, not the usual shape of saplings that had been uprooted from amongst friends and half smothered by the heavy hand watering of a novice gardener. What could this dirty green be that solidly flapped in the winds of...... Flap! Recognition dawned on Safia. Of all the cheek! She purposefully took the last few steps, her gait acquiring the purposeful stealth of a cow approaching a trowel full of juicy hay.

Getting no response to her two "ahems", she slapped the back of the green sharply. The back straightened and turned quickly, showing a salt and pepper beard on which last night's gravy and this morning's paan juice were mingled. A terrorizing clean upper lip and a green and white check scarf thrown casually round the neck under the green cap sitting snugly on the clean shaven head.

"Oh please! Not a *Maulvi*," mumbled Safia to herself.

"How dare you!"

"The clergy when found at fault take the easiest form of defense—offense. The trick is not to be intimidated by the strategy." Abbas had written in one of his editorials.

"How dare you!" Safia turned on him with full force. It was a cow who had found that the hay mixture contained quinine. "What are you doing, eyeing the young girls?"

"Just that. It is my job to keep an eye on everything, especially these so called new experiments."

"Oh really? Why don't you come inside then and look properly. Why hide yourself in a henna bush."

"You dare question me, a *Maulvi*, a man who represents the Prophet?"

"Really! And where does the Qur'an say that the *Maulvi* is the Prophet's representative?"

"You dare to question my knowledge of the holy scriptures and have the audacity to call *Kalaam Paak* the Qur'an, you slut!"

Something inside Safia snapped. Her hard held resolve not to ever loose her cool in an argument with a fundamentalist gave way to the hot seething temper rushing from the base of her spine to the medulla oblongata, to reach the pituitary and give the cerebrum a six pound punch.

"Yes and I also call you a dirty debauch and for a man like you, I have this cure." The slap rang out loud. A crowd of curious onlookers had gathered. A quarrel between a low class woman and the local butcher or *nanbai* was interesting but common. Something that one could afford to forgo. Now an upper class woman quarreling with a mullah would remain the highlight of the season and an eye witness would always have a ready audience.

Safia was shocked at herself and turned to escape further interaction.

The *Maulvi* shouted at her back "The curse of Allah be on you and your family. You shall answer for this." The girls who had crowded near the hedge were being shunted back by a cane wielding Nafisa *aapa*, a look of strong disapproval marked on her pudgy features. The whole incident kept coming back to Safia. Feigning a calm she did not feel during the *vazu* and the mid-morning *namaaz*, the thread insistently rang in her ears. "You shall answer for this." It was not an empty threat. It carried a cool confidence, which accompanies the assurance of knowing that one would be heard and followed.

Gathering the pile of copies and her bag, Safia walked out of the empty staff room. Normally, Nafisa *aapa* accompanied her up to Nishat Ganj, where they both shopped for the day. Today she had mumbled an incognizable excuse and hurried out. Safia sighed. What was that line of Tagore that Abbas often hummed "*Jodi tor dak sune keu na ashey, tobe ekla chalo re* (If they answer not to thy call, walk alone)"

She was walking out alone when she heard a soft patter behind her and turned to see a frail girl following her. The girl stopped in mid-path, uncertain, taking a step forward and then retreating two steps. "Surely this was not how Lenin had visualized his great treatise 'One step forward, two steps back.' Safia smiled at her wild thoughts and the girl thinking that the smile was for her smiled back.

"What is it Parveen? You have something to say." The shy girl nodded her head. "Well, you won't get through it by nodding your head. Out with it my girl." Parveen gave her another hesitating smile and held out her right hand. Then remembering her manners, the left hand joined the right. Two hands held out a rumpled paper lotus, the kind Safia had taught them to make from waste paper.

"Why thank you Parveen, but for what?" Parveen looked meaningfully at the lotus, turned and scampered back to the tamarind grove, where a group of girls were waiting for her. Their gestures and nods told Safia that this was a contributory gift and Parveen had been selected by the group to present it. Nonplussed Safia looked down at the lotus on which was scrawled a single word in raw ink—*shukria*. A solitary word that made a world of difference. As Safia turned towards the gate, her steps were lighter but her grip of the ground firmer.

Crossing the railway line, Safia hurried through the snoozing bazaar of Nishat Ganj. Afternoon siesta is strictly observed in every Muslim locality. She had nothing to buy and wanted to reach the safety of her home as soon as possible. A low dignified voice followed the quiet polite cough, "*Bibi!*" It was the voice that struck terror in Safia's heart. Too polite, too dignified to be real even in Lucknow.

It had to be put on, but for what? She turned around and stepped back creating an arms distance between herself and the stranger. He *salaamed*, keeping his eyes down.

"Ahmed *bhai* requests you to please step up to the *nanbai's*."

"And who is this Ahmed *bhai*?" Safia enquired.

"Please follow me," was all the answer she received. Suppressing an instinctive urge to make a dash, she followed the man who stopped at the wooden steps and inclined his head motioning her to climb them. Seeing her hesitate—no unaccompanied woman would be seen dead on the upper floor—the *nanbai* stepped up. "Nothing to worry about Begum *Sahib*. Please go up." The heavy bamboo curtain shut out the afternoon blaze and Safia blinked her eyes trying to adjust to the dim light. In the haphazardly scattered wooden chairs sat a lone figure, clad in white with a green and white check kerchief thrown carelessly round their neck. As her eyes adjusted to the dark, recognition dawned on her.

"So it is you, but I was told to meet one Ahmed *bhai*."

The stranger who had saved the two pieces of Burmese *chappals* from the railway track *salaamed*. "*Chappal* retrievers cannot be named Ahmed?" There was a mirthful enquiry in his eyes.

"But Ahmed *bhai* is a known goon of Lucknow......" Safia could have bitten her tongue.

"It's alright. You have heard about me, that is in itself a compliment. I have requested you to come here because I do not want you to feel threatened in anyway. You have done the right thing and nothing will happen to you. That is Ahmed *bhai's* word."

"I think my husband is quite capable of looking after me."

"He will have to, in the house. But what about the road? Women who have questioned the clergy meet with mysterious accidents."

"You mean I might be lynched on the road?"

"That would not be so bad. But being maimed or disfigured would be pretty bad, wouldn't it?"

The casual tone sent a chill down her toes. "Who would....?"

"It would never be found. With time, people will accept your accident as the will of Allah. Do not question me. Please continue to take this route. Under no circumstances, change it till I say so. *Khuda Hafiz*."

Walking down Safdar Ali Road, Safia felt someone following her. She turned twice only to find a lone bakerywala leisurely riding his bicycle strapped with the big tin box and then to collide with a *burqa* clad woman hurrying down to catch the last local train. Bodyguards? She reached home safely.

"There is a call from Bubu's," Abbas glanced up the galley.

"When do we go?"

"Immediately. The sooner these showdowns are over with, the better."

The main *Deewankhana* which was rarely opened during the day was lighted. Usually Bubu entertained the family and intimate friends in a rectangular room which, she insisted on calling 'seeloon'. It was a black and green gathering of all shades. The black ranging from liver black to the shiny pitch black and the green from the filthy, bubbling muck of a village ditch to the bright duckweed covered pond. The variety in the headgear, the large curling turbans, the skullcaps and the tasseled *topi*, showed that the entire hierarchy was there. For once, the gathering had representatives from both the Shia and the Sunni sect. Bubu was sitting behind a muslin curtain held up by two women.

A cackling and cawing, almost like the quarrel for a resting place between the crows and the parrots on the old Ashok trees lining the *Chaman* underlined their entry. The *Shahi Imam* raised his hand that held the baton, given to his forefathers by Nawab Safdarjung, the founder of modern Lucknow. The crows and the parrots stuttered to a quiet. Then began a long vulgar speech, sprinkled with dirty abuses that made Safia's ears burn. How could a man of religion speak such language? She shifted her weight from one foot to the other. Slowly her senses numbed and all she could hear was the guttural, Arabic pronunciation of the unending stream of abuses that formed inside the betel juice greased red cannon and volleyed out of the white bearded mouth. Safia suddenly felt Abbas' hand wound round her waist. His grip was firm and possessive. Shocked at this open defiance of manners before the religious heads, *Imam Saheb* stopped in mid-sentence, the open mouth showing the broken, *missi* blackened teeth.

"*Lahaul-e-vila-koovat*," he spat. "This is the same boy who was leaving for England twelve years before?" he asked the muslin curtain.

"Yes, I am the same man and yes, I did commit the three crimes."

"My coming had no effect then?"

"No! And shall have none now."

"You have decided that without knowing the reason of our coming?"

"When has religion stepped into the privacy of an honest man's house to do any good."

"I am sorry to confirm Begum Sahib, that your son is a good looking Satan."

"I am flattered. I thought clean shave was un-Islamic. Now can we hear why you have honoured us with your august presence?"

"Honour, my foot! We have come to seek justice. Do you know that woman you are so unashamedly embracing has dared to raise her hand and slap a Mullah!"

"What!" Abbas' hand dropped from Safia's waist and she felt her spirits dropping like a bird, hit by a bullet in mid flight.

"*Ji haan*," *Imam Saheb* relishingly chewed each word. "Narrate the incident." The Nishat Ganj *Maulvi* jumped up and narrated how he was watching the school's activities, for God forbid, they might be teaching *kufr* to our girls. This witch in woman's garb grabbed him from behind and without so much as a 'may I please,' gave him a sharp slap. Abbas stepped away from her and she felt like the injured bird hitting the hard earth.

"So what do you say now?" *Imam Saheb* asked.

"That is not all," the younger one tittered. "She has been seen wearing the sacred green and white check scarf in her foot and what is more she gossips with that ragamuffin Ahmed at the *nanbai*.

"No, I don't. I….." Safia intervened.

"Shut up." All the years of training of the *azaan*, the prayer call resonated round the room. "No woman speaks when the *Imam's* are assembled."

"Safia, I am very angry with you," Safia's heart stopped beating. She could almost here Lady *Sahib's* stiff upper lip crackling into an arrogant smile. Her son was proving to be a man after all. "I have asked you again and again, taught you, cajoled you and even given you at least a dozen demonstrations but you refuse to listen. How many times do I have to tell you, not to slap a man? Always punch him in the nose and never once. A punch must be followed by three or four quick hard punches. A slap does nothing while a punch on the nose, even from a light hand would at least numb him for a few seconds. It is not enough to insult, you must give real pain, cause a serious injury."

The *Imam* stood up and the congregation followed. "You shall either divorce her or be ostracized from the community."

"Which community?" asked Abbas. "Oh you mean the Muslim community, or is it the Shia one or the Syed one? I have never seen them function as a community except during the *Moharram* when they gather round large *tazias*, built on lies of miracles which never happened to shed crocodile tears while really drawing malicious pleasure out of the martyrdom of a great man. Where is the community? Do you ever meet to help each other? Do you sit and plan what is good for the Muslims of India? Do you ever think that the world has just emerged from a World War and that a new world is in the process of being born, a world with a new system, a new policy. Have you ever tried to think what role the Muslims would play in shaping this new world? Let alone the world, think of *Hindustan*. We are on the brink of independence. Have you ever thought what would be the form of independent India? The young old India, that has the second largest population in the world. India, that has a mixture of so many races, religions, civilizations. We have so much to give and we are not even aware of the treasures that we possess. Have you ever thought about these things? Some Muslims are demanding a separate country. True that the Muslims of Lucknow have so far made no comment on this. Jinnah's two meetings have been utter flops. Nevertheless, they shall keep coming, because they are riding the wind of madness and will not let go. Have you tried to make people understand what partition would mean? Have you made the Muslims think, even selfishly, what harm they would come to, if this madness becomes a reality? No! You continue to live in the sixteenth century when Muslims were the rulers. We are not the rulers anymore, but this is our country. Think of it as a whole. Stop living in small cells looking down your seldom found Turkish noses at the Hindus and their numerous sects. Allah knows we have as many if not more. People listen to you. Do something about things that matter. Don't make petty incidents major issues *Imam Saheb*, it is a dangerous habit."

The *Shahi Imam* drew himself to his full height. Even at five foot nine, he was dwarfed by Abbas. "You are right. People listen to me and as Allah is my witness, you shall not find shelter in Lucknow."

He stepped out with the majesty of his position, his black robe sweeping the white marble steps, the green and black entourage following him.

Abbas ran down the steps and stood before him. "*Imam Saheb*, it is true that people listen to you, but they also listen to reason sometimes. But it shall not always be like this. Slowly with time, reason and logic will replace fundamentalism."

"We shall see *Ameerzade*." *Imam Saheb* put out his baton and gave Abbas a push.

Giving way, Abbas smiled. "This is the only word that could have heckled me. Clever of you to use it."

"No point in getting worried now, after the dye is cast. More important is to think and be prepared what it could fish out."

"That is what is worrying. Maybe because of the fatwa......"

"There will be no fatwa. Bubu will see to it."

Safia glanced at Abbas, slowly stirring her tea. He seemed very sure of what he was saying. She waited, knowing that he would elaborate. "Enough donations shall be sent to all those concerned and the clergy shall be placated."

"But if the fatwa can be stopped with money, it can also be given for money."

Abbas inclined his head adding in a far away voice. "It is often the case. Have you never noticed that no law of the *Shariat* ever stops the rich from doing any wrong? But that is not the issue at the moment. I have to find some way to open a debate on this issue—Interference of the clergy of any religion in the fundamental rights of the citizens of this country. Education is a fundamental right and not a privilege of the rich. No religion can intimidate or threaten people into giving up education."

"Till now they have been doing just that. This stand, if accepted, would heavily curtail their powers. Nobody likes a smaller kingdom Abbas."

"I know. That is why the debate. An open discussion would bring a transparency into the arguments being given by both sides. The people will then decide which side to support. That is why the keepers of Islam do not ever want a discussion. That is why a fatwa."

"I only hope that Mujtaba *Saheb* is not intimidated by the stand of the clergy. Why what's the matter?" She asked Abbas who was already picking up his *shervani*.

"You have hit the nail on the head. If I am able to persuade Mujtaba Hussain to publicly speak on the subject, then a discussion can be generated. It does not matter if our stand is defeated. Discussion in itself would throw up many different views and each view shall be weighed and examined by the general public. Discussion is the beginning of a solution. I must talk to Mujtaba *Saheb* immediately."

Mujtaba Hussain was livid. He waved Abbas into a chair and without acknowledging his greetings started talking. Abbas who in the long walk to the school had been planning what to say to convince him to support his views, relaxed smiling, admonishing himself for not taking into account the natural reaction of an Indian father whose daughter had been ogled at by an outsider. The two put down their heads to work out what Mujtaba *Saheb* would say in his speech and where he should say it. Mujtaba *Saheb* was a convincing speaker and as he himself often said, there could be no inspiration like a cause to make a Muslim give his best oration. It was the venue that caused a slight altercation. Mujtaba *Saheb* was of the opinion that work must be started at the lowest level and he must begin to speak from the smallest and the most insignificant mosque and work his way up. In the process, the discussion generated and the arguments given from both the sides would spread and diversify, involving a large cross-section of the community. As opinions will be formed, people shall take up the battle and speak out in favour of logic and reason.

Abbas disagreed. "What you are trying to do is form a political base, to have strong support at the grassroots level. That is a good strategy for a war that is expected to be long drawn, a struggle that might last years. This is a conclusive battle, where winning is the only way. It is certain that if we begin from the smaller mosques, the clergy shall be alerted and shall see to it that you are not given an opportunity to speak in the bigger mosque. Yes, don't look so surprised, you shall be physically stopped. That is why we must start at the top. Take the bull by the horns. What is said at the top shall, by the process of gravitation, trickle down. What happens at the lower levels has little chance of making it to the top and all possibility of stagnating at the base. Let us begin at the top and catch them where they are least expecting us to attack. The success of an attack is directly proportionate to the awareness level of the opponent. That we dare to attack the highest, most secure fort is proof of the truth of what we uphold. If we manage to put the clergy on the defensive, half the battle is won. The masses shall do the rest.

Mujtaba *Saheb* apparently agreed. He glanced at the huge grandfather clock in his room, opened the lower drawer of his table and brought out the white net skullcap his daughter had so lovingly embroidered for him almost twenty years ago. Twenty long years and still no change. He sighed. Well, we must keep trying. He picked up his silver headed rosewood cane and turning to Abbas said, "No time like the present."

Abbas nodded in the affirmative and both of them walked out of the school gates together. "Should I......do you.......?"

"No, I want to be alone to consolidate my strength. As you said, this battle cannot be lost at any cost."

Abbas nodded and raising his hand in a silent *salaam*, he moved in the opposite direction. The battle would not be won by a single man's attack. There must be a number of people who would stand up and demand that Mujtaba *Saheb* be allowed to speak, people who would physically protect the old man in case of an attack and people who would take his word beyond the Juma Masjid into the narrow, dark lanes of Lucknow, where it might be expected to show a thin ray of light.

Mujtaba *Saheb's* speech at the Juma Masjid was the crowning glory of all his oratory exercises. Before the *Shahi Imam* could get down to speak—in fact he was only in the middle of the opening sentence, saying that he wanted to bring to the notice of the gathering, the way people of religion were being attacked—Mujtaba *Saheb* had got up and said that he agreed that the *Maulvis* were in danger and since the matter concerned his school, would he please be allowed to speak. He had started with agreeing with the *Imam*, permission had readily been granted and Mujtaba *Saheb* took the centre stage.

"I need not remind the gathering that Islam had been a storm of liberal and progressive ideas, that it had brought about radical and much needed changes and that Allah had bestowed the Holy Qur'an as a book to be referred and read by every Muslim. So generous was Allah that he instructed that even criminals, murderers, a woman of loose morals and even those openly operating a brothel should be allowed to read it. No one can deny the fact that Prophet Mohammad's first wife, *Bibi* Khadija was an educated woman, operating her own business. She and his other wife's daughter *Bibi* Sayeda, were all educated women, who moved amongst other women and taught them the Holy Book. Small insignificant being that I am, I am trying to follow the Prophet's example because if Allah had wished to deny education to the woman, he would have restricted them from reading the Holy Qur'an. India is on the brink of achieving freedom. The Muslims have to participate in building its future, they must be educated and healthy to make their contribution towards building a strong nation. A healthy mother means a healthy son. So I introduced the morning drills. There is nothing hidden or underhand about it. Anyone could have sought permission to be present during the morning assembly. Why would anyone want to hide in the hedge and look at the girls? It is not me or the girls who have anything to hide. It is the man in the hedge who had to something to hide. The Holy Book says that while a woman should dress modestly, in a way as to not attract the attention of strangers, so should a man never look at a woman who is not his mother or daughter. If he needs to address one, his face must be turned away. Brothers, from the minute a girl leaves her house to come to my school, till the moment she steps back into her house, she is my daughter and my responsibility. Her parents have entrusted her to my care. I shall not allow anyone, even a *Maulvi* to ogle at her. Safia Abbas Jafri was under my instructions to find out what or who was driving away the girls from the drill. True, I did not instruct her to slap the reason when discovered, but it was he who provoked her. Can any woman from a genteel family tolerate being called a 'slut'? Yes, I have witnesses to prove that. Still, I shall make her apologize but only after the *Maulvi* in question has apologized to her and has been removed from his position in the Masjid for carrying on this un-Islamic activity. He shall have no right to lead a prayer, no moral right to teach the scriptures and no right to perform the *nikaah*. Knowing the *Shahi Imam* and his love for our religion, I am sure he would stand by the dictates of the faith. He shall be our guide and by his decision to punish the wrongdoer, show us the right path."

Mujtaba *Saheb* bowed low to the *Shahi Imam* and sat down. The murmuring in the gathering became louder and anyone who has handled crowds would have understood that they were rumblings of anger. *Shahi Imam* had enough experience of understanding the moods of the general public. When he rose to speak, he neither condemned Mujtaba *Saheb*'s speech nor did he support it. He opened a different subject—freedom and patriotism and its meaning in Islam. At the end, he delivered an emotional *khutba*, calling on Indians of all communities to unite to build a powerful nation, to support and help each other to overcome the problems of the new, independent India.

The *khutba* was acclaimed by the Press as an example of the contribution of religious heads in building India. The fatwa did not come.

Every tea shop and kebab corner became a venue for discussing Mujtaba *Saheb*'s speech. Moral indignation was high and cartoons appeared on walls, followed by the Urdu Press deriding the clergy, praising Mujtaba *Saheb*'s efforts and in one stroke achieving for him what he had not been able to attain in more than a decade. People lined up to admit their daughters in the school and Safia joined forces with other teachers, taking extra classes to help new girls cope up with the syllabus and other activities.

The liberals were happy. It was the first firm step of separating religion from personal life. The leadership in his party had congratulated him. He was already a member of the central committee, buzz was that he would probably be elevated to secretary level or be made in-charge of the minority cell. Abbas, though happy at the success of the first round, was alert and probing around for opportunities to open a second round. He knew that the clergy too was on the alert. Nobody liked ceding ground. He knew that he must keep up the pressure so that the support gathered in the victory of one battle is not lost by the time the second one is fought. Continuous, lively discussion was the one way to keep the support alive.

* * * * *

NINE

It was midnight. The streets of Lucknow were enveloped in an eerie and unending silence punctuated by the sudden rasping of military boots, keeping vigil on the monsoon drenched muddy streets. Nothing unusual; it was just another night during the '47 curfews. The severed country, the flow of refugees from both sides, the tales of horror wrecked by the 'other' community, the revenge taken from innocents, the checked riots but the still smouldering hearts full of hatred. No more for Lucknow the melodious *thumris*—"*Raat kahan pe kati Sainyan* (Where did you spend the night, beloved?)" Nobody dared to step out after dark. The well-lit by-lanes of *Dal ki Mandi* wore a deserted look, its pavements shaven off the flower, paan and *attar* sellers, its parapets unadorned by the smiling faces, underlined by the tinkling of the inviting and welcoming ankle bells. Why *Dal ki Mandi*, this was the condition of the whole of Lucknow. The coffee house which opened at eight in the night and closed at five in the morning, now opened at eleven in the morning and closed at six before dark. The waiters, not used to these unearthly hour, kept yawning the whole day, waiting for customers who never turned up.

It was time for Safia to go to bed. In fact she should have done so an hour before. Her work at school required her to be up at five in the morning to finish with the household work. But strangely enough, she felt a nagging, an irritation at the thought of going to bed. Like something was about to happen that required her to be awake, a foreboding of some impending disaster. She prayed silently as she combed her hair. What could be happening at the big house? Why was there so much shouting before dinner and why was she sure she heard Ladli's voice shouting back? That wretched Bengali girl, who never spoke except with her large black eyes. The only one who had stayed on. In four years, she had opened up only to Safia, causing her sisters-in-law to snigger about the unity of a class. Ladli was being beaten. But she was used to being beaten and hardly ever protested. What could be new today? Safia shivered at the creativity of Lady *Sahib's* cruelty. The frozen silence that followed the noise was even more frightening. At her mother's house, even the big black buffalo was severely scolded only when she kicked a bucket full of milk. Later, her mother would in a fit of remorse give it a large chunk of peanut cake.

Safia rose to switch off the lights. As if on cue, there was a loud knocking on the door. The sheer desperation of the banging, accompanied by loud gasping gave her heart a cold squeeze. All her senses told her to ignore the cry for help, yet her feet led her to the door. Removing the iron U that slipped into the bolt, she noticed that her hands were shaking. "*Ya Ali*," she murmured the Shia talisman for help and protection. Damn! Not again. She had promised Abbas that she would get over these beliefs. The chink between the doors revealed nothing. Had she imagined the whole thing? Impossible! It had been so vivid. She opened the door and then as her eyes got used to the darkness, she saw a female form lying on the muddy slush outside the doorstep. It was Ladli but she was stark naked. Safia closed her eyes in disbelief. When she opened them, she saw a hand stretching itself towards her. Quickly she tied her hair into a knot. What if it was a genie? They were attracted to girls with long hair. She recalled the fascinating tales woven round the warmth of the open furnace, in the long dark nights of the desert winter, flavoured with roasted peanuts and spicy green peas. The grim warning that came at the end of the tale—"So girls, never leave your hair open after evening. Always oil and tie it in plaits or else a genie would see your long tresses and start living in them and then there would be no help short of cutting them off to get rid of him."

The hand reached up further and she saw Ladli's naked breast, full and firm, with a deep black gash in the centre. The extended hand fell lifelessly back, almost as if the last atom of hope had been squeezed out of it and the effort to reach up had proved too much. The splashing patter of running feet, several of them, followed the splash of the hand in the puddle. A glimmer of a torch flicking the ground moved closer. Ladli shivered, made as if to get up and then fell back listless. "She went this way, to *Chhoti Bahu's* house." The harsh sound of Bishan *Bua's* throat clinched matters.

Bending down Safia gave Ladli's still body a severe shake. "Ladli get inside." The desperation in her voice must have communicated itself to the lifeless heap of flesh, for Ladli made an effort to move and Safia pushed and dragged her over the two steps. Giving her the last shove, Safia banged the door shut and collapsed on it, putting up the chain with one shaking hand while the other groped for the iron U. She managed to slip it in place just in time. Bishan *Bua* was already banging it, her dry 'grain in the stone pestle' voice admonishing, "Give us that whore *Bahu Sahib*, Lady *Sahib* commands it."

"Go away, come back in the morning." Safia was astounded. How could her voice sound so confident when her insides were shivering like jelly?

"Don't be adamant *Bahu Sahib*. Don't force us to do something that might belittle your prestige," the grind persisted.

Prestige! The very word got Safia's hackles up. From this woman, who was her mother-in-law's spy, the woman who reported the visits of the *dhotiwala* to *Chhoti Bahu's* house in her husband's absence. The poor Punditji, who came to teach her the Devnagri alphabet. How humiliated he had been? In a trice, Safia slipped the U and unhooked the chain. Throwing the door wide open she said, "Go away, or let the curse of a Syedani be your lot." *Sura-e-yasin* came naturally to her lips. She started reciting it with all the vigour, and belief of a purebred Syedani. The group behind Bishan *Bua* backed away while she herself stood her ground for a couple of minutes, then suddenly finding herself alone, began to tremble and stumbled back mumbling, "Mercy *Bahu Sahib*, mercy on this sinner."

When it all came out, it really didn't amount to much. Ladli was three months pregnant. Her crime was that she openly claimed that the child was Syed Wali Jafri's. She had been beaten to change her statement but she refused to comply. She didn't want anything; only that the child should not be called a bastard. This wasn't much, so why should she lie? Safia had no answer to that. How could she explain to the girl that had she wanted money, things could have been settled after a bit of haggling. It was the desire to give the unborn child a name that was threatening the prestige of the upper class.

At around seven, there was a cautious knocking on the door. Safia, who had hardly slept, was up in a trice. A sheepish Bishan *Bua* was standing outside. "Lady *Sahib* wants to come down and discuss something with you."

"I'll come with you then," Safia offered.

"No, no, she would rather come herself," Bishan *Bua* shot back, hurrying towards the main building.

Safia was not asked to sit down after making her *salaam* to Lady *Sahib*. She knew she was to be questioned. To equalize her position, she pulled up a chair. The green eyes glinted but swallowing her anger at this obvious discourtesy, Lady *Sahib* began, "So, you open your doors to people who are thrown out of my house?"

"I didn't realize that people who are thrown out are chased," replied Safia equably.

"You prefer to listen to that whore than to me?"

"I prefer to listen to both of you and form my own opinion."

"Why are you hiding the wretch here?"

"I am not hiding anyone." Safia thanked her stars. At her wits end, she had asked Ladli what was to be done. Ladli had offered the solution. She would leave before dawn to live with one of the Bengali girls who had been sold with her and had had the luck to marry a cook in an English officer's house. Remembering Abbas' advice—"When in doubt, depend on the horse sense of the Indian farmer"—she had acted on Ladli's advice. Ladli was gone. Whatever fretting and fuming Lady *Sahib* could do, would not bring back Ladli.

Yes, Ladli was safe and so was Safia. However, only for four hours.

At the stroke of ten, the heavy ceiling fan stopped whirring. It was evening by the time she realized that something was amiss. All the windows in the big house were lit! Then why was there no electricity in her portion? It was the 'grain in the grinding stone' voice, dipped in glee that answered her queries. "Lady *Sahib* is resting, she is not well; poor thing after yesterday's excitement. Yes yes, your side of the electricity had been disconnected. Lady Sahib's orders. After all, she is the owner." Last night's fear of the Syedani's curse had clearly receded.

Safia walked back to her portion, visualizing the pile of the high school papers she had been assigned to correct—her first big assignment outside the Sajeda Hussain Muslim Girls School. One rupee four annas per answer sheet for two hundred answer sheets—enough to see her through winter. She had planned to work through the night. Lighting the earthen lamp, she picked up a palm leaf fan. In the dim light, the moving fan made strange shadows. Suddenly Safia was alert. With every twist of her wrist there was a glint on the discoloured wall. What could it be? Then she smiled. Of course it was her diamond ring. Poor, lonely solitaire, trying to maintain its glitter even in its fallen circumstances. Yes, that was it. That is what she had to do. She had to sell the ring and get a separate connection for her house. She had always believed that jewellery was security, so why not sell it and buy comfort. The next morning was the first of the many times she had to sell her jewellery.

Abbas was back. His tour of the North West Frontier Provinces had been very successful. The constantly warring tribes had agreed to declare a truce. After all, everything boiled down to economics. These tribes lived hand-to-mouth, subsisting on the meagre output of agricultural pockets and grasslands of the inhospitable Hindukush ranges. Looting had been a way of life for centuries. They had existed as the eagles of the rocky terrains, swooping down suddenly on the unsuspecting prey. Buddhism had come and gone but Islam had survived through a policy of noninterference. When other avenues seemed to open up, they were willing to give it a try, especially as they came through a Syed. The Muslim tribes had immense faith in the proximity of the Syeds to the Allah. For centuries, no Syed dared to venture in their areas. Denied of formal places to worship, they killed Syeds in the belief that prayers offered at their graves would find favour with Allah, with Syed *Saheb* as the go-between.

Safia was enjoying listening to Abbas. He seldom spoke and when he did, conversation with him was interlaced with long silences. This non-stop conversation reflected his excitement, similar to the one of a horse trainer before he steps into the field to break a thoroughbred. He was already being called the 'successor of Badshah Khan'. Success was heady, even though there was still a long way to go. Women rights, even Islamic rights were unheard of. He would slowly have to convince them all. He had already made a convert, Aasim Haashim. A young man, who had wanted to marry a French woman, but had been forced to marry an illiterate tribeswoman instead. Though he had got over the French affair, his heart still yearned for the companionship and warmth it had given him. Aasim would have given his right hand to educate his wife.

"What is the matter? You do not seem too happy about Aasim educating his wife. See, one has to accept that charity begins at home. So does education and freedom. No point in gaining national freedom if we keep our women in shackles. What would be the meaning of freedom for half of the population then?"

Safia changed her position. It was time to explain. There was a sound of polite coughing from behind the curtain. When Abbas was at home, the main door was always open.

"Yes Bishan *Bua*, come in."

"Lady *Sahib* wants to know, why you have not come to *salaam* her," Bishan *Bua* enquired, her hand folded under the cover of her *dupatta* respectfully.

"I shall make a call in a few minutes." Abbas got up to wear his *shervani*. Bishan *Bua* coughed again, reminding Abbas that he had to give her permission to leave.

"Doesn't your mother ever talk in normal terms like, meet me, see me, visit me. Why is it always the formal—to *salaam*, pay respects, get an audience," Safia enquired brushing the *khaddar shervani*. Abbas smiled. He was a great believer in the *Panchsheel* principals and had made his own derivatives—'Don't arm either sides and conflicts shall be milder and would be resolved in the nonviolent way.' A statement from him to either side would certainly be a strong weapon.

"Oh by the way," Safia continued as an afterthought, "your mother and I have had something of a tiff."

"What! You have managed to disobey her again?" Abbas' smile took away the rebuke from his comment.

"No, only provoked her."

"What is there to choose between the two? Anyway, thanks for the warning."

God! That cough again. Abbas had been gone about ten minutes. What could Lady *Sahib* want now?

"Lady *Sahib* is calling you." Bishan *Bua's* usual politeness had an air of nonchalance. 'Calling her', this was not normal. Something very drastic was up at the big house. Picking up her *dupatta*, Safia slipped her feet into her Burmese slippers.

Her elder sister-in-law did not acknowledge her *salaam*. She had obviously been crying, her red nose still sniffing which she kept pressing in the pink muslin *dupatta*. Bubu and Wali *bhai* merely nodded. "It is all her doing. She is the one who gave shelter to that whore or else........."

"Or else? You would have killed her, aborted the baby?"

"Don't be disgusting Abbi."

"Why didn't you say this to Wali *bhai*, when he was raping the girl who was in your protection? Safia did no wrong in sheltering the poor girl."

"I told you he was completely under his wife's thumb," Wali *bhabhi* sniffed.

"What is done, is done. I have called you here to find a solution. A child in the womb won't sit still."

"Oh my Allah, why doesn't doomsday swallow me," wailed *bhabhi*.

"Perhaps because it isn't time yet. We are Muslims, aren't we? The Prophet has allowed four wives to bring down prostitution and this is probably such an occasion."

In his teens, Abbas had been fanatical about Islam. Waking with the first *azaan*, he was among the few Shias who knew the Qur'an backwards. In his Marxist days, this knowledge came handy.

"But to have a wife from that class. Disgusting!" Wali spoke for the first time.

"You had no problems sleeping with that class. Frankly you would be doing little else with any woman."

"I refuse to sit on the same table with that woman."

"You needn't," said Abbas "Wali *bhai* would maintain her in a separate house. It is a possibility though that he might spend more time there." Safia turned red to her ears. Six years of grass-root level of organizational work and two years in jail had certainly dried up the Lucknow politeness.

"I think Abbi is right. Marry the girl if she can be found."

"Wali *bhabhi* screamed and promptly fell off the chair in a swoon. Safia rushed to her while Lady *Sahib* eyed the two with disdain.

"Oh she shall be found. Party cadre would begin the search immediately. She shall be here within forty-eight hours." Abbas was jubilant. If a man from a respectable family could be persuaded to right a wrong and marry the girl he had compromised, then it would be a step forward in getting Muslim women some rights in this society.

"Then we will fix the *nikaah* for day after tomorrow."

"Shall I arrange for the *Maulvi*?"

"No. I shall ask the *Shahi Imam* to send someone. He is family and I would rather not have this talked about till the *nikaah* is over," Lady *Sahib* was candid and clear.

"Right," Abbas who had won a major battle cheerfully agreed.

Wali *bhabhi,* not having received any male attention, had got up and sitting on the *divan* was whimpering and rocking herself.

"I'll leave you home and then go down to the party headquarters. This business of finding Ladli might take some time. Don't wait for dinner," Abbas was gently hustling her out.

"But Wali *bhabhi*........?"

"Tch, come on. Don't you know when the audience is over? She shall be alright. Bubu will give her a pill of opium and she shall feel much better after a good rest."

The next two days hung in a fog for Safia. Ladli had been found the next day. She was still wearing Safia's sari. Safia gave another one, asked her to bathe and then sent her to the big house. The poor girl was absolutely nonplussed by this turn of events. In the few broken words that she could manage, she called Abbas her protecting angel. Safia oscillated between pride and fear. The girl really had a sensuous body and Abbas was after all only a man.

Weeping men look horrible. Women don't look beauties, but with men it is different. From early childhood, they are schooled to be 'men' and keep their emotions in check. The poor things get no practice. For the woman who is a witness to their seldom letting go of emotions, it is worse. They too have no practice of consoling a man. They cannot ask the master to shut up, they cannot be openly shameless and cuddle them nor can they offer the proverbial shoulder.

Safia felt the sense of helplessness creeping over her. She had never in her wildest thoughts imagined that Abbas could break down like this.

Half a dozen guests had gathered in the small drawing room of the big house. Lady *Sahib* and other women of the house were seated behind the curtain. *Shahi Imam*, with another nondescript *Maulvi* was present. Ladli, draped in red was sitting strangely calm and collected. Stranger still, Wali *bhabhi* was equally calm, rather jovial, cracking jokes as she prepared paan. Safia had a sense of misgiving, which she quickly thrust aside. The *nikaah* was over within three minutes. Paan and sherbet were being served, when Kasim came and whispered something in Wali *bhai's* ear.

"What!" The surprise in Wali *bhai's* voice seemed genuine enough. Kasim's breaking down too seemed real. Then why did Safia feel as if the whole questioning, even Lady *Sahib's* cold enquiry of what was amiss had been rehearsed.

"The girl is carrying a child!" Wali *bhai* exclaimed.

"Good god! Of all the treachery," said one of the guests before all pandemonium broke loose and Abbas' "But you knew about it" was lost in it. When some calm was restored, it turned out that Kasim was laying claim on the baby and on Ladli. Ladli was standing near the bamboo curtain while *Imam Saheb* questioned her.

"You are pregnant?" *Imam Saheb* asked curtly. Ladli nodded. Abbas moved to say something but was stopped by *Imam Saheb's* broad hand. "Who is the father?" Abbas relaxed. After all, there was nothing to worry about.

"Kasim," Ladli's reply was like a bombshell. Abbas looked as if he had been hit. The few seconds he took to find his bearings was enough for *Imam Saheb* to begin the *talaaq* proceedings. Ladli quietly took the one thousand and one rupees *meher* from Wali *bhai*, *Imam Saheb* cutting in to say that Wali Ahmed Jafri was not obliged to make this payment under the Islamic law but being an upright man, he wanted to honour his commitment. Ladli could leave or marry Kasim as he was willing. Ladli shook her head and chose to leave. She raised her hand to *salaam* Safia and then walked to Abbas. A neoconvert, she still carried in her blood the traditional Bengali custom. Pulling her *dupatta* over her head, she reached for his feet.

"Don't," Abbas stepped back. Ladli looked up in hurt surprise. "Why did you? How could you agree to this? I was with you," Abbas continued in a choked voice.

"Yes you were, that is why I managed to get so much money. Lady *Sahib* was turning me out with just fifty."

"And is that all that is important……money?"

"But isn't it? I was being offered only a fifty. Because of you, I have got a thousand and these silver ornaments. I can now go back to my village in East Bengal. I can buy back our land, maybe more. Perhaps I shall even be able to find my family."

"I wanted to change so much through you. I wanted to help Muslim women get some rights, wanted that the men should stop treated them as possessions for pleasure."

A hurt look shadowed Ladli's face, "And I thought you wanted my happiness. *Salaam*."

Ladli left. That evening, the *Shahi Imam* himself presided over the last *namaaz* of the day. He spoke at length over the growing tendency among some Muslim young men to distort and deform the *Shariat*, even change it. Thanks be to Allah, the laws were His own words and no man possessed the strength to change them.

Next morning, Ladli was found murdered in the most disreputable quarters of old Lucknow. She had probably been murdered for the money and the silver ornaments. The police took its time in handing the body to Abbas who had just returned from the faraway graveyard for the pauper where Ladli had been given a quiet burial. Irfan had been the other bearer besides two Hindu comrades who stood behind Abbas and repeated the *Namaaz-e-janaza*.

"So the coup was not successful?"

Abbas lost his temper. "It was not a coup. It was an effort to give some honour to womanhood."

"An honour in which the Muslim woman is not interested."

"What do you mean?" Abbas was perturbed.

Pandit Katayan was on his fourth cup of raw tea. Taking a long, noisy sip he looked up at Safia. "Did you know what Abbas was going to do?"

Nervously she glanced at her husband. "No. That is, I did have some inkling......."

"Based more on your imagination than his explanation. See even your wife has not been taken into confidence. Is it not important to make the woman realize what you are about? Isn't it important that she should agree and struggle for what is her right?"

Abbas had come in contact with Katayanji at the Lucknow central jail. He had become a major influence. Abbas had been a founder member of the Marxist Party of India, but was also a member of the Congress party and in his ideology had been something of a centrist. He had come out a radical Marxist, often questioning the lukewarm struggle of nonviolence. Katayanji, with his khadi dhoti, naturopathy, Vedas and theories of making Prophet Mohammed the eleventh *avatar* of Vishnu like Buddha had been made the ninth, was in the neighbouring cell. His own community, the Kanyakubj Brahmins had ostracized him but he was not deterred. That Muslims also ridiculed his theories was of no consequence to him. His chosen guinea pig was the Indian Woman. He conformed with the Aristotelian theory that a man's personality is developed in the first five years of his life. In those five years, it was the mother and only the mother who was the major, perhaps the only, influence. Change the mother and you shall have a changed man. Not one to be secretive about his research, he had given it the best exposure—discussions at the Hazratganj Coffee House. The news— Katayanji was out to reform and change the woman—had spread like wild fire. The case was taken up by the *Katha Mandals* in temples to the *Arya Samaj* get-togethers. Cartoons had appeared comparing him to the fourth century sage Vatsayan, the writer of *Kamasutra,* whose name rhymed with his. Doors of the inner quarters had been promptly closed on him, without anybody bothering to find out what change he was talking about. This country loves its status quo. He seldom managed to get samples of guinea pigs and rarely got the chance to get down to dissection. Abbas was a new recruit and a source to a sample of the rare guinea pig.

"For centuries men have been telling women what she is, how she should be, what her ambitions, her character, her desires, her aims should be. She had been put into the mould made by men and his society, Now you, another man wants to change that. Therefore, you decide what is best for her. Why not take her into confidence? Why can't she review and analyse her situation, why shouldn't she take the initiative and protest? Why can you not see? You are as much of a male chauvinist as your ancestors. All of them were sons of pigs," he added, calmly licking and then lighting the thin cigarette he had so painstakingly rolled.

Safia looked up, shocked to hear the worst abuse possible for a Muslim. The Hindu scholar would certainly be thrown out now. Abbas stood up and she pictured the wizened man, thin like the cigarette he was sucking, being bodily picked up by her six feet plus husband and chucked out.

Abbas walked the length of the courtyard and back. He then stood before Katayanji and said, "You are right. I am a son of a pig and a knighted one at that," he mumbled in an undertone.

"Right. Now that you accept it, lets get down to change it. Now don't look so hopeful. I am not promising you a change of parentage, but I can certainly try to give it a face lift." A look of expectancy flitted across Abbas' face, quickly engulfed by the prevailing sorrow. "Stop gloating over your failure. It was not the first. No chance of it being the last. The best thing for you to do is to cut your losses and to move on."

"Katayanji, I am so frustrated…..."

"Which incidentally is the luxury of the rich. Surely your ideology had taught you this much. Coming back to Safia, why didn't she know what you were going to do?"

"Well, there really wasn't time. I did want her to know and understand but….."

"But decided that she being your wife would naturally do what you want."

"No. There just wasn't time, really."

"Just my point. There never is enough time in spite of all good intentions. And even if you had years at your disposal, which you don't, it would still be impossible to reach out to every woman, every person you wish to convince."

"So I sit quietly and let one half of my community trample over the other half?"

"For Pete's sake, use your head and your legacy."

"Which one?"

"Both! Revolution in USSR was brought about by the tons of leaflets distributed amongst the factory and farm workers. Incidentally, Muslims happen to be very proud of the fact that they possess the Book, so give them another."

"Come of it, Katayanji. Eighty-five per cent of this country's population is illiterate and that is a calculation of the whole mass. I believe the illiteracy rate would be higher among the Muslims and if it was based on the gender calculation, women would still be the greater losers."

"And you believe that a book necessarily has to be read to make a difference?"

"Well, isn't it?"

"My dear Abbas, a book is a solid document, with longevity surpassing that of the pyramids. It shall be read by those to whom it shall make a difference, whose unquestioned authority it shall challenge, whose powers it shall question. It shall be there in shape, form, weight and size; it shall be impossible to deny its existence. It cannot be ignored. A concrete book can either be accepted or rejected. For either, it would have to be discussed. This discussion is our trump card because it shall lead to curiosity to know what the original document says. Curiosity is the mother of invention as they say. This curiosity shall set about inventing or rather reinventing the woman's position in society. Everything said and done, that is what we want, don't we? That the woman, decides for herself what is right for her because she has to live it. You have written a book and it had put the clergy on the defensive. But no one can survive on *Fireworks*. They are just a flash that don't really light up the darkness, only intensify it. It is time a flame was ignited—one that would keep burning because it would be continuously fed with new ideas, new concepts, new beliefs and most importantly new definitions. Let us light a flame Abbas and let us keep it burning. Life is short, there is no time to waste over failures; we have to keep trudging on."

* * * * *

TEN

The decorated tonga leisurely moved into the spacious portico of the Charbagh Station. Syed Murtuza Mehdi stepped up and signalled the thin tongawala, who loving pulled the emaciated horse to a stop.

"*Huzoor* would like to go to the city?"

"No, the Sheldon Palace," Syed Murtuza Mehdi answered gruffly. Shuttling between Karachi and Ajmer had been enough and this time it had been Karachi, Ajmer and Lucknow. A night in the unreserved compartment had worked wonders on his perpetually aching back. Held straight for almost eight hours, it refused to bend, turn or twist so that now he moved and turned corners like a wild boar.

"Do be seated, Sir."

"Yes but what about the fare?"

"Eight annas *huzoor*," replied the tongawala easily.

"Eight annas! It is daylight robbery. I will give only four annas."

"Be generous, Sir. If I get a little more, my horse shall eat well at night and he will pray for your family and dear ones."

"None of your Lucknow sop. I don't get taken in by it."

"*Huzoor* is obviously an outsider."

"I am from Ajmer."

"Sir, don't let your temperament become as dry as the Thar desert."

"Four annas or nothing. Don't try to get round me. I am originally from Benaras."

The tongawala gave up. "Be seated Sir, obviously mother Ganga would have dried up had its course run through Rajasthan."

Ignoring the jibe, Syed Murtuza Mehdi got into the back seat, lifting his feet while the coolie adjusted the small trunk and the food hamper. In the last eighteen months, he had developed the attitude of reacting only to things that involved him. Life in Karachi had taught him this. The promised country had turned out to be the proverbial pot of gold at the end of the rainbow. Luckily, a teacher still commanded respect and a couple of his students from the rich Sindhi community had arranged a house in the heart of Karachi. Even the thought of the refugee camps was throttling. In spite of the house, claiming his property, getting jobs for his sons and having to prove his identity at every point....what could be worse?

The borders were now safe enabling him to make a last trip to this wretched country and go back to his homeland. He had chalked out all the corners that had to be tied up and God willing, he would be able to handle even the most difficult one. But he had not bargained for this addition. He knew that Safia was not happy. That she had to work in a school to make ends meet, that she was living in a damn outhouse and that Abbas had become something of a jail bird even though the country had its much awaited Independence. But the latest was the last straw. Why didn't the foolish girl write to him or to her brothers? One of them was still here, posted in Jodhpur, working for the Indian Police. Poor child! Must be too ashamed to even put it down on paper. How could she write to her family that all her sacrifices had got her nothing? All the self-denials had led to more demands, that she forsook everything a human being lives for, till the final sacrifice is asked for. That she is even denied her own faith and blaspheme against Allah's gift—the *Shariat*. To find herself all alone in such circumstances. Why did he have to be so far away from his only daughter? What with a casanova for a father-in-law and the mother-in-law acting like a she-dragon, her parents and family migrating to the new homeland, what else could the poor child do except grit her teeth and make the best of a bad situation that continued to get worse. No more! Now she would have her father beside her. With God's help, hadn't he managed to prove that he was a rich landlord and thus entitled to a big claim in Karachi. Three palatial houses vacated by the Hindus. The houses had been exhorted of the ghosts of the Hindus who had been killed on the premises. A proper *Qur'an Khani* had cleansed the heathen ambience and any one of them could match the grandeur of Safdar Manzil.

"Where in Sheldon Palace, *huzoor*?" The tongawala enquired.

"Safdar Manzil on Nazir Hasan Road."

The tongawala chirruped the horse to a stop. "You are a guest of Sir Safdar Jafri?"

"No, Abbas Hasan. Why?"

A fleeting expression of terror crossed the tongawala's face and was quickly covered with a mask of indifference. "I would be grateful if you get down here Sir."

"But why? How do you think I am to carry my baggage to Safdar Manzil?"

"I am sorry Sir, but I cannot be seen associating with anyone connected to Abbas Hasan or his family." The tongawala had already put the food hamper down on the dusty road and was lifting the trunk.

"Associate? How dare you think that the *Najeeb-ur-tarafain* Syeds would associate with the likes of you. You are merely doing your job."

"Maybe so. But after the fatwa…….."

"What fatwa?"

"You don't know Sir? Then you must be warned. The *Shahi Imam* of Lucknow has pronounced a fatwa. No Muslim is to associate with Abbas Hasan or his family, or he too would be included in the fatwa. If I were you, I would turn back and put up somewhere else."

"I am the wretched man's father-in-law. It is my duty to redeem him and my daughter."

"Then God be with you. No, I won't charge anything. After all, you are Abbas *bhai's* father-in-law."

"What is that you said?" asked Syed Murtuza Mehdi, holding the four anna coin between his thumb and forefinger.

"The fatwa has been passed and must be obeyed. But Abbas *bhai* is a fine man. There are not many like him. He organized the tongawala's union and got us living quarters. Even the Prophet Mohammed was condemned in the beginning."

"So you think that he is right to blaspheme the Faith?"

"Who am I to think anything, only an illiterate tongawala. But Abbas *bhai* has a following. Give him my *salaam*, say Sher Ali remembers him in his prayers."

Syed Murtuza Mehdi turned, hamper in hand, the trunk balanced precariously on his head, he remembered the boy of fifteen who had trudged from Jaunpur to Benaras to complete his High School. Even after giving him two degrees and three palatial houses, life had a strange way of repeating its course.

Trudging his way through the overgrown path, Syed Murtuza Mehdi reached the dilapidated dirty moss green door that must have been brown once. Lifting his fist to bang loudly, Syed Murtuza Mehdi almost toppled inside as the door was flung open suddenly.

"God have mercy on us, don't you know how to enter a gentleman's house?" Precariously balanced on the wooden frame, with a deep voice, broad forehead and piercing eyes, stood an insolent looking man doing nothing to help him. Syed Murtuza Mehdi tried to speak in a dignified manner.

"Is the lady of the house at home?"

"Hear this one. Walks straight in and wants the lady of the house. Why, may one ask does *janaab* enquire about the lady of the house?"

"Oh, *Abba*! Irfan, this is my father."

"Well why didn't he say so? With an iron trunk on his head, how was I to know."

"Abbas seems to have made himself so popular that I was not able to persuade the tongawala to drop me at the house," replied Syed Murtuza Mehdi, thankfully surrendering the box to Irfan who deftly slipped behind him and shifted the weight on his head. Syed Murtuza Mehdi heaved a sigh and turned to his daughter, who covering her head, bent to pay her respects. Blessing her for happiness, Syed Murtuza Mehdi's voice choked and Safia also started sniffling. Irfan quickly deposited the trunk on the verandah and turning his tousled head grinned, "The Shias wail at any given time. It is a practice to appear in full form during Moharram. See to the morning tea *bhabhi* while I wake up Abbas *bhai*." As Irfan sauntered away, Syed *Saheb* raised an enquiring brow at Safia.

"That is Irfan."

"Does he live here?"

"No I only sleep here sometimes when I am too drunk to leave," Irfan turned back to reply.

"*Lahaul-e-vila-kuwat*."

"He helps Abbas with the Party paper. Don't think anything about him, he enjoys shocking people."

"Huh! Funny hobby."

"Isn't it? In fact, I could tell you some more of my hobbies, like………"

"Oh shut up Irfan," Safia intervened hurriedly. "You were going to wake up your Abbas *bhai*."

"Right. He might thank me for saving him the emotional let up."

"Thanks for the concern, I am up. *Adaab abba*."

"*Adaab*," came the curt reply. Safia glanced at her father. Acknowledgement without blessing. Signal of impending trouble.

"You seem to be sleeping well after the fatwa," Syed Murtuza Mehdi enquired tersely. Abbas smiled and kept quiet. Safia marvelled for the umpteenth time at his capacity to smile where a grimace would have been more appropriate.

"Don't you think you should have a bath before breakfast *abba*? I will have the water warmed in no time. Shall I open the trunk for a fresh kurta pyjama?"

"Yes my child," he thankfully handed her the keys. While her father was in the bath, Safia flitted from the kitchen to the make-shift dining room in the verandah, to the bedroom and the guest room. Her eyes deliberately avoided Abbas' eyes which sometimes raised from the morning paper to glance at her.

"Safia, don't fidget, I am not going to ask you any questions."

"I wish you would. It is so important to say something."

"Is it?"

"Well, of course. How else do we communicate?"

"That is a different question. One doesn't have to speak to communicate."

"If one doesn't speak, how can one ask, how can one know?"

"Wait! Just that. Wait for him to let you know. He will, because he has come for that. Don't get worked up before knowing everything."

"Do you know?"

"I can guess, but I am not telling. Today you have to take a major decision."

"But……"

"And it is going to be only your decision."

"Someone should learn from you how to get a person worried without saying anything. I won't stand for it anymore. You have to tell me."

"Wait."

"Oh she won't have to wait any longer. I shall come straight to the point." Syed Murtuza Mehdi, dressed in a crisp kurta pyjama, smelling of talcum powder, seated himself on the high dining chair and stared pointedly at Irfan who smiled and stared back smugly, scooping the cream from the top of the milk into his tea.

"This is a family matter," Syed Murtuza Mehdi said coldly.

"Nothing about Abbas *bhai* is private anymore. I am a reporter and the first quality of a good one is being nosey. I am not going to vanish.

"Please Irfan…" Safia murmured.

"Yes, I think you should leave." The serious tone of Abbas worked and Irfan gulped down the oily tea.

"Nastiest cup of tea I ever had. Well, so long."

"What an insolent young man! Well, now to more important things. You perhaps know that with God's grace I have received three big houses in Karachi."

"Really? I thought you were entitled to only one," Abbas interjected.

"The government in our homeland is benevolent. I want you to come back with me and live in one of the houses."

"But *abba*, in a secular country the Muslims are up in arms demanding Abbas' execution. How do you expect an Islamic regime to accept him?"

"I wasn't talking about him. I want only you to accompany me."

"But how can I, in this condition?" Safia blushed at having to mention her advance stage of pregnancy. "And when and how does he join me?"

"He doesn't. You take a *talaaq*."

"What!"

"The period of *Iddat* can be spent in your brother's house. The final *talaaq* can be handled through correspondence."

Safia turned to Abbas. "You knew about this?" Abbas nodded.

"And what about my……"

"*Meher*? We shall waive it. With a bungalow for a dowry, you will be able to find a suitable man in Karachi."

"I was not talking about *meher*. What about my consent?"

"What do you mean 'your consent'? You are my daughter, you would not wish to live with a non-believer. Anyway, in case of *talaaq* a woman's father or brother take the decision. Your consent or dissent is not required."

"You knew about this too?" Safia again questioned Abbas. "You know that a woman has a right to reject or accept a proposal but no rights when it is a question of getting out of the contract."

"Really Safia, I am quite at sea about what rights Islam has basically given to a woman and which in the process of giving, it has taken away."

"Well, you can't remain at sea. You will just have to find land because I have to live, we have to survive."

"Who has to survive?" Syed Murtuza Mehdi enquired.

Safia sighed. Why were parents so much bother, so much responsibility? One didn't want to make them unhappy but they had a habit of being over possessive, of taking decisions about their grown up children as if they were still babes in arm. True they had made sacrifices for them but was it right to demand total subjugation later on. "*Abba*, I am not leaving Abbas, nor this country. Not for any bungalow, not for any well placed man and yes, not even for you."

"I am warning you. In a few years you will have to come to your homeland, bareheaded and barefooted, because these Hindus are going to drive out all the Muslims."

"If that happens, I shall not come begging at your door step. I shall stay with the rest of my bareheaded sisters at the refugee camps."

"Well, one thing Abbas has certainly given you. In my house, you had no tongue in your mouth, now it is a yard long."

"In your household I was only a woman, now I am a person."

"Don't you think you have said enough Safia?" Abbas intervened. "Surely you have not come all the way from Karachi to acquire a divorce for your daughter, Sir?"

Syed Murtuza Mehdi had the grace to look ashamed. "No, I came to speed up Shahid's migration to Pakistan. All his other colleagues in the police force have received their orders but the Home Department is strangely quiet about his case. Shahid did make enquiries but was informed that his file has been sent to the chief minister's office and has not been returned."

"But why didn't Shahid inform me? I have very cordial relations with Pantji. I could have got him an appointment."

"Shahid wants to migrate to Pakistan. He has a bright future in the Police Force there. He does not want to spoil it by taking your help. You enjoy a reputation in Pakistan that would frighten *Iblis* and information has a way of travelling long distances."

"That is true," Abbas agreed. "Very astute of Shahid. Well, we do the next best thing. You come with me to the chief minister's residence. We will see if he gives us an audience. Shelve the doubts. You can always claim in your homeland that as Safia's father and a devout Muslim, it was your duty to return me to the true faith."

"That is what I told the tongawala," Syed Murtuza Mehdi blurted out before he could check it.

"See, you already have it on your mind. Keep repeating until you are convinced that it is indeed a fact. Let us hurry. Pantji is a stickler for punctuality and leaves home at 9.30 sharp. Safia, my *shervani* please and *abba*'s coat. Give me some money too."

Safia opened the old cupboard and gave the Indian wife's call 'listen'. Actually the Muslims have adapted it from the Hindus like so many other things. All Indian women make their husbands name-less. This is their way of getting back at the in-laws who call her by her husband's name—a married woman is forever so and so's *dulhan* or wife, till she graduates to being so and so's mother. Poor men are always on the alert, lest he answers the wrong woman's '*suno.*'

Abbas got up glancing apologetically at his father-in-law. Safia seemed busy digging under a pile of clothes. This is where she kept her money and the notes had got into the uncanny habit of travelling up the folds of saris and losing themselves.

"Why are you doing this?" Safia asked without turning.

"He is an old man, he needs help."

"Even after the way he tried to break us up?" Angry tears glinted in her eyes.

"In a close relationship, time often erases bitter incidents and only the sweetest of the memories remain. He is your father. You would soon forget his miscalculations because after all you, have proved him wrong and emerged victorious. A winner enjoys the pleasure of forgiving. But then comes the regret, for not having made that small effort that could have helped the relationship to survive. Then you would make twice or thrice the effort but fail to blow life into a relationship that would slowly dwindle into being just a face saving family connection with no real love or warmth. Don't grudge him this demand that he has not made. Don't make him small by waiting for him to ask for our help."

"But then he might not be grateful for this favour."

"Better to give and cheated of gratefulness than be a miser and not give at all."

"It really doesn't matter," Abbas said suddenly and Syed Murtuza Mehdi glanced furtively at his son-in-law. The two were walking down Sikander Bagh Road on way to the chief minister's residence. "You are her father, you have a right to think of her well being."

"She doesn't think so. She spoke as if I was her enemy." Syed Murtuza Mehdi wiped away a tear.

"No, she doesn't think that. But she does feel that she has right to make her own decisions."

"What would the world come to, if women start taking decisions?"

"We would have to wait and see, won't we?"

"Not me. I shall be living in an Islamic state. Anyway, now that she is irrevocably yours, please take care of her."

Abbas stopped in mid-stance, "I can't promise that. I can't be a liar. My path is such that I can't make any 'taking care' promises. She shall take care of herself and I shall be with her as much as I can."

Syed *Saheb* shook his head. What was happening to the world? No pretences. Not even for the sake of an old man.

Abbas was filling the Visitor's Register when the Chief Minister's Personal Secretary Bholanath came running out. "The CM wants you inside immediately. Leave the register, just come." Grabbing his arm, Bholanath almost dragged Abbas inside with Syed Murtuza Mehdi bringing in a bewildered rear.

"Why are you roaming the streets like a ram in heat?" Pantji did not believe in beating about the bush. Bang on the head, was his technique. Only sometimes he banged so hard that the poor fellow turned to pulp. Abbas turned red at the vulgar reference to his manhood. "Don't you know there is a fatwa decried on you? You could have been lynched on the road. Walking down alone, with a non-descript old man. Some bodyguard eh?"

Syed Murtuza Mehdi visibly flinched at Pantji's onslaught. Fond of a stiff manner himself, he took pride in calling a spade a spade. But then he had seldom been at the receiving end and it hurt.

"This is my father-in-law, Syed Murtuza Mehdi. He wanted to see you and I had to accompany him."

"Why walk? The rickshaw pullers are on strike? Bholanath, some tea."

"Oh stop being a boor Pantji. I reached here alive in one piece, so drop being the over zealous chief minister. You personally would love to see the last of us communists."

"You are right."

"So why the act?"

"Nehruji's instructions. Why does your father-in-law want to see me? Lets see, your name sounds familiar."

"Perhaps because his son's application has been lying on your desk for the last eight months. Name is Shahid Mehdi."

"Oh! You are ACP Shahid Mehdi's father. And why didn't he come to see me himself?'

"Perhaps because he is afraid," suggested Abbas. "You are quite a frightening person. In the communist circles, you are known as the perpetual 'No-er.'"

"My head shakes because of an injury received in a lathi charge."

"True, but you must admit that it shakes in the wrong direction. Very off-putting indeed."

"Maybe. Coming back to your brother-in-law, I have been waiting for him to come and meet me. The front office has standing instructions to let him in whenever he comes."

"That is kind of you, Sir. I would be grateful if you would let me know why you will not sign his application for migration."

"Oh, so he speaks. Well since Shahid is so afraid of me, I might as well tell you the reason. Perhaps you can convince him to stay on." Pantji took a big gulp of the black tea and grimaced. "No life without sugar. It was the summer of 1945. A demonstration had been scheduled outside the Nainital Secretariat. It was a peaceful one and we were not expecting anything but a token reaction from the British Police. They had got used to us Congressmen and though the entire government of the United Provinces was inside, we knew that the most that would happen from their side would be shutting of the windows. We had been shouting juicy slogans for an hour and our throats were getting hoarse. The leaders had delivered the speeches and the crowd after the usual clapping were quieting down, getting ready to disperse. No one was prepared for the next event. From nowhere appeared a group of mounted police, led by a handsome young officer. The crowd, taken unawares, scattered in all directions. There is not much flat space in Himalayan towns and small groups become easy targets for the sure-footed horses. Baffled by the sudden onslaught, I also ran but then turned back to help my injured friends. There were women too in the crowd. Most of them too scared to run. We had not faced the mounted police since '43."

Abbas started to speak but Pantji held up his hand to stop him. "Wait! There is more. Suddenly I saw an extremely old man running towards me. He was being chased by an extremely rough looking policeman seated on a chestnut gray, the horse as handsome as the rider was ugly. A blow caught the man and he was dragged down, falling on his back, his hands thrown asunder, mouth open in a silent scream, eyes cringing in terror for the anticipated blow. I ran in his direction, wanting to throw myself on him to save him from the blow that would surely have killed him. The hand was raised and the whip sang through the air. They were too far, I couldn't make it. In a fit of escapism, I covered my eyes. All was suddenly pin drop silent, waiting........waiting for the death blow. In the silence, a single word rang out. "STOP!" I can't describe the voice that gave the order. It was like a pistol shot from a revolver with a silencer. Have you ever heard a revolver with a silencer being fired? It goes zrrrrrrrrrp, but is as effective as the loud rapport. Just as this curt, low order had been. The policeman's hand stopped in mid-air and he turned, looking surprised at his officer. "He is an old man, a push would have driven him away, why whip him to death. Our orders are to disperse the crowd, not to murder common citizens." The young officer in command gave the order. Everyone heard him and slowly moved away as he followed at a canter, waving his baton of authority, asking everyone to disperse. And I deprived of a heroic act, blessed him. Next day, I found out his name and stored it for future use, when India would be Independent. Well, the future has become the present and as expected India is free. Syed Murtuza Mehdi, that young officer was your son Shahid Mehdi.

We need police officers like him. Officers who have sharp brains and strong bodies but who also possess a heart; who implement the law but give a soul to authority. Discipline without compassion amounts to cruelty. We need him here on this side. Why does he want to leave? He is not a Punjabi or a Sindhi. He belongs here with us."

Pantji got up and stood near the window. He seldom made personal appeals. Shuffling through the files to cover up for the burst of emotions, he felt a strong hand on his shoulder. Turning he saw Abbas standing behind him. "Don't Pantji," he said softly.

"Don't what? The CM asked gruffly.

"Don't stop those who want to go. Give them the freedom to make a choice. If they stay, good; if they leave, they really were never ours."

Pantji thought for a moment. "Bholanath, please bring the file of applications for migration of police officers. You are a good man, Abbas. Why do you stick with the commies? They will never be any good. Why don't you cross over. We could do with men like you."

I was thrown out of the Congress in '39, remember? I could have apologized and stayed. But I made a choice. There is enough crossing over going on at the border. I would rather stay put."

"Hunh! So be it. No one can say I did not try, with you or with your brother-in-law. Ah! The file. So I shall sign and stamp it and safe journey to Shahid." Pantji handed the signed and stamped application to Abbas who, glancing at it, passed it on to Syed Murtuza Mehdi.

Smiling, Abbas addressed Syed *Saheb* who was a little aghast at the speed of events. "You see, not all of them are bastards. That is why I stay. Let us go."

"Oh Abbas," This was Pantji from his desk, "You are not going anywhere."

"You mean?" Abbas half turned towards the chief minister.

"Just what I say. There is a warrant for you."

"Oh really. So I have walked in to get myself arrested. What are the charges?"

"Here is the warrant, you can read it."

"For causing communal disharmony, unrest and tension. How very original! I never would have believed that I would qualify for this. So where do I go?"

"Stay put. The jail van is on its way."

"But you can't do this. My daughter, his wife is in the family way. She has no one with her."

"Don't plead *abba*, not before the bourgeoisie. I suggest you leave Lucknow immediately. This might harm Shahid's prospects in Pakistan. Go to him. He would know what is to be done next. Pantji, as an 'A' class prisoner, I am in the 'A' class I presume, you have still not got down to changing the shoddy British rules, I demand another cup of tea and the morning newspaper please."

Pantji rang the bell to summon Bholanath, his shaking head expressing the remorse he was feeling, "I am sorry Abbas, I wish you would listen to reason and join the Congress. Think of Safia......."

"Spare the histrionics Pantji. In my ideology, we are prepared for the worst and this is still not quite there. *Abba*, ask Safia to pack a clean pair of kurta pyjama and the incomplete manuscript of my new book. She knows where it is. Give my love to Shahid, I hope he will do very well in his new homeland. We shall probably not meet again, so take care."

Syed Murtuza Mehdi embraced his son-in-law. "I accept Safia's point of view, you are certainly worth giving up the world for. But son, see the proof of my point of view. Most of them are ogres."

"Oh no, they are not," Abbas smiled at Pantji. They are merely wearing ogre masks, which might scare the humans but would not frighten the real ogres when they come. And come they will! Their faces more dreadful than any mask can be, their manner brazen and gloating, their aims fundamentalist and sectarian. The world would stand a better chance if we were to face them as strong humans rather than disguised demons, because they would see through the disguise and tear it off, knowing that the disguised were shitting in their pants with fright. Then, having torn down the defenses, they would jeer at the faceless, spineless authority. They would surge forward, trampling all of us to dust, the few remaining humans along with the disguised, the masked and the faceless. But this class never understands. Today they hold the reigns....unfortunately."

* * * * *

ELEVEN

"How can you be sure this time? After all you have been in love before several times."

Sir Jafri looked at the black velvet surrounding the picture of Kaaba. His new found indifference to religion, all of them, gave him a sense of distance so that he could view them without prejudice or bias. He wondered how close did hanging photographs of shrines bring Islam to the idol worship of the so called 'kafirs'. Perhaps Abbas was right in saying that it was impossible to believe in a God that was omnipresent but formless. The thought reminded him of Abbas. Strange, this man whom he almost feared to call his son. How could a progeny's stature grow so much higher that his father's? He had visited him yesterday in the jail to find out about the status of his bail application. But Abbas had merely smiled and quickly changed the subject, enquiring about his plan of talking to Bubu about his decision to marry Sylvia. That is why he was here, because Abbas declined to talk of himself or Safia's future till that was settled. His wife's rustic brazenness that bordered on insolence irked him. He resolutely brought back his gaze on her and straightened up a bit. He had to take the bull by the horns.

"You are right. That is why I know that this is the real thing."

Zeenat Begum's eyes became alert gimlets. One has an upper hand if the opponent takes a hypocritical stance. There is an advantage if he is trying to hide and take a detour or trying to find by-lanes to surreptitiously reach the destination. Beware when he admits his folly and throws in all earlier ones in the admission. One is then on equal grounds. The opponent has chosen the straight road and was hurrying towards the destination. Not a situation very much to Zeenat Begum's liking. She would have to use all her wits to delay him from reaching there. It was time to advance with care.

"Who is stopping you from continuing with your...er, love affair?"

"Moral ethics. Sylvia is carrying my child!"

It was not the bombshell that one would normally have expected from such an information. Rather like the damp cracker—a fizz and no pop. She had already been alerted by the *Shahi Imam*. Years of generous contributions to various masjids and madrassas and any information concerning her would find its way to her network of spies. She knew of his decision and had sent down Bishan *Bi* to request him to step up to the 'seeloon' on his way for the evening stroll. He had been a bit surprised because usually she just barged into his parlour after confirming that there were no outsiders. But he had agreed saying that he was coming to meet her anyway.

"This is still going to far."

"I love a woman. I want to marry her. She is with my child. I do not want it to be a bastard. What is the far and near of these facts? The *Shariat* allows me four."

She did some quick thinking. Wildly, she hunted around the dark closed abysses of her mind for a strategy, a process to stall if not stop this step that would bring an end to her reign.

Sir Jafri, finding her deep in thought, had stood up and almost reached the door before she realized that this would probably be the last chance she would have to talk him out of his decision which that would lead to her doom.

"You had promised not to bring another woman to this house. You had said that I shall always be the queen of this house."

Sir Jafri remembered the first night he had spent with his beautiful bride. A young foolish man, believing that beauty in a woman was the only reason for loving her.

"That was a long time ago."

"Which you think is enough reason to break a solemn promise. Your oath is like the fruit preserves, to be thrown away after the season?"

"No, time is not the only reason. Look, I am very lonely here." He put his hand on his heart. "The country is free, my friends have moved on. Some to England, some back to their estates, others even further, to heaven."

"You have a family. You have three grown up sons....bless them!"

"True, and the youngest one was really a friend. A friend I let down because of you. Yes, you stopped me from contesting the ban on his first book *Fireworks*. Giving way to your nagging, I publicly burnt hundreds of copies of the first creative work of my son. All because you wanted to be on the right side of the *Ullema*. More than a year before India achieved freedom, he tried to persuade me to return the knighthood. He tried to make me understand that I needed to identify with my own people, find my own feet in my motherland so that I could stand without the support of those who had enslaved her, sucked her dry. He gave me the example of Rabindranath Tagore who gave up the knighthood to protest against the Jallianwala Bagh massacre. Today, India sings his song as the National Anthem. Again, it was you, who would not let me do so. Sylvia, that undefined mixture as you call her, believed that Abbas was right. But not you, his mother. Why is there a myth that a woman knows her child best? Why do we continue to believe in it? My knighthood was your crowning glory. Lady *Sahib*! That is how you liked to be addressed publicly and Begum *Sahib* would have been a come down, something common, ordinary, Indian. Well, the support that propped me is gone. The rulers have gone back home and I, with no feet and probably also no spine, am left groveling in the muck that they have left, marked forever as the *chamcha* of the oppressor. I let my boy go to jail when I should have resigned in protest and joined the freedom fighters. Sylvia has helped me analyse my life, my past. I have to do what is right and shall not be cowed down by anyone. She told me that if I continued to remain silent in the face of injustice, then my conscience would do the speaking for the rest of my life. Well, it has started goading me. I see my son, alone, trying to manage without luxuries which are his birth right. I see my daughter-in-law working outside for a few rupees. See her wearing old, darned saris to work. They don't come here anymore, not unless I ask them to. They are fed up of your petty politics. You wanted it this way, well you got it. So be it."

"Abbas or your dear daughter-in-law have nothing to do with your affair with that Anglo Indian."

"Don't you understand? This is as much as my conscience would take. I cannot add the weight of another sin on it. Sylvia is carrying my child and it must have a name—my name. It must have its rightful share in my property."

Realization hit Zeenat Begum like the sudden electric pain of a colliding elbow and she cursed herself for not seeing it before. That was it! The slut wanted a share in what was hers—Lady Jafri's. She wanted the money that Lady Zeenat Jafri had cringed and saved, the property she had added with her business acumen. She played again, hoping that it was not the last card. In a game of wits, the biggest hurdle was that one did not know how many cards one possessed or what was the worth of each card till it was played.

"You were happy enough to deny your own son any right in your inheritance."

"Only because you prevailed upon me to stay on the right side of the Muslim clergy, to project myself as a good Muslim. Like a weakling, instead of standing up to you and shooing away the *Ullema* from my private life, I took the easy way out. Well, not anymore. Day after tomorrow, I am drawing up a new will and I shall leave Abbas his share."

"You can't do that. You cannot leave ancestral property to someone who has been ostracized by the community. The *Shahi Imam* has pronounced a fatwa that demands his head and condemns anyone keeping any relation with him. Even his wife has been granted permission to divorce him. The government has arrested him and he has been charged with causing disharmony and unrest among communities. You cannot leave him a penny. It is against the *Shariat!*"

"You forget that more than half of my property has been bought with my personal earnings. I can leave it to anyone I want. Regarding the *Shariat* and this so called fatwa, I am going to contest it till the highest court. This country is secular. The Constitution that is in the process of being written and shall become the backbone of its governance will proclaim it so. A country can have only one system of law. Personal laws of any religion shall have no place in a secular set up."

"Why don't you call the *Shahi Imam*? Three of us can sit and discuss this. Maybe he can find a way so that we can give something to Abbi on the sly. I do not want to cut him off completely. I am aware of his circumstances."

A soft, mild smile, slowly spread on Sir Jafri's face. A knowing, understanding smile. He was quiet but his eyes spoke and what they said was so stark that Begum Zeenat quickly lowered her eyes. Never again was he going to act on her advice.

" Never am I going to trust the decision of the *Ullema* and abide by it. Nothing shall ever be done 'on the sly' while I am alive. Every step of mine shall be visible, every action open and transparent. I am personally going to file the application for Abbas' bail and shall be his lawyer when the case comes up. It is never too late to change and though I know that I shall not be able to right all the wrongs in the short time left to me, I can at least make a beginning."

She changed tactics.

"Why don't you ask him to come here? Abbas I mean. Once he is out on bail, three of us can sit down and talk. He is very upright and his ideology might not allow him to accept anything from you. He might even oppose you marrying this woman."

"Tell you the truth, it is not possible to face someone who is as honest as him. I am proud to have a son like him and ashamed of being his father."

Zeenat Begum heaved a sigh. That end was safe so far. Now she could talk to Abbas and get him to stop this catastrophe.

"But I talked to Katayanji and he persuaded Abbas to meet me. Yesterday I spent an hour with him at the Lucknow Central Jail."

So much for hope. Zeenat Begum tightened her insides resolutely. She would not, could not give up that easily. "And what did he have to say?" It was important to know. Well informed is well armed. What had her son, who had always stood with the right, say to this proposal of marriage and inheritance?

"Nothing much. He said that I was wrong to have carried on an affair behind your back. He had asked me two years back, in Allahabad to make a clean breast of it. He did not seem very much interested in a legacy nor in the proposal I made to him."

"There is another proposal? My! A lot seems to have been going on at the outhouse."

Sir Jafri carried on, ignoring the sneer. "I have to take steps to protect the child I father at sixty eight. I cannot hope to live for long, though I am in excellent health. I was hoping that Abbas would stand guardian to Sylvia's child and see that it gets its share in the inheritance."

"And…?"

"And nothing. Abbas refused."

Good. If her son was not on her side, he was not on the side of the enemy. What needed to be done could be planned and sorted out in time.

"But Katayanji managed to persuade him to discuss the whole proposal with Safia before taking a decision. Apparently Safia has been able to make him see things in a different light. I have received a note from him this morning."

"And what has that woman been able to persuade him to take for himself and for her?"

"Strange as it may sound to you, Safia does not fit into the craving, grasping mould of the woman."

"Meaning that I do?"

"I did not say so."

"But that is what you meant. All my grasping has been aimed at making you and this family richer."

"No, it was aimed at making you richer because that is what you wanted. Money, because it got you power, more control over other mortals. The more you were able to control the lives of others, the happier you were. It did not matter that none in your family was happy. It did not occur to you that it would take one small decision by someone to cut off your control string. A tiny decision, not to depend on money for happiness. Safia and Abbas have found that happiness. Coming back to the point, Abbas does not want a share in my property. He only wants what I have already promised him—the outhouse."

"But the outhouse has so much land with it!"

A ghost of a smile flitted across his face. "Yes Abbas has said so much. In his note, he points out that this would be the first thing that you would say. How well he knows you. He does not want the land, only the four dilapidated rooms. But I shall not stop at that. I shall still leave him half of what is mine. Let him refuse to take it or give it away to his party. I must do what is right, now at the very end. What is important is the final point in the letter."

"And what is that?"

"He has agreed to be the custodian of Sylvia's child and its inheritance, even adopt the child if Sylvia wants to move on in life. But he also wants Sylvia to be taken care of. He says it is the honourable thing to do. Strange that an out caste, someone who is considered a disgrace to his community, should tell a judge what is honorable?"

It was like a slap across her face. Abbas, her honest, truthful, forthright son, one who always sided with the oppressed, fought the battles of the downtrodden, could not tolerate lying, cheating and injustice, he had decided to side with this injustice—the insult and public humiliation of his mother and his family.

"I am getting late for a meeting."

"With her?"

"Your satire does not heckle me anymore. No, I am not meeting her. I am meeting one of my junior lawyers who now has an independent practice, to discuss the will and the guardianship."

She did not try to stop him. Her mind was busy elsewhere and working so fast that it did not even register his departure. That was that. Sylvia and her child would get a share in the family inheritance and half of Sir Safdar Jafri's personal property. The other half would go to Abbas. But then, he may not be satisfied with this much and might contest his denial from the ancestral legacy. He was a capable lawyer and stood a fair chance of winning. All this façade of not wanting any property was only a put on. She knew that every man wanted to possess, because possession was power. If that happened, where would it leave her and her two sons and two daughters. Steps had to be taken and fast. No time to ruminate the pros and cons.

* * * * *

TWELVE

I

The man coughed to tell Lady *Sahib* that he was on the other side of the bamboo curtain. Standing behind the curtain, she seemed stiff and motionless. She did not want to speak. Her voice might give away the fear she was feeling inside. Fear of losing everything that she had so carefully pieced together, of seeing her tightly closed fist prised open and its power snatched away. Whatever the extent of her apprehension, she had to go through this alone. It had to be an impeccable plan and the first condition of an immaculate scheme was that there should be no witness to it.

It was not that the man had never taken instructions from the weaker sex. He shifted weight and cleared his throat. He was nervous only because of the class. *Imam Saheb* had asked him to reach on time and not ask questions. Only those related to the job. It would have been better to get instructions from *Imam Saheb* but then as he himself had admitted, each minute lost in receiving and passing instructions was an hour forgone in implementing them. Anyway, who was he to question? His payment and of course, the clear-cut instructions, was all that mattered. He did not like using his head and as he had found, neither did they who gave him assignments. He appreciated it when a watertight plan was laid out before him. He could carry out a prepared plan with a clear conscience.

Lady *Sahib* was speaking. Did he sense a tremor of fear in the voice? No, he must have been mistaken. No fear or else replaced in a split second with relief and anger. It was natural, the anger, but why the relief? Why now, before the action?

He heard the whole thing through. It was all of five sentences. At the end of them, he found his hand damp with his own sweat.

"This is what you want for both of them?"

The man had over the years cultivated a process of understanding emotions without looking at the face of the person he was talking to. The jerk of the knee, the small movement of the thumb and the little finger, the scratching of one's palm, inclination of the head, all told him the manner in which his queries were being received. It was because of this instinctive capacity of reading the person that had brought him so much success. He heard the almost inaudible extra breath outside the rhythm of respiration. It was an appreciation for exact detail.

"No! Only for her. He is only to be…...."

It was left hanging in mid-air but was understood, judging by the quick nod of agreement from him. "Good. It is safer. Big names always invite more attention, enquiries and deeper investigations. The authorities feel it is their duty."

"As if their sense of duty would make a difference."

"Quite. Now, if I could have more explicit instructions. A photograph would have been extremely helpful."

"*Imam Saheb* told me you might want one. Let me make myself clear. I don't have her photograph and I am paying you twice your price, just for this one shortcoming on my side."

"I am sorry. Please go on. You have already described her. Tell me when and where shall I find her."

"Not her, them. They have to be found together. That is why you won't really need a photograph. You do know him by face, I presume. Before you leave them, you have to take off his diamond cuff links, the gold watch, a diamond and ruby tiepin and whatever cash he is carrying. This is important. The motive has to be robbery."

"He would be wearing all these things?"

"Oh definitely! Always trying to impress that woman with his wealth and good taste."

"You want them returned to you?"

"No, keep them. A bonus if you do your job well."

"I have never failed."

"So I was informed. That is why you are here. I also know that this is the toughest one you have handled. It also comes with the highest risk factor."

The man was silent for a few seconds. Looking away from the curtain, he ventured tentatively, "Have you....have you tried talking to him about the outhouse?"

"Don't you dare bring him into this."

"It would be advisable to talk to him."

"Since when have the likes of you dared to advise people like us? Don't get above yourself just because I am talking to you."

"His persuasive powers are well-known. Wait for him to come out of jail. Maybe he can prevail upon your.....not to take this step. Then you won't have to go to such extremes."

"You are being paid the sum you wanted. What is your problem? Getting cold feet?"

The unaccounted relief he had felt in the cold voice seemed to be subsiding. He pressed on. "The Muslims are encircled by seclusion of doubt. No longer does the man on the street trust us, no longer does this country count our leaders as its leaders. Stories both true and false about Muslims are being spread and believed. If it is ever found! Let him persuade *Sarkar*."

"I do not want to persuade anybody. No one is reliable."

"No one can doubt his integrity. Anyone in Lucknow would willingly swear by it. Even those who have pronounced the fatwa!"

"They are all on side. Men! They are all united. I want an end—a permanent one."

So that was the reason for the relief. She was ending a long chapter, one that she had learnt to live with. Reaching the end had been painful but once having arrived, it had kindled the hope of a new beginning, where she and she alone would take decisions, give orders and rule. The mistress with no master.

He knew that no backtracking was possible. "I am here. You can be rest assured."

"I never do. Not until I have the results to my satisfaction."

"An advance was promised."

"Certainly. It is on the table. Collect it on your way out and do count it."

Dot on cue, the door behind him opened. He had been dismissed. A chilled gust entered the room and stopped in mid-path, almost as if it had collided with something colder than itself.

II

"Why have we stopped here?" Sylvia parted the thick curtains of the buggy just enough to peep out. "It is still not the guava orchard."

"Why are you so nervous today. I would have thought that you would be calm in the assurance that everything has been decided."

"I don't know. The apprehensions that should have vanished have returned. They are faceless and formless, yet they are there, frightening in their undefined presence. I am unable to fight them, to drive them away even when I know that everything will turnout all right. It will, won't it?"

The childlike, nervous query brought a smile to Sir Jafri's lips. He reached out for her hand that was agitatedly tying and untying her scarf. She let him hold it for a minute then deriving strength from his warm grasp, she took it back to the knot, tying it for one last time before saying quietly, "It is still not the answer to my question. Why have we stopped here?"

"I'll ask. Basharat, Why have we stopped here?"

"*Sarkar*, the winter rain has begun and the road beyond in not a *pucca* road Sir. It is full of puddles. The earth is lose and the wheels shall sink. The buggy might get stuck *Sarkar*."

"Oh, all right. Drop us here and you park at a safe place. Come down Sylvia, it shall be a longer walk today to reach your favourite fruit."

"Raw guavas are not my favourite fruit. It is the baby who loves them—hard, green, raw and bitter sweet."

They walked in companionable silence for some time. Once inside the orchard, Sir Jafri walked ahead clearing the way and raising branches for her.

"You have something to tell me and are debating whether to say it now or keep it for another meeting."

"It is remarkable how you always know what is going on inside me."

"Nothing remarkable about knowing the feelings of the man I love. So go on, say it."

"Its nothing really. Only that I had a talk with her, with Zeenat and she has taken it rather well. You know, no tears, no tantrums, no ranting and raving, not even the cold fury that she whips up when she has not decided whom to vent it on and keeps it alive till she finalizes the target. It was almost as if she knew the whole thing and only wanted a confirmation from me. Having got it, her mind was already on its way to making some other plans."

"I have a strange feeling of foreboding."

"My dear, this is the first time you have admitted being afraid of anything."

"I have to be, because you are."

"I am not afraid, but yes I am a little uneasy. How could she have known? Who could have told her? I have not discussed this with anyone except a *Qazi* of a non-descript mosque. It was he who advised me to wait for a month after you had converted."

"You never told me that it was the *Imam* who had advised you to wait?"

"Well it was a meaningless detail. But how does it......what is the matter? You look terrorized!"

"Time! That is what they are trying to do. Buy time. You should have insisted on an immediate *nikaah*. We must go back, immediately, to safety. But where can I go? Which place would be safe? Yes, Sheldon palace. Take me there, now!"

"You want to live in Sheldon Palace? Why? How? Lord Sheldon shall be leaving in a week's time. Everything in that house has been packed or sold. Lord Sheldon himself was telling me the other day that he is being served his meals in enamel plates because all his tableware has been shipped to England."

"It is still an Englishman's house. Nobody can dare to enter it without permission. I shall be safe there. I must leave The Carlton Hotel and move there. I shall beg him to let me stay. You come with me and persuade him. Please."

"Don't be ridiculous Sylvia. You are carrying my child. My only child that shall be born out of love and not lust. I shall not let any harm come to you or to the baby."

"The baby!" She faltered and stopped, her eyes glazed and unfocussed, staring into faraway nothingness, where undefined, floating images were taking a form. "Yes, that is it. It is because of the baby that she is worried. She does not want it. She shall not let it become a reality."

"Now you are being silly Sylvia. This not the first time that a man has fathered a child out of wedlock. Indian women are used to it and Muslim women more so, because they accept the *Shariat* as the God's word and it allows more than one legal wife."

Sylvia stopped and turned to face him, fixing him with an aghast look. Was it possible? Was ever such ignorance, such naïveté possible in a man who had talked, heard and punished so many criminals, had seen so many shades of human character. Could a man who knew so much still believe that a woman's sensibilities in the face of scorn and humiliation were any different than that of a man? Did being a woman lessen her sense of dignity and her feeling of outrage? Why did men assume that if they had slept with a woman she stopped being a person and only became his shadow with no right to vanish in the dark? She would never have a wish outside his wishes, feel no degradation in the secondary position, never become a non-person in her own eyes and never rebel. Why were they so sure that she would never think beyond his thoughts, have emotions he did not know, entertain reactions to his actions that he could never imagine, yearn for revenge to balance years of degradations, make decisions that he should fear and attack with a strategy and ferocity that he should have had a foreboding of?

This sudden dawning of this ease scorched a truth in her brain. She would have to protect herself. Much as she loved him, she could not depend on him to look after her. She turned and trudged back to the buggy mumbling to no one in particular. "We walked far. Why did we have to walk so far. Where is the buggy? Why can't we see it from here? Do not come to meet me at Sheldon Palace. Come only at the time of the *nikaah* with the *Qazi*. This earth is so loose, makes movement difficult, slows progress."

Sensing her agitation, he hurried towards her trying to calm her down. "Keep quiet Sylvia. Control yourself and don't run like that…. the baby….."

"The baby, yes the baby. I want it so much. Don't let anything happen to it."

"Sylvia stop!" He put his arms round her but she continued to move, dragging him with her till he had to use all his strength to make her still. "There, there, calm down. He embraced her and tightening his arms tried to soothe away her fears. She came willingly and held him tight. Just for a second and then her body tensed and she screams. Sir Jafri felt a sharp pain in his neck and heard the crunch of his collar bone breaking. He still managed to turn and caught a glimpse of a man throwing away a club and a glinting blade replaced it. Instinctively he tried to fall on Sylvia and felt the man kick him roughly to one side. Two heavy punches landed on his ear and jaw. He saw Sylvia screaming and trying to run and the man doggedly, calmly follow her. The last he saw was the vague figure of Sylvia receding from him....far....further....before all went black.

Basharat saw a hunched figure walk out of the grove and move towards the river bank. Five minutes later, he heard a soft splash. Who ever it was, planned to cross over to the Ujaryaon village. Not necessarily because they lived there. Merely that crossing water meant putting the dogs off the scent. Not for nothing had Basharat worked for a judge for twenty five long years and haunted the grounds for eight hours everyday.

He continued to crush the tobacco crumbs on his palm, carefully adding the lapel full of lime, humming line from the popular ballad of *Shirin Farhad*. Testing it for crispness, he pulled his lower lip and placed the mixture carefully in the cavity. Leisurely he got down and patted the horse to assure him that he wasn't going to be far and walked into the orchard.

In the clearing he saw a small pink mound. As he walked by it, he couldn't help stealing a glance. The knees were pulled up as far as possible, as if to squeeze shut the large gaping gash on the abdomen, like the mouth of a demon finishing its aperitif of fresh blood. The lips were open in a silent scream and in the eyes there was still life.

Basharat turned his head away and hurried the few steps where a still body lay face down, only the hands sometimes making clawing movements in the mud, trying to hold on to something precious. He lifted up his master and got under him, the way he had often helped bring out sinking buggies in his footman days. Heaving the not so heavy body, he trudged slowly outside the grove. With great care, he deposited him on the seat. Sir Jafri slumped to one side. Basharat propped up the other seat to stop him from rolling down. Closing the door and bolting it from outside, he jumped to his seat and clicked. The horse remembered that it had brought two passengers and looked at him enquiringly. Basharat shook his head at the horse and saying, "No, we are not taking her," pulled the reins hard and gave the horse a sharp flick of the whip. The horse neighed, put down its head and moved.

India was now a free country and the new government had proclaimed equality between all classes. As a servant, Basharat had no choice but to obey his master's commands. As an equal, he was entitled to have an opinion about these commands and Basharat did not approve of his purebred Syed master marrying a *firangi* leavening. He patted the horse's rump lovingly. Why, he would not allow even this horse with its Arab strain to mate with a lowly mixture.

* * * * *

THIRTEEN

She had been expecting the summons for the last two days. When they hadn't come, she knew that it was not because Mujtaba *Saheb* had not heard about the fatwa. He was turning the whole episode in his mind, looking at it from every angle, weighing the pros and cons, all the time hoping for something to happen, something that would divert public attention, perhaps change the course of events and take the decision out of his hands. Maybe he had been hoping that she would resign herself to save him from the shame of having to throw out a teacher he had personally approached and appointed.

Whatever might have been the reason for the delay, it now seemed to have sorted itself out. Safia reached the door of Mujtaba *Saheb*'s office, which usually was never closed but today it was not only closed, its curtains too were tightly drawn. She knocked and waited. After a full minute, Rasheed opened it from inside and stepped aside to let her come in. He normally *salaamed* all the teachers but today his one eye looked her in the face and then looked away.

"Come in Safia. Please sit down. Rasheed, close the door as you go out and stay there. I am not to be disturbed."

Safia sat down and smiled at Mujtaba *Saheb*'s back. He was making a severe effort trying to find something in the bookshelf that held only about thirty old volumes. She remembered reading somewhere that it was far easier to appoint people than to fire them. Should she make things easier for him? He had given her a job when she needed it. Trouble was that she still needed the job, now more than ever so that she could save up for the two months without pay. She wasn't even sure she would be able to rejoin work with a baby at home. She resolutely squared her jaw. She knew what was coming and she wasn't going to make it any easier for him by saying so herself. She wasn't going to resign. She would have to be fired, with the reason for the termination of her services spelt out clearly in black and white. Proof of the injustice meted out to those who did not toe the accepted line of religion.

"We shall not get this over with unless you begin Sir."

Mujtaba *Saheb* turned. Safia had never seen him looking so tired. He grasped the back of his high chair and fumbled for words. Slowly looking up he said, "My hands are tied Safia."

"Only as long as you think they are. Otherwise anyone should feel free to take their own decisions. This is now an independent democratic country."

"I have opened this school to educate girls. Not to turn them away from God."

"And my presence here, one who is *namazi* and a strict Muslim, would turn them away from God."

"I have worked hard to persuade Muslims to educate their girls. Each one of these four hundred and thirty girls are the result of my constant toil. My reputation of being a devout Muslim and shall never give way to anything that would remotely harm our religion has been my strongest support. I do not want all my labour to go waste. I cannot afford to tarnish my reputation. It would be the same as putting a blight on the school's name."

"You are trying to give education to the Muslim girls so that they would be more acceptable to their educated husbands?" Safia knew that she was on dangerous grounds. She could be turned out for touching this subject.

But for once Mujtaba *Saheb* gave a ghost of smile and nodded, "I myself would not have been able to put it so well."

"And acceptance by men is the end to all female desires. You think she should not have a better status, any more rights, any more empowerment than that?"

"I have set out to educate women. My work is defined. It does not include meddling with the *Shariat*."

"And you accept that an educated woman would still accept everything as it is handed to her. The education that you are giving shall never turn her into a reasoning, logical, analysing being that all education aims for. This reasoning, logical being shall never see or realize the lack of reason and the contradictions of the *Shariat*. She shall never understand that God by himself could never have been so unjust to one half of his believers. The one who treats colour, race, labour, status with equality, would He treat the two sexes so differently? Why do you want man to have the right to accept or reject a woman? Why don't you want some riders put on his constant effort to insult the woman who sleeps with him, begets his children, looks after his house and hearth? Why does not she have the right to say the triple *talaaq* and be rid of an unjust partnership."

Mujtaba *Saheb* was quiet for a while as if debating whether he should come out with the truth or not. Then he gulped a big swallow of water from the silver glass and fixed his eyes on her. "*Shahi Imam* was here yesterday. I either throw you out or else not only would he personally go to the house of each student and make the parents withdraw their daughters, he would also lead a mob of Muslims and set fire to everything combustible in the building."

"No, No! That shall not happen. Not because of me." Safia had risen up and was shivering as a chill of apprehension ran down her spine.

"Then please my daughter, leave!"

""I shall leave Mujtaba *Saheb*, even though I badly need a job and the money. But you must give me a letter terminating my services."

"Why Safia? So that you can show it in the progressive and liberal circles and run me down as a reactionary conservative whose entire effort to bring education to the Muslim woman is nothing but a sham?"

"Why are you so afraid of how you are perceived amongst the progressive muslims? They are hardly a handful and you have decided to side with the majority. Why then does it matter?"

"Safia, as God is my witness, I would give my right hand to see some changes in the *Shariat*."

"But what use is your right hand to the liberals or for that matter to God? It is your support that would have made a difference. But you wouldn't give that now would you?"

"Blessed are those who have the strength of character to stand with right though outnumbered."

"I don't understand you Muslims—the educated ones. Most of you believe that some changes should be made in the *Shariat* to provide space for the freedom of the female. You live in dread of what might happen to your sisters, mothers, daughters. You know that the

Shariat puts absolute and ultimate power in the hands of the clergy where the women are not represented. Yet, you choose to do nothing about it. You believe that in your abstaining to caste your lot with either side, you can safely maintain the status quo. You are wrong! Fundamentalism spreads like the plague. The dark alleys of apathy are its breeding ground. *Khuda Hafiz* Mujtaba *Saheb*. Do not throw away your copy of *The Flames*. Come to Hazratganj tomorrow. A bonfire of the book has been scheduled by the *Shahi Imam*."

* * * * *

FOURTEEN

I

It was a night of darkness, a night of light, a night of union, a night
of separation, a night of pain, a night of pleasure, a night of joy, a
night of sorrow, a night of creation, a night of destruction, a night
of warmth, a night of chill, a night of sharing, a night of loneliness,
a night for welcoming, it was a night of rejection.

Twenty eight days before Abbas had been arrested for his latest
book *The Flames*. The Muslims had been up in arms and a statement
had been issued in the name of Sir Safdar Jafri, publicly disowning
him. The new government had its duty to protect the minorities
and anyone making an attack on their culture and personal law had
to be duly punished. The formation of Pakistan had given birth to
a new cult that had never existed before—The Hindu chauvinism.
The Partition had given a choice to the Muslims and those who had
decided to stay in India had shown faith in the basic secularism of
their country. But they were still insecure, sheepish at being part
of the whole that had demanded partition and got it. Jawaharlal
Nehru, Gandhi and the rest, in that order, had agreed to divide the
country. The first, because he was losing time and wanted to get on
with making a tryst with destiny, the second because he was losing
energy and the fight seemed to have gone out of him. Instead of
handing over the reigns of the freedom struggle to someone who
had more energy resources in him, Gandhi chose to hand over one
third of the country to an English educated buffoon who boasted of
having created Pakistan single-handedly with the help of a stenog-
rapher. He had asked for a lot in the hope of getting some. When
Lord Mountbatten informed him about his getting the lot, he had
been too surprised to thank the Imperial representative. Migration
had begun but those who chose to stay on, prided themselves for

having chosen secularism over fundamentalism, cultural unity over religious unity, motherland over the promised land and co-existence over ghetoism. True, they had chosen all this, but they also had a lot of expectations and the greatest one was that the Hindus would be grateful to them.

The Hindus were sharply divided. One portion would have been happy to see the last of the Muslims leave for wherever, the other was ready to make room for them and treat them as equals. The second half was committed to protecting the Muslims who were clearly insecure in the slim passage of the divided sea. This half was more vocal, educated, filled the English press or the press that mattered, made up most of the writers, poets, and prided themselves as comprising the intellectuals. They were also in the majority in the government. Nehru was a known socialist and a Muslim supporter. It was his duty to protect the interests of the Muslims. He knew that Abbas was right. He also knew that the other three writers who had contributed to writing the book named *The Flames* were responsible intellectuals who had the interest of the community and the country at heart. He also knew that had these four remained with the Indian National Congress, they would have been assets today and would have then contributed more towards the development of their community than a measly book that was burnt in bonfires at roadside corners. He discussed the problem with Pantji, the down right secularist, the person in-charge in Uttar Pradesh. Pantji was always level-headed and had a blinkered attitude. His vision always centered at on one point at one given time and at this moment it was focussed on the First General Election to be held in sixteen months time. That the Congress would form the government was a foregone conclusion, but the Muslim vote was important. A few writers more or less did not matter. Nehru, on the other hand, wanted these writers to be safe. Personal security, black cats, Sten guns and karate had not arrived on the scene. The central chief and the provincial one put their head together and reached the conclusion that one out of the four writers, the one who had conceived the project of attacking the Muslim Personal Law through short stories and creative writing, should be arrested. The other two, were to be let off with a warning and the fourth, a woman and a doctor could be spared on those very grounds. Women lynching was still not fashionable and even the fundamentalists had enough ethics not to stoop so low, as to physically harm a woman. So the official circles believed.

Dr Zahida was left to device her own security. The Mullahs still spoke about her every evening after the last *namaaz*. Why they bothered to talk about a lost woman to an all male gathering remained a mystery. They would have been more effective had they talked to the women. Islam believes that it is the men who should be held responsible for the actions of their women. Goaded on by the lower clergy, young boys stood at the corners of Zahida's route to the Civil Hospital. She was thick skinned enough not to let their comments disturb her. It was their self-righteous egos that got under her skin. They should have been at school rather than hanging around paan shops, waiting for a woman with ugly leukoderma marks. Leukoderma, that had brought a haunted look in the eyes of a beautiful six year old child. Lukoderma, that had prompted her to bow her head at innumerable *durgahs* and shrines. Leukoderma, that seemed to grow every day making the dark areas blacker and the white ones more opaque. Leukoderma, caused by generations of cousin marriages, that had made her hide herself in the dark corners of her father's library, that had turned a chirrupy child into an introvert adolescent, who chose for herself the hard road of medicine, asking her father to spend her dowry on the post doctoral work in England. Leukoderma that had so shot down her value as an attractive ware in the marriage market that even her sexual abuse had only led to disbelief. Who would find her attractive enough to rape her? The rape was one of the stories of *The Flames*. She had finally got it out of her system and she was satisfied that it had been publicly burnt. She smiled at the boys mouthing taunts and comments taught by the madrassa teachers. The degradation of the Muslim mind began with its association with the semi-literate *Maulvi*. In the last few years, she had taken pleasure in shocking people around her. She had cut her hair. Not the fashionable Edwina bob, but a proper boy cut, wore trousers in public, openly smoked, rode a bicycle to work and worse, spoke to men who accompanied their fifth time pregnant wives about not to have so many children. As if it was up to him, poor thing, to stop the will of Allah!

Safia was in pain, the pain of childbirth. Zahida refused to beautify facts and pain for her was never beautiful. "Pain of creation, my foot!" She retorted to the progressive men who tried to indulge in discussing the greatness of woman in her motherhood. All women hate their husbands when they go through labour pains. What comes out is not beautiful. It pees, yells and hurts her breasts regularly and worse, sleeps for twenty-two hours a day. It is much later that the aesthetics of creation begin and by then most women have either lost the will to create or have again been led in the direction of creating something she did not really care about.

"Is your wife joining the party school or is she busy preparing another lump of meat? She would ask the flustered comrade. Her sound scolding had the nurses on her toes and often so scared the woman on the table that the baby came a good quarter of an hour early.

The frequency of the pains was not increasing. Labour had continued for six hours now. Zahida put her ear on the swollen womb willing the baby to move down. The head was down, the position right, the heartbeat was regular. There was nothing wrong with the baby. This called for other measures, but for the first time Zahida wanted to manage without them. "Oh come on girl, a patient is a patient, don't go all gooey hearted on her. It is more important to save the woman from this pain than spare her feelings." She took a deep breath and put her hand on Safia's head. The tired woman had slipped into a restless slumber. She opened her eyes and ran a dry tongue over her parched lips.

"Is it over?" She whispered. Zahida laughed "Not yet and perhaps not for a long time."

"Oh God, why?"

"Because you are not cooperating, not really relaxing and how can you when you have heard the horrible news."

Safia was alert "What news? I have not heard anything. What has happened?"

"Oh dear I am sorry, I didn't know that you had not been informed." Zahida turned away and smiled. But for the Leukoderma she would have made a remarkable actress. Safia grabbed her doctor's coat. "Tell me, you must, is it……..has Abbas…….." Zahida put her hand on the stomach. Good. The intensity of contractions had increased. Now for the rest of the dose.

"Don't take it like this. Everything will be all right. We will get the most experienced lawyers, take up the case to the highest courts, don't you worry."

"But what is the case? What are the charges they are framing on him this time?"

"It was expected. The Muslim clergy have met the prime minister and requested him to ask Abbas to leave the country."

"Leave the country? But where would we go, what will we do?"

The contractions were speeding up. Zahida had been right with her natural practicality. Safia now wanted to get this thing over with and get down to dealing with more pressing problems. The delivery was over in half an hour.

The baby, a girl, was washed, wrapped and fed. Safia was sponged and given a hot drink. She should have slept but when Dr Zahida came in, she sat up and looked at her enquiringly. Not one to mince words—when an English classmate had begun to take too much interest in her, she had turned on him and said, "You are not going to marry this blackie and this spotted blackie is not going to sleep with you, so buzz off." 'To the point' was the rule of her life. She did not ask what Safia wanted to know. She also made no show of enquiry about her health. She was the doctor, wasn't she? She knew how the patient was feeling. No need to indulge in formalities.

"It was a lie." Zahida said simply. "Please try to understand Safia, it was you who made me do this. You were indulging yourself in pain, perhaps psychologically trying to identify with Abbas and take away some of his discomfort. You did not want the labour to end. It was necessary to galvanize you into action, so that you would desire to get out of this placid pain and get on with the real pain, the pain of existing, pain of living, the pain of being and the pain of trying to change it. By the way, have you seen the baby? It is nothing much to look at now, because fundamentally all babies are manufactured in Japan. But she will be a beauty. Take it from a woman who has delivered more babies than any living female. Yes, weasels and rabbits included. Why so aghast? All of them, even yours, are mine."

Safia reached to take her hand, "You are my messiah, my baby is your gift and will remain yours always."

"Don't go all soppy over me Safia. You know I do not like dramatic dialogues. Leave them for the narrations of Moharram." Zahida was back to her usual brisk self.

"Well, if that be the case, don't stand on my head chattering. A woman likes to rest after labour. Why so aghast? Two can play the game of being brunt."

"Oh la la, we are quick to learn."

"When in Rome as they say…."

"Great! Two of us would make a great team." Mumbled Zahida as she briskly walked out of the room. Safia dozed to the lullaby of her flat heeled sensible shoes making a soothing clatter.

II

The rumblings in the Muslims continued, the sporadic comments and stray incidents of violence took an organized tone and Zahida felt the heat of anger and discontent around her. It was a month since Abbas had been arrested. His bail application had not yet been entertained by the courts, neither were the charges properly framed. Those baying for his blood had slowly become wise to the game the government was trying to play. It was biding its time until the anger and the sense of outrage would calm down. Meanwhile it was keeping Abbas safe in the lock up. Helped by the clergy, frustration was building up in the community. If it was impossible to reach Abbas then the next best thing was being debated. Sir Safdar Jafri might have been a good alternative, but he had already been attacked by a robber and almost killed in the process. That left Safia and Abbas' child. As the *Shahi Imam* had said in one of his speeches, the progeny of a snake is also a snake and Islam puts no restriction on killing a future snake before it acquires fangs.

Left to her own devices, Zahida might have found a solution to the anger that was slowly reaching the boiling point. The administration, however, had to step in. It had a duty to fulfill. Zahida was served a notice. She was not to step beyond one mile of her house.

"But the Civil Hospital is three miles from here. How do I work?"

The inspector shrugged his shoulders. It was really none of his business. He was a Hindu and simply followed orders. "Please sign the receipt so that I can leave." Zahida signed and waited for her lawyer. She had been leaving for work and had made plans to move Safia in her house. She would have to get someone to fetch Safia, someone who was not afraid of mobs, someone who knew the lanes of Lucknow like the back of their hand, someone who loved Abbas and Safia and would stake their life for them. A long list of names and faces floated before her. Mentally, she struck them off until she had only two names left. One, who had no contact telephone and would have to be hunted all over Lucknow, from the wretched bars to the elite hotels. The other was a wizened nondescript man, the last real scholar of Sanskrit, the waif of a man who could stand up to any mob and no one would have the guts to touch the hem of his *dhoti*. He picked up the phone himself and recognized her voice. Dispelling with the formalities, he cut Zahida in mid sentence. "Come to the point *Doctorni Sahiba*. You are not one to stand on ceremony and I really do not have the time for them. Why are you calling this man when you should be busy slitting stomachs?" Hearing the full story, he sighed and said, "Bad timing. If the communists cannot time a baby, how can one believe them to time a revolution? I will reach the Civil Hospital in an hour. Meanwhile I shall try to find Irfan."

Katayanji reached the OPD just as it was beginning to spill over. He walked straight to the crowd that parted, bowed and *salaamed* the old scholar. Someone dared to ask if all was well with him. "People don't visit a hospital when all is well with them. Incidentally this is not the Sikander Bagh you know." His retort silenced any other queries. He had the ward number and wanted to find it without having to make enquiries. He knew half the crowd outside were not patients. But they were not idle bystanders either. He did not have time to judge if they were curious onlookers waiting to carry bits of information to all the corners of the city or were they here for something more sinister. A nurse had been following him for the last few minutes. Wanting to shake her off, he turned towards her suddenly splitting his lips to show the large ugly teeth. "Have designs on this *chhaila*, my girl?" The girl blushed and moved one step back, then glanced around quickly, stepped forward and said loudly "Ward number 78 is vacant, you can wait there if you like." Then she lowered her voice and added, "She has been discharged, very early in the morning. It was not safe to keep her here. The crowd outside are not patients."

"And she went.......?"

"I don't know where, but she was alone."

"Naturally. You let her go at an unearthly hour and expect the family to be playing the brass band outside. I shall see what can be done."

Coming down the betel juice spewed staircase, he almost collided with Irfan. Katayanji gestured to keep him quiet and Irfan started speaking with great gusto about his latest poem. To anyone it would seem like a senior scholar and critic was trying to shake off an over-enthusiastic puppy poet. At the turning of Jopling Road, Katayan stopped. "It is safe now. Where do you think she could have gone?"

"There are her students, but I doubt if she would put them to danger. She might have gone to some relative's house."

"Better chance of finding her at Zahida's."

"No. I have been there."

The two stood at the street corner paan shop, digging into the long list of friends, comrades, students and relatives. It was mid-morning. Katayanji hailed a rickshaw and circuited eastern Lucknow. Irfan managed to dislodge an acquaintance from a bicycle and rode to the western side. They agreed to meet at the same spot at three.

III

Safia had walked out alone from the gates. The Medical Superintendent had been right. Nobody expected her to be alone and her casual exit proved to be her best disguise. Begging is a habit and learnt with difficulty. She was penniless, yet she had not been able to ask for money from the nervous nurse who had escorted her to the hospital gate. Carrying the day old baby, she dragged her legs towards home. Her eyes stroked the soft skin of the baby. Her lower abdomen was tender and as she walked, the thick sanitary towel became heavy with blood.

A rickshaw stooped near her. A *burqa* clad woman was sitting at one end of the seat. As Safia looked up, the woman silently beckoned her to climb beside her. It was the size of the hand that first alerted Safia. Her glance travelled down and she saw the broad pyjamas and thick-soled shoes peeping from beneath the black hem. Safia stepped back and would have fallen but for the baby. The large hand lifted the *naqab* a few inches "Please Safia *aapa*, come quick." It was Zain who extended his hands. Safia handed him the baby and tried to get in. Her swollen legs suddenly buckled and she collapsed. The rickshaw wala jumped down and holding her by her waist, lifted her to the seat. Zain held her firmly and the rickshaw began its slow crawl against the hot winds. The turn to Nazir Ali Road brought hope surging back. She quickly started planning where she would keep the baby's cot, the baby had to be fed, first thing. Then she must write to the court and get an appointment at the Lucknow Central Jail. Abbas must see the baby and together they must give her a beautiful name.

It is strange—the process of childbirth, the simple biological process of continuity. If the woman is happy with her man, if he loves her and she loves him, the pain she goes through comes with a bit of regret—This is one thing she cannot share with him. She wants to hurry through it so that she can reach the stage that can be shared, where the pain has turned into a three dimensional being, a soft, brown visual. If it is only the woman who loves and not the man, if for him the nights spent in her bed is only a physical release, which if suppressed would have taken the course of a nightfall, if he gives only his physical being and not the warmth of his heart and soul, the woman understands this. The absence of the warmth that fulfills. The absence of love and desire, the presence of lust alone. Lust that does not satisfy, lust that is a glutton that gobbles its fill. Lust that only awakens a yearning for completeness. If this were the case, the woman goes through the pain hoping that the coming child would be the beginning of a warmer relationship. A beginning that would build ties, some sort of a bond that would sustain her, give her the light, the air and the room to photosynthesize her existence into a life, so that she can open to the dawn and the dark of the being, of loving, of surviving and of resurrecting. What high expectations from a poor, helpless lump of meat. Hope! Yes hope, the last and the most beautiful of beings to emerge from Pandora's box, so unidentified that even the *Navarasas* leave it alone, yet so necessary that each *rasa* needs it for its own existence. Hope that waxes and wanes but never quite extinguishes, hope that survives death in vague beliefs and superstitions, of chance meetings in dreams, in the familiar glance of a stranger, in the cool foamy touch of a Himalayan spring in the placid flow of the Ganga.

Again, she might be as uninvolved with the man as he with her. A woman is usually raped on the bridal night. The entire process of loving and being loved, is lost in the matter of fact way intercourse is conducted. For the man, a few hard jumps, for the woman a bruised and bleeding vagina. With time, she would get over the physical pain only to be overtaken by another pain. A pain that swings from the mental to the physical, squeezing her mortal being as she exists with a man who cannot even mildly arouse her. Her arousal and her expectation of receiving pleasure is considered a sin and she has to keep her breath, her groans and her grunts of pleasure, suppressed in a tight ball, inside herself, till the man has had his fill and rolled over. The realization that this has activated the seed inside her, that someone could use her like this, that she, without making any contribution, was saddled with bearing an undefined form. How? Why? She asks herself. When the baby comes, when the first pain begins, when the human form makes its first movement downwards, most human forms make a habit of moving downwards from then on, she begins by disliking it that slowly grows into a hatred, travelling through disgust, anger, self pity and loathing. The biological process takes its course. Thankfully, the Homo Sapien is still enough of an animal. She hides the hatred for the child and the loathing for the man in the superficial activities like bathing, clothing, feeding the baby. Suckling gives her more pleasure than innumerable nights of lovemaking. Thus begins the first bond with a human being for the woman, a bond that she nurtures and protects more for self-defense and self-satisfaction and even more to justify her existence.

If the child is a male then it is the first real love for her. Enveloped in the Jocasta complex, possessive and grabbing, she detests the way her baby grows to manhood, connives to keep females of all ages away from him and gloats in his need for her. If the baby is a girl, the woman sees a rival in her. The rest of the family rejects her and it becomes easy for the woman to sideline her. However, if the man tries to form a bond with the girl child, the woman sees all the caresses, all the love that should have been hers by right, being diverted to her daughter. She feels scorned before the usurper whose existence she has brought about. The woman, helpless against the man who is out of reach, becomes Clytemnestra who tortures Electra because Agamemnon is not approachable.

The rickshaw was slowing down at the gate of the outhouse of Safdar Manzil. Zain jumped down and Safia was struggling down with the help of the rickshaw wala when Zain hurried back and whispered, "The gate is locked Safia *aapa*."

"What do you mean....? This gate is never......" But it was. With a big black iron lock and the gate was also padlocked, for good measure. It had been done in the last forty eight hours when she had moved to the hospital. But why and who would? Justice Jafri had said that this portion belonged to Abbas or rather her. Bubu with all her determination would not dare to take any step against his wishes, even now when he was totally paralysed and bedridden..... Or would she?

"What are we to do *aapa*?" Zain enquired. Safia looked up and down the road. The morning commuters had come and gone. Whom should she call? Who would come? How to take this household insult to the public? Well, as Abbas said, when being chased by a buffalo in a treeless field, there was no way but to turn back and hold its horns.

"*Bhaiya*, you had better go to the main *kothi* and enquire. Perhaps they have done this for safety." Zain nodded and slipped behind a tree to remove the black disguise. He spread the *burqa* under the tree and turning away said, "You better feed the baby *aapa*. I will get the rickshaw wala to park in front you."

Sitting down on the black cloth, Safia lifted her *chikan* kurta and tried to give the swollen nipple to the baby. Its lips searched around, sensuously feeling Safia's rounded breasts and then suddenly the toothless gums made a hard grab at the swollen nipple. Safia jerked as a wave of pain and pleasure surged down to her vagina. The baby continued to suck for about three minutes. The first feed that should have been celebrated with drums, songs, sweets and jewellery. The formal welcome given to the continuity of life by the living, the resonance of knowing that we shall always be here, whatever doom the religions might predict. Conducted in the shade of a tree where even the chirping sparrows had retired in the shadows to escape the scorching June sun. No one blessed her, no hand threw gold and money in her lap, thanking her for nurturing the family seed for forty weeks, for giving it its first life source. The baby gave a final tug, spilled most of the overflowing milk and loosened its grip. Safia lowered her kurta. She was herself so thirsty and hungry. She had heard that women became ravenous after feeding. She yearned for a pan full of *haleem*, but would have settled for some *dal roti*. Zain was taking a long time. What could be happening? Then she saw him coming down, slowly, taking one marble step at a time. He was slouching and he was alone. Head bowed, he stood before her. When in trouble think of the worst, but this was far beyond it. Begum Zeenat had refused to give the keys to the house. In the last twenty four hours, Sir Jafri had disowned Abbas. How did a man, paralysed and confined to bed, who could only produce guttural sounds to attract attention, disown someone? No one had dared to ask this question. The fatwa had asked all Muslims to cut off ties with Abbas. A special line had been added for her. She was to divorce Abbas immediately. It would come into force at once. The period of *iddat* had been waived off. She would be free from the minute she pronounced the wish to be free of the contract. If she didn't divorce him, the same fatwa would apply on her as a party to the crime of blasphemy against Islam and the Holy Qur'an. The *Ullema* had come a full circle. Some years back they had demanded that Abbas divorce her, promising all support in helping him get out of paying *meher*. Now it was the other way round.

Safia sat there, her mind refusing to function. She had heard that if during meditation one is able to empty one's mind of all thoughts, even for a split second, the relaxation achieved was more than a long deep slumber. Here her head had been empty for what seemed like hours and all that was happening was a surging numbness in her limbs, her body, her brain, her heart and her soul. She seemed to be sinking. Deep and dark was the abyss through which she sank. She had not begun at the top, she was not reaching the bottom, it was a travail from nowhere to nowhere. It did not even have the energy of nothingness, from which new life begins. It was just a floating into the non-existent, a road to nowhere, a bridge that did not lead across. Zain's cough seemed to come from a long way.

"*Aapa*, I'll go and find the others. You do not lack supporters, but we will have to be careful and find out who is with us now. You shall be alone here." Safia nodded and saw the rickshaw turn and go back on the road that had brought her to this point.

She should have asked Zain to get her something to eat or at least water. On the dry grass, she saw some brown pellets. This tree probably fell on a goat path. We are so busy trying to see what is at a distance that we forget to see what is in our immediate vicinity. Involved in widening our circle of friends, of forming new bonds and of breaking new grounds, we forget that there are existing ties that need to be nurtured, need to be looked after lest they dry up leaving a deep dry moat around us. A deep gash beyond which forms can be seen but not touched, counted but not loved, visualized but not felt, not embraced. Gashes, that allow no communication to take place, no love to envelope the soul and keep it safe, no warmth to bring the brain and the heart in tune with the body. Gashes, that with time fill up with slime, dirt and dust; too filthy to clean, to offensive to touch.

It was the third tug on her *dupatta* that registered. The end seemed to be caught in something that would not let go. Safia gave a sharp pull and with the *dupatta* came a small goat falling pell-mell on its unsteady legs but not letting go the tasty morsel. A shrill scream accompanied the goat's fall and a grubby child of about seven appeared from behind the tree. Scampering up to the fallen goat, she picked it up and glanced at Safia. "A young goat should not be hurt. Suppose it had become lame?" Safia gave a non-plussed smile. The little ragamuffin had shiny black currant eyes and sun bleached mangy brown hair. That was all that was visible under the dirt. Suddenly the child smiled, "Is that a baby?" She asked pointing to the bundle. Safia nodded.

"What is your name?"

"I am Rasso. This is Akram and he is mine." Funny how poor Indians provide casual names to their children and definite ones like Akram, Parvati, Sundari to their animals. Perhaps because their own children just come and are another mouth to feed, while an animal is a provider and entitled to receiving more thought and love in its name. Rasso was examining the kid. Satisfied that nothing was broken, she put it down on the ground. It scampered straight to Safia's *dupatta*, sniffing it delicately before taking a nibble. Rasso squatted down beside her and said, "How beautiful you are......but how tired you look." The simple observation brought tears to Safia's eyes and then tears began to chase each other in a mad race.

"Why are you crying? Are you hungry? I cry only when I am hungry, but now that *abba* has a regular job, I am not often hungry.

Amma makes lots of chapattis every night and there are enough left-overs for the next morning. See, she has given me one to eat while grazing Seema."

"Who is Seema?"

"Akram's mother, didn't you know? Amma will be coming with her in a little while. She has lots of milk in her udders and is not be left alone to graze. The milk would be stolen. I could give you my chapatti….some of it….because I like to give a piece to Akram."

"*Ei* Rasso! You bastard! Where have you vanished and where is Akram? I told you not to go far with Akram. He will be stolen." The high pitched scolding came nearer with each word.

"Amma, someone is here, under the tree."

"So? Instead of getting Akram's stomach full, you are wasting your time chattering with outsiders……… you just wait………! *Salaam Bibi Sahib*." The woman stopped in mid-sentence and quickly put out her hand to cover her head with a dirty sari *pallu*.

"You know me?" Safia asked

"But I live in the huts behind the big house. Haven't you ever seen me?"

How often do the poor look up to the minarets of the palaces of the rich, drawing warmth and joy from the life that would never be theirs. How seldom do the rich look down from the minarets to recognize those crawling creatures as human beings.

"I know everything. Lady *Sahib* is capable of doing anything, even cut her own hand if she doubts that it would go against her. Do not weep Begum *Sahib*, your husband will not always be in jail. Come to my hut. We are poor but whatever is there, is at your disposal. Come *Bibi Sahib*, the sun is getting high, the baby should be inside."

It was the generosity of the miserable and carried with it the di-rectness and horse sense of the common man. The woman took the baby and deftly shifting it to one arm, extended the other towards Safia. Supporting Safia, she began to walk calling out, "Rasso you stay here and look after Akram and Seema. Call if someone comes to make enquiries about *Bibi Sahib*."

"What is your name?"

"Zamurad."

Safia stopped suddenly and stared at her. "What is it *Bibi Sahib*, what is wrong?"

"Nothing. A *darvesh* told me, years back, that I would come across an emerald that would save and protect me. I spent weeks trying out different emeralds in the hope that my luck would change. I did not understand that it might be a person. Perhaps always suitable stones defined people of that character, who could make a difference in our lives." The dark woman blushed and turned purple. "But I still had better not come with you." Safia turned to go back under the tree.

"Why *Bibi Sahib*? Do you think *Saheb* would be angry with you for going to a Sunni household?"

"Don't be silly Zamurad, you know *Saheb* doesn't believe in all this."

"Then it is our humble dwelling and our meagre means?"

"You are richer than anyone I know Zamurad. No, it is just..... you know there is a fatwa on your *Saheb*. I am included in it. *Saheb* has been asked to apologize. He is not going to do it and I am never going to leave him. Anyone who shelters us or helps is also included in the fatwa. I do not want any harm to come to you.

The poor woman looked down at her broad dirty feet then she looked up, her eyes glinting with swallowed tears. "Often, me and my family have gone hungry. More often, we have not had a roof on our head. I have lost two children because I had no money for their medicines. The *Imams* have never bothered to find out how we are. Why should we bother now about what they say?"

"True, but his followers can be rough and violent."

"So can I. Let them come and touch anyone in my house. I will split their sides, drag out their entrails, fill them up with red chillies and hang them to dry."

The visualization was so vivid that Safia had to smile. "That's better. Keep laughing Begum *Sahib*. Come, you must eat." They had walked only a few steps when a mild noise erupted from behind. Safia turned, half expecting an ominous crowd coming for her. The tightening of Zamurad's arm told her that she was thinking the same thing. Together they turned, Zamurad's hand going towards her silver *kardhani*, a beautiful ornament that jingled with every step making simple movements sensuous. A lethal weapon that can be loosened with a single tug and swung like a Kung fu baton.

It was Katayanji, hurrying up to her, his unstarched *dhoti* held high to give him freedom to move, followed by Zahida, Irfan, Zain,

Ramlal and so many more. There were young boys getting down from cycles, each with a hockey stick, a group of tough looking men with Ahmed *bhai*. Katayanji held her by her shoulders. "Are you all right child?" Safia collapsed on his emaciated chest. "I am giving you just thirty seconds to control yourself and then we get down to work."

"What shall we do?" Zamia enquired.

"I am going to sit on a *dharma*. This is my struggle and I shall fight it out." Safia said with determination she did not feel.

"By sitting on *satyagraha*?" Katayanji enquired.

"Why not?" she shot back.

"Because *satyagraha* is all wrong, right from its conception. That is why the freedom it got us has taken away a chunk of the country. It worked because Gandhiji understood that basically we are a lazy people, who would never be able to pick up guns and drive away the British. The best we could do was loll outside the government offices. It worked because the Englishman hates a mess and that is what we were creating. He left because he could not stand the mess anymore. Your family is Indian; its members can take any amount of mess."

"Shall we talk to Lady *Sahib*?" Ventured Irfan.

"Don't be silly. Go begging from the unjust and give them an invitation to be cruel."

"Don't just keep countering every suggestion Katayanji. Find a solution and do it fast." Zahida brooked any further idle discussion.

"*Doctorniji*'s orders. Ahmed *bhai*, can you open the lock? Take care the lock and the padlock do not belong to us and would have to be respectfully returned. Please see that they are opened and not broken."

A packet of small instruments materialized. The two imposing looking locks were opened in a jiffy and Zamurad, who seemed to have taken charge ran ahead, opening cupboards and changing sheets on which the baby was placed. Rasso ran to get milk while Zamurad lighted the *chulha* and prepared tea for the gathering.

With tea and soggy biscuits from a passing baker came the news that Abbas' bail application had come up for hearing in the morning court and had been accepted. He would be released the next day.

"Well you brat, you bring struggle and deliverance, hardship and release at the same time. True representative of life, I bow my head to you." Katayanji opened the closed fist of the sleeping baby and put a four *anna* coin in it. "Well now to complete the work. Do not look so surprised. I am a writer. I can't construct a story without a climax and I can't end it without catharsis." Irfan caught Zahida's eye and pointed a finger to his head. "No, I am not ga-ga Irfan, unfortunately not." Katayanji sighed gathering the two opened locks, chains and padlock and walk towards the main Safdar Manzil.

* * * * *

FIFTEEN

I

It was an emergency meeting of the Executive Council of the Party. It had been called to review the backlash to Abbas' book. But it was taking place six months after Abbas' release on bail. The delay was caused by the absence of most of the executive members who had been on an official visit to the Soviet Union. The first of the icing, that came with the bitter cake of joining the revolution. India was preparing for its first General Elections and though the entire world knew that Nehru would form the government, the Party had to receive instructions on how to contest those elections and maybe come out as the main opposition power. The communists in India had until now believed in an armed revolution, one that would establish the dictatorship of the proletariat and do away with the bourgeoisie. They had seen the success of the "Long March" in China, the struggle that had killed thousands of Chinese but had given birth to a Red China and established Mao Ze Dong as its undisputed leader. The Indian Communist dreamed of such a struggle, their poets wrote about the red dawn, their painters painted red morns.

In Moscow, they were told to put those dreams into the cold storage and contest the elections. India was a democracy. Advantage must be taken of the fact that the party had been allowed to surface and all imprisoned comrades were set free. The elected members could work towards bringing about changes through the democratic set up. USSR realized that India was an emerging power and it was important to have it on their side. Nehru was a self-proclaimed socialist and that seemed enough for now. The visiting delegation had also been instructed that India was a multi-religious country and that they should, under no circumstances, hurt the religious sentiments of the masses, especially those of the minorities. This meeting was a result of the visit and six months long instruction and evaluation.

Since the Executive Council comprised only of men, they thought only of the men and the men in the Muslim community were crying blue murder.

"It is preposterous. It is obnoxious. You have put back the party by thirty years."

"May I remind you comrade general secretary, that the party has still not completed thirty years of its existence in this country. Impossible to take away thirty years, from a body that has not lived that much."

"Comrade, I would thank you to restrict your acid humour. We have gathered here for a session of self-criticism and you are the one who has to be critical."

"Even though I do not find any action of mine to be worthy of a session of self-criticism?"

"Then it is our duty to remind you of your act. You dared to publish a book without the party's approval. You took upon yourself to be openly critical of the *Shariat*. Not merely criticize it, you make it clear in this book of yours that it is these laws that are responsible for the sorry state of the Muslim women of the country. Not satisfied with this much, you attempt to rewrite the *Shariat*, calling many laws outdated. You have successfully managed to alienate twenty per cent of the population from the party, the portion that could have been in our hands, had we played our cards right. Your book has destroyed our bases with the Muslims believing that we are out to kill their belief and destroy their religion. They no longer trust us. The *Imam* of each and every God forsaken mosque is giving long speeches against the Marxist party and its single minded agenda for destroying Islam. Posters appear on the walls of the Muslim localities announcing jihad against the Marxist party. The colour red that should have inspired confidence amongst the poor classes is today dreaded like the reincarnation of the devil himself."

"Don't you think you are being a little harsh comrade?"

"Harsh! Harsh you say, after you have lambasted all the work we had put together brick by brick. Comrade, you had no right to write *The Flames* and none to publish it."

"Wait comrade, this is supposed to be a session of self-criticism. Give me a chance to indulge in it. Remember it is I who am supposed to criticize and me again who has to prescribe the punishment. This is what Marx wrote and this is what Lenin practiced."

"Don't throw Marx and Lenin at us. Get on with whatever you have to say."

"Right. I will do as you say, even though you make me feel like Professor Schiller did, way back in Oxford. He fined me five pounds, my monthly allowance for getting a puncture in a borrowed car and returning after the hostel gates had been closed. But why mention my aristocratic background. I must remember that I left all that to join the freedom movement and then the party. So let us begin with the charges. I shall begin backwards, the last of yours being the first of mine."

"You say I had no right to write *The Flames*. Well, I am a writer, first and foremost and have every right to put my thoughts on paper. My desires, my pains and sorrows, my hopes and expectations, my anger and my disillusionment. I have to write what I feel for the moment, because I am answerable to posterity. I do not want to burden my soul with guilt when future generations question me, and question they will, of my complete silence on the one subject that hogs the Indian masses—religion. I cannot and will not put on the ostrich act for immediate paltry gains and forsake the ultimate goal of a complete revolution. As to why having washed my soul in ink, did I need to publish it? Well, let me make it clear. Writing is not a purgative for me, to be used to purge my system of thoughts and ideas so disgusting to the party leadership. It is and shall remain a means of communication with the minds of the people, minds that have to be influenced, convinced and brought to the point where they make a choice to side with us. I would like to clarify that I do not support the production of puppets. The masses have brains and a conscience and more than that, a right to make their own choice. For centuries, the clergy of every religion has dictated what it thought was best for the community. That is why we are stuck with the *Manu Shastra*. Who would have followed the Prophet if he had not proclaimed himself a Prophet and said that the Qur'an was the God's own word? What would have happened to his social reforms if he had not claimed that they were God's bidding? Imagine the scrabble for the prophetship if he had not said that God willed him to be the last one. The masses have to see these things objectively and make their own choice. As a first step, exploitation in the name of religion has to stop. You claim that I have destroyed the base which was arduously constructed by the party brick by brick. Comrades, we have never had a base amongst the common man. It is only the upper class aristocracy with a desire to live life differently and let us admit, sometimes to shock their own class, who formed the party. They became the leaders and today form the core that makes the decisions. The common man is totally missing. I have not destroyed any base. I have simply tried to jerk the masses out of their centuries old reverie. Yes, posters and banners are being put up on every street corner in the Muslim quarters. Their propaganda is strong, their machinery well oiled. So, are we going to be cowed down by a few wall graphics? Surely when we set out on this road, we did not expect to be accepted with open arms. We knew that brickbats would be more and would hit harder. But we have to keep treading the path of justice. Justice for all, including the women.

Yes, I consider many laws of the *Shariat* outdated. It is time they were repealed and new ones written in their place, laws that would be more human, more contemporary. Life cannot stand still, but that is what the Muslim clergy has been successfully doing and we have been abetting. I have not attempted to re-write the *Shariat*. I have only made a claim that there is an ardent need to do so. I hope the Muslims would understand and get down to doing it. Yes, most of my characters are Muslim women, suffering because they are socially trodden upon. True, the Hindu women also suffer, but the Hindu social customs do not have rigid laws to support them. So one Raja Ram Mohan Roy can get down to reforming the Sati custom and succeed. The Hindu is allowed to change his laws according to the social needs. Why shouldn't the Muslims get the same benefits in a secular, democratic country? Law and religion are two separate entities and have to be treated as such. Such a step might cut down our membership but it would establish us as the spokesman of the downtrodden, especially women. Need I remind the august gathering that in his first speech on the radio after the success of the October Revolution, Lenin addressed women as a separate entity? I quote: 'Women of the Soviet Union, from today your rights are equal to that of the men.' Comrades, I think I have answered all the charges you so meticulously framed against me. I absolve myself of all the charges levied."

"Absolve! You absolve yourself! Well, Well! We had been hoping that during the open criticism, you would realize your follies and prescribe a punishment for yourself. Since you do not do so, we are left with no option but to take the decision ourselves. Comrade Abbas Jafri, you are expelled from the party for a period of six years. During these six years, your conduct shall be watched and dialectically analysed. If you are found to be making an effort to overcome your past follies of anti-party activities, you shall be re-instated as an ordinary member, with the usual duties and responsibilities. I now close the extraordinary session of the National Executive."

II

"You can't sit like that, holding your head and expect me to go about my work as if nothing has happened."

"Why Safia, I never knew you were superstitious about these things," Abbas mumbled with a watery smile.

"For God's sake, tell me what happened at the National Executive."

"Nothing really. They had their say and then I had mine and then they had theirs again."

"And then you had yours again. Don't lead me into a rigmarole of says. Tell me what was the outcome."

"I have been thrown out."

"What! But how is it possible? You are one of the senior members. You have done so much for the party."

"It is not important what I did for the party. What is important is that at this point the party is not in a position to take any setbacks. They say my writings set the party back by thirty years. Oh Safia! I can't bear it. I can face anything as a soldier of the party. I would have understood if they had dropped me from the General Council and made me a common ranker. But to be thrown out of the organization which is my life and my soul? The shame of it....I feel totally helpless! Alone! Naked!"

"Don't, my love! Do not torture yourself like this. Surely there are other organizations, other avenues that you can join. Organizations that need you, where you shall be able to do similar work."

"How to bear the shame of having compromised? How can I accept that all that I stood for has proved that it does not need me?

The party has thrown me out but how can I throw away my ideals and become a renegade?"

"But that is what you have been called today."

"Maybe. But they are human and can make mistakes. Is that reason enough to discard the entire ideology?"

"Then let us continue to work for the ideology. If that is what is important, why do you need the party. Let us leave everything and go to some remote village. You wanted to show me the Himalayas. Let us go there. Not as visitors or tourists but as people who want to work for the development of the highest ranges."

"I cannot dream anymore Safia. My dreams have dried up. I have no existence without a cause and my cause has been taken away from me."

"Nobody has the power to take away a cause. What is your cause? To bring about a social and economic change. Well, let us begin with a village."

"It is no use. I wish I had continued my practice with Baba and kept politics secondary to other things."

"I never knew that the wish to work for one's country could be a hobby."

"I have gone past mockery. Your satire will not arouse me."

"What will? Frustration is the luxury of the rich. We are too far gone Abbas. We cannot turn back now and we cannot stop and wait. We can but go on—go on the path that leads we know not where, to find we know not what. Tread on we must, because what we leave behind is ugly and sinful. What is beautiful and rightful must lie beyond. So dear one, remember '*Jodi tor dak sune keu na aashe, tobe ekla chalo re.*'"

"Can you do it?"

"Yes. With you beside me, I can survive in a remote Himalayan village without an identification."

"Forgotten by the cause we have lived for and yet continue to live for it?"

"Yes, even that."

"What about Sitara?"

"What about her. She will be with us. She is only six months old. We shall decide what to do with her in a few years."

"It is the beginning of spring. If we have to leave for the hills, we had better do so now. I must talk to Katayanji."

"Yes he has travelled all over the Himalayas on foot, even to Tibet. He shall be able to advise us where to go. Where work need to be done and where we can be safe!"

"Yes, safe. Self-preservation, first and foremost. I had better go immediately, so that I can return before it is dark."

"Do you think we should contact Irfan? We could ask him to accompany us. He can look after us and I can look after him."

"True. You alone can control his drinking bouts. I'll look him up at the Golden Fox. Sure to find him there in the evenings."

"Bring him along if you will. We can discuss the plans in the night and tomorrow we can set about implementing it. Take this *dushala*, the evening breeze still has a nip in it."

"Thanks, I will. Lovely smell of mango blossoms in the air."

Safia smiled. She watched Abbas' light step, his broad shoulders moving up and down, his neck stretched forward giving his tall frame a slight slouch. She leaned against the door. Victory for a woman, the most complete one is to steady the faltering steps of her man, to show him the familiar path of truth, to egg him on to continue to walk on it. To move beyond only to turn and beckon him, assuring him her camaraderie. True, no battles are fought alone, no victories won single-handedly. She need not be the one to wage a war, but it would be because of her that they would be fought. She might never be the flame; she would remain the calm, still bowl of oil, silently feeding the flame to light the road to progress. It would be because of her that the flame would have a permanence and not fizzle out after a flash. She, who would be born again and again, because the world could not get on without a *Jagatdhatri*, the being that could absorb all that was dark and emit light for the world to see its way. She was the victorious, the empowered, the extraordinary, the omnipotent, the manipulator. If God is there and is responsible for the synchronized manipulations of nature, then that God must definitely be a woman.

* * * * *

SIXTEEN

I

Sitara was asleep. The deep, carefree sleep of childhood which was so short lived. The train taking the known route was moving in an unknown direction—the direction to the unknown. She had travelled this route so many times. Crouched in the lower birth of the three-tier third class compartment, Safia recalled the innumerable demonstrations, the *satyagrahas*, conferences and seminars she had attended. She had made this journey innumerable times sometimes with Abbas and at times alone. Being alone was never a problem because there was always hope. The separation was only for a short lapse. Time that could be divided into years, months, days and hours, compartmentalized into the past and the future. The present always a few suspended moments that whiz out from the future and zip into the past. The present, that time could divide and sub-divide, to be handled and managed with dignity and pride. Present, that had suddenly become an unending space with not even a make belief horizon at the end of the vision.

No vision now. Only survival. Strange how the wheels of the train took up her thoughts and clanged 'survival…..survival…..survival.' But for what? For whom? For Sitara who was such a mite, helpless, two year old. It was a dark night outside. Dark, like the night when she waited for Abbas to come back with Katayanji and Irfan. Night, when they would plan a future in a Himalayan village, the night when she and Abbas would set out on a new journey, the night when they would burn their dreams of changing the world and set out to change a small village, the night when a new cause would be born. The night that never came.

Instead, came a lump of bones and flesh, covered with a grey and white *dushala* with large patches of red. A mass they said was Abbas. They….who were they? Katayanji, who had discussed the plan and accompanied Abbas to the Golden Fox in the hope of digging out Irfan, who was now shivering with dry gasping breaths faintly resembling sobs. Irfan, his drunkenness kicked to a stupor. He looked at the body and then at Safia and spread his broad hands, jerking his head and shoulders as if to shake off a persistent sleep that showed him such horrible nightmares. And Ahmed *bhai* and so many more remained grim quiet till Lady *Sahib* walked in followed by her entourage. Taking her son's head in her lap, she broke down for the first time. Touching the mouth where blood had oozed out and dried in thick crusts, she wept—wept for full five minutes. Then raising her head, she addressed Katayanji—a single word—"How?"

"The fatwa……carried out at the Golden Fox."

"The man?" she asked candidly.

"Caught and killed by Ahmed *bhai*."

"Two deaths," Safia whispered, "for nothing."

"Nothing, you say! Nothing! After goading him on for years, you witch, you have got your own way." Safia had always known that Lady *Sahib* never let up. But nothing had prepared her for this. The tight grip that Lady *Sahib* kept over her life did not loosen even when she was faced with the death of her dearest child. She took a deep breath and quietly started giving instructions. "The body has to be buried. No! Not the family graveyard. The *Imam* would never allow it. A corner at the general graveyard would do. Everything has to be managed before daylight, as per the dictates of the Holy Book. See that a widow is here to break her bangles and dress her in white. Inform me after everything is ready."

"Lady *Sahib*, won't you hold your grand daughter?" Katayanji made a last plea to the retreating back.

"She is nobody to me. Neither is that woman. My son is dead and the link between her and the family is broken. These two are neither a part of the family nor do they have any right on the property. The funeral over, get this place vacated."

Lady *Sahib* had been true to her word. On the third day after the burial, Safia had been served a notice to vacate the premises. Sir Safdar Jafri, a dead mass of immobile flesh, lay helpless on the huge bedstead, only his old eyes had dimmed with tears that flowed and spread into the crow feet wrinkles, as Safia bent down to *salaam* him. Such had been the velocity of events that Safia had not even had time to grieve her loss. Lady *Sahib* had acted in accordance with the *Shariat* and it had in turn fully supported her. Safia's lawyer had not even been able to get the case admitted into the lower court. The last appeal had been made at the high court, which had upheld the lower court's decision. The Muslim Personal Law was not to be meddled with and the case was dismissed. Two years had elapsed in the struggle to keep a roof over her head. Eight years before, she had been welcomed with a lotus flower. She had been thrown out with not even brick bats following her. The complete silence had the finality of a grave, like the mound of damp earth over a fresh grave where the grass had not yet had a chance to grow. The make belief of the continuation of life.

As she walked out carrying the last bag to the waiting tonga, it was only Sitara's lisping chatter that accompanied her. "Where are we going Ma, why are we leaving home? When will we come back?"

As Safia climbed the back seat of the tonga, she saw a window open on the top floor of Safdar Manzil and then close with a definite bang. So much like her own life. A window had opened which she had not planned for. But when it did, she had opened her arms to the fresh gust of freedom and revelled in the sensation of it stroking her mind, her heart and her soul. She did not expect it to stay with her without giving anything in return. As God was her witness, she had never allowed herself the right to measure and weigh the sacrifices she made for it. No sacrifice was too big, no yearning too intense. The promise was of liberty and wasn't that how it was described? Yet in spite of everything, with all its demands and all her willingness to fulfill them, it had forsaken her—the woman! So certain had she been that she would soon reach out and have it in her hand and press it to her bosom. Liberty! Gone so suddenly, so definitely, like the window closed. Why was she alive then? How was she to live without the hope of possessing it? How was she to turn back and subscribe to what she had rejected? Submit to the bonds she had broken? Would ever a day come when the *Shariat* shall be re-written to give voice to the women? When shall God decide that he no longer wanted to be used by men? When shall any religion have a female Prophet?

II

It was at Zahida's that Razaak *bhai* and Katayanji talked with her about moving out of Lucknow.

"Delhi! But why Delhi?"

"It is a bigger city and it is the national capital."

"But whom do I know there?"

"At the moment you don't need acquaintances. What you need is anonymity."

"Yes. You and Sitara are completely unprotected. What might keep you safe is moving to a place where no one knows you."

"Lady *Sahib* has always been very powerful and now with Justice *Saheb* totally paralysed, she holds all the reins."

"She has won the case. Why should I matter now?"

"You and Sitara would always be a threat. And there is still a higher court, you know."

"As if I had the resources left to appeal in the Supreme Court."

"You are still here."

"And she would feel safer if you weren't."

"What do you mean?"

"Don't forget what happened to Sylvia and Justice *Saheb*."

'But you can't mean that it was Lady *Sahib*......."

"There is something like a definite doubt. We have to preserve ourselves so that the struggle can continue. Our absence is not going to help the cause in any way. I wouldn't want anything to happen to you or Sitara."

"No! Of course not." Unknowingly Safia grabbed Sitara to her breast. She dropped her rag doll and turned to look at her mother. How much could a child of two understand? Hopefully nothing. Then why was there a knowing look in Sitara's eyes? Why did she wake up at night and snuggle up to Safia—not to find protection but help her fight off the insecurities—hush the dry sobs that racked her tired sleeping form?

It was the fear for her child—Abbas' only living proof—that clinched the decision. Safia was in the midst of putting her certificates and degrees in order when Katayanji had returned. He carried a fat envelope that he put on top of the certificates.

"This has to go with these. It is equally important."

"What is it?"

"A letter for Mrs Govind Ram. She is the wife of the owner of the National Cloth Mills and has recently opened a performing arts institution, Gandharva Kendra. I believe she would be able to give you a job. I have explained everything to her in this letter. Go straight to her. She is usually home till eleven in the morning."

* * * * *

SEVENTEEN

I

"I can see that Katayanji makes no difference between his detailed travelogues and a simple letter of introduction," Mrs Govind Ram grimaced on opening the letter. "How does he expect someone to read eight pages of Hindi first thing in the morning?" An extremely beautiful woman, she was amongst the few on whom temper sat well. After the first few lines, she was on her feet and glanced at Safia doubtfully, then back again at the letter. As she read, she reached absently for a switch near the *divan*.

"Eh," she asked the liveried servant.

"You rang Madam."

"Oh yes, bring some tea. Milk for the child and some toast and jam." The servant threw a curious glance at the guest dressed in a crumpled sari, in which she had obviously slept, hugging a skinny but good looking child, accompanied by a wrought iron trunk that she carried herself. Mrs Govind Ram's, "Well? Get going will you," scurried him out.

Mrs Govind Ram folded the letter and looked up. Safia found herself looking in two large blue brown eyes that reflected strange lights—because they were filled with tears. "Don't Mrs Govind Ram. I am too far gone for pity. I have no tears left for myself and no words with which to console you."

"You are right. Let us not waste time on self-pity. Let us pick up the bits and pieces and add new ones to them in the hope of making a whole. I shall give you a job....Oh, don't thank me yet. I need an educated woman. Most of my staff are barely literate. The artistes come from Rajasthan and Madhya Pradesh. I give them employment for seven months, a dormitory accommodation and vegetarian food." A look of appreciation passed her eyes as Safia whipped out a pen and writing pad and started jotting facts. "The artistes practice seven hours a day and put up sixty shows of *Ramleela* and thirty of *Krishnaleela*. They are paid half their salary for the months that they are here and the balance when the troupe shuts down for five months. You shall look after the payments, supervise the food, keep track of attendance and of course see that no hanky-panky goes on between the male and the female artistes. In short, you would be the manager, and yes, there is a director and a music director. They are not included in the rest of the team. They are paid much more and treated differently. When we perform in other towns, they travel second class, stay in the best rooms and get more free time. The rest are trash, to be treated like it. They are more or less dogs to whom we give a regular ration and sometimes throw an extra large bit like a bonus in the form of a Diwali allowance." Pausing for breath, she opened a packet of Dunhill and raised her beautiful eyes to meet Safia's. The smirk in them changed to surprise. "You smoke? Oh come, no one could have mistaken that greedy look in your eyes. Go ahead, help yourself."

It was the first time that Safia smoked a Dunhill and as she would laughingly admit later on, it tasted like chicken shit. There and then she made the decision—it was going to be Panama for her—always.

"There is something else that you have to do Safia. Do away with your married name. It is advisable to be safe."

"I had thought that Delhi is too big for recognition."

"True, it is big and gets bigger every day, but it is also more in-human, more unjust and more orthodox. Do not endanger yourself and do not trouble those who want to help you." The quiet threat was veiled with a smile. "You must have had a maiden name. Muslim girls have such lovely second names, much nicer than the *devis* and *ranis* of the Hindus.

"Yes, I did. I was called Safia Dilshaad, Mrs Govind Ram."

"Beautiful! You are Safia Dilshaad officially."

"Yes Mrs Govind Ram."

"If you are Safia to me, I am Amrita to you."

"Amrita, the life giver," Safia said to herself softly.

"And Safia, I have an inflated ego. For your own comfort, do not pump it any more. I shall be Mrs Govind Ram to you and you shall be Saidani *Bibi* for all of the troupe and the workers. But in private, we shall call each other by our names, not the names of the clans, caste or husband. How is that for anonymity?"

II

Amrita was known as the dragon amongst her artistes. She knew this and revelled in it. The Director, Satya Patwardhan, was a classical *kathakali* dancer. He was also an expert of Indian folk dances and used a mixture of both in his choreography. A decade back, he had been a member in the Uday Shanker's Dance Troupe and had toured the world with him. The experience had brought out a latent quality in him—that of visualization. No more solo performances for him. He needed space and used it with an ingenuity that had so far been absent from the Indian stage. Coupled with the richness of traditional forms, he and his troupe had quickly become a household name in the upper circles of Indian society. Amrita knew she was lucky to have him and paid him six times the salary of the other artistes. Which was just as well because he blew it up all on drinking and was perpetually in debt. Later on, Safia was to learn that it was Amrita who paid a couple of artistes to lead him to the bars where he could conveniently blow away a weeks pay in a night. That way he never managed to save a penny and stayed put with her. But Amrita was a miser with praise, always managing to convey with a look or a nod that the choreography left much to be desired. Patwardhan was an egoist and could not digest criticism. He stuck to his guns and refused to alter anything on the directions of the money supplier. He was the only one in the troupe who could tell Amrita to her face that she knew nothing about the arts and that she would have been better off buying Benarsi saris and gold jewellery. At this, Amrita would pointedly glance at the huge twenty thousand rupees stage settings, being built for the latest production. Their battles were the comic relief in the otherwise grueling routine of the troupe.

Prashant Mukherjee or Masterji as he was fondly called, was the music director. He was the typical 'Bengali Babu', calling Amrita who was some ten years his junior '*Ma*' and secretly loving her. His voice bore the richness of the deltas of the Ganges and years of rigorous training of Dhrupad. A master teacher, he claimed that no one in this world possessed a bad voice. What they did have was a bad ear. Masterji and Patwardhan were a perfect team, understanding each other's desires without saying them. Stage is where the unity ended. Masterji and Amrita never quarrelled. When Amrita raved at the troupe—she did so once a week just to be in good form—he would stare at her with his large sad eyes which seemed to ask, "Oh beautiful one, why is it that your tongue does not match your looks." Masterji could play anything from piano to *sarod*, from flute to violin. While Patwardhan looked with disdain at any other dance drama or production being put up in the capital, Masterji was to be found in each one of them. Humble to the core and always willing to teach, he could be caught singing an old *Baul* song in the lawns of Sapru House, to an admiring group of young music students. Patwardhan expected the female artistes to keep him happy, often cutting down drastically from the roles of dancers who refused to oblige. Most women came from ambiguous backgrounds and did not mind crossing the middle gravel patch between the staff accommodation to the director's quarters in the dead of the night. Masterji was said to have been married. No one knew what became of his wife. As proof of his once marital status, he had a fourteen year old daughter Manjari who kept house for him and called him Baba. Masterji was loyal to his absent wife and completely devoted to 'Ma' or Amrita. His evenings were taken up in teaching vocal music to Manjari, who at the age of fourteen possessed the voice of Begum Akhtar and the range of Gangu Bai Hangal. Try as she might, Amrita was never able to persuade Masterji to let Manjari join the troupe. It was one thing that Masterji would not give. It was the one thing that Amrita never stopped asking for.

The rest of the artistes were dancers and singers from Rajasthan and Madhya Pradesh. They were ordinary peasants, most of them landless, who like all Indian peasants sang and danced on an empty stomach. For the first couple of years or so, Patwardhan and Masterji had toured these two states in search of talent. Later on, they started coming on their own after the harvest when work became non-existent in the villages. An audition took place at the beginning of the year. The ones employed signed a contract for seven months, at the end of which they could go back to their villages and cultivate their land or work as hired hands. The money they saved was enough to free their bit of land from the clutches of the local money lender. This made them forever indebted to *malkin* and they kept coming back year after year to save enough money to marry off a daughter, add a room to their village house or complete the *shraadh* of their dead. Desire for better living conditions soon became secondary to the headiness of public applause and recognition. Success on the stage, greed for prominence in highlighted roles and they remained with the troupe for several years, giving Patwardhan the scope to experiment and Amrita the right to treat them as her permanent subjects.

Amrita had been born in a Kayastha household. Her father, Dinanath Saxena and his father before him had all been in the government. His forefathers had served the last of the Moghuls. Proof of this was the proud *haveli* in the Kucha Ghasiram, in Chandi Chowk. When the tottering Moghal dynasty was cleaned out, they managed to switch sides and served the British. Amrita had been born a beauty and as she grew, her fame spread beyond the walled city. The Kayasthas are an exception among the Hindus; they don't marry for money. In the girls they look for beauty and in the boy, his family's political contacts. Amrita possessed both, plus an education in St Mary's Missionary School. By the time she was twelve, marriage proposals had started pouring in. Her father was in no hurry. Fond of his drink and delectably cooked non-vegetarian food, he nursed every concept like a glass of mature wine. Marrying a daughter was a very important concept to him.

When Amrita was fourteen, she had a clear inkling that she was being followed. A buggy was immediately put at her disposal for commuting to the school. The feeling refused to go away and as her mode and speed of conveyance increased, so did that of her follower. The coachman was never able to catch anyone and soon everyone in the family began to believe that she was having premonitions, which either meant that she was getting weak in the head or too proud of her looks. The womenfolk, most of them beauties of their times, took her in hand and gave her such a drubbing that she stopped talking about the stalker. Her father's long talk explaining that premonitions were the first step to schizophrenia was frightening enough to scare away any misconceived phantom. God save women from male psychiatrists. For good measure, she was also given a doze of isolation. She was left to herself and was constantly under observation so that she got into the habit of looking up or turning around suddenly even when she was inside the house. How insecure can a girl's family make her feel!

The stalker seems to have been waiting for this precise moment. A note was found smuggled in her notebook. It professed a Govind Ram's—what a name—undying love for her. The person had no sense of writing a love letter, which was in Hindi, hardly a language of love. Amrita had said as much as she had scornfully handed the letter to her father. She had been proved right, hadn't she? The person—he never became Govind Ram to her—clearly confessed to having followed her for nine months.

"Well, at least his intentions are honourable," Amrita was shocked to hear her father referring to the line about wanting to marry her.

"You think it is honourable? A bania making proposals to us!"

"I can't say anything till I have found out who this Govind Ram is."

In the next forty eight hours, all the Govind Rams of the walled city were questioned and it was some task. Apparently, every other bania named his son Govind Ram—perhaps in the hope of pleasing both the Gods in one go. Trust a bania to find ingenious ways of stinginess. The right one was finally found and his father was summoned. Amrita's father had made a vague guess that had proved right. He was from the family that owned Bhagyanath Industries. A family that had begun from dirt in Calcutta, the city of industries with the proverbial '*lota*' and '*kambal*'. Salt, sweets and cloth had been added within a short span of seven decades. A true bania never switched or closed a business. He merely expanded or added new ones, keeping the earlier ones intact. The present generation, that is Govind Ram's father, was expanding into paper—the latest gold. Amrita's father had grown up learning about the banias. Many a times, he had managed loans from them for impoverished Englishmen, who could never understand why the salary that promised to make nawabs out of college graduates failed to give them a decent living. They yearned for the East India Company and cursed monarchal democracy, which in any case had no meaning for these 'blackies.' Dinanath knew the money lending class in and out and came down heavily on the man whose son had tried to compromise his—Rai Bahadur Dinanath Saxena's—daughter.

The banias, in the years under the British rule had also undergone a change. They were no longer the cringing moneylenders whose shadow on the house was considered an ill omen, who had to wait in the verandah and bear the humiliation of seeing water being sprinkled to cleanse the area where they had stood. The *Arya Samaj* had brought about an equality of sorts in the Hindus. The railways accorded mixing with the Punjabi banias who were better off financially and socially. The British had allowed them to keep horses and buggies unlike the *Badshah* who made them walk or hire vehicles. The banias had not forgotten the humiliation and the fact that in spite of being Vaishyas like them, the Kayasthas had aided and abetted that humiliation.

Laxmi Narayan was not cowed down by the show of strength. But he gave his son four resounding slaps, just in case. The son offered no resistance, only stared at Dinanath with lovesick eyes. The father knew that new winds were blowing. India was reaching out for freedom. A bania was heading the struggle for independence. The same bania who had brought the element of business, the give and take, the haggling and bargaining, into the freedom movement, conveniently relegating the head strong demand for complete *swaraj* of Lokmanya Tilak to the backfires. Laxmi Narayan was shrewd enough to know that he need not have been summoned. At Rai Bahadur's behest, a police party could have gone from the Darya Ganj Police Station and put him in his place. Ordered by Rai Bahadur never to look at his *haveli* again, he resignedly got up to leave. Govind Ram promptly collapsed on the floor, mouth foaming, eyes showing white marbles. Laxmi Narayan in a fit of emotion started beating his head, his beady eyes shedding bean sized tears. When the pandemonium had calmed down, business was discussed. The son refused to eat or drink until Amrita was promised to him. After an hour of fasting and everything being thrashed out, he ate with such gusto that on the wedding day he sported a paunch that made his first and last ride on a horse quite uncomfortable.

Dinanath's family was seeped in debt. Even the *haveli* was mortgaged and the interest had not been paid for several years. Laxmi Narayan agreed to pay all the money and the wedding expenses. His returns would come in the form of newsprint. He would have the sole right of supplying paper to all the government offices and the sole agency of importing and supplying newsprint in Delhi. Amrita, of course, was not consulted but merely told that she was to be married six months from that day. She would be rich and with her looks would be able to persuade her husband to give her many jewels and servants. Amrita protested feebly, not because she was not a strong person, but because all of her sixteen years had not taught her what to expect from a marriage and ignorance, as for many others like her, was bliss.

In her early thoughts when Govind Ram had not become visible, she had referred to him as 'the person'. Later, she was grateful that the Indian customs did not allow a woman to pronounce her husband's name. Even in her thoughts, the name Govind Ram was repulsive and she trained herself to refer to him always as 'the person'.

How to live with a man one hated? A man who only wished to possess her body. A man who believed that a woman had no brains and had none of his own outside account books and ledgers. Had he had some of his own ideas, concepts or beliefs, she would gladly have made them her own. She wanted to be moulded. She knew she was a shapeless lump of clay. It was the day that she realized that this lump of clay was beginning to dry up into a permanent shapeless form, an amoeba frozen in mid-movement, that she decided to do something about it.

Her mother-in-law's scream of disgust on seeing the *tanpura* entering the holy portals of her house was enough to prepare Amrita for the long drawn battle that prompted 'the person' to set up a separate house. With the *tanpura* and *tabla* came Khan *Saheb*, who had taught Amrita music for years and slowly the tedious hours of *riyaaz* became her only solace. But a short lived one. Now that they had a house to themselves, 'the person' turned up at all hours, giving vent to his perverse desires. He arrived with red high-heeled sandals for her and made her parade naked, wearing only the sandals. He never wanted to waste energy in giving her pleasure and entered her only at the very last minute, squealing like an overfed pig being led to the butchery. Sometimes he came while sitting on a chair and jumped in rhythm with the jerks of the ejection. Her breasts ached as he sucked and bit them, pinching her naked buttocks, pushing his thumb inside her arms and rubbing his penis on her thigh to hurry up his own climax. Two years of this and she decided to talk to him. The blow had been so hard that she had rolled off the bed, hitting her head on the floor.

"Don't dare talk like this. It is not for the woman to question her master's desires and how he quenches them. Don't you ever discuss these dirty things again!"

How can a woman allow that dirty, bad smelling appendage, down their clean insides, down their throats. To think it was supposed to be extreme bliss, the final ecstasy….well maybe for the man, who should be blissful and ecstatic at getting the chance to put that filthy thing inside. No wonder women bathe more often and douse themselves with all kinds of fragrances. How else is one supposed to get over the jellyfish smell of that equipment? How wrong it is to say that one gets used to things? One never does. One only learns to ignore, to overlook and to numb one's senses. But, that is not a permanent state of affairs and very soon, one comes back to reality—that one is really fooling oneself. With this realization comes the gush of loathing. For him, but more for herself. For having accepted, for not having the guts to rebel, for not having the resources to take a stand and live it.

* * * * *

EIGHTEEN

Safia's room had become an extension of Amrita's office. She talked, read, wrote letters and got her beautician to come there to massage her. Her moods were mercurial. Sometimes she would turn up everyday laden with boxes of pastries from Wenger's and would not allow Safia to cook anything. Safia had been frightened of using a gas stove. Amrita had brushed away her 'but the gas cylinders are known to burst and set fire to the whole house' logic. A gas stove and a coffee percolator was added to Safia's kitchen. Amrita was addicted to coffee and could not stand the instant powder version of the brew. Safia's routine was always at her disposal and though she missed the lazy pace of Lucknow, she loved the unpredictable Amrita. Sitara had become Amrita's very own property. She bought her toys, clothes, often turning up with books meant for ten year olds for a child of three.

"Well, how was I to know?" She would ask, irritated by Safia's indulgent smile. Safia was always non-plussed by this. Amrita had an eight-year-old daughter and seemed to be an indulgent mother. Safia had often accompanied her to Kashmiri Gate and Connaught Place where she shopped for Geetika. How could she not know what books were right for a three year old? True, Safia had never seen her buy books. Any mention of her daughter and Amrita clamped up like the rusted lockers of the Railway Cloak Room. None of the troupe members had seen Geetika and the way Amrita behaved about her, gave Safia a nagging feeling that deep inside her, Amrita really looked down on her employees and did not want to mix her family with the Kendra. Well, Safia was herself not in any mood to build too many bridges. Sitara had adjusted well to the new life and played quietly while Safia did the accounts. She also enjoyed the rehearsals and became the darling of the troupe members.

It was a still cool night of the early summer and the fourth day of Moharram. A year had passed since she had left Lucknow. Safia had not been invited to any *Majlis*. She did not know any Shia Muslims in Delhi and she missed the *Marsia* and *Nohakhani*. Detest her as she might, even Lady *Sahib* had accepted her capacity of giving a heart rending narration of the incident of *Karbala* and following it with the soulful melodies of the *Marsia* of Meer Anees. Safia had spread her papers on the floor of the balcony and was checking the attendance register of the artistes and calculating their salaries. Sitara, sitting beside her on a mat, was drawing with crayons on a white file, the most recent gift from Amrita.

"*Ma*, is it nice?" she sat back and asked.

"Yes my darling, it is very nice."

"Then don't I get a prize?" Safia smiled at Sitara's innocent query. Managing the Kendra was hard work and she was grateful for it. She did not want her brain to take a break and wander back to the known past or ponder over unknown reasons. In her busy schedule, she had invented a game of placing goodies in out of reach corners, to be brought out, only if Sitara had been good. Even small things like toffees and biscuits became prizes to be earned by keeping quiet and obedient.

"So what does my dear one want?" Safia had a guilty conscience about this arrangement but could not find another one till Sitara began school.

"Sing me a song." The request was so well timed that she started singing the *Marsia* immediately. From her heart tumbled the hot desert winds, sweeping over the family of the Prophet's grandson Hussein, his sister, brother, wife and infant children. The small caravan, camping near the river *Karbala*. So close to the source of fresh water, yet so far. The waters guarded by the armed forces of Yazid holding out the eternal choice—vote for Yazid as Caliph or die; perish of thirst or live a compromised man. Beg for water and be spurned or agree to ancestral caliph-hood and return alive to the Mecca. How many times during its existence has Life brought its lovers to the same cross roads. Blessed are they who have chosen to live by not compromising rather than die a death of oblivion. As she sang, tears started rolling down her cheeks, each line bringing another one—she wept calmly with the deep understanding of herself. A woman who had kept the fires inside her, burning for so long that the embers had frozen. What flowed out was the pure river, cleansing her soul and her mind.

She started as a hand was placed on her head. She was lying on the rug she had spread on the small balcony outside her room. She jerked up to see Masterji sitting near her, his daughter holding two glasses of steaming tea. Manjari put down the glasses and gathering Sitara with a bribe of candy, took off to Masterji's quarters.

"It is good to weep, better to sing and best to do both. If you can follow this bash with a strong cup of tea, then it is the closest you can get to heaven on this earth. Try and see." Despite the melancholy, Safia smiled and picked up the glass. He waited in expectation and laughed gleefully at Safia's incredulous expression. "I am right, am I not, hunh?" As Safia nodded, he joined her, sipping noisily and making a face, "I have neither sung nor wept, it doesn't taste right to me." As if to make mends, he began to hum. Closing his eyes, he repeated it and then sang a line. Impatiently he opened his eyes and said, "Well go on. How many times do you expect me to repeat a line. How shall I finish the song?"

* * * * *

NINETEEN

Masterji teaching classical music to her was a natural outcome to Safia's work at the Kendra. When the troupe was not performing, evenings would find Safia and Sitara in the single room accommodation of Masterji, learning new songs, ragas and *bandish* from the maestro. Amrita often joined them during the lessons and it was the final bliss for Masterji that *Ma* should be learning from him. But long discussions on theory, practice and variation bored her.

The Kendra shut down in the beginning of April for the summer break. The dormitories emptied within two or three days. Safia stayed on because she had nowhere else to go. She was alone in the Kendra with only Masterji and Patwardhan for company. This was the time Patwardhan and Masterji held long sessions to chalk out the new productions and improve the old ones. Patwardhan missed his usual group of artistes who accompanied him in his drinking bouts. He was also lonely without any female company and moved around the Kendra like the ghost who had forgotten its graveyard.

Safia was sitting on the floor of her room, sorting a pile of cloth bits. New costumes had been made for the *Ramleela* and Safia had asked the tailor to give her the left over pieces. So engrossed was she in her work that she did not notice Patwardhan who came in and sat down in one of the two chairs. It was only when he coughed that she looked up. Seeing the ease with which he was sitting, she realized that he must have been there for a while. The fact that he did not bother to feign guilt at barging into her privacy got her hackles up.

"What are you doing in my room?" she growled.

"I need some ink and the office is locked," he answered not taking his eyes off her hands still holding the bit of cloth and needle. "I did take off my *chappals*," he added referring to her fastidious mopping of the floor.

"Well, you could have asked for the ink from the place where you took off your *chappals*."

He looked up, a little confused as if he had lost his bearings and then spoke in a rush, "Look Syedani *Bibi*, I don't have any ulterior designs on you. I am a man enough to know when a woman can belong only once. You did and still love Sitara's father. There is no room in your life for another man. You were so engrossed in your work that I did not like to disturb you. The only folly I committed was to gesture Sitara, who saw me at the door to keep quiet."

A little non-plussed by his forth righteousness, Safia got up to open her cupboard and brought out a bottle of ink. He glanced at it as if he did not know what it was meant for and then looked back at the pile of cloth pieces.

"The ink you came for," Safia reminded him impatiently.

"Huh, Yes yes." He took the bottle and absent-mindedly placed it on the stool. "What is that you are doing?"

"Oh that, just making some stuffed toys for Sitara. This is the mother tortoise and she has many children."

"Of different colours?"

"Yes. That would teach her to recognize colours and shades."

"But they have a movement in them." He picked up a finished piece and moved the flippers and its head.

"I've put little springs in the joints."

"Ingenious," he said more to himself than to her. Then deep in thought, he got up and walked out without taking her leave or saying a word of thanks, leaving the ink bottle sitting on the stool.

"Artistes." Safia shook her head and smiled.

She had not seen Amrita for the last six days. She rarely came to the Kendra during the summer. When Delhi emptied itself into Shimla, Mussourie or Nainital, Amrita stayed put, enjoying the heat, pampering herself with summer goodies. She bathed with sandalwood paste, decorated her hands and feet with henna, wore crisp starched cotton saris and downed glasses of sherbets and hummed the couplets of Zauq, "*Kaun jaye Zauq, Dilli ki galiyan chhod ke* (Who would go away Zauq, leaving the alleys of Delhi)" Her absence gave Safia the time to finish the innumerable chores she had been keeping for the break.

On the seventh day, Amrita barged into Safia's room, cursing the heat and fanning herself with a sandalwood hand fan in spite of the whirring ceiling fan. Her driver followed with a thermos full of ice and a bag of lemons. No synthetic squashes for Amrita. Cool after three glasses of lemonade, she answered Safia's question.

"I had to come. Patwardhan has been working on me. Not that way stupid," she brushed Safia's scandalized look. "He was at my place four days before and has been calling me every day."

"What does he want? Another salary hike."

"No, strangely enough no! He has been after my life telling me that I have been misusing a talent. That I have buried a genius and am not even aware of having done so. How am I supposed to know the talent of each artiste? He is the director, isn't he? He had the audacity to call me a rich undertaker." She got up and started pacing the room. Safia smiled. It must be one of Patwardhan's momentary attachments and he probably wanted a better deal for the artiste.

"Stop worrying Amrita. Sit down and let us call Patwardhan here. I am sure things can be sorted out."

Amrita gave her a strange, doubting sort of glance and sat down on the *divan* only to jump up at Sitara's scream.

"*Aayee*! Amrita aunty has killed my children."

"Now how did I do that?"

"These, this crocodile and this big tortoise, are my children. You sat on them. Thank God they are not dead."

"What all has been going on behind my back," laughed Amrita, "and how can you have a tortoise baby? You are a human being."

"Well, I did. This is my daughter named Zero Fairy and these are her nine children, my grandchildren. They are very naughty and wander off in all directions and she has a lot of trouble finding them and keeping them together. So she has to tie one to the other, like this and the last one she ties to herself. But she doesn't always remember which one comes first and which comes next. But I don't know after that. *Ma* has not completed the story," Sitara explained.

"That's good. Then I can hear it with you," Amrita added, settling down with a cushion in her lap.

"Amrita, I have enough on my hands without adding bedtime stories to it."

"But I have come just for that—a story. Please will you tell me the story of the tortoise and her brood."

Safia began, a little embarrassed but soon the story was flowing out. "There was once a she tortoise named Zero Fairy who lived in a village named 'Mud'. This village was called so because all the houses in it were made of mud, its cows and goats were mud coloured, its cats and dogs wore coats of mud and wonder of wonders, even its human beings had skins to match the colour of the mud. The only thing that was not mud coloured was the golden wheat that they harvested at the end of winter and they called it "The Gold". The tortoise had a happy existence till the day she realized that she was all alone. She became depressed and sad at her lonely state. She talked sometimes to a shoal of carp living in the pond and they asked her the reason for her long face. When they came to know the reason, they laughed and they danced and they sang, with a cackle and a tinkle and a bang. So merry did they become that the tortoise was really put off and was just walking away in a huff when the oldest and the ugliest carp caught her hard humped shell and said "Don't be a silly-billy, all you have to do to drive away your lonely state, is to lay some eggs. When they hatch into a brood of baby tortoise, you shall have so much company that you shall then beg for solitude. So the tortoise named Zero Fairy went ahead and laid a batch of eggs on the sandy sunny side of the pond and when they hatched she had a brood of nine tortoise."

Safia continued the story, manipulating the stuffed toys to make it interesting for Sitara. She finished with the nine colours and the nine basic digits to be added to Zero Fairy and make number learning simple for the child. When she finished, Amrita looked at her and asked incredulously, "And you just made it up, like that?"

"Oh come Amrita, there is nothing to make in it. Trouble arises when Sitara asks me to repeat a story and I have forgotten its end or the middle and make up a new one and Sitara remembers the original and gets very upset.

"Why don't you write them down?"

"Who has ever heard of writing down these silly ramblings."

Sitara got up and peeped into the balcony, half of which served as the kitchen and coming back said matter-of-factly, "*Ma, tehri* is smoking."

"Allah, now the lunch is ruined. Really Amrita! I had promised Sitara *tehri* for lunch and look what you have done."

Amrita ran to the balcony and yelled for her driver. She enjoyed yelling at servants. When he had run up, she questioned him, "Where had you vanished?" As if the poor man was responsible for burning the lunch! "Run down to the coffee house and get *dosas, idlis* and *vadas* for lunch. Where do you think you are going? On your way out, tell Directorji to be here in forty five minutes, not before that, understand?"

While Sitara covered the small table with a tablecloth and Amrita brought out the plates and spoons, Safia scraped away the burnt rice and vegetables and soaked the pan. They were finishing lunch when Patwardhan arrived and settling down on the floor, brought out his packet of *bidis* and looked up enquiringly at Amrita.

"You were right, we have been misusing a talent."

Safia got up to put on the coffee percolator knowing that Amrita could not stand South Indian food without washing it down with coffee.

"Coffee can wait Safia. This is more important."

Apparently coffee after South Indian food was also a fad of Amrita and not a necessity as she had earlier made out. Well, thought Safia, she had a lot to learn. She sat down to listen to a long casting and recasting reshuffle. Patwardhan seemed to be elaborating on a new production and its cost and Safia was surprised that the drama being discussed seemed to be quite a low budget one. Amrita was listening and apparently agreeing and only made a few general enquiries when there was a question of inviting somebody called Kumar Dutta from Calcutta. Another surprise was that Patwardhan was advocating that some other director should be called in to help out in the new production. What was going on? It couldn't all be because of the heat.

"So what do you think?"

Safia jumped at Amrita's sudden question, "Well I.....It seems good, not too many people involved and not a lot of funds needed either for stage sets and costumes. Seems quite workable."

"Good. Then when can you take charge of the puppet troupe?"

"Me! Puppets......how?!"

"Well, obviously it was you and your work that we were discussing. Kumar Dutta shall teach you the proper making and operation of puppets. We'll write to him immediately and if he is available then this is the best time to begin. Your salary shall be raised, though not much immediately because I do not know how the puppet troupe would fare, seeing that it is a novelty. But then perhaps that is what will make it do well. Masterji shall do the music and….."

"Amrita hold it! I know nothing about puppets and running an entire troupe….."

Safia stopped aghast at the whirlwind scheme.

"To begin with, the troupe is going to be only five or six people. Patwardhan, of course, shall help and Masterji too. Its settled, lets get down to the actual work. How about beginning with coffee?" Amrita opened her bag and brought out a pinch of cardamom seed and her packet of Dunhill. Safia got up with shaky knees to put on some coffee. Five months later, she was confidently discussing the lighting for her first puppet play "Soldiers of Rock."

From the deep green of Bengal had arrived Kumar Dutta. Part of the arrangement with him was that the Kendra would arrange three shows of his three new puppet plays. His first show and Safia was astounded by the strength of puppet characters, the last and she was unashamedly wiping away tears, identifying and sympathizing with the plight of "*Shroopanakha*" the vamp character of *Ramayana*.

Kumar Dutta would remain quiet long after a question was asked, ruminating the pros and cons of his answer. The master puppet player loved his puppets so much that it was rumoured he slept with them. Safia almost believed it catching him once lovingly combing the hair and talking to one of his mannequins. She asked him about the play "*Shroopanakha*" and he told her to use the 'if' and 'but' method to known stories. When he saw the confused look on her face, he explained, "Everything that shall be said today, has been said before. The trick is to say it in a new way, to give a new meaning, new colour. Epics are one of the greatest supports of the performing arts, so are folk tales, legends, fables, *jatak* tales and of course, the history. Read them and hear them but always when replaying them, subject them to your own sensibilities, your very own interpretations. And the best way is to introduce the 'if' and 'but' technique. *Shroopanakha*, the woman was lost on the day her brother Ravana said that he loved her the most in the world. What after all was her folly? Widow of a man who was killed on the day of the wedding. Ravana had hated and feared him, probably agreeing to the match to catch him off guard. Left alone she had no option but to come back and live on the generosity of the murderer. Alone, brooding on her plight, she chances upon two good looking young men in Panchvati. The epics are full of men marrying more than one woman, making overtures to married women, kidnapping and forcing them to co-habit with them. But when a woman dares to profess love to a man, she must be taught a lesson. Even the sage Valmiki must make her the laughing stock of generations to come. So Laxman has a good time with her and then asks her to get lost. Not having any other refuge, she goes back to the original sinner and in her anger she loses the target. She points her finger not at Rama or Laxman but at another woman, Sita."

Puppets are not like a play. The director and playwright not only create characters, they also creates the actor, body, voice, movements. The mannequin master is more like a God and a God must shop with care, he explained while a scandalized group of customers stared at him and a bored shopkeeper with a 'they-come-in-all-types' expression served them in a narrow lane of Kinari Bazaar. Safia learnt the use of different kinds of foam, glues, papers, paints and improvised brushes to give different textures and finish to the surface of each puppet. Small, intricate cut outs became gigantic palaces with the play of shadow and light.

Patwardhan took over her voice training, something that she found much harder than controlling puppets. Frustrated with her ineptness at controlling her own vocal chords, she asked him how long would it take her to have as variable a voice as his. With a superior smile he replied, "With daily practice and care and not eating sour and oily stuff, I believe it should be........"

"Yes?" Safia had pressed on hopefully.

"Maybe about five years."

"Five years! When do I start performing?"

"In a few months. You don't wait for it to reach the zenith. You make do with what you have and keep working on it."

Between Kumar, Patwardhan and the administrative work, Safia had no time to think of a play. Three months into this rigorous training and Safia could see that Amrita was getting restless for her to deliver. She lay awake at night and tried to think of a new theme, something that had been untouched, something intricate in its simplicity, something grandiose in its starkness. In the dark night, staring at the moonless black sky, praying for insomnia, because she had so much to think out, she glanced upon a group of stars, not a constellation, some that had simply collected together to show her the form of a young girl, with a hammer and a chisel. A memory from the happy days of story telling. She had got up in a rush and sat down with a pen and paper.

Three days later, she knew she had chosen well, when heavy-eyed, she had read out the script to Kumar Dutta, Patwardhan and Masterji and Kumar had nodded his head and said, "Do it well."

Masterji had started the music score and she had started auditioning the returning artistes. The mornings would now be devoted to the Puppet play and the afternoons to *Ramayana*.

Six weeks of hard rehearsals and Safia knew that the play would be a success. So did Patwardhan and Masterji, both of whom stood by her like rocks, helping her tide over normal, natural hitches. Amrita too could see that the play would become an asset to the Kendra and she wanted to open it with great fanfare. Lt Governors, Mayors and even ministers had inaugurated the annual *Ramleela* and *Krishnaleela*. But this time, she wanted to go over their heads and have the Prime Minister open the first show of the puppet play. She had written to him thrice and though he enjoyed a reputation of replying within the week of receiving a letter, there had been no answer from his side. Safia could understand that Nehru was still a socialist at heart and though his mentor Mahatma Gandhi had kowtowed with the biggest industrialists of his time, Nehru was still an advocate for the public sector and did not want to be seen hobnobbing with the capitalist. The artistes were getting restless. A scheduled opening date is as much of an incentive as a full house. But Amrita refused to schedule the play without the prime minister. At the end of her tether, she played the final card. She wrote a long letter accusing Nehru that his love for children was really only a publicity stunt, otherwise why wouldn't he want to come to her show, when she was trying out a totally new concept of theatre and education for children. No one else had even thought of something like that and she was ready with a play, waiting for him, the promoter of the cause of children who could not even find time to reply.

It worked. Like so many of Amrita's brazen ideas. Nehru agreed to come, fixing the date for 25 November.

Sapru House was booked. The play was well rehearsed and slick, the welcome planned and working on dot. Why then did Safia had that nagging of misgiving as if everything was too well fitting, too smoothly oiled. Something would fall out of place at the last minute and bring the whole structure down like a house of cards. Try as she might to shut it out, something in her past was telling her that something in her past was about to resurface into her present. What could it be and how was she to prepare herself for it?

Three days before the show, Safia got up at her usual time to put the milk can outside. Sliding the bolt, she hugged her shawl tight. The winter chill had set in and it was dark at five in the morning. Opening the door, she saw a shadow leaning on her door. The shadow slid as a solid mass as the support of the door was removed. Her loud screams awakened the artistes in the dormitories who rushed with whatever they could lay their hands on, one of them appearing with a empty rubber hot water bottle. Manaki was lying on the floor, half inside the room, dressed in a thin sari, her body damp with the morning mist and inching towards fever.

Manaki, the second voice in the puppet play. She sang all the songs while Safia rendered the dialogues. Manaki, a tribal girl from Madhya Pradesh, whose father had taken a loan on his small bit of land for his elder daughter's marriage, had brought Manaki—all of sixteen years—to the Kendra to help pay off the debt and perhaps save up enough for her own wedding. A natural artiste, Manaki had learnt the steps with ease and managed to get bit roles. Her laughing eyes had met the bold heavy lidded ones of a Rajput boy, leading her heart strings to get entangled in the golden ovals of Panna's ears. Panna and Manaki had married and been given the single room with common bathrooms allotted to married couples. The land had been transferred from loan ledgers to ownership ledgers of the landlord and Manaki's family had become landless labourers, migrating from one region to another, living in makeshift shelters, grateful for the back breaking work and meager wages that helped to keep body and soul as one entity.

Panna had been jealous of Namdev, ever since he had been selected to play the male voice. When open flattery did not work, he tried to advise Safia that the play required a mature artiste and that Namdev was a novice compared to him. Safia remembered Patwardhan warning her that a director should remain aloof. She should listen to everyone but act only on her belief. It was after all her play. Safia had smiled and told Panna to mind his own business. Not meeting with any success, Panna turned on Manaki. He tried to persuade her to give up the role. Four years at the Kendra and Manaki was an artiste through an through. Her heart yearned for important roles that would bring her success and acclaim. She knew that with her dark skin and broad tribal features, she had no chance of playing an important role in the Aryan version of *Ramayana* and *Krishnaleela*. She refused to give up her one opportunity to stardom. Noises of frequent fights and quarrels from their room became a regular feature. Yesterday Safia had seen large, purple bruises on Manaki's arms and face and had taken Panna to task, warning him of dire consequence if he did not behave. Instead of frightening him, the warning had made him throw all caution to the winds. Late in the night, he beat up Manaki and pushed her out of the room. Alone, embarrassed and shivering, Manaki had reached Safia's door but her tribal pride had not allowed her to knock. She waited for someone to come out and had passed the night in the bitter cold of the ascending winter. By mid morning she was running a high fever, her voice reduced to a husky whisper, body burning and shivering in turns. By noon, she was delirious and had to be moved to Lady Irwin Hospital.

Amrita was beside herself. She ranted and raved, cursing the entire breed of artistes, shouting at all of them to get lost and then bursting into angry tears, sobbing out abuses on her fate and Safia's luck. Patwardhan smoked *bidi* after *bidi*, accepting responsibility for not foreseeing that it could come to this. In the fourth attack of her weeping fit, Masterji ventured near and in his usual humble manner said "*Ma*". When Amrita did not reply, he repeated it and she jumped up and almost hit him screaming, "Don't stand there *maing* me like a goat."

"I was only suggesting *Ma*," he began a little uncertainly.

"My whole reputation is at stake, my whole world is crumbling around me and all that man can do is bleat like a goat '*maaaa*'!"

Safia saw Masterji's hurt look and turned on Amrita. "Calm down Amrita, calm down at once. At least listen to Masterji. If what he says is workable, we shall act on it, if not, we can reject it."

"I know it is going to be some silly suggestion. Alright, lets hear it."

Masterji drew himself to his full height which wasn't much, but he seemed to look down on Amrita and all of them. "I was going to make a suggestion, but if that is your attitude, I had better not." Nodding at Safia, he moved to the door. Amrita humphed as if to say that she knew he didn't have a suggestion that was any good. Safia ran after him. "Please Masterji, don't leave. I am at my wits end. At least tell me what you were suggesting. Please for my sake."

"Nothing much, I was only saying that Manjari could take Manaki's place."

There was a stunned silence and then everyone was speaking at once. Patwardhan was slapping Masterji on the back, Safia overcome with the turn of events was explaining to no one in particular, "She knows all the songs. The music has been composed by her father you see and she has a very good voice, been learning music since she was a baby."

Patwardhan's grinning, "We know Manjari's background Syedani *Bibi*," checked her and she laughed loudly at herself. When everyone had quietened down a bit, Masterji turned to Amrita "There is a condition *Ma*."

"Anything. Anything you say. We'll pay her more than the others."

"Sometimes, something might not be about money Madam." This was Patwardhan at his arrogant best.

"Oh! Well, of course, we shall adjust Manjari's timings so that she can attend school." Amrita corrected herself nonchalantly but stopped when she saw Masterji shaking his head.

"Safia, will you promise to keep Manjari with you? She shall never go on any trip without you, not be forced to work in any production which you are not directing."

"Of course, Masterji. You know that Manjari is like a younger sister to me. She is from today my responsibility just as much as Sitara is."

"Anyone would think I was a Madame from the red light area," grumbled Amrita. She was too relieved to be really angry.

* * * * *

TWENTY

The twenty-one wick brass lamp was in place and its base was decorated with saffron, red and white petals of marigold, rose and jasmine. This was no ribbon cutting ceremony in an institute of Indian Arts. Two girls in red bordered, handspun silk saris were standing on either side of the gates of Sapru House, with a pot of sandalwood paste and rose water sprinkler, seven children in seven different Indian costumes were grouped to offer the prime minister his favourite red rose, while Amrita herself waited with a flower garland for the traditional welcome.

Safia had just come out of the bathroom. The butterflies that had been fluttering in her stomach since morning had turned into gigantic moths and she had just thrown up. Angrily, she told herself that this was her payback for laughing at artistes suffering from stage nerves. Patwardhan caught her half way to the stage, "Have you tried nibbling a biscuit?"

"I don't think I could swallow anything," she whispered.

"Try it," he commanded and brought two soggy digestive biscuits from his pocket. She did as she was told simply because she had no energy to argue. Miraculously, the moths settled down and became a dull crawling ache. He raised his hand to silence her when she would have thanked him adding, "Take your place at the stage, the ambience will help to calm you."

Masterji, Manjari, Namdev, all were in place. Safia joined them behind the black backdrop, the mannequins sitting in line, waiting for their entries, as alert as the actors. She wished them good luck and felt them smirk back at her. She smiled at her wild thoughts and it helped to quieten her nerves. There seemed to be a constant sound of gurgling water with sudden splurge like a smooth mountain brook suddenly taking a deep plunge. It seemed to come from across the heavy velvet curtain. Following her train of thought, Masterji mumbled, "The audience."

It struck half past six and on dot the drums outside started playing the welcome beats. The prime minister had arrived. Two minutes later, there was a sudden hush and a scraping of seats in the auditorium as everyone stood up to greet him. He must have said something funny because the whole auditorium erupted into laughter. The lights dimmed and there was a sound of everyone sitting down, the curtain slowly rising. The show was on.

Safia was operating the puppet of the Himalayan girl Sumera. Daughter of a famous court sculptor, having learnt the art from her father, she is denied the right to practice it because she is a girl. In the small Himalayan kingdom of Chhitkul, it is a sin to give a hammer and chisel in the hands of a girl. As Safia performed, a wrenching, throbbing pain formed in her chest. The loneliness of an artiste, denied the natural outlet of creativity, seeing people around her produce mediocrity, knowing that she can do much better, forced to bow to the will of an unfair, biased society that reserved all its prejudices, all its injustice for the female.

She poured her own solitude into the yearning heart of Sumera who rises to defend the land from the invading Tibetan forces. A woman rising up to protect another, the motherland. Sumera's effort that turns into hundreds of stone soldiers that stood guard on the mountains creating a vision of a fully armed force, ready to attack.

The prime minister was to leave after twenty minutes. Safia had been prepared for a disturbance. Most of the audience on that day had turned up because of him and were expected to follow him out. The play was to pause when the commotion started and resume after five minutes. When the disturbance did not come, she glanced at Masterji. He too was a little mystified but he had been too long in the show business to let an absent disturbance spoil the show. He gestured her to go on and she continued giving life to the mannequins.

The comic scenes of the cowardly king and the queen running away to the safer plains, leaving the poor struggling masses to the mercy of the invaders brought laughter at the right puns and Safia relaxed, her mind divided, one that concentrated on the show and the other dwelling on the memory of the night Abbas had told her the story. A storm had been raging outside and Safia had always been afraid of thunder and lightening. Abbas had told the story to divert her mind. When the story had ended, the storm outside had passed and calm, cool, dripping peace from shiny wet leaves had descended. The play had ended with the carved stone soldiers coming alive in the morning mist, confusing and frightening away the invading forces. On the high mountains of Chhitkul village, beyond the Sangla valley are the remnants of the stone soldiers, silent, firm and undefeated they stand even today. Proof of a young artiste's love for her motherland, proof of the merging of myth and reality. Strange that the storm outside had not abated. It seemed to be raving and lashing, like a roaring sea, banging its head on the rocky edge. It took her a minute to recognize the applause of the audience. Before she could react, Patwardhan was running towards the group of four performers urgently whispering, "The prime minister is coming on stage to meet you." And ran to the wings to help the stage hands roll up the curtain.

Manjari helped her to stand up as Pt Nehru walked up the stage. Memory of Abbas' unfulfilled promise of getting her personal copy of *The Discovery of India* signed by him came like a honeyed ache. As she bent down to address a low *salaam*, he seemed to stop for a second. Whatever he had expected, it was not this. He hurried up replying with the grace of a man used to good manners of different cultures.

"What is your name?' he asked in chaste Urdu.

"Safia Abbas Jafri," Three years of careful anonymity was thrown to the winds.

"Abbas Jafri? You are Abbi's wife? Why?....How?" He checked himself and asked, "You are alone?"

"It was her daughter Sir, who presented you the bouquet at the entrance," Amrita answered for her.

"Of course. I should have guessed from her wavy brown hair. Come and meet me." He turned to his secretary, "When do I have time this week? Safia come to Teen Murti House day after tomorrow in the afternoon."

"Sir you have a meeting at four with…....." fumbled the secretary.

"Prepone or postpone it. Better if you can manage to cancel it. So I shall see you day after tomorrow at four and do bring your daughter. I am fond of children," he smiled at Amrita.

He turned to leave and most of the crowd followed him out. Safia had been told about the feeling of desolation that follows a successful show, a vacuum after frenzied activity. A small soft hand slipped into hers and held fast. She looked down at the green brown eyes. A part of Abbas that would always be with her. She pressed the small hand. Comrades always. Suddenly Sitara was the most popular person around. Gifts of chocolates and toffees materialized, people were asking her to come to their house and bring 'Mummy' along. A woman's introduction, forever changing. However big or small might be her contribution to life, for some she would always be Sitara's mother.

Amrita had returned to the auditorium and was walking towards her. Safia patted Sitara's hand before letting it go and almost ran towards Amrita. Holding her hands in a tight grip, Safia could only say, "Amrita, how can I ever thank you?"

"You could begin by thanking the financer." The voice, like fungal mould dipped in oil came over her shoulder, so close that she felt its breath on her nape. She would have turned and given a sharp retort when she caught the angry, disgusted and somewhat humiliated look of Amrita. So, she was to meet Govind Ram at last. Slowly she turned and moving away from him, joined her hands. "*Namaskar* Lalaji".

Govind Ram grimaced but let it pass. "So how about thanking me? I am the money supplier you know, indirectly your employer."

"I am employed by the Kendra and Amrita is the one who has done so much for me."

"Oh don't thank her, she has her own selfish motives for doing anything for anyone."

"I have never found them Lalaji."

"You will, you will. But lets not go into it now. You could start thanking me by not calling me Lalaji." He smiled.

"Stop making a fool of yourself and stop humiliating me before my staff," hissed Amrita.

"Govind is my name," he grinned ignoring his wife. "For second ,you could have dinner with....us." His pause had an innuendo. Suggesting that he would have liked a tête-à-tête.

Patwardhan had never really liked Govind Ram. Masterji was a true Bengali and did not like men talking to women without adding a suffix of a relationship. As if in mutual agreement, both of them ventured close. Seeing them , the other artistes also moved up so that Safia, Amrita and Govind Ram were loosely encircled by the entire staff of the Kendra.

"Let's go home Safia *Didi*. Mustard fish loses its flavour if it is kept too long." Manjari tried to get things moving.

"So what do you say, shall we have dinner Safia?" Govind Ram was enjoying the situation, knowing that she was being embarrassed by the presence of so many spectators. He was trying to beat her into submitting to his will, banking on an Indian woman's natural dislike for a public scene, their distorted sense of shame and honour that made them tolerate years of physical and mental abuse. It was a test of wills.

"She is Safiaji to you," Amrita interrupted again.

"Oh lets not stand on ceremony between friends." He interposed with mock irritation.

"Leave her alone. She is not interested."

"Tut tut Amrita, such bad manners. So what do you say Safia…. ji? What is fish without a tang as that chit of girl just pointed out. Celebrate the success while it is still heady eh? Let us go to Maiden's. They have got a chef from Lucknow who serves excellent Mughlai cuisine. But you shall be able to tell us if its really authentic. Let us go there for dinner."

Safia did not need to look up to see all eyes boring at her. Questions unasked glistening in them. Was she one of them or would she, if the opportunity presented itself, reject them and move on with the rich. Safia smiled to herself for having to prove herself again and again. She picked up Sitara and turned to Govind Ram. "We are poor artistes Lalaji. I would not be comfortable eating in a Five Star Hotel. Don't waste time all of you. Pick up the instruments and pack up the puppets in their boxes. Hurry, Sitara is almost asleep."

Everyone galvanized into action. Manjari took Sitara on her back, while Safia picked up a drum and moved to the door, loudly giving last minute instructions and announcing next day's stage call time.

Amrita was glowering at her husband who smiling through his defeat and cautioned her, "Well next time then. Remember, I hold the purse strings."

"If you have finished making a fool of yourself, we might move." Amrita started for the side exit where her car was parked.

Out in the cold night, the artistes started joking and laughing, recalling small mishaps of past shows, pulling each other's legs and giggling at snide remarks. Someone started singing in a shivering voice, another stopped a lonely peanut seller hurrying home. Armed with bags of warm roasted peanuts and sesame candy for Sitara, contented at having given a good show and been praised by the executive head of the state, the group trudged the half mile to the Kendra. Safia was laughing away with everyone when she stopped short and looked at herself in surprise and then with anger. Masterji who had stopped with her, put a hand on her shoulder. "Don't be," was all he said.

"Don't be what?"

"Don't be angry with yourself for being happy and don't be surprised at finding happiness. It is always there somewhere."

"I never did think I could be happy without Abbas."

"Those who suffer the loss of a partner believe so. But Safia, how long can life be a comrade of death? Sooner or later they have to part company. Life has to return to the living. Do not grudge yourself this happiness. It does not mean any disloyalty to Abbas."

"What did Lalaji mean by being my......our indirect employer?"

"Just that."

"But the Kendra is built on your father's land. You say so often enough."

"Yes, and his money for the structure. The long and short of this is that when I couldn't take anymore of this person, I had a long discussion with my father. He agreed to give me this land, bought in some whim and quite resalable because of its position. It was four acres. He then talked to this person who came shivering in his pants thinking that I had been complaining about his perverseness. When he understood that it was money that was being demanded, he turned the businessman that he was and drew up a deed. He agreed to loan me an amount to build the Kendra, but I have to repay it at 10 per cent compound interest. Safia I had thought that I would be able to pay it back in five years and here it is almost ten and I am not even half done. I don't know what happens. Shows are arranged, money is earned, installments are paid back and yet I remain in debt. If only I could pay his last paisa, I would be free. But when will it happen? When?"

Safia held the anguished face in her hands. "Soon, I promise you. I shall stand with you and together we shall earn enough to pay him and buy back your freedom. We shall do it. We have to do it!"

* * * * *

TWENTY-ONE

The guard escorted her through the security check and to the first steps of the visitors room. He coughed politely to get her attention. "The prime minister does not like his personal guests to be escorted by armed guards. It is undignified, he says. Cross the visitors room to enter the garden. You shall find him there." Safia nodded and climbed the steps of the Teen Murti House. The visitors room was a little dark and when her eyes got used to it, she saw several people waiting. It was going to be a long wait. A slim, smartly dressed woman stepped up to her. "Madam, are you Safia Abbas Jafri? Please walk through." She gestured smiling at Sitara who was clutching a red rose. Safia walked on the lawn and saw him sitting at the furthest corner, on a folding chair, under a Molsari tree. She had almost reached him before he glanced up from the files.

"Ah Safia! Welcome. Do sit down. What is it? You look worried. Anyone misbehaved with you?"

"Panditji, you are sitting here all alone, no security for miles. Suppose someone was to....you are important for this country."

"Thank you my dear. I can't see anyone wanting to kill me. Don't be taken in by the visual absence of the guards. They are hiding somewhere in bushes. I have told them not to bother but Sardar Patel refuses to listen. He believes that the home minister's primary duty is to protect me. I can't work with security breathing down my neck. So the compromise. They hide behind the flower shrubs. And how is my little one?"

Sitara bashfully extended the rose she had carried all the way in the bus.

"I am already wearing one in my *shervani*," he said with a twinkle in his eyes.

"But mine is prettier," insisted Sitara.

"Of course," he said incredulously. "Why didn't I see that?" With finesse, he withdrew the fresh rose bud and replaced it with Sitara's crushed one. "Now, have you ever seen red pandas? Would you like to see them?" Holding Sitara's hand, he led her to the cage where the lazy pandas came to life on seeing him. He opened the gate and two of the pandas jumped on his shoulders. Sitara squealed and clapped her hands. "Hey you behind the bush! Come out and take care of the child." A hulk appeared sheepishly from behind the greenery and Safia moved away with Nehruji taking a round of the lawn.

"How many troupe members in the puppet repertory?"

"Four Panditji."

"Only four? But I heard so many different voices. It was all your voice. Good. Do you have a passport....no....why not? Go down to South Block tomorrow at eleven and meet the secretary of external affairs. He would have instructions about what to do."

"You have done well for yourself. Don't you ever go back to Lucknow?" He asked over a cup of tea.

"Nothing left to go back for."

"This is what happens in the Marxist Party. They make a scapegoat out of the most innocent man and then feigning self righteousness wash there hands off him."

"You don't do too badly yourself. It was your government that arrested Abbas for writing *The Flames*, remember?"

He had the grace to blush. Then after a pause, he added, "We had no alternative. But it was the Marxist Party that had ignited *The Flames*. They are the ones who divide humanity into classes, the ones who don't believe in religion and openly claim to be atheists. It was their duty to stand by him."

"Everyone was passing the baggage called duty. But everyone knew that what *The Flames* said was right. Those flames shall flare up again, from another pen, from another heart, because injustice cannot be given the garb of religion. Providing each sect its own kind of bias cannot be the definition of secularism. Just as winning the elections on male appeasement can never bring about a true democracy. You see Panditji, you are good at doing the balancing act. You manage to stand erect on the slim wall between the fair and the unfair. But a few of us decide to take sides. We like to see things as white and black rather than be satisfied with a constant gray. Abbas belonged to that category. He paid for his choice, first by his humiliation and then with his life. I suppose I don't get the foreign tour now, do I?"

"I asked for it, but it still hurts. Sit down Safia, you have a right to be agitated. I have no business to sit on judgement on your principals. I am sorry." How could anyone be angry with this disarming man? Little wonder that he had initiated the concept of disarmament in the Third World. "Tell me, how are you really? Are you happy with the Kendra?"

"It is good work and I am safe....almost." She remembered the slimy, leery face of Govind Ram.

"We shall take care of that. Safia, thank you for trusting me."

There are people who give their protection when it is asked for. They are worthy of the gratitude and respect. But blessed are those who extend help and security without being asked. They are the answers to long forgotten prayers.

Had it not been for Amrita, Safia would have been blown away by the typhoon that almost instantly blew up after the meeting. Safia's troupe was invited to perform in Belgrade at the Children's Festival, followed by a long tour of the Soviet Union. Amrita accompanied her from office to bank counters to travel agents, tidying her papers and putting things in order. When she saw the pile of papers, she would be expected to show at each airport, Safia almost swooned.

"Please Amrita, I can't do it," she panicked.

"Its last minute nerves," Amrita soothed her.

"For Pete's sake, I am not getting married. I can't manage all this alone. Why can't everyone carry their own papers?" Safia argued.

"Fancy expecting Masterji and Manjari to take care of papers and Maithili who cannot even read and write. Let me concentrate Safia, I have loads to do."

"Why can't you come with us? You can pay your fare and the rest can be managed. Things would be so much easier. You have travelled abroad so many times."

"You think I don't want to. This is the first time my institution is going abroad in an International Festival. You think I don't want to be there?"

"What's stopping you?"

"I can't."

"Why not?" Safia persisted. "Why are you being so mysterious about it? One would think you have a dark secret hidden away somewhere."

"What if I do? Not everyone is free like you and not everyone can tell everyone everything. I have a right to my privacy. You might be going abroad but you don't own me or the Kendra for that matter."

"Amrita, it was meant to be a joke. Perhaps ill-timed but please treat it as such. I am sorry."

"No I am. One of my black moods. If you were to leave me, I would know that I asked for it."

"Don't you go finding a replacement behind my back. But why are you in a black mood today?"

"Because you are free and I am like a bird tied to a string with as much flight as the length of the string. Fly some, roam some but always keep within limits little birdie. That is the general. The particular being that 'that person' has given me an extra hard drubbing. Don't look so shocked. You know I am beaten often and the unfairness of it gives me a black mood."

"To torture those who work under you? Has it never occurred to you that if you were to hit that moron back, you might end up in a better mood?"

"Don't try to make a leftist out of me Safia!"

"There is nothing leftist about self preservation. Have you read the *Female Eunuch*? Grier is not propagating leftism, just equality between sexes. Anyway, did he have a reason? Not that any reason is good enough for wife bashing."

"Yes," Amrita said quietly. "Sleuths from the home department were at his office and have pointed out to him that his business was delving too much into lawful loopholes. The government had looked the other way, till now. But it might be obliged to hunt deeper, especially if he did not keep within limits in other matters besides business. The threat was heavily veiled but quite clear. It was also apparent who had sent them. That man loves his business too much to allow it to be harmed in anyway, but he had to show that he hated his womanizing tampered with. So, it was me at the receiving end as usual." Safia reached for her hand. "Don't feel sorry for me, it is my fate."

"The day you will accept that there is nothing like fate or destiny, you shall learn how to change it."

Amrita smiled. "In the meantime, lets change your trunk. You can't go on an international flight with an iron box. Lets shop for a decent suitcase, one with a number lock."

"Oh no, not something more to remember," grumbled Safia. But her heart was soaring. When saris, sweets and requests for a dinner had not stopped coming, she had presumed that the prime minister obviously had too many things to keep him busy. She had passed on the gifts to Amrita to return to the sender. Amrita knew her husband but a strain had slowly become noticeable in their friendship. Safia had made it amply clear to her that she was not interested in any man, least of all her husband but the coldness had grown. Safia had realized that passing the gifts had not been the most diplomatic thing to do. It was a public proclamation of the fact that her husband was a womanizer and in spite of accepting her straight forwardness, it made Amrita feel awkward and small. Both of them tried to cover it up by making fun of Govind Ram and his romantic overtures, but Safia could sense an aloofness creeping into Amrita's attitude. She happened to be tied to the man they were making fun of.

Realizing that this could not go on, Safia had decided to move out of the Kendra and seek a job in one of the other institutions opened in Delhi. She had a couple of offers that she had earlier brushed away. Now she knew that the bitterness would only increase and that she should leave before the situation became completely unpalatable. She had planned to complete this trip and leave on the pleasant note of having taken the name of the Kendra overseas.

Amrita was telling her that Govind Ram had received clear instructions never to interfere in the Kendra again. "I am going to have a hard time because he grabs things with his teeth and doesn't let go till he has bitten off a sizable chunk. If he is forced to let go, he goes around like a bad tempered bull dog waiting to dig his fangs into a soft target."

"Come with us Amrita. You shall be able to take a break and forget everything, at least for some time," persisted Safia.

"I wish I could. I really wish I could, but I dare not."

That line kept coming back to Safia in a monotonous beat till it became an unbearable din in her head. What was it that could frighten a strong woman, that could hold her captive and terrorize her? True that there was no 'why' about fear and often the most trivial of memories became the basis for phobias that grew to madness. But it was difficult to imagine Amrita in such a situation. The regular domestic violence was no more than a joke to her and often left Safia wondering if she was really hurt by it or enjoyed it like a violent form of lovemaking. So many times Safia had helped her wash and bandage her wounds. She knew no threats of violence, even murder could frighten Amrita. If anything, it made her perversely obstinate. Then what could the fear be?

Sometimes a small incident can make a deep etch on the subconscious. The conscious memory of the happening is erased but the etch remains deep and more definite than memories of stronger and more important events. One day, this deep etch takes hold of rest of the brain, guiding it to the place or point from where the excavation can begin. An effort to root out the real cause of the insignificant incident having made such a deep and lasting furrow.

Safia was rushing from the South Block to Shastri Bhawan, to Connaught Place, while the government servants and bank clerks took their time in telling her each requirement, one at a time. Safia decided that everything was slipping through her fingers without Amrita, who had called in to say that she would not be able to come to the Kendra today. Not a single of her papers seemed to be complete and they were to take the next morning flight. Bearing the auto rickshaw wala's grumbles, she guided him to the Kautalya Marg Bungalow. Alighting at the gate, she realized that this was the first time she had come uninvited after the first visit. Without really saying so, Amrita discouraged anyone from making impromptu calls on her. Safia debated for a second whether she had done the right thing. Perhaps she should have made a phone call. But the deed was done and the Gorkha recognizing her, was already opening the gates.

It took a long time for someone to answer the door, as if the household was not expecting any callers. Safia was raising her hand to press it again when she heard the bare feet of Anusuya hurrying towards the door. "Oh! *Memsahib* forgot to tell me," she said opening the door wide.

"*Memsahib* doesn't know." Safia stepped in

"But the….." Anusuya stopped uncertainly.

"Its an emergency. Don't worry. Is she in the back lawn? Safia was already crossing the hall and the gallery to reach the back garden. This was Amrita's refuge when she was in the house. Safia opened the back door having seen Amrita lying on the large swing under the mango tree.

"*Memsahib* I tried to stop her," Anasuya called from behind her and Amrita straightened up holding what seemed like a very large doll.

"I am sorry Amrita, I didn't want to bother you, but I am totally lost and I......." She stopped seeing the contorted face of Amrita. Was it anger or despair? Disgust or sorrow? Hatred or fear? Whatever it was, the sheer nakedness of the emotion made Safia look away from Amrita's face, down at the limp doll, its lolling head and dribbling mouth.

"Well now you have discovered my dark secret. Yes, this is Geetika, my eleven year old daughter. She is a total spastic. Her mortar nerves do not function but her brain is alive and sensitive. She loves me and I love her and we are a world together. She gets fits of fear and no one can control her but me. That man hates her and does not want anymore children from me. Not while she is alive. Recently, he has discovered that he can get her to have a fit if he beats me in her presence. Nothing he can ever do to me will ever bring me to my knees, but when he threatens to kill her, I am afraid. She is so helpless; can't move, can't scream. I am frightened into submission. This morning too she saw me being beaten and she went wild. Normally, she is looked after by Anusuya but this morning she went completely out of control. Here on the swing, close to my heart—she perhaps thinks that she is back in the womb and slowly she calms down."

"How wonderful to be loved like that Amrita. It is obvious that she wants to protect you. I don't know anything about her brain or her nerves but her heart is in the right place. It does not tolerate injustice. Geetika, I am Safia Auntie."

"Don't you feel any revulsion, any disgust? Don't you really?"

"No. And Geetika feels none from me. See, she is smiling at me. Stop pitying her Amrita and stop pitying yourself. She is a beautiful child who loves you to distraction. Don't hide her. Be proud of her and let everyone know that she is yours."

"Why? To see the pity in their eyes, see them look the other way, act as if she doesn't exist?"

"Yes. Tolerate those who do that and find others who won't behave like this, who shall either love her or learn to love her because they love you. Amrita, give people a chance. Once you stop being ashamed of her, your husband will not have this power over you. Don't put on act of being an extrovert while being an introvert of the worst kind. You will find that you have so many people on your side that your husband shall be afraid to touch you or her. Do you think she would come to my lap?"

"I would rather you told her a story. She loves them."

Out of Safia's purse came a bit of paper, a needle and a thread and from it she wove a story of a flying ship. She fashioned a boat with wings, captained by a prince who wanted to see the world but got lost in the clouds. The boat was ready as she finished the story and she placed it in Geetika's lap. Anusuya picked up Geetika and strapped her to her wheel chair, but when she removed the boat, Geetika made loud gurgling noises.

"Well you have made a conquest," said Amrita. "No one has ever made this kind of bond with her. Till now she only had me and it is because of her dependence and that man's threats that I can't go with you."

"But surely he would not harm his own daughter?"

"I have seen blood in his eyes. He can do anything, especially if I am not here for a gap. But what are you doing here? The banks close at half past two."

"That is why I came. Amrita, I can't handle it alone. But now I really do not how to ask you to help."

"Exactly as you are doing. Come lets go."

"Amrita should I.......would you......? I mean can I stay with Geetika while you go and handle all this?"

Geetika's dribbling mouth smiled and she made as if to lunge towards Safia.

"She wants you to stay and she has never done like this with anyone except me and Anusuya. So stay and I will be back in an hour or so. Safia, in case......."

"No one shall even touch a hair on her head while I am here."

Amrita nodded and turned to go. Then she stopped and turned back and asked in a strange far away voice. "Why is it that we cannot form bonds out of our shame and humiliation, Safia?"

"Because there are no bonds of shame. It is only in pride that bonds are formed. From today you are going to be very proud of Geetika and she is going to be proud of you."

Safia's first flight and she was a baggage of nerves, dropping papers, submitting wrong ones, getting tongue tied and wooden legged as the Custom officer carefully scrutinized each of her features and compared it with the photograph in the passport. The last flight from Tashkent to Delhi and she moved with the ease of a seasoned traveller, persuading airport officials into not charging her for extra baggage, signing documents with the ease of a popular artiste who had given innumerable autographs.

She was waiting in the lounge of the Tashkent airport when a young officer walked up to her and pointing at Sitara, shyly presented her a furry bear. Used by now to receiving gifts from strangers, Sitara stretched out her hand, while the officer explained with gestures and broken English that it was a gift from his son, who was Sitara's age, had seen her show and wanted a real baby elephant in return. While Safia and the officer laughed, Sitara walked up to a shop selling perfumed candles and came back with the request that Safia fashion out an elephant out of the largest one. Paying her last dollar, Safia bought the candle and sat down on the floor. With her nail file she proceeded to fashion a plump *Ganapathy* out of the block of wax. A crowd gathered around her and some cameras clicked. She finished with many 'ohs' and 'ahs'. Sitara gathered the elephant God and haltingly uttered '*Spasiba*' handing it to the officer, who insisted that Safia carve Sitara's name on the back of the sculpture.

The noise on the microphone was blaring something in Russian English that was repeated in Russian and the entire crowd started making wild gestures, some picked up her hand baggage, others ran with Sitara and a fat man bodily picked her up to make her stand in-spite of her troublesome sari. She caught the flight back home in the nick of time.

Home! The one room with an attached bath and a veranda, part of which had been converted into a cooking area.

* * * * *

TWENTY-TWO

Reaching home and settling down, Safia pondered about Amrita, who had been conspicuous by her absence. Patwardhan had come to the airport with a thick wad of notes in case they had to pay duty on something. But the custom officers had turned up their noses in disdain on learning that the foursome was returning from USSR. None of their baggage had even been opened. On the way back, Patwardhan had revealed that a new dance drama was underway and that Amrita came regularly to the rehearsals often accompanied by her daughter. Good. So Amrita was learning to treat Geetika as a person and not as some unknowingly committed crime that had to be hidden away in the dark corners of some cupboard. But why hadn't she come to meet her? The artistes had arranged for a formal welcome and Amrita had paid for the flowers and the sweets but she had not come herself. Didn't she care to know how the troupe had fared. Perhaps she had become so involved in the new found joy of accepting Geetika that the Kendra and its accomplishments too a back seat.

Well, first things first. She had to clean the room and sleep off the jet lag. The thirty two shows and constant travelling had taken its toll and each of her bone was telling her that it had been sorely misused. Changing the sheets of the *divan*, she dipped the immersion rod in the iron bucket, picking up the broom to sweep the room while it heated the water when Amrita barged in.

"For God's sake, live up to your image. Here you are just back from a trip abroad and I can't differentiate between you and the sweeper woman. Why have you tied your head with a black cloth, like the commandos?"

"I have to sweep the floor, clean the cobwebs, wash the bedsheet and..."

"Spare me please. Geetika is in the car. She wouldn't let me come alone."

"Geetika is here and you take this long to tell me? Why didn't you bring her in right away?"

"Well I…"

"You were not sure that she would be welcome?"

"I was sure about you but Sitara…she might be frightened."

"Stop being such a stuffed shirt Amrita and send for her."

Sitara, who was almost asleep sat up at the commotion. When Geetika was placed beside her, she moved to make more space, staring at her then tentatively touching her arms, legs and face. Suddenly she climbed down from the *divan* and dragged the biggest suitcase to the centre of the room. Opening it, she brought out her favourite toy, the bear, given to her at the Tashkent airport. Climbing back, she snuggled the bear to Geetika's neck who smiled and gurgled. With the suddenness of a light put out, she fell on Geetika and was asleep.

"She is an angel," Amrita smiled through tears. "They both are and we are angel mothers."

"Lets not get into this mutual flattering campaign before I have had a bath. I shall take ten minutes."

"Take more. You smell of black bread and vodka." Safia aimed a towel at her before disappearing into the small cubicle. When she emerged a strong smell of coffee and fresh *pakoras* welcomed her.

"Why Amrita, I didn't know you could cook."

"I am a Kayastha remember? And a much better one thanks to you."

"Thank yourself. Advice is the easiest and the cheapest thing to give. You are what you were. Nobody undergoes drastic changes. Some traits in our characters are obvious and some latent. Our only contribution is to keep juggling these traits to find the best permutation combination to suit a particular time or a situation."

"You have so much confidence in me. It is rather frightening."

"Yes, confidence of others is rather intimidating. So is love. There is the constant fear of losing it. But Amrita, those who are afraid of losing the love of their loved ones work hard to keep it intact. Those who lose it are the ones who had taken it for granted."

"What about you? You lost love, didn't you?"

"Do you think so? I never lost Abbas' love. I lost Abbas and that is not the same thing. I still have the joy of having had his love and confidence to the very last."

"Don't lets talk about the past. You know why I am late today. I took Geetika to a special school. They are confident that she can be taught to read."

"How wonderful Amrita! Which reminds me that I too have to take Sitara to the corporation school. I hope I am not late and find that admissions are closed for the year."

"A government school! For that angel! Are you out of your mind?"

"But Amrita, I can't afford a public school and then most of the Indian population sends their children to these schools."

"Let them. I am not talking about the scum of this earth. It is Sitara we are discussing and she shall be going to the Modern School. A new principal—Mr Kapoor—has taken over and he is reforming the whole system of education."

How can one explain to the rich that there can be things out of one's reach? How to make them understand—those who live in closeted compartments, within so many walls—that a mother might not want a wall in the one relationship she was left with. If Sitara was to go to a school patronized by the cream of the Delhi society, she would spend seven hours in the company of children who never really experienced any desires. Their wishes were fulfilled so fast that they had no chance to mature into desires. She would mix with the class that her father wanted to overthrow and that had wanted to destroy him and her. Slowly, Sitara would get tuned to their likes, wants, thoughts and aspirations. But each day she would be coming back to this single room accommodation of a staff artiste of the Kendra, scantily furnished, barely livable, what the rich condescendingly called 'functional'. With time, without conscious realization would come an abhorrence for the life that her mother could give. A wall would grow, brick by brick, dividing blood between two ideologies, two perceptions of life that could never co-exist.

"No, I don't think I would like that Amrita. Not that I have anything against your Mr Kapoor. It is only that I don't have faith in public schools."

"But you can't put her in a government school. That would be murder."

"Perhaps a way shall be found."

And strangely enough it was. The puppet troupe received an invitation from the Carmel Convent and the warmth of the atmosphere there made Safia approach Mother Superior right then. Even Amrita was surprised at the smoothness of events fitting themselves into each other. It was not easy to get admission in this school and once Amrita got over the initial shock, she entirely took over the arrangements. Not that she was an expert. Ten sheets of brown paper were bought to cover three copy-books, six sets of clothes for six days of the week and three satchels in case Sitara had a change of mood over the colour. It took Manjari's frank innocence to point out that Amrita was overtaking the rights of Safia *didi*. Amrita went into a black mood and refused to come to the Kendra for four days. Knowing her, Safia would have left her alone to work herself out of her dungeon but something came up that required her immediate attention.

A letter summoned her to the ministry of education and culture. It was a short note from the secretary and Safia had gone out of curiosity to find out how the official side of education and culture functioned. The meeting had lasted a good forty minutes in which he explained to her what plans the ministry had about culture in general and the performing and fine arts in particular. The plan was to open three national academies of literature, fine arts and performing arts. They would function as the apex body to oversee the functioning of the state and district level bodies to promote and preserve the cultural heritage of each region. Decades of erosion and the onslaught of ridicule that had been heaped on the Indian arts by various conquerors had to be washed away and the true face of Indian culture had to be re-discovered. It was the brainchild of Maulana Abul Kalam Azad and the central government had accepted it.

Safia heard everything in awe, her heart crying out for Abbas, the man who had nurtured similar dreams about the greatness of a united India.

"So what do you say?" The secretary asked her politely.

"It seems an ambitious plan, too big perhaps, but one that has to be undertaken and the sooner the better. But why are you telling all this and asking for my opinion?"

"Precisely for that, to get your opinion. Since we now know that you like the concept, we can make a concrete offer. How would you like to join as the assistant secretary for performing arts?"

"But you can't do that. You can't leave me and the Kendra in the lurch. You come to me asking for alms and when I have helped you stand on your feet, the first thing you do is walk out on me. Why? Because you prefer to be a clerk. How dare you even think of such a thing when the Kendra needs you so much? Why you seem to make a habit of deserting those who rely on you, even your family."

That hurt but Safia bided her time, waiting for the steam to blow off and temperatures to cool. But Patwardhan who had accompanied her, did not possess her patience. Nor was he Amrita's friend. His *bidi* packet was empty and in his agitation he had forgotten to buy one at the bus stop. Both of them had known that it was not going to be easy.

"If you would be quiet and listen to her, you might find that her plan is for your benefit."

"Don't tell me to be quiet in my own house."

Patwardhan got up. "Alright, we shall talk when you decide to come to the Kendra."

"We! We shall talk! I didn't realize that both of you were so thick. Is there something else brewing without my knowledge and under my nose?"

"Amrita you are sick! I had come to discuss with you how I could help the Kendra become independent. The independence that you used to yearn for. Well, you just made up my mind for me. Your room shall be vacated by tomorrow."

"Go to hell and stay there," shouted Amrita at her back.

She was in Safia's room before the evening and gave way to bitter sobs on seeing that Safia was almost packed. "I am sorry, please forgive me. I promise not to interfere in the future or even plan anything about Sitara. I can't let you go, I need you."

"No you don't. What you need is a packet of tissues. Use them, chuck them. My turn has not come yet, but it will."

"You have every right to be upset with me after my abominable behavior. But I really do need you. What will happen to the puppet troupe? It depends on you."

"I shall train a replacement."

"Can I please hear your plan?"

Safia turned and faced Amrita and seeing the defeated look on her face took the two steps to reach and hold her shoulders. "Don't look like that. I am not really going away. Not even to the hell you so wanted me to visit. Now listen carefully. The government is planning to give away a lot of money in grants to groups performing Indian dance and theatre. With the background of the Kendra, I can help in securing a grant for you. You shall no longer be obliged to take money from your husband. Between the two of us, we can make this institution the premier institution of dance and music of the country."

"But how will we manage without you and what shall become of me and Geetika?"

"As I said I am not going anywhere, not even leaving the city. Surely for bigger gains we can make these small sacrifices."

"You are the biggest sacrifice that life has asked me to make."

"Then you are in for many surprises. I must be going. I have to find a room before dark."

"No you don't. You function from this very place till you are given the government flat. And Safia don't forget to write a note of thanks to Nehruji."

"You mean….?"

"Of course. You don't think anything you do would make these idiotic bureaucrats sit up and take note. They are too busy tying reels of red tape to every file and scheme. It is he who has done this for you."

"So this is what he meant when he said that he would find a permanent solution to my insecurity."

"Stop browsing over your do-gooder. He is a politician. Just as a bureaucrat cannot think of anything original, a politician cannot think of anything without a motive."

"Not this one. Because he is really an intellectual masquerading as a politician."

"Whatever. You are on your way to becoming a bureaucrat, that much despised clan who send their children to public schools. You might have chosen Modern School for Sitara."

"I am glad I didn't. Sitara is doing very well in Martaday and I am still something of a conservative. I don't really like co-educational schools."

"Stop being so prim and proper and lets make a list of things we have to buy. Saris would top the list because a bureaucrat must be properly dressed."

"And well informed. I have to start buying books."

* * * * *

TWENTY-THREE

"Are you sure you want to do this?" Safia had read and re-read the proposal and each time it seemed to multiply in size. She had taken two months over it and had at last decided to call Amrita and discuss the whole project with her.

"I would not have submitted it to you if I wasn't dead serious." Amrita had shot back.

"Maybe. You have been receiving the highest grant and it has been hiked every year to match the budget that you have submitted with your proposal. But I have never found you this ambitious."

"Everything has to grow, even ambitions."

"But this is colossal. To actually want to build a university of arts."

"True. In time that is what I aim for and I have the land."

"Amrita you don't just need land for making a university."

"That is all that Rabindranath Tagore had at Shantiniketan."

"You can't compare yourself with Gurudev!" Safia was scandalized.

"Oh, don't go all Bengali over me. I know it is the 'in thing' and that you are obliged to do justice to occupying a room in a building named after him. Let us be North Indians and treat him as a man. A great one but a man none the less and not a demi-god."

Safia kept quiet. It was no good arguing against this regionalism that had slowly been raising its head, sure and certain like communalism. Another 'ism' to cope with. Whatever happened to the 'isms' of the arts? Realism, naturalism, symbolism or surrealism? She brought back her mind to the issue at hand, that of Amrita asking for the moon.

Safia debated with herself and repeated, "I still think it is too ambitious."

"What is it you really have against the proposal? Don't you want that there should be a university for arts in North India or do you believe that North India doesn't have the scholarship and the artistes to support this kind of an institution."

"I shall not go into the details of what I think about your project. The only thing that I can say is that the government would not have the kind of funds to support such a huge project."

"So that's it. Govind said as much."

"Who said?" Safia had heard so much of 'that person' that the sudden cognizance of his name came as a shock and suddenly the picture was clear. It was Govind Ram, working hard behind the whole proposal, scheming and plotting to get....what? What was it this man wanted?

"So it is basically your husband's idea."

"Well we both worked it out together."

"And since when have you both started working things out together?"

"Damn it! I can't be expected to keep you posted about the way my marriage is going. After you left, I was all alone and…....."

"And he made himself available."

"Look Safia, don't get personal. I admit that this whole thing is on the ambitious side, but I am not expecting the government to fund it completely. Do whatever you can. Govind was sure you would not be able to manage the whole amount."

"Govind seems to know a lot about everything. And may I ask, from where are you going to manage the rest of the finances?"

"Well, Govind says that he would be able to manage the rest of the funds from his other business contacts, the Karnanis, Jains, Lakhias and others."

"So why can't he manage the whole amount from them? Why try to dip into the governments meager resources that should really go to the artistes who survive through their art?"

"Well, getting even a small grant from the government for this kind of an institution would lend it a lot of credibility and be a great help in raising funds from other sources."

"I shall do what I can Amrita. In case of big projects, my job is only to see that the file is put up with proper noting. But I still think that you should give up this 'become-the-North India's-Tagore' thing alone. It is advisable to begin at the bottom and work oneself up. That way one has one's feet firmly on the ground."

"Don't you think you should do your job and leave me to do mine."

Safia understood the state of things. It was eleven years now since she had moved out of the Kendra. She should not expect her relationship with Amrita to remain the same as it was more than a decade before. No relationship can remain stationary. Any impulse was bound to generate a movement that would disturb the existing state of rest. The relationship would then either move forwards or backwards, yield positive or negative results but never return to the stationary zero. Amrita had every right to depend on her husband. Safia herself had pleaded his case several times. Why then was she so upset now? Simply because Govind Ram had made a few passes at her in the remote past. Yes, very remote past. He had been put in his place. After Nehruji's death, she had the protection of being a government servant. Why then did she feel a sense of apprehension growing inside her? Was it for herself or for Amrita? Had she not noticed his continuous presence by Amrita's side at all the major art events of the capital. As a businessman he must have been watching the fallout of the formation of the republic and the slow decline of the rights and wealth of the Rajahs and the Nawabs. If he wanted to provide jobs to the deposed artistes who had earlier survived in the feudal courts and were now virtually on the road, then he was really a philanthropist with excellent business acumen. He was trying to do what the government was handicapped in doing. So why was she disturbed? He was not asking for the entire money and even if he was, it was a decision that the expert committee had to make. Why should she worry?

It came to her as an accepted realization, in a mellow and forgone sort of a way. Twice while thinking about Amrita's proposal, she had thought about it as 'his'. That perhaps was her worry. She didn't want what was Amrita's to become her husband's. Perhaps she knew in her subconscious that she would not have the same rights over the Kendra if it slipped from Amrita's hands to become Govind Ram's property.

Well, if that was the case, she must make a conscious effort to view things impersonally and the best time to begin doing so was now. Pushing aside her personal thoughts, she pulled her chair to the desk and began to write. "An unusual proposal, that on the face of it seems too ambitious. However if it comes through, would provide sustenance to a large number of artistes and training to an even larger number of students. Can be reviewed for partial support."

The Kendra's support in the top industrialists multiplied overnight. It was almost as if the big wigs of all business houses had suddenly woken up to performing arts and in their great concern to promote them, had chosen the Kendra to dump their excess money. The fact that Govind Ram managed to acquire Income Tax Exemption for all donations made to the Kendra, crossed out the last misgivings.

The Ismanis suddenly discovered that they had a grandmother who had played the *dholki*, possibly at family weddings. The percussion wing was named after her. The Mittals dug out a daughter-in-law who sang *bhajans* and the Gargs took a lead in paying for the auditorium. It was going to be the best in the city, with not just sliding seats, carpeted gangways and balcony. It would have a huge stage, airy green rooms, imported lights and excellent acoustics.

"Such an auditorium has never been seen in North India and it is mine," Amrita had gushed, showing each nook and cranny to Safia. Her enthusiasm was catching and Safia felt her misgivings being washed away by its deluge. Two more floors were being added to the main building of the Kendra to accommodate the music and dance classes. One of the inner lawns was being converted into an amphitheatre. Famous gurus like Birju Maharaj and Ustad Ishtiaq Hussain Khan would be joining soon. *Odissi* dance was the new fad of the Delhi high society after Indrani Rehman introduced it with great fanfare. A guru was being brought all the way from Cuttack. The Kendra would soon begin to produce their own staff artistes for the dance dramas and do away with the illiterate country bumpkins.

The flow of money from the business houses seemed endless and work was progressing at mind boggling pace. Later Safia would look back and curse herself for not biding the voice that persistently mumbled 'when....when?' inside her heart. Not only had she insisted on not listening to that voice, she chided herself for being self-centred and perhaps a little jealous of the success of her rich friend in a field that really was not hers. So hard had she tried to quieten that voice that when the cyclone came it caught her totally unawares!

She had ignored other warnings too. Patwardhan and Masterji had come to her office to inform her that they were planning to leave the Kendra. They had been vague about the reasons, saying that they would not compromise their art. Since this was a pet dialogue of Patwardhan, Safia took it with a pinch of salt. When they stayed put the following week, she had been assured that it was a routine tiff between the worker and the employer. Later on, she could have kicked herself for not remembering that Masterji never talked in terms of finalities and when he did, there was no possibility of a compromise.

Two weeks after their visit, Safia was at home, trying to finish an article she had promised for *The Illustrated Weekly* before leaving for office, when the call bell rang and continued to ring as if unhinged. Opening the door, Safia formulated the choicest abuses she could think to greet the caller, when Amrita almost fell in.

"The Kendra is shut down and the artistes are on strike," she began without ceremony.

"What! How? Who?"

"You! Yes, you! Patwardhan had been planning this for months and he was with you a couple of weeks back, wasn't he? Didn't he say he wanted to leave? You didn't even bother to inform me? Why? Because you were supporting them."

"I had no clue about the strike. He talked about leaving the Kendra and I merely suggested that he try other means before resorting to such a major step."

"Well, this is one of his other means."

"Stop this bickering at once Amrita."

"May I come in?" Govind Ram was smiling, the angular, oily smile that he had cultivated ever since he took over as the Chairman of Bhagyanath Industries.

"You just have. You can sit down. Now Amrita, suppose you tell me calmly what has been going on."

"Will you allow me?" Govind Ram didn't wait for anyone's answer and embarked on the story. What he told and what Safia interpreted amounted to this:

Govind Ram had generated the large amount of funds, both donations and loans and in the circumstances it had been natural that he become the Managing Director of the Kendra. The industrialists felt more comfortable in dealing with a man. Amrita remained the

Executive Director. The artistes had not taken kindly to this but they had no right to like or dislike any change in the management. They, after all, had not been effected and Amrita still managed everything. He visited the Kendra only on the seventh of every month which was the pay day. The expense of running the Kendra had shot up given the fact that the number of employees had increased tenfold. Efforts had to be made to cut down the deficit so that it could become self reliant and he, Govind Ram, didn't have to dig into his pockets. So he had merely pointed out that salaries for off days should be deducted, contracts should be made for eleven months instead of seven to take on more shows. Artistes should be divided into three categories and paid in those grades depending on their talent, expertise and parts assigned. Being the MD it was his duty to make as much income as possible. But look at the artistes! They are on strike and threaten to form a trade union. Whoever heard of an artistes' union? All his life he had heard that the artistes were creative people, who could sing and dance on an empty stomach, who dealt with the spiritual and shunned the materialistic. But these artistes! Why he had even taken insults from that man Patwardhan, when he was only suggesting that they use some revolving lights, you know to give a disco like effect in the new dance drama. Pray why shouldn't those lights be used when the equipment was there, bought at such a high price? But he has to be told not to teach what he has not learnt. These are the tastes of the public and after all the Kendra is catering to them isn't?

Safia took a deep breath and smiled at him. "I understand everything now. I think you and your contribution have been greatly misjudged. What you really want is that the Kendra should function in a well organized way. Get assignments, fulfill them, produce goods that are salable, meet dead lines with each employee fulfilling a well defined role. In short function like a well organized industry."

"Exactly madam. I am so glad you have understood everything so soon and so clearly."

"Precisely Mr Govind Ram. I have understood everything. You want to run an industry of performing arts, or turn performing arts into an industry. Yet you do not want to give the employed artistes what you would be obliged to give to an industrial worker."

There was a silence—so heavy and solid that it could have been banged and sounded.

Govind Ram gave a hurt sigh. "I told you, she has a background and she has to live up to it." No raving and ranting for him. He had his own smooth way of slipping in and staying in till he wanted. This meeting had been designed to test the level of his influence and he was at his soggy best. He had managed to get into the Kendra, become its MD and slowly seep into its roots like the slimy damp, eating it from below, slow but certain, with no cracks showing on the outside till the day the whole structure came crashing down. He was now trying to make an inlet into Amrita's emotions. His first move of pointing out that Safia had a background for being on the other side had hit the mark.

"So whose side are you on Safia?" Amrita asked. She had to ask because she had a right to know. Safia had to answer because she too had to know—know who she was, what she really stood for, what bonds the years of desk work had deformed, what ties wrapped and put away in dark cupboards of forgetfulness, what comforts had replaced denials, what weights tied down her urge to live and planted in its place the lukewarm wish to survive.

"I am not on anyone's side, till I have talked to the artistes."

"After all we have told you, you still have to talk to the artistes? So that you can make up your mind to support or condemn us?" Amrita was livid.

"I have to know their reasons. They must have some, perhaps many for taking this extreme step. You too shall have to talk to them."

"Me? Me, talk to those bastards? All artistes are like dogs and I throw bits of leftovers to them. They can take them or leave them but they cannot ask for more."

"Seeing that this is your attitude for them, its really a wonder why they have not rebelled before."

"You seem to identify so much with them."

"You forget that I was one of them. I was never one of you."

The silence descended again and as Amrita and Safia scowled at each other, Govind Ram intervened in his greasy voice, "You forget that you are not one of them now. Neither are you one of us. You are a bureaucrat, something of a *Trishanku*, not belonging anywhere. In the end, these artistes shall come back to us because we are the givers and shall detest you for having shown sympathy without really doing anything for them. Empty sympathy is the favour that does not make people grateful but vengeful."

If for a moment Safia had ever doubted Govind Ram's business astuteness, she thought otherwise now. He knew how to conquer on the strength of money and had learnt to dissect everything, even emotions, before making an investment. He did not wait for events, he planned to make them happen. This scene was one such event, where he had carefully worked on the psyche of one of the opponents to bring the showdown to his choice of conclusion.

Packing off Sitara to school, Safia flagged an auto rickshaw to reach the Kendra. The artistes were sitting outside the locked gates. She was immediately surrounded and bombarded with pleas, reasons, causes and details of the strike. It was only when she was rescued by Patwardhan and Masterji and given an empty fruit crate to sit on, that she slowly began to piece together the whole body of events.

Trouble had started when Amrita began absenting herself from the rehearsals and her place had been taken up by one Puranchand. Manager of the pickle and preserves unit of Bhagyanath Industries, he did not have a clue about performing arts. He openly ogled at the girls, who complained to the director, he made regular rounds of the dance and music classes on the pretext of seeing that the gurus stick to the syllabus. He could never understand why the Diploma course was of five years. Surely all this leg shaking could be mastered in six months. Why weren't two girls in the same class learning the same *Toda* or *Khandi*? Why couldn't the classical vocal music teacher, teach *alaap* to the student who had not mastered the *sargam* of the raga. He had his own concepts of beauty and insisted that the most good-looking girl should be given the main roles. Patwardhan, in spite of his sexual frolics, worked with a love for the stage. He had a strong instinct of knowing what would look good on the stage and did not think he had to explain his reasons to anyone. Indeed he did not know how to, because there was no logical explanation for these choices. Puranchand's over enthusiastic 'Why?', 'Why not?' and 'Do explain to me' managed to get under Patwardhan's skin, who snapped at him to shut up and let him work. There was one hell of a row.

The world of music was undergoing a revolution. Fundamental instruments were being replaced by the synthesizer. Playing an instrument with the push of a button was very exciting for Puranchand who insisted that it should be included in the orchestra. Masterji made no comment on this. In fact, he did not have an opportunity to since he was not consulted. He had several years before, saved up for a piece of land across the river Yamuna. He began building a house on it and one day, with Manjari and the few bits of furniture he possessed, he quietly moved to his new house.

Girls in the dance troupes were always let off from rehearsals during their menstrual cycle. Puranchand started deducting their salaries for these days and when there were protests, he insisted on knowing the reason for their day offs—a sure way to embarrass a young girl.

When the number of artistes had increased, the dormitories had become overcrowded. Amrita had reassured the artistes that new rooms would be added and that it was only a matter of time that things sorted themselves out. But when the rooms were ready, they became offices for Puranchand, Amrita and Govind Ram and three were converted into guest rooms constantly occupied by the guests of Bhagyanath Industries. The living conditions deteriorated but the management refused to look into it.

Impossible to believe that Amrita did not know of these developments. They had periodically been reported to her and she had looked the other way. The last straw had come with the stopping of the bonus from the sponsored shows. Amrita had never viewed the Kendra as a money spinning contraption and had distributed almost half the income from sponsored shows to the artistes. She had also never really run around to increase the number of shows. Puranchand was a person of sales and pickles could very well be replaced with performances. On a commission basis, he hired two good-looking girls who spread a network of shows involving colleges, schools, clubs, associations and even wedding receptions. The network was so extensive that even Amrita was left aghast at the turnover. The artistes were on their feet practically seven days a week with matinee shows added on weekends. Not that the artistes were upset by the round the clock routine. They were performers and were happiest when on stage. The gold pot at the end of the rainbow was the bonus money. Cunning Puranchand had persuaded them to take it at the end of the year.

At the closing of the financial year, Puranchand had taken the accounts to Govind Ram, who had gone through them in detail, suggesting a few more calculations and some clarifications and then submit them to *malkin*. When Amrita saw the five figure sums that each artiste would be entitled to, she wanted to know the total amount that would go to the artistes. Puranchand was ready with the figure and hearing the huge figure, her heart turned a little green. Govind Ram had made a quiet entry and on queue Puranchand presented the requisition for the annual installment of the loan of the building, the stage equipment and the auditorium. Govind Ram sighed and murmured how all their labour was not giving the desired result—self reliance for the Kendra. They were, alas, miles from the target! Inconspicuously, Puranchand pointed at the huge amount going away as bonus to the artistes. Govind Ram praised the benevolence of *malkin* in distributing to the artistes all that they—the management—earned. Puranchand was a persistent one and enquired why, when all the artistes were receiving regular salaries for performing, should they be given a bonus just for that. The contract did not mention any bonus. Govind Ram had in between let slip that his own financial position was at an all time low because he had imported machinery for his electronic unit.

Amrita had, as if on her own, come to the conclusion that the artistes would not be paid any bonus this year. Puranchand had immediately embarked on the exercise to placate her conscience pointing out that even the best industries gave away bonus only when they made profit. Instead of expecting a bonus, the artistes should work hard to make the Kendra independent. It was their duty since that is what they had been hired for.

Amrita agreed and asked Puranchand to collect all the artistes in the rehearsal room, explain to them the debts on the Kendra and the reasons for the 'no bonus' decision. The artistes had gathered in the hope of receiving the salary for the last month and the bonus for the full year. Most of them were still farmers and had been intending to leave in a few days time. The announcement of 'no bonus' had caught them as unprepared as a Thar desert tribe in a raging flood. Patwardhan had been thinking of leaving and Masterji was planning to open a music school in the trans-Yamuna area. But to leave without the hard earned bonus?

It was a flash strike and each member had signed on the formal ultimatum being submitted to the management. Amrita had had a change of heart but her decision to backtrack had quickly been stemmed by Govind Ram. The MD took the platform and called the artistes ungrateful wretches, who would spit and lick it. The fat was in the fire and the artistes had been sufficiently incited. The management had threatened the angry artistes with dire consequences if they did not pick up their salaries and resume work. There were still a few commitments to be completed. The threat had spread the fire to the areas that had so far not been involved. Within minutes, the classes had closed down and the teaching faculty was down with the striking dance drama artistes. Amrita had again shown a willingness to talk to them but the management led by Govind Ram had been able to convince her that it would be her personal defeat if she bowed down now. In future, she would never be able to control this 'riff-raff'. Let them suffer for some days and they shall come back to you with their tails between their legs.

Somehow, each word uttered within the closed door found its way to the agitating artistes. That *malkin* had called them 'riff-raff', closed all doors of a settlement. Seething tempers mounted to the point of no return.

* * * * *

TWENTY-FOUR

It was around this time that Bhadralok reappeared. He had been to Punjab for the Party Congress and was visibly angry that a strike had been called without his permission. His plea was that a strike needed a lot of the 3P's—Preparation, Planning and Paper work. It should not be impromptu because then it might fail and be a set back to the International Leftist Movement. But when he saw that the simple minded artistes were not in a mood to discuss International-ism, he changed his tactics and rendered a fiery speech, deriding the capitalists and calling for unity amongst all artistes to wage a war of just rights.

It was debatable whether the artistes understood any of this but they clapped and cheered at the right moments. The arrival of Bhadralok apparently made Govind Ram and the rest uneasy and for first time in five days the police was informed. The arrival of the police frightened the guts out of the poor artiste peasants, who had vague, intermixed hearsay memories of *gora saheb*, police, jails and beatings. Some of them were just slinking away when they stopped in mid-retreat. There eyes opened wide as they stared at Bhadralok walking with firm strides towards the police jeep. The ACP emerged and warmly shook hands with Bhadralok. Then arms on his shoulder, he walked towards the squatting artistes.

"*Chhi Chhi*! Artistes and striking like uncultured, illiterate labourers. You are *Saraswati putras yaar*." The ACP was a middle aged, pot-bellied man, fully aware that this duty would not get him free lunches.

"I told them so Sir. Actually the strike happened in my ab-sence."

"What are gifted *gandharvas* like you doing on the road?" the ACP asked.

"Trying to get a square deal," someone shouted and the ACP stopped in his tracks. Patwardhan had been shocked into silence on seeing Bhadralok being hugged by the policeman. In his youth, the Left and the police were always on the opposite side. It took him a full twenty minutes to realize that twenty years had passed and the Left had undergone a change in their aims. They were now for democratic social change. They had to be on good terms with the protectors of the law. Many of the law enforcers were sympathizers and that is how it should be. Once the new system came into force, the new state would need a police force to maintain law and order, wouldn't it?

"We are trying to get justice. Even *Saraswati putras* have to eat."

The ACP turned and subjected Patwardhan to a cold glowering. "Who is this red hero?"

"Oh, he isn't red. He is not even a trade union member. At least not one of us," placated Bhadralok.

"So a red in disguise perhaps. Listen sonny, do you know that the police has to be informed before calling a strike. Why didn't you inform us?"

"I have been telling them this. Why don't you sit down sir and let me talk to them. Have a paan." Bhadralok led away the ACP and seating him under the *Jamun* tree, turned back grumbling, "Now look where you have landed me. I shall have to go back to the PHQ and report this matter."

The ACP jumped up from the makeshift seat. "Why? Why do you have to go to the PHQ?"

"Well the whole matter has to be reported. This development has to be discussed, further action and strategy chalked out."

"But why at the PHQ? Why can't you discuss it with me? Throwing your weight around eh?"

It took a while to clear the wrangle. PHQ for one meant Party Headquarters while for the other it was the Police Headquarters. After much smirking and back slapping, Bhadralok left, leaving the artistes in expectancy and the policemen in slumber at the gates of the Kendra.

At four in the afternoon, on the seventh day, the contingent of reserved police for public demonstration descended and took position around the agitating artistes. Almost simultaneously another cavalcade of cars brought members of the party accompanied by Bhadralok.

Bhadralok was a Bengali who had had some basic training in theatre. He had migrated to Delhi some six years back and failing to get admission in the National School of Drama had formed his own theatre group PAT, People's Action Theatre. About the same time, the party leadership was discussing the importance of a Left platform of theatre. The Indian People's Theatre Association, the official theatre wing of the party had disintegrated and they did not want to revive it. Yet the party could not deny the importance of having such a wing and the meaningful role it would have in propagating its ideology and gathering a crowd during election campaigns. It wanted a new forum that would have the party's backing but would be able to function as an independent body. PAT had been un-officially adopted by the Party.

'Comrade B', as he came to be known in the inner circles of the party, became a card holder and given the task of peeking into the mushrooming cultural organization, their functioning and problems of the artistes. The party accepted the American diktat that there was no business like the show business. Big business meant workers that needed to be organized. To give his intuition credit, Bhadralok had had an inkling that unrest was brewing at the Kendra but had not expected things to boil over so soon. He was unable to decide whether the strike was a windfall or an uninvited dust storm.

The senior comrades had descended from their cars and sat down on the naked ground with the artistes. This was the attitude that had endeared them to the strikers. Someone who could ride a car and sit with them as equals was a novelty and the artistes were ready to give them their complete trust. Safia had not known the background of Bhadralok but the arrival of the senior comrades was like a gush of known breeze. It was almost as if inside an imprisoned but fresh water spring had found an outlet and gurgled out with relief. Now things would move in the right direction. She soon began to regret her first reaction and tried to close the outlet lest the spring flow itself dry.

They started with detailed questioning of each artiste, their backgrounds, their tenure and their salaries. At the end of each interview, the comrades shook their heads, frowned and sighed. Having talked to all of them, they turned to Safia and learning that she was a government employee, looked her up and down. Turning to the artistes, one of them asked blandly, "What is she doing here? Don't you understand? She is a spy of the bourgeoisie. She is here to find out your plans and report to her bosses."

Patwardhan got up to protest but Safia holding his hand held him down. "You are right. Now that all of you leaders are here, I am not really needed. I am at my office, in case you need me."

"We won't," she was curtly dismissed. Safia understood that she was considered on the wrong side of the fence and so long as she was there, she had no right to be telling those on this side how to till their land. But to be called a spy was humiliation of the worst kind.

Patwardhan accompanied her to the Academy. Walking down the shaded Ferozeshah Road he began to speak, more to himself than to her. "It is perhaps time to go back. I belong to Maharashtra and had come here searching a chance to carve a niche for myself. Maybe also because there are so many like me in Maharashtra and I was afraid to enter into a competition. This place was like finding a chance oasis in a desert. Well, I found it and lost it. It is time to move on. The Indian Council for Cultural Relations has asked me to take up the post of dance teacher in Mauritius. Try as we might this strike is doomed. Why do struggles that have the right people to support them, are the voice of a just cause and are based on honourable emotions fail to succeed? The Leftists are as much of opportunists as the other political parties. They can see that the artiste does not form any vote bank. Soon, very soon after making a credible show of effort to get us our rights, these people shall leave us to our fate—the fate of the disorganized, creative rabble."

The comrades spent marathon sessions, generously sprinkled with lunches and teas with the management. All the while, the artistes sat in the scorching sun. Initially, Amrita had not wanted to have any truck with the commies, but Govind Ram had persuaded her and the comrades had gone in as the representatives of the artistes. It never became clear who had nominated them to talk on behalf of the artistes. They knew nothing of the reasons or problems that had led to the agitation.

The strike had lasted for almost a month. In the last two days when the comrades had come out of the Kendra, Puranchand had run out before them, shouting at the *chowkidar* to summon their cars.

When the artistes had tried to find out what had happened inside, they were told to have patience. This was after all a grave matter and would have to be dealt with carefully and delicately. The fact that their agitation was a grave matter had satisfied the artistes for some time. The cars whizzed past and Bhadralok had stayed back to give the artistes a gist of the discussion and the fiery speeches the comrades had made before the panel of industrialists and how each one had trembled in his chair remembering the strike in his own factory and the way the trade union leaders had handled it and led the workers to victory. His narration and demonstrations could compare with the best war enactments in the court of Nebuchadnezzar. He always concluded by assuring them that the cause of the artistes was in safe hands and tomorrow would bring a red dawn—*Lal Salaam*!

Almost a month into the strike and the artistes began leaving. Their reason was simple—the strike and the bonus could wait but not the crop. If someone had tried to keep them together, if they had felt the strength of united suffering, they might have forgone one crop. But the end was nowhere in sight and the comrades were almost happy to see them go. On the surface, they continued deriding artistes for not being organized, having no unity and no love for their cause. They quoted Lenin as having said that organizing artistes was like weighing live frogs. But they made no effort to keep the frogs together.

The management had timed their attacks well. They knew that a peasant could forgo money but not his crop, that he lived in the dread of his land turning barren if not tilled for a few years. In a week, the strength was reduced to half and the negotiating tables had still not yielded any result.

Exactly on the thirtieth day, the end came. No one saw the stone being thrown but the dozing silence of the midsummer afternoon was shattered by the splintering of the huge tinted glass window. Everyone had taken a second to react to the fact that a stone had been thrown at the Kendra, aimed at the hall where negotiations were taking place. Only the policemen had reacted with the speed that belied their lazy postures. On cue, they had jumped up and rained blow on the stunned artistes whose first reaction had been to run. The policemen had followed them, rounding them in an organized manner and had thrashed them while men and women rolled on the ground. Then some of them had picked up the only weapon available. As stones were flung at the policemen, they had no alternative but to burst a few tear gas shells. In the chaos, the comrades had emerged from the conference room and vanished inside their cars. The cars had moved before the artistes could start shouting death curses on their names.

Next morning, Bhadralok had appeared with full security, getting a feel of what it would be like when he became a minister, and delivered the decision of the Party.

"The artistes of the Kendra had no registered union and as such were not entitled to stop work and strike. In-spite of this, the party had agreed to look into the matter because it was a struggle of the oppressed working class by the capitalists. But the party does not and would not condone violence. Most of the artistes had neglected to keep a copy of the contract made with the Kendra, nor had they demanded a renewal when the contract period had been exhausted. They also did not possess any written commitment of the management entitling them to the bonus. The party thus has no way of knowing who was right, the management in not giving the bonus or the workers for demanding it? On the face of it, it seemed that the demands of the artistes were unfair and unjust. The management had been on the point of terminating the services of all the artistes, however, the intervention and the constant presence of the trade union leaders had forced them to review their decision and re-employ the artistes. Once employed with renewed contracts, the artistes could under the guidance of the party form a union. Then, in an organized manner, under the guidance of the party, the union could fight for the just causes and the rights of the artistes. *Lal Salaam.*"

The decision by the party had the finality of the mid-monsoon shower. Most artistes ignored it and started packing their bags. Several shows had been cancelled because of the strike. The Kendra found itself with just a handful of artistes and a long list of commitments for the coming season. Govind Ram arranged a meeting with the Virmanis, the vegetable oil kings of Kolkata. The Managing Director of Virmani Oils suggested that an advertisement should be placed in the papers of West Bengal that was teaming with artistes of all kinds. Conditions in Bengal were bad and worsening, with the constant flow of refugees from Bangladesh. Artistes could be hired for a pittance, with no contracts or commitments. Most of them would have no support or influence in Delhi and care could be taken to select only those who did not speak Hindi.

At an exorbitant price, Balraj Singh, an average level music director from Bombay was hired to set the score for the Dance Dramas and it was recorded. All productions would now be performed on recorded music.

Patwardhan joined Masterji. He purchased a motor cycle and drove around giving home tuitions of dance. One night, his motor cycle collided head on with a truck coming from the wrong side. His head had been crushed like an egg shell. The driver vanished in the dark with his truck. The body was found only in the early hours of the morning by the police and though Masterji had made the identification, he had not been able to give any proof of a blood connection. The body was not handed over to him and was cremated by the police.

Thus ended the first and the last effort of the artistes to unite against those who would forever control the purse strings of the show business.

* * * * *

TWENTY-FIVE

The artistes' strikes had been the last eventful incident. The prescribed art functions still took place in the Capital. The annual dance, music and theatre festivals, the State Awards, scholarships, grants and fellowships were organized and held as usual. Safia's own life had become as monotonous as a government servant's can be. Sitara had graduated from Miranda House College and joined the Delhi School of Economics. With blinkers on, she had completed first the Post Graduation and then her PhD. Somewhere in the process of growing up, the happy chirrupy child had become a quiet, deep thinking individual. In her own quiet way, she took decisions, just informing Safia and rarely asking for her advice or suggestions. This brought a seeping unhappiness that seemed to settle down around Safia's heart because she had always expected Sitara to be her best friend. Sitara's decisions always proved right so she had nothing to complain of.

Deep inside her, she had that nagging feeling that with each passing day Sitara was drifting away from her. She tried to look back, analyse the past and dig out the reason for this drift. Perhaps she herself had not been a very happy person, a person brimming with life. Perhaps she had, unknowingly given Sitara the feeling that caring for a small child all through her life was only a duty that she was fulfilling. Maybe Sitara's adolescence had been spent in fighting and then coming to terms with the contradictions that existed between her own mother and the mothers of her friends. Her unorthodox views were an embarrassment to her daughter who wanted to conform, to be like others. Or maybe she in her own need for companionship had treated Sitara too much as an equal. An equality which the child was not capable of handling, that had matured her too soon and in the direction opposite to her own. Whatever it may have been, though Sitara obeyed her every wish, Safia was deep down a little afraid of her own child.

At twenty seven, Sitara had a PhD and a job at the Lady Shriram College. The Congress Party had lost the General Election for the first time since Independence. Safia was beginning to worry about Sitara's single status when she turned up with a young man and introduced him as Wasim Zakaria. Later, she had informed Safia that they were intending to get married.

Safia had nothing to complain of. Wasim came from a middle class, respectable family of Hyderabad. He was fairly good looking, had studied in London on a Commonwealth scholarship, graduating in social sciences and was now employed at the UNICEF, earning five times the salary that Safia did after more than two decades of service. Safia wished she had been taken into confidence, told about the first few meetings, the coming together and the proposal and their joint ambitions. They must have some or how else does one decide to live together. Wasim, on the other hand, more than made up for Sitara's quiet privacy. Very fond of good food and possessing a vast collection of jokes which he told in Hyderabadi Urdu, Wasim visited them often and soon became good friends with Safia. His natural acceptance of Abbas' memory and calling him *Abba* warmed Safia to him.

Wasim had been brought up at his maternal grandparents. His grandfather was a jack-of-all-trades who had invested in the Banjara hills when no one was willing to look that way. Though he proclaimed that he enjoyed constructing houses, he was in fact among the earliest businessmen who realized the importance of built up houses. A lawyer by profession, he had soon given up the vocation, unable to stand up to the glib talking Hyderabadi counterparts. He was a migrant from Amroha who had soon dissected the geography of Hyderabad. His sixth sense told him that the Banjara hills had an important role to play in the economics of the Nizam city. He made a tidy fortune that he carefully invested in the name of his four sons. His only daughter was married into a well-placed family. Everything seemed to be going well until it came out in the open that the son-in law was a supporter, no a militant supporter, of the Telegana movement. How shameful to be fighting for a separate state for those half clad savages, the Telangi tribal. His daughter, brought up in the true Islamic culture of treating everyone but their own particular clan as barbarians, had come back to her father's house. She was eight months pregnant. Wasim was born here and his mother married again. In his infrequent visits to her house, he found her happy. He grew up in the strict religious atmosphere of his maternal grandfather's house, recited the *namaaz* five times, finished post graduation from Osmania University, took a Commonwealth scholarship to United Kingdom and cherished his hatred of any organized activity for change. His dislike for change going up to his refusal to cast his vote in the University student body elections.

Safia came to know all this and accepted it with a feeling of misgiving. She also noticed other things of less consequence. Sitara had always called her *Ma* and she liked it because it was the Indian way of addressing. Wasim often pointed out that she should be *Ammi* as it was the Muslim way. He also objected to Sitara's name and said that he would have preferred the Arabic version of it. Safia convinced herself that a change would occur in Wasim's rigid attitude. She too had had a strict Islamic upbringing. So why wouldn't Wasim change? Had she not adapted herself so easily and happily to the liberal way of life? The healthier way. Safia never stopped to think that what had been very natural for her as a woman would be impossible for Wasim, simply because he was a man. His manhood demanded that he reject everything that a woman suggested. Though accepting and adjusting to classes and their different approach to similar problems, Safia did not understand the one basic division between a man and a woman, that of their psyche.

One day Safia was jerked out of the morning reverie on finding a plump *Maulvi*, complete with a pointed beard and checkered kerchief entering her drawing room. His loud voice that mispronounced almost all the Arabic words got under her skin. After he had gone, Safia prepared herself for a long argument and was stunned into silence when Sitara quietly brooked all of them saying, "This is my faith and my inheritance. You had no right to keep me away from it."

How is one to explain that faith is not inherited; that there is a fundamental difference between religion and faith? Faith comes with belief and this belief has to be based on knowledge, with logic to support that knowledge. The ritual bound link, that one has with one's religion of birth, is very different from the emotional but firm belief that one has in one's faith. The firmness of faith comes with years of understanding of human nature, delving into the study of societies and civilizations, dissecting the requirements of each moment of existence that set the pattern for the rules and laws most suited to carry on the one important work given to humans—celebrating life. The pattern that changed with every blink of the eye, making it imminent that the rules and laws supporting it should be revised and reconstructed. Having lived these reviews and reconstructions all through one's life, it is desirable to look back at the end of it and judge if one had lived it honestly or only truthfully. It is then time to analyse, segregate and finally to pass on what one had created to the next generation.

The firmness inherent in subscribing to a faith one has sculpted, can never be achieved by reciting a few lines in a language one did not understand, accompanied with gestures one could not logically justify.

Safia had never wanted to give a single religion to Sitara, but she had tried her level best that she should possess a faith in humanity, goodness, truth, freedom and in the fact that nothing can last forever and has to undergo changes just so that it can survive. Religion was no different. Safia had thought that a person should be taught the scriptures only when they could comprehend and rationalize. Now it seemed someone had overtaken her and usurped her duties and the rights of the plural faith. In her desire to belong, Sitara had chosen to belong to Wasim rather than to her. Perhaps it was just as well. Had not she herself decided to belong to the ideals of her man, rather than her family? God grant that Sitara might find the same joy as she had and that it may last much longer than her happiness.

The wedding had been a quick and easy affair. Wasim was a devout Muslim and did not believe in the ritualistic fanfare of the Indian Muslim weddings. He proudly proclaimed that Islam had given the world its shortest marriage ceremony and adding anything to it was blasphemy. What did strike an odd note in Safia's heart was the manner in which he had calculated the price of all the gifts received, especially the diamond set that Amrita had brought for Sitara. Surely, Islam preached austerity in personal life. He got on very well with Amrita who had turned up only because Sitara had personally gone to invite her. Though Safia and Amrita had not been on talking terms since the artistes' strike, Amrita had not allowed the estrangement to interfere with her participation in wedding, chattering away with most of the guests, insisting that Wasim call her 'Ma-in-law' and giggling like a girl when Wasim cheekily called her "My Sauce."

A month after the wedding, Wasim had been posted to Geneva and Sitara had moved with him taking up a job at the International Labour Organization. Everything was well-settled and seemed to be moving at a normal happy speed. Safia had a lot to be thankful for but a voice inside her often whispered that when one has to keep reminding oneself of this, there is definitely something wrong somewhere.

* * * * *

TWENTY-SIX

I

All the way to Amrita's house, Safia had been preparing herself how to condole Geetika's death. Thousands of sentences formed themselves in her mind and were rejected. Death was a reality that remained most difficult to accept. What could one say to those left behind? It was Sitara who wrote to her from Geneva, having learnt of Geetika's death from a friend in Delhi. Safia marvelled at the distance that can exist in the same city. However, she did find it strange that no information about Geetika's demise had appeared in the newspapers.

Safia had never seen Amrita hysterical. All her outbursts of any sort had an undercurrent of control that bellied hysteria and only added to the excellent histrionics. But this was real and prepared though she was, Safia could hardly have imagined something so devastating. Amrita wept as if to empty herself and with a kind of determination that refused to be deterred from its aim; that of emptying its body of its last drop of moisture, its last breadth.

Safia tried to calm her down, knowing that a collapse was at hand. Unable to handle Amrita herself, she shouted for someone to get a glass of water. She dare not let Amrita go; knowing that she was almost unconscious. She was persuading Amrita to sit down when a familiar slimy voice made her turn.

"So Madame Amrita is at it again."

Choosing to ignore the jibe, Safia addressed him, "I am so sorry to hear of your loss Lalaji."

Govind Ram looked her up and down and cocked an eyebrow, "Mine?"

Safia let it pass. "Do I have your permission to ring the bell? I think Amrita should be given something to drink."

Govind Ram smirked, "I'll do that for you." He picked up the intercom. "*Memsahib* has had a fit. The usual."

"Does this happen often? No wonder Amrita is so thin. Have you consulted a doctor?"

"Waste of time—his and now yours. I have the cure. Ah! Here it comes."

As Safia stared at him trying to phantom the innuendo, a servant appeared with a large pitcher of water tinkling with ice cubes.

"Well, what are you waiting for? Give it her."

As Safia looked from one to the other, the servant approached Amrita and emptied the pitcher on her head, shoulder, back, everywhere.

Almost instantly a sharp slap rang out and Safia found herself pinned to the wall.

"She is a guest Deju, let her be....just this once. Do not slap these servants Safiaji, they are all black belts. I said let her go Deju and leave."

Finding herself free, Safia ran to Amrita, still jerking and shivering from the cold deluge.

"There was really no need to do that," Safia wiped Amrita's face.

"Shock treatment! That is all that she responds to. Now that the dance drama troupe and Kendra have gone defunct, she has no outlet left for her hysterics. I really want to know why such a fuss is being made about the death of a cabbage. Mind you, she lived a good thirty plus years. Most mentally handicapped are dead by twenty. She lived longer because she got good care, food, and medicines. But in spite of everything, she is better off where she is. She had nothing to live for. Why so much unhappiness over something that was so natural? One cannot change the law of nature. I do not like this vulgar show of grief. I must say, I prefer the western way of dignified grief. All this show for mass consumption is rather disgusting, isn't it?"

Safia listened. Embracing Amrita and cradling her head on her chest, she said quietly, "Let's go inside."

Amrita's large eyes looked at her from below and the dead expression turned slowly to that of incredulity, "But there is none!"

"What does that mean?"

"What she says. There is none….no inside. She has a room, but I would advise you to sit here and not for very long." Making his last words sound like a veiled threat, Govind Ram left the room.

The threat and the tone got Safia's temper rising but it only helped to calm Amrita down. She began to talk normally.

"After the dance drama troupe closed down, he slowly got rid of the teaching faculty. The Kendra showed no income for three years and declared itself bankrupt. But you know all that. It was your job to know."

"True and I did try to find out what had really happened. You never answered my calls, nor wrote back. The official enquiries about the grants were all answered by him."

"Did it never occur to you that I might not have received any of your messages? That all my mail incoming and outgoing were, still are, being censored. It is unbelievable but I am a prisoner, in a prison with narrowing walls."

"I never…..it never……."

"Occurred to you? How could it? Amrita the arrogant *malkin*! He judged me like a good shopkeeper would judge a new product. He understood that my backbone was the Kendra. Once that was gone, I was like a lost boat with a torn sail."

"But Amrita you can't put all the blame on him. If the Kendra was everything to you, why didn't you stand up for the artistes? Why did you stand and watch while people—who would have kept the kinder going—were treated like dogs."

"Because I am myself a bitch. Wagging my tail, I followed the dog that licked my mild scratches and told me they were fatal wounds. Little did I realize that the lick had rabies and would soon lead to my mental derangement."

"I am sorry it happened that way. No one could have shown you sense at that time but I did expect you to remain human."

"I told you I was a mad bitch, snapping and biting at the hand that held out a scrap."

"You can't wash away your sins by admitting them. No possession is big enough to commit murder for."

"What do you mean?"

"Was it not enough to remove all the artistes, to throw them on the road? Did you have to get Patwardhan murdered?"

"I didn't. Believe me I did not. It is true that I had some inkling that it was being planned….."

"And did nothing about it."

"I did try to warn him……"

"Stavrogin psychology. You know that a crime is about to be committed. You know the people who are involved and you do nothing about it. You keep mum. Why? Because deep inside, you accept that it is a way out—the easiest way out. Well every action has a reaction…. Newton I think—the cycle has completed itself. Your one support, one support after the Kendra crumbled, has been taken away."

"Yes taken away…..she didn't die….she was taken away."

"What do you mean? Amrita your face is ashen—don't pass out on me. I can't take a repeat of Govind Ram's treatment."

It worked. Amrita gritted her teeth and closing her eyes fought for control.

"You know of course what has been going on here."

"And what has been going on here?"

"You really do not know?"

"Amrita please."

"Well, to cut a short story shorter, he has another woman."

"What's new? He always had one."

"Not this kind. Not one who occupies my whole house."

"She's here? She lives under your roof?"

"No. I live under his and her roof. She occupies the whole house."

"And you?"

"Have been shunted to what used to be my dressing room."

"And you just mooch around. Why don't you throw her out?"

"I can't. Disintegration of the Kendra has given him all the power. In the first three months after it was officially defunct, he changed all the servants. All my contacts were cut off, my telephone disconnected, my car taken away. Even my friends—I had very few in any case—have been discouraged from entering this house. He has taken away everything. I am left with only one power. I will not give him a divorce. Battles about this had become a daily fixture. Geetika had become completely silent, maybe her heart had come to terms with the futility of her wordless screams. One day, he was banging my head against a table. I opened my mouth to scream for help, knowing that none would come. Then suddenly I was free. I saw him being thrown on the floor. Geetika tottered for a second before becoming a pile of flesh, bones and cloth on the floor. My baby had stood up. She had defied all the laws of nature and stood up to help me. But he was up and had picked up a pillow, and was pressing it down with his foot on my baby's face. I tried to get up but everything went black. It must have been only for a few seconds because when it was light again, he was leaving the room and my Geetika….why was she staring at me like that? I crawled to her and took her crumpled form in my arms. "Its okay, *Ma* is safe, don't worry, don't stare like that, shut your eyes. Sleep….sleep my darling and she, obedient as always, slept a long dreamless sleep forever.

The dead do not tell tales. Nobody believed that it could have been anything but natural. Nobody wanted to believe or was concerned enough to think that it was anything but normal. She suffocated herself on her pillow. Do not weep Amrita, she is happy where she is, do not blame yourself, you did all you could do for her for 36 long years. A few noticed his strange nonchalant behaviour. They mumbled, 'Poor Amrita, so much beauty and such an unloving husband'. Another added, 'Pity her father is dead and she doesn't have a brother. They would have put him in his place.' But would they? We depend so much on our fathers and brothers that we forget that they belong to the same class—men. Would they help their sisters speak? Won't they be afraid that giving voice to their sisters could lead to speaking wives? And who in his right mind would want that?"

II

It took a long drawn battle of three and a half years to get the possession of the two lower floors of what was once the Gandharva Kendra. Three favourable judgments from the courts, before Govind Ram realized the futility of fighting on. The fact that Amrita insisted that she did not want a divorce worked in her favour. She came out, a pious Hindu woman, honouring the seven birth commitments to her lord and master. All she wanted was a separation and a settlement of property.

Safia worked hard, digging out artistes who had once worked with the Kendra and now lived in obscure corners of the city. Most of them were unwilling to support Amrita, gloating over her misfortune, calling it the revenge of providence. However, some came, agreeing to appear in court in support of Amrita. Masterji was the last and the strongest one to appear for Amrita and openly condemn Govind Ram. The case was keenly followed by the Press and Amrita became a woman charged with a fire to win. On the day of the last Press conference, when Amrita announced the terms of the out of court settlement with Govind Ram, Safia remembered the effort it had been to persuade the same Amrita to begin to fight. The defeated lonely Amrita, who stared in space, yearning for the daughter who could not speak, walk, laugh or even sit up, but who was hers, all hers.

Safia had not done it on her own. It had been a sudden dark shadow that had crossed Amrita's eyes. It was for a split second but it was there and Safia had taken the decision immediately. She would never have been able to explain what it was that she saw in Amrita's eyes, but she knew that Death was close at hand and she had to act. She had to push it away to make the orbit of life bigger, longer. It was an impulse and Amrita though in a daze had agreed to let Safia take decisions. Presumably taking Amrita for a walk, she had brought her to her small flat. As far as Govind Ram was concerned, the arrangement suited him perfectly.

It was in her flat, when Safia was in despair, having used up all her means to ignite a spirit in Amrita that Masterji had turned up. He came himself. Safia had been afraid and embarrassed to approach him for help. He heard from some other artistes and came. They did not exchange a word and Safia, after tea and a few futile attempts to start a conversation, sat silent with them, staring from one to the other and back to her hands, keenly examining the wall hangings and teacups she saw everyday. Masterji left, as it grew dark. He was back again after three days. It was very early in the morning. Old, thin as always but now with a dried up, parched exterior, dressed in a coarse, handspun, new dhoti, he put down a small earthen pot on the table. The pot was covered with a piece of banana leaf, tied with a red thread. Extending his hand, he grasped Amrita's and led her to the waiting auto rickshaw. Safia ran out after them. She was not sure what Masterji was planning and she doubted if Amrita was up to whatever would take place. Masterji turned and smiled, then shook his head and said, "Don't you trust your old teacher? Well come then, three can fit into this contraption."

The auto rickshaw brought them to Nigambodh Ghat. He paid for it and nodding in Safia's direction, he walked down the steps to the river Yamuna. A couple of ghat pundits jumped towards them but stopped when he turned and told them, "Can't you see I am a Brahmin? Get away crows."

Safia had strange apprehensions and stories crowded her head, stories of senile old men, drowning their beloved in the hope of purifying them or meeting them in the next birth. But before she could say anything, Masterji handed Amrita the earthen pot and uncovering it asked her to empty the parched rice, bits of banana and flowers into the flowing waters. For the first time a question dawned in Amrita's eyes.

"It is Patwardhan's *shraadh* today. Do this for him, so that his soul might overcome its doubts about you and be at peace." He folded his hand and stepped back.

Amrita looked long at the rice and the flowers, then she looked further at the serenely flowing water. Then very calmly, she tossed the pot into the water and said, "Just this much for peace? Surely not." Climbing back the steps, she accosted the group of curious onlookers, "Never seen a woman kick religion aside to make way for herself, hunh?"

Masterji smiled at Safia's surprise. "It is on....the battle is on."

It began at the lowest courts. After every verdict, Govind Ram took a stay from a higher court but Amrita fought on, until only the highest court was left. Govind Ram's anxiety of losing the entire Kendra seemed to be becoming a reality and he stooped down and suggested an out of court settlement. He proposed one floor of the building and the back lawns, Amrita asked for three and all the grounds, he enquired how his staff was to enter the building if she controlled the grounds, Amrita said it was none of her business; they could fly for all she cared. Several meetings, browbeating and walkouts later an agreement was reached. Amrita got two floors and the front and back lawn, with enough space to build an open air theatre. Bhagyanath Industries now used a side lawn for entry. On the ground were the administrative offices and Amrita's living quarters. The classes were on the first floor. Masterji started music lessons, a teacher was appointed for *sitar* classes and a student of Patwardhan joined to teach *kathak*. Anusuya, who had been summarily dismissed after Geetika's death, appeared like a conjuror's trick and took over the running of Amrita's home. From a sprawling bungalow, Amrita was in a two-roomed accommodation. But it was hers and she was free. Safia blessed Amrita for fighting for her freedom, even though in some corner of her heart she had to admit the truth. More than Amrita's will, it had been the Hindu Marriage Act with its various amendments and updating that had made its women supportive, providing the Hindu women the right to maintenance, property and a legitimacy to live with dignity. She wondered when Amrita's Muslim counterpart would enjoy the same benefits under a unified civil code.

* * * * *

TWENTY-SEVEN

At fifty-six a heart attack was nothing to crib about. Though it had been a massive one, Safia had survived. "I could have the attack all over again," she had mumbled, when she had opened her eyes and seen Amrita standing near her bed. She must have been heard because Amrita started crying. Why had she thought of Amrita when that suffocating pain had criss-crossed her body? How had she managed to stagger towards the phone and rung up Amrita? Why had Amrita—who never answered the phone herself—come to the phone on the second ring?

Seventy-two hours later, she was allowed to walk. Supported by Sitara and Amrita on either side, she laughed mirthlessly as she took the first faltering steps. "Thank God it's just walking. Imagine my fate had everything been brought to the 'first' level and I had to learn the alphabet again!"

"You are on your legs again. I have been praying for the last three days. I am so glad you are not paralysed."

"Thanks. This is good enough for me."

"Well not for me. Take some weight of my shoulders *Ma* and put it on your legs. They are meant for that you know."

All three of them were laughing.

"Its like...."Amrita stopped in mid-sentence.

"The old times," completed Safia. "When did you arrive Sitara?"

"Only just. You might have warned me."

"How? It came so suddenly."

"You never intended to inform me. Amrita Aunty told me that you didn't want me bothered."

"I would have informed you....afterwards."

"And what good would that have done?"

"What good is this doing?"

"Stop it both of you. Sitara you can't blame your mother for not wanting to trouble you. After all, you and your husband have not been on the best of terms with her."

"Is that true? Is it me and my husband or just my husband? *Ma* if he has not come up to your expectations, why hold it against me? Why is it that I am clubbed with his follies? I am an individual, a person, am I not?"

"Seven years in a country that insists on calling its salesmen and chairmen, salesperson and chairperson and my daughter has become a person. Well I am quite happy for you. I am sorry; I should have looked at it from this angle. Anyway welcome home."

"Where is hubby dear?" Amrita enquired. The in-laws by relation are always better equipped for their roles than the actual ones.

"Talking to the doctor," replied Sitara shortly.

"Now if that isn't sweet. Here he comes, welcome home son-in-law."

"Oh, my loving 'Sauce'!" Feeling intruders, Sitara and Safia glanced at each other. A look of camaraderie passed between them.

"Don't you think it is enough walk for the first day, *Ma*?"

"Tch tch Sitara, back to your old ways?"

"I have a right to call my mother whatever I want."

"Okay, have it you own way". Wasim agreed indulgently. "Lets move *ammi* to the bed and have a heart to heart talk."

Safia looked at Amrita who took the queue, "I think it is enough excitement for the day for Safia. Why don't you take the keys and go to her flat. Have a bath, rest, whatever and come back in the evening or better still tomorrow morning. Come, I'll send for my car and see you off."

On the face of it, the reason for their having come to India was Safia's health. No one had informed them. How then had they landed right in the nick of time? Safia had a strange feeling that her heart attack had provided them the much-needed opportunity for burning all their boats in the west. They were staying at Safia's small, low-income group flat. Five weeks later as Safia prepared to rejoin work, she wondered aloud how long Sitara and Wasim intended to stay.

"For good," Sitara informed her, with a deadpan expression. Answers to all queries were short and to the point. Sitara had cultivated this exactness to questions in her college days but now her answers carried with them a stiffness that had been absent until now.

Safia decided to take the bull by the horns. In reality, she had no other option. "You must tell me your plans. You can't unconditionally keep living in this house."

"Why?"

"Because I must know and because I too am a person."

"Alright. I will ask Wasim to find a place for us. It might be difficult—maybe when I have a job or maybe when……." Sitara's indefiniteness was a novelty.

"When will Wasim have a job?"

"He never will. At least not in the near future."

Safia swallowed this information with a mouthful of tepid tea. "Don't you think its time to come clean Sitara?"

"If you really are well enough to……"

"I have never felt better. I have seen life. Nothing you tell me can really shock me."

She could not have been more wrong. Wasim had been doing fairly well by European standards and very well by Indian ones. Four years passed comfortably with only one sorrow in Sitara's life—that she had not been able to conceive. Then Wasim made some contacts in Dubai and Abu Dhabi. Late night meetings became normal and weekend flights to the Gulf and even to India. He had never informed Sitara about visiting Asia. It was by chance that she had opened his passport and then been accused of prying.

Reduced to a secondary status because of her barren state, Sitara bore everything quietly, knowing that she had not fulfilled the one duty that is the primary one for a woman. She had kept her questions to herself only to be alerted when he started bringing large wads of hard currency usually dollars and refused to put them in the bank. They were paid in German Marks and payments to foreign employees came in cheques. Wasim successfully waded through her questions and was always on the alert so that even her round about queries yielded no information. Three year passed.

It was when he came late in the night and informed her that they were leaving for India that she had sat down refusing to budge until she was told the truth

"Well stay put and be arrested," he said throwing things pell-mell into a suitcase.

"But why? What for? Tell me Wasim."

"Only if you begin packing."

Then it had all come out. Wasim had become part of a child traf-
ficking racket—smuggling children for adoption, prostitution, camel
racing. They came from Bangladesh, India, Nepal, and Pakistan. He
was not the pivot, only one of the stooges.

"Well, get out of it. Just spill everything, turn an approver and
keep away from these men," Sitara had reasoned.

"And be killed. You think it is so easy to get out, so simple to spill
everything. Their men would kill me."

"And this is your Islam that you claim freed mankind from
slavery?"

"Stop your gloating. We shall be taken for questioning, but the
truth shall be out. The European police are thorough. The Indian
police have some information about us and once the police here get
their facts, they shall alert their counterparts in other countries. We
have to get back to India before they alert the Interpol."

"The Interpol! It is that big then?"

"Of course it is. Why do you think I am so jittery?"

"I am not going. I am not involved and if the need arises, I shall
be one witness against you."

"You are going because you are involved."

"But I never even knew that this racket existed."

"Well several children have changed hands in your name—because of you being barren."

Sitara remembered the way he had insisted on keeping the medical documents and results of all the tests of her being barren when
all she had wanted was to forget the fact.

"How dare you? How could you use me, my sorrow, my shame
this way?"

"I am your husband, I have every right to use you."

"Or misuse," Sitara struck back as she began to pack. Even as a
common criminal, he did not forget the true faith. The faith that
was pliable for anything that concerned men and solid like a rock
where it dealt with women. "Excessive devoutness is a sure sign of
guilt." Now where had she heard this before. Of course, from *Ma*.
"Do we carry that?" she had pointed to the neat pile of green at the
corner of the cupboard.

"Of course! How else do you expect us to buy our way out of
this wretched continent?"

It had been literal. They had taken short flights, often diverting their route, somehow entering East Europe and travelling by train and bus to finally reach Bucharest and then on to Moscow to take the final flight to Delhi. Officials at each Airport had been curious to know their haphazard route and their unwillingness to move out of airport lounge between connecting flights. The answering process had made them practically penniless.

"Now what?" Safia had turned to the future in the hope that it might not be as frightening as Sitara's past.

"I don't know. All the money is gone. I left my job without a notice. All my degrees and certificates are there. So are his."

"What about Wasim?"

"He is selling my jewellery to concoct a lost suitcase. Once that is done, he can claim duplicates. I am trying to retrieve mine. Your heart attack was well-timed for me. I am claiming that you were on your deathbed and that I lost my senses. My one thought was for you. If the plea is accepted, I can withdraw the money in my bank."

"God! But you are brave."

"Once you have found out that you have been wrong about everything, fear of committing another wrong recedes. You know that at the worst you shall only be proved wrong again."

"Don't be so depressed and don't try to put on a brave act. Let down these walls you have built around yourself and go out into the world. Meet people. Not all of them are unworthy of your trust. A decision can have long lasting repercussions, but not ever lasting ones. A way shall find itself out."

"Out of what? A criminal record, wasted years or a bad marriage?"

"Everything. For the moment, stay with me."

"There is no where else to go."

"Shall I say that I am happy my baby is back to refuge?"

"Which she should not have left in the first place."

As things turned out, it was almost a year before Sitara's degrees and savings could be retrieved. The flat being congested, Safia decided to sell it and buy a bigger one with all her saving and those of Sitara's. The new place was registered in Sitara's name.

* * * * *

TWENTY-EIGHT

The world was watching. The administration was tense. There was every possibility of flash communal riots. The ones that happened in a flash, but seemed to have years of preparation behind them. Riots in which shining revolvers, AK-47s and bombs find themselves on the streets. The Muslim world waited with bated breath and watched with an unblinking eye. It was going to be a supreme verdict. One that would change the pattern of sociology that would prove to the world that it was on its way to redefining laws and making them human friendly. A step towards the primitive man—the creation of God—the one that was loving, friendly and yes, more human.

The fundamentalist world was sure that no one would dare to touch the very fundamentals. Why the world would be crumbling down, wouldn't it? The liberals and the progressives hoped for a change and prayed that some one else would initiate it. They would then be there to give it conditional support. The common people prayed that the storm would blow over without breaking on their heads.

Returning from the All India Radio after participating in a discussion on traditional poetry, Safia noticed that there seemed to be more than usual policemen. Patrol jeeps could also be sighted, frequently moving at a snail's pace. On an impulse, Safia asked the auto rickshaw driver to turn towards Minto Bridge. As she entered the walled city, she saw several policemen, grouped at corners. At other places, there were piles of bamboo shields and coils of thick rope for barricades. Well, it seemed that the administration was not leaving anything to chance.

"Am I glad that you are back safe," Sitara embraced her awkwardly. Demonstrations of love still embarrassed her and she seemed more at ease in Wasim's absence.

"Did you expect me to spend the night at the Radio Station?"

"The city is ready to burst into flames."

"No it isn't. I went all round the walled city in the hope of seeing a riot."

"You what? *Ma*! But the BBC has reported this in their Asia bulletin."

"The BBC is not the gospel much as Wasim might like to project it as one. It gets pleasure in projecting this, a country of cow loitering streets, snake charmers, impoverished Nawabs and yes, communal riots."

"But there is tension."

"Lots and everywhere."

"When is it due?"

"Any minute now."

It took another half an hour for the verdict to come. It gave a seventy six year old woman, a right to live and die with dignity. It took just about the same time for the Muslim world to be up in arms, claiming that it had every right to treat its women like chattel and questioned the authority of the Supreme Court. Who was the Supreme Court after all to order them to be more human towards their women folk?

Somehow, Shah Bano seemed familiar. Shah Bano, who had picked up the remains of the battle that Safia had once tried to fight and perhaps given up too soon. Shah Bano had fought it to the end and won. Or had she? This was the apex court, the highest place for appeal. If it had upheld her plea and the high court's favourable verdict on it, then that should be it. Surely, the Indian Constitution entitled each individual this much. In any case, what had the poor woman appealed for? She had been summarily divorced at the age of forty six, with a pittance for a *meher* and five children. She had worked hard all her life to make good human beings out of them. Now her old bones ached for rest, her sunken eyes looked at the judges begging for a dignified end to a long life of drudgery and indignity. The three judged bench, headed by the chief justice himself, saw her pain and destitution and ordered her husband—long married to a girl half his age and father of many more children—to pay her a measly Rs 179.20 every month as maintenance to the shrunken old woman who had once shared his bed and life.

'The judgment is against the *Shariat*, the Muslim law!'

'It is an insult to the minority community!'

'It is communal. It is a calculated attempt to merge the Muslims into the Hindu majority!'

'It is against secularism!'

'It is direct interference in the practice of one's faith!'

'It goes against the Constitution!'

'The Muslims would rather die than allow these changes in their *Shariat*!'

Members of Parliament flung their allegations at the young prime minister. He enjoyed a gigantic majority in the Parliament, having come riding on a sympathy wave whipped up because of his mother's murder. However, majority is not synonymous to maturity. He held hurried discussions with Hindu leaders of Congress who were supposed to be close to the Muslim community. They shook their heads and told him to be careful. He was treading the red-hot coals, very much forbidden to the kafirs.

He parleyed no more. He also thought no more. To do him justice, the poor man was a pilot and not a politician. In flying an airplane one had to take quick decisions. He did not understand that in politics one had to buy time, hum, haw, and keep mum. Then dilly-dally and keep mum some more, set commissions and panels for review and placate people into lethargic waiting, leading to mass forgetfulness and short spells of mass amnesia that would last till bigger and different issues raised their head and the earlier ones could be shelved. He was new to politics and believed that to speak was to make a commitment and once commitments were made, they had to be honored. He was there through a process of negation and there was no help for it because the Indian masses still set great store by families and heredity. So he got down to speaking and though his advisors had started him on the path of speaking a lot and not saying much, he was still not quite there. He was more adept at deciphering the different whirring of plane engines rather than screaming parliamentarians. He was polite enough to let himself be shouted down, believing that shouts meant strength and this show of muscle really got his goat. He agreed to introduce a Bill in the Lower House, Bill for the Protection of Muslim Women.

As a finale, the Muslims played their trump card. In one sweep, they took away the right of everyone, whatever their religion, creed or ideology. No one had the right to speak except the Muslims. It did not concern them after all. Everyone else quickly agreed and neatly subsided in their chairs.

A young member of the Parliament, Arif Mohammad got up to speak. He was from the Congress Party. In his student days, he had been president of the Aligarh Muslim University Students Union. It was not scheduled that he would speak and the decision was taken a couple of days before at an evening tea party. Being a Muslim, it was expected that he would condemn the judgment. Strangely enough, he took the opposite line. He not only supported the judgment but also condemned any effort to quash it and introduce the Bill. He made statements that clearly aimed to free Islam from all the shackles of fundamentalism.

"Religion is always taught in parables. We have to take guidance from them and frame social laws accordingly in tune with our times. My faith had always been progressive, especially on matters relating to women. Any suggestion of reform upsets fundamentalists. The people trying to quash the Supreme Court's judgment are trying to take a short cut to heaven by making this world a living hell for our poor and illiterate women. This judgment would be sacrilege if it challenged the unity of God or the Prophethood of Mohammad."

How could the protectors of Islam bring their faith to such basics? It would mean removing all divisions and barriers, it would mean treating all Muslims as human beings and more than everything, it would mean giving equality to women. The best way to counter a progressive move is to show the other party its hidden skeletons. ZR Ansari, also from the Congress Party and minister for environment, got up to counter Arif Mohammad.

"Amongst us, neither do they burn nor are they burnt. Look on the other side, every day they burn, everyday they are burnt." He began thus referring to the dowry deaths amongst Hindus. "How can we tolerate that after divorce our ex-wife may share her bed with another person and get her maintenance and pocket money from us? If a divorced woman continues to get maintenance, why would she ever remarry? She never would and shall daily have a new man at the expense of her husband. She will enjoy life with other men at the cost of her ex-husband. How can we tolerate this?" The Indian Parliament and its august members were discussing the morals of a divorced woman rather the maintenance or support to be provided to her by her husband. At the end of his speech, Ansari played his trump card. "If this was to become the state of affairs in this country, if this interference and these bids to make changes were not stopped, the Muslim men would rather die before seeing the *Shariat*, the God's word and instructions tampered with."

Now this was a grave threat. None of the liberal Muslims all over the country countered it. Yes, it might happen. Some fanatics might publicly burn themselves. The Indian government could not have the death of Muslim men on its conscience. Ill-treatment of divorced Muslim women and their financial conditions did not matter.

Then the young prime minister got up to speak. And when he had finished, he had the credit of having put back history, sociology and justice right where they belonged—under the boots of the men and in the elastics of men's pants. They dare not change their position for fear of being caught with their pants down.

All of the communist parties had openly supported the verdict, calling it a major breakthrough in the process of giving equal rights to women. But the din created by the Muslim men made them see red and sent all of them cowering for cover. At the end, they lamely said that changes in the Muslim law should be brought about by the Muslims themselves—meaning that the mullahs should sit down and give their women a more economically sound deal.

The poor young executive head of the state had been counting on the Marxists. They were still a force all over the world and hadn't his mother and grandfather before her depended on their support and got it. But when they turned tail, the poor man started talking—nay jabbering—and in his nervousness, he reversed his initial welcome of the verdict. He corrected himself and said that what he really meant was something quite different. That divorced women who were destitute and not well-off should be looked after by the relatives and if they did not have relatives who could support them, then by the community, organizations could be formed to help divorced women etc., etc. He promised to bring in a bill to this effect; Bill for the Protection of the Muslim women, who being from a different community could not be protected in the same way as their Hindu or Christian counterparts.

Eleven years back his mother had retained her prime minister-ship by making wily-nily of the judiciary. She claimed that she knew best because she and the majority of her parliamentarians were the people's representatives and thus had the supreme power to guide this county. Eleven years later, her pilot son navigated this country through the troubled seas of gender war to the calm waters of male superiority and female complacency.

* * * * *

TWENTY-NINE

Dinner had not been a comfortable meal. It never was. The atmosphere was always edgy and awkward. Wasim was arrogant in an effort to project that he was not rattled by being caught in criminal activities. He seemed out to prove his manliness in the fact that though he had been wrong, he had got away with it. He now had a job, a small one in a printing press, but it was there. Sometimes Safia had the feeling that Sitara was almost sorry for having opened up to her and oscillated from a very warm to almost cool behaviour. Usually Safia made up for the dampness by talking about nonentities like food or Ghalib's poetry and of course the weather. But today, the urgency of the subject to be discussed stopped her from dwelling on anything else.

Wasim was on a night shift and left after dinner. Safia made it a point to talk to Sitara only when Wasim was on night duty. He had often remarked on this coincidence. He had hinted that it gave Safia a chance to talk to Sitara and this was what she waited for impatiently.

When she glanced at her watch and the wall clock for the fourth time, Wasim smiled meaningfully and mumbling, "They are both correct," got up to go.

Sitara saw him to the door and picked up the *paandaan* from the sideboard. Sitara had stuck to her three paan daily quota in spite of Wasim hating paan. It was a small way of maintaining her identity and Wasim indulged in patting his back for being progressive enough to allow his woman the freedom to eat something that he detested. He still called her a cow or a goat.

"I have something to discuss with you."

"I know. But I wish you wouldn't make it so obvious." Seemed like it had been a wrong beginning but it had been made and there was no going back.

"I wanted to talk to you alone."

"He has a right to leave when he wants."

"Quite. I would have liked to talk to him but I was not sure how he would react."

"No one can be sure of Mr Wasim's reactions."

This was getting out of hand. Sitara's bitterness seemed to be growing and though Safia admitted that she had enough cause to be bitter with the world, she had hoped that with time the bitterness would be replaced by logic, which would lead to her taking some concrete steps about her relationship with Wasim. That Sitara often did not know her own mind was obvious by the way she vented her bitterness on her nearest one. A typical case of mislaid identity, not courageous enough to punish the tormentor, she systematically constructed walls around her, alienating her loved ones and those who might have become her friends.

Safia checked herself. All this could wait. She had to begin work as soon as possible. There was no time to hum and haw. She had to take the bull by the horn.

"Sitara I am very concerned by the turn the Shah Bano case has taken."

"Poor woman, I feel so sorry for her."

"Just for her?"

"But wasn't she appealing alone? I didn't know that there were many of them."

"There weren't but it has effected many."

"Really! Who?"

"You and me to begin with. What's wrong with you? Can't you see that this decision would have given you some rights. Not just to breathe and survive but really live, with dignity and self-respect. We women are living on a narcotic—a narcotic called complacency. Come out of it Sitara, come with me."

"Where?"

"Indore. The poor woman is alone there. We must go to her. Make her feel that what she has done is right, that we stand by her. We must help her. She is old and not very educated. But she had the spine to stand up and challenge all that we have succumbed to. We are crawling insects living the life of bisexual worms. She alone is human with a brain, a heart and yes, a will. Let us give her support."

"Just you and me?"

"Other shall come. Sanskritayanji has written to me from Lucknow. He will be there. He is a force to reckon with. Dr Zahida too shall come."

"Really *Ma*, you are banking on these puffs of ancient wool, who have one foot in their graves. Half of them shall pop off while making their speech."

"Since when has a desire for change become the prerogative of the young? Do you think you have a better chance because you expect to be here longer?"

"Well, it does seem a logical reason to think of changing something, that we shall utilize the changed version longer."

"Precisely my point. So how about seeing to it that the change materializes. How about helping it to concretize?"

"I shall have to talk to Wasim."

"Do that. I want you to. I hope he too will come."

"I am not sure. He happens to be very dogmatic in his approach to religion and he has been very upset by the Supreme Court's decision and satisfied that it has been over-ridden by the Parliament."

"But that is what this is all about. Law and religion are two different things. How can they be clubbed together? The demands on law keep changing as society keeps churning itself. According to Islam, all thieves should have their hands cut, all rapists lose their noses and you should be paying one third of your income as taxes. No Muslim thief or rapist is punished that way and Muslims are quite happy to divide their income into various allowances so that they do not have to pay any *zakaat*. Why then should the personal law remain static? Why should social and personal law be compartmentalized? Because men want to maintain their superior status in their homes. They know that a family is the smallest unit of the society and if they manage keep a hold on that, then they can keep control on the society. Why should a daughter inherit one-third of her father's property? Why is it so difficult for her to get out of a marriage while a man can say *talaaq* three times in one breath and be done with it. He can marry again and again. Why as a Muslim are you not allowed to adopt a child you have not borne but can be a mother of? Why can a grandfather disinherit a grandchild if the son dies before him?"

"*Ma*, are you trying to revive your battle through Shah Bano?"

Safia took a moment to collect her wits. Then she looked squarely at Sitara and said, "No. My battle has long been lost. But the war has to go on. A war, which calls every broken, battered, disarmed soldier to fall in rank. Come child, we have to stand united for justice."

"*Ma*, I think I will come with you. I must talk to him. Try to convince him."

As Safia walked to her room, she felt a twinge of pain—no a kind of vibration like a string reacting to a high frequency sound wave in the center of the chest. Well, if her heart had decided to remember being musical after all these years, who was she to protest. When she woke up refreshed, she really had no cause to complain.

She was still in the habit of waking up early and when Wasim was on night shift he came in around four in the morning and had a cup of tea before going to sleep. The kitchen sounds woke her up earlier and she dressed quickly. Decisions were to be taken today and a strategy evolved.

However, she was not prepared for Sitara's scream that rent the air and the crash of crockery that followed. Quickly she opened her bedroom door and ran to where Sitara was lying on the floor. Wasim stepped in her way and gripped her as she collided with him.

"Let her be. I shall deal with her later. Get out of this house, my house, immediately."

"Wasim don't do this. *Ma* is not well enough".

"Well enough to plot against me when I am out of my own house."

"This is my house too."

"We shall see that in court. Trying to throw me out of my own house so that you two can live here and enjoy yourself. A sinful widow and a dirty divorcee."

"But I never...."

"Yes you did. You are plotting with Sitara how she can be the owner of my property, how she can throw me into the streets. What kind of a woman are you? You are plotting to sell your only daughter's soul to the Satan. Have you forgotten that it was I who took pity on you and your daughter? I married her even though you were an outcaste of the community. Everyone I knew was against forming any links with you. I believed that I was doing a service to Islam by bringing a lost soul back to the true faith. And this is how I am repaid. What have I got in return? Her barrenness! I have no child to carry on my name. It is my Islamic duty to propagate. I can marry again. I need not even divorce her. It is the goodness of my heart that I do not do this. I still keep her as my wife. And you? You plan to take her to support that senile old woman, who should be passing her days praying for mercy from her maker. With one leg in the grave, she has the cheek to challenge the law of God in a court of mortals. God's will shall prevail. By any means He shall see that His law survives. When the whole of the Muslim world is condemning this woman and the rest is maintaining their own council, you choose to support her. Well not from this house, my house. Leave it at once."

"I will. Sitara get up. We shall leave."

"Oh! Is that so? Does Sitara want to leave? Then I am afraid it shall take some time. Let me get a *Maulvi*. If she wants to leave, I shall willingly divorce her. But since it is she who wants to leave, she gets no *meher*."

"We'll see about that. Come on Sitara."

"*Ma.... Ammi.....I....*"

That change, that small change of a single word and Safia knew that Sitara had switched sides.

"Don't say it, I know. You do not want to risk it. But remember daughter, it is sometimes better to take risks willingly rather than have them forced on you. I hope that time would never come for you."

"Now that you know Sitara's decision you can leave."

Safia turned to her room. As a parting shot, she heard Wasim instructing Sitara. "Tell her to take all that she can. What she leaves shall be thrown out and burnt."

"I have only one request Wasim. Don't ever use violence with my child."

"If she is a good wife and a good Muslim, I shall not need to. But sometimes women need to be reminded their place."

Safia glanced at Sitara who lowered her eyes to hide—her own drugged state or to avoid her mother's destitute state.

"At least get her a taxi," Sitara's last plea was to her husband. Safia braced herself for his reply which she knew would be loud enough to reach her ears.

"Ha! The great militant libber. She can jolly well find one for herself."

When will women stop pleading with men?

* * * * *

THIRTY

As the train pulled out of New Delhi station, Safia clutched her bag and hung on to the bathroom door. The train was crowded. It would be, until they crossed Uttar Pradesh. Seeing her jerking, a woman whispered something in a young man's ear and he got up grumbling. The man next to him immediately made himself more comfortable, taking up half of the space. The woman smiled at her and asked her to sit. Safia blessed her and her son and squeezed in. The train stopped at every god-forsaken station. It was a passenger train, the only one she could manage to squeeze in. The train would take her to Jhansi and then turn towards Rajasthan. She would have to get a connection from Jhansi to Indore.

As Safia straightened her back, her mind began churning the incidents of the last seventy two hours. She had met Amrita and her state of helplessness. What was really holding her back? Why are we, as people, so willing to abide by commitments that others make for us? Why are we so afraid to consider the responsibility of committing to anything ourselves? Why do the young still prefer arranged marriages? What is it that they are afraid of? Surely, an arrangement made by someone else should appear more intimidating than one's own decision. Or is it the fear of responsibility, of being saddled with the mark of having made a wrong decision?

"Tell me Amrita, why don't you want to come with me? What is it you are afraid of? What is it that is holding you back? Geetika is gone, Govind Ram has given up all pretense of a tolerable relationship. The Kendra is nothing more than a dance and music school. The dance drama troupe does not exist anymore. So what is keeping you? This woman has waged a single-handed combat. The courts have supported her. By any call of justice, she should have been a winner and I should not be asking for your support. Then a naive prime minister gets scared out of his wits because a set of clergy has screamed 'Boo'. Let us not let this happen. You have always fought for your own rights and have suffered because there has been no one to support you. This is your cause as much as this woman's."

"No it's not. You cannot deny that I am a Hindu. How can you expect that I shall identify with this Muslim woman's battle for equal rights? Why, I don't even know what she is fighting for."

Safia was stunned into silence. Then she gathered her wits and got up to leave.

"Have you talked to Sitara about accompanying you?" Amrita asked her back.

"No. I wanted to know your decision. I somehow believed that there would be no question of you saying anything but yes. I had planned that we could then talk to her together. But I shall talk to her tonight."

"Don't."

"Why?"

"Please Safia. It is for your sake that I am saying this. Don't talk to her."

"Why? Do you think…."

"Safia, you have been without a man for too long. You have to a large extent got rid of the influence a man has over a woman. You have even forgotten that he has one. Taking a few guidelines from the few years that you spent with Abbas. You have developed and formed your own character. It is you—the complete you. None of us is really 'Me'. We are all reflections of our husband's personality in a much abused and cracked mirror. However much we might like to be our own self, we can only reflect what is most around us. Sitara is no different. Let her be or her mirror shall get too crowded. If there is one image, the mirror has a chance of a survival, but too many contours and the mirror is blurred where images merge to become a kaleidoscope, where no design is stable or discernible. Most of us settle with our split personality. Some do not and wage an unvanquishable war to find one intact form. I don't know which plight is worse."

Safia who had got up to leave put down her bag and sat down on a stool. As she reached for Amrita's hand, she saw the dark brown marks of nicotine and something else. An unnoticeable tremor seemed to pass through the hand as it came into her strong grip. Somewhere her mind knocked—marijuana. She looked at Amrita who smiled sheepishly and opened her mouth to speak. Safia raised her hand to check her. This was no time for discussions on smaller addictions. Even to herself, Safia's voice seemed to come from somewhere remote, yet her thoughts were so intimate and immediate.

"Whenever I see a master piece, I have this inner craving, a deep yearning to reach that level of passion as the creator of that work, that peak of mastery. To be able to reach out and touch life and love it with that intensity. I often ask my soul—shall I…? Will it be an all-consuming love? Shall it be hindered by the mundane functions of living? Why is reaching out to life and living it, so different from one another? Why does one make a God out of a human being and the other just a vegetable—one of Van Gogh's potatoes.

Shall I burn a searing passage through the years lived? A road on which others shall tread and discover many new corridors leading to better settlements, that possess the allocation of new ideas and fling open yet new avenues, till a whole maze of galleys come into being; where novel concepts and fantasies overlap with each others, and great dams and dykes lie still or quivering to build an Ankara of mental abstractions to bless mankind for centuries to come. When the dust of time dulls the conquest of passion, the imagery is lost and only the visual rules, forcing life to begin coveting the conventional, another brave shall stealthily and silently reach towards the sorrowful candle to rekindle the flame of passion even as the world around roars 'Stop thief! Check the robber! Pursue her, arrest her, kill her.' She shall move ahead chanting, 'I am burning a passage for the first time, I am treading on the path so far untrodden; I am novelty, I am the Prophet, I call for a settlement in a place from where no thought has soared and returned to roost.'

Thus is life kept evergreen by death that is so necessary for the existence of life. Death without which life is incomplete, that which gives a consummation to life.

I ask myself—Why then do people weep at death if it isn't the end, end to all that is beautiful? Yes if one looks at life and everything connected with it as a straight line segment, then certainly there has to be a beginning and an end—a birth and a death—two well-defined ends. However, if life was like a circle—a death-a birth-a life-a death—then who could say where the circle begins, because the end merges with the beginning and within itself, it encompasses space—the deliverance that is nothingness—the root of all energy from which again life or is it death is reborn? The finite, always part of the infinite, the removal of which has never lessened the infinite. Treading into the infinite, one often comes across the already taken and felt. But we know not and pick it up with care and love it and tread on it tenderly, lest we trample something delicate or the path turn out too soft and the mud buckles under the wait of our deliberations. Stealthily and softly as we progress, so involved in the contemplation of our own discoveries that we miss out the indulgent laughter of the infinite. 'Drift along, oh mortal! This piece of known. Thou shalt not falter or fall, nor the ground give way under thee to reveal an abyss thou shalt dare to leap in or jump across. Thy fate is to transverse this finite and no more.'

But those who advance with resolution and firmness, whose steps are steady albeit obstinate; who shun the advice of those who tread the accessible and the realized finite, not to reach out to the unknown but just to keep moving. The infinite observes with curiosity. 'Yes you tread what you think is the unknown. On the path known and the beaten track, thou shalt be able to find unknown routes trodden by caravans lost, who have in the trains gone by, dared to prowl the abstract course. You might find treasures lost or deliberately buried and then preen that you have created them. But never mind the misconception, for it shall be yours to give to the present, to your world, to your part of life—to the small miniscule of the whole that is infinite.

As life beckons death or death call out to life and the infinite circle is reoriented again and again, the old and the new, the known and the unknown, the perceived and the hidden, heard and the unheard, all lose their definitions and merge into the infinite. And Time? Time that man has taken so many centuries to perfectly capture, divide and record, stands stationary. There is no past and no future....only now.

What anyone can do is only a repetition of what others have done before Amrita! And for each action, there has been a percentage of ascent or descent. Let us not rejoice in the ascent nor be intimidated by the descent. What is important is the action and that is what I want to do."

"It is your action and your right to take it. Why are you persuading me to join you?"

"Don't you think there is only one divide on earth—mine and thine? My property, my beliefs, your religion, your commitments. Into these two halves fall everything—family, land, money, faiths and yes, even ideologies. Today you are thinking that all this does not concern you, but soon very soon you shall see that the two halves are two concentric circles and the area where they overlap shares the same light and darkness, the same fates and the same destiny. That region is inhabited by the woman. Don't think this will stop here. Very soon, the Sati shall be revived. Some woman somewhere shall be burnt like rotten wood. People will say that she was a Hindu, just as they say about Shah Bano that she is a Muslim. How wrong they would be. She would really be like all of us—just a woman.

* * * * *

THIRTY-ONE

With the hot dry winds from the sandy desert would flow the sound of the single stringed *ektara*. Safia had always loved its sound, perhaps because it was her earliest association with music and story telling. The melodious sound of the single vibrating string and the clanking of the wooden stick on the innumerable iron bangles on the wrist and arm—signal of a dervish coming. The serenity of the dervish's face, the tranquil sound of the *ektara*, the sombre lyrical narration and the distribution from the bag carrying an unending supply of sugar candy. But why was she thinking of the *ektara* in a crowded train? Nobody could be playing it in this sweat and grime. Maybe she had slept for a few seconds and a vision from her childhood had crept into her dreams. But the sound of the *ektara* still came—vivid and clear as the rumbling of the train, as the snoring of the fat man next to her. She craned her neck to look for the player—must be a beggar making his round of the passenger trains. He must be far away because she could not see him. Then why did the sound seem so close by? It was getting closer and louder. She suddenly felt a gripping desire to see the *ektara*. Where could it be and who was playing it in long resonances and why only the *ektara*? Each resonance was followed by another, after long still gaps and grew louder. Yes louder, almost near her left ear. Safia's hand involuntarily touched her left ear, traced a path down the earlobe, her left jaw, and stopped at the pulsating artery. Strange! The *ektara* seemed to be playing very near the artery, though not quite there. Safia smiled to herself. Well, her body seemed to be growing musical at the end of its day. All at once, restlessness came over her. She must get up and go. But where? Anywhere; she must walk and keep walking, put a restraining hand over the *ektara* and shut down its resonance. A part of her brain told her not to be silly. There was no *ektara*, no resonance and no need to muffle it. But the urge became fanatical. Her whole heart…... Heart? Yes, that was it.

That was where the *ektara* was located. That is where the waves were coming from, steadier and more definite than before now that she had at last managed to locate them. So why had her heart decided to be the *ektara*? And why in this suffocating compartment? Having become a musical instrument, why did it want her to perform a waltz? Why urge her to walk? Well, she could not oblige it. Safia resolutely shut her eyes, hoping that the music would die. It did and was replaced by a slow, dull pain. Oh God! Not on the train. She could not be getting a heart attack on the train! She had to reach Indore. She had not come this far just to kick the bucket. This useless exercise could have been carried out anywhere—why here? She had to live. Safia began chanting the line with the wheels of the train—'Have to live–have to live–have to live'. The pain seemed to subside as if lulled by the mantra and she persevered, willing it to pass. The cool night became hot and humid as she sweated, luke warm drops running down her chest and back. The chanting seemed to be getting slower. God! I must be dying and my senses are losing their grip over my body. No! It was the train slowing down and her chant instinctively kept time with it. A station approaching. Safia glanced at her wrist watch—one in the morning. Could this be Indore? The train was scheduled to reach here at six in the evening but was running seven hours behind schedule. As she craned her neck to catch a glimpse of the name of the station, a loud murmur started in the coach, 'It is Indore. Get up! It is Indore I say, tie up the bedding.'

So here she was. This part of her journey, the easy one, was over. Safia got up gingerly remembering the doctor's instructions of no sudden jerks. However, her heart lurched anyway and seemed to become still. Almost simultaneously, her breath seemed to stop and the air seemed to have become solid, refusing to flow in. As suddenly as it had stopped, it made a rush inside and her lungs filled to bursting as her heart tumbled into an irregular movement. She was planning the maneuver to the carriage door, when her bag was lifted from her shoulder. She turned quickly hoping to catch the thief. It was the young Sikh man who had vacated the seat for her at Jhansi. "You look very tired Auntyji. Let me help you."

Safia gratefully surrendered the bag and followed the Sikh who skillfully skipped over sleeping bodies and pushed away vertical ones. A living proof of how the destitute Punjabis had survived the Partition of India.

"Is anyone meeting you Auntyji?"

"No son, I shall be meeting someone."

The man gave her a curious look. She did not seem weak in the head. Having assured himself, he walked towards a bench. "You better sit, Auntyji. I'll get you a cup of tea."

Relief came with the syrupy tea and the boy smiled as she thanked him. "You don't look a casual traveler?"

"I am not. I come with a purpose." Suddenly the urge to talk to someone, anyone, became uncontrollable and the whole reason for her being here spilled out. The smiling Sikh became serious and grim. When she had finished, he picked up her bag. "Come on Auntyji."

"Where? I can't go to Shah Bano's house at this time and I know no one in Indore."

"That is why. You are not safe. Come, we'll meet the Station Master."

The crumpled piece of newspaper who answered for the Station Master was least interested in hearing their story. The Sikh persisted and at the mention of Shah Bano, the crumpled newspaper seemed to crease out. He listened, glancing from one to the other, and asked, "How many people in Indore know that you are coming?"

"None," replied Safia.

"Good. But not good enough. Information network of the other side is strong. Please stay in my office while I see the train off. When it is light, I shall escort you to her house."

"There is no need to do so. I can take a cycle rickshaw. I have the address."

"Shah Bano is not allowed to meet anyone. She has given the affidavit asking the Supreme Court to review its decision, or else she shall be withdrawing her case. She is never left alone. You shall have to wear a *burqa* and pose as a strict Muslim come to reform her. Maybe then you might stand a chance and be allowed to meet her. I am a Muslim and I am with you in this just cause. Please do as I say."

The Sikh gave him a long stare. Then turning to her said, "I think he can be trusted Auntyji. Take care of yourself and if you get to see Shah Bano, tell her that I, Gurdeep Singh, a Sikh from Hoshiarpur, stand by her. Though maybe it is not my business."

"But of course it is your business. It is the business of every justice loving being. Thank you for being with us."

As the train chugged out, Safia felt marooned on an unknown island, from which the last boat had just pulled out with no promise of return. She felt a chill run down her spine and shivered. "What's the matter? Are you cold?" It was the station master returning after seeing the train off.

"No. Just someone walking over my grave."

He gave her a quizzical glance and put a saucepan of water over the electric heater. "Never got used to the station tea. Your bedding has obviously not been opened."

"There was no space."

"Never is. Why don't you move to the chair and I'll open it on the sofa....er, bench."

Safia smiled at the correction and got up. Her heart again did the mid-air somersault.

"What's the matter? Are you ill?"

"No. I am just a little nervous I suppose."

"Don't be. You can't afford to be. Not with the purpose for which you have come." The simple, matter-of-fact statement steadied her and she sat down on the chair. "It is a false affidavit, given under duress." Imtiaz Ali spoke after a long silence in which he prepared tea and cleared the saucepan before handing her a chipped cup. "It has to be," he added taking a sip.

"How are you so certain?"

"When faced with a dead end, one has to remain affirmative. Uncertainty can cause devastating accidents. Good."

"What is?"

"Good to smile, better to laugh."

"There is really nothing to laugh about. This is no comedy."

"Isn't it? I had gone to meet her—Shah Bano. She is a distant cousin and I am a devout Muslim. So it was possible. She offered me tea. She never had on my earlier visits. When I refused, she insisted saying, 'Please do. I am now a rich woman, receiving one hundred and seventy nine rupees and twenty paisa as maintenance. You better have the tea while the going is good'. When we were alone, which was only for a few minutes she kept quiet for a few moments and then burst out laughing. At herself? At the world that took cognizance of her after so many years? At me, who met her but rarely and had now come to view her as something of a rarity, a museum piece? The courage of the destitute to laugh at themselves."

He was suddenly quiet and not having anything to say, Safia tried to plan her modus operandi. The rush of events had not given her enough time to make a plan of action, while what she would probably need here would be two or three courses of action, for she was sure to counter failure at least once. To be honest, except for trying to contact Danial Latifi, Shah Bano's lawyer and leaving a message on his answering machine, she had not done any sensible planning. She did not feel unsafe. The worst after all could be a lynching, but she did feel unsure about the extent of support she would be able to gather for Shah Bano. Well as Abbas would have said, '*Jodi tor daak sune keu na aashe, tobe ekla chalo re.*' So here she was, alone but not lonely. This stranger station master seemed to be on their side and the Sikh boy, though not present, had extended his support. Coming back to the gentleman sitting before her, he seemed honest and forthright. But seeming is faraway from being. Was he or was he not a supporter for Shah Bano's cause? And if he was today, how long would he remain so? So many people had flipped sides, making mincemeat of commitment and throwing it to the vultures.

The polite cough brought her back to the present and he smiled apologetically. "I'll have to leave now. I want to say one thing—I am glad you are here. I had given up on the educated Muslim women. They say one thing and retract it before you have turned around. Shah Bano's only hope is women like you or those in the same position as her."

"You mean?"

"An illiterate housewife from the village Manakpur, of district Badayun in Uttar Pradesh has made the first open expression of support—'It's all very well for the Mullahs to defend the *Shariat*. But when a poor girl gets divorced who is going to feed her. Especially if her relatives themselves are poor.'" He raised his hand to stop her when she would have spoken. "You don't have to agree or disagree. What you need to do is rest. Try to sleep. I am going outside. The Vindhyachal is due and then several others. I shall be gone until dawn. I have to keep an eye on the signal man—he's a new fellow." He had returned to his crumpled newspaper state and frittered out.

Safia sighed and glanced at the cotton mat and old pillow that was to be her bed for the night. Her head was aching and the left shoulder was beginning to feel numb after the throbbing pain. She should rest; she had a long day before her perhaps. Or it might turn out to be a very short one, with her not being able to see Shah Bano. Then what would she do? Wait? Wait for Danial Latifi, Shah Bano's lawyer to knock the doors of Supreme Court and get Shah Bano the freedom to live. The woman had begun her fight from the middle. She should have started at the beginning. Sought the Muslim clergy's permission to live, before asking the courts to tell her husband to provide for her food and other needs. Would Danial Latifi be able to get her and others like her a meeting with the frail woman?

She got up from the wooden chair and made for the raxine covered wooden bench—the sofa. "Now to decide which one is more uncomfortable," she smiled. Yes, humor is the essence of life. She suddenly tottered and would have fallen if the wooden bench had not been so close. She gripped it with both hands and kneeled on the floor. As her body began to give way, her brain charged on. Yes, that was it—the poor destitute woman—that is where the crux of the matter lies. Everything boils down to economics and that is why the poor woman would support this fight for economic justice—the same reason why men would continue to oppose it. It has to be the women who do not know where their next meal would come from, who have to stand up, have to be convinced to fight and fight they will, because they have nothing to lose. She had been wrong in believing that the educated and the well-to-do would rise up. Why would they, who had for centuries believed themselves as the upper class, the genteel, the privileged? Why would they take up arms for those whom they have considered the scum of the earth, little more than worms, to be used and crushed? They lived as parasites and they knew that there was no survival for them minus the host who maybe receptive or hostile. They must cling on.

Strange how progression in life makes one lose focus of the very fundamentals—food, clothing and shelter. The common woman struggled for these, together with her man—working away her body to dust, yet giving man credit for being the provider. She would be the pivot of this war—the war that would prove to the world that the law of the land is subject to evolution, the same as everything else.

She must write all this down. All her thoughts must be put on paper and she feverishly reached out for her handbag for her notebook and pen. A part of her brain questioned her—what is the big hurry? While the other urged her on—'Quick....be quick.'

* * * * *

THIRTY-TWO

I

"What are you doing with those books?"

"Making a pile of them"

I can see that Sitara."

"Then why ask?"

"Why are you making a pile of the books?"

"Then ask that. To make a stake."

"A steak?"

"Not that one, a stake, to burn."

"Burn all those books?" Wasim put an expression people do to show surprise instead of anger at a child's mischief. The child is never fooled.

"Today is Sunday. What better day to burn all of *Ma*'s possessions." Seeing Wasim's expression, Sitara sighed patiently. "You are the one who said that everything that belongs to *Ma* shall be burnt. And perhaps somewhere I agree with you. I have to live with you and we must agree on major issues if we have to co-exist. *Ma* is my past. She can be wrapped and packed away or burnt at a stake. Memories can never be as important as the present and certainly not more important than the future. Problem is there are so many of them—these books—practically all the books in this house are hers. And there is the other problem—how to burn her crockery, her refrigerator, furniture and pots and pans and….."

"Hold on Sitara. I never said all these things have to be burnt."

"But you did. I heard you and so did *Ma* and then as I said, I quite agree with you. So to continue, how do I get rid of her gas connection, her telephone, the artifacts she collected all her life and the two paintings by Hussein….do oil paintings burn?"

"But Sitara I didn't say....I mean, I did say but I really didn't mean that they have to be literally burnt. Look, I was very angry. You know I am touchy about my religion. Everything else has been taken away from me. I will not let this country take away what is most precious to me—the *Shariat*. When your mother openly supported this attack, I lost my cool and I suppose I said more than what I really meant. Take it easy. Let's go out somewhere and talk this over."

"So Ma was right. You know Wasim, when *Ma* embraced me for the last time, she whispered in my ear, 'Don't worry; he won't carry out any of those threats. He loves possessions too much to make this kind of a sacrifice—even for Islam.'"

"Sitara, you don't really believe...."

"I didn't and I did. For the last forty-eight hours, I have been oscillating between the two. Forty-eight hours like a pendulum and I could not take it anymore. I ached for stability. I knew the equilibrium was not for me. I could never have managed the two extremes and survived in the centre position. I could have compromised and remained stuck to one extreme. But your extreme is as unsafe as my equilibrium. You are really not there. In fact, you are nowhere except with yourself. You are not really a fundamentalist; it is too tough to be one and puts you with the unfashionable crowd. It even asks you not to have an educated, professional wife who does not observe the purdah. Fundamentalism is too demanding on personal life. On the other hand, you cannot be progressive. It demands excessive and continuous self-analysis and one does need basic honesty for that. Honest is one thing you would never be. I prayed that *Ma* would be proved wrong. That you would pass this test and really burn everything. It would have made me very unhappy but restored my faith in you. At least, you are reliable as far as your religion goes. You would have got rid of *Ma* in any case. This incident gave you a valid reason—protection of Islam, undying devotion to the *Shariat*. So I am left with no choice. I am the pendulum that has just discovered that the other side is sealed. I have to change my cycle and find a new place to rest."

"I think you are unnecessarily making a big issue out of nothing. If I were you...."

"Which you are not and because you are not, none of my issues shall ever be big enough for you. You shall always revel in the advantageous position that a man has in this society and fight even the smallest concession a woman might demand. The *Shariat* as you practice it, is not a right, it is a means to practice your male chauvinism."

"Sitara," as Wasim advanced towards her menacingly, she picked up the decorative carved wheel and pulled out one of the spokes. A long ice pick glittered in her hand.

"Don't even think of it Wasim."

Wasim stopped in his tracks. "You would......"

"Just as you would. Go back to your room and stay there until I have left. Yes, I am leaving you. If a woman with an ailing heart can think of supporting a just cause, the least that I can do is stand by her."

II

"I am sorry. I did not mean to bang my head against yours. Did I hurt you? I am afraid my head is rather big and a bit hard."

Amrita held Sitara's shoulders and steadied her. "I think both of us have been rather hard and yes, big headed too. I had come to discuss that with you. But it seems that...."

"I am leaving this house."

"Not like this. You are not. Come inside."

Four hours later, Amrita's lawyer had made a detailed list of all that belonged to Sitara—taken the original receipts of the installments for the flats and left after taking Wasim's signature on everything.

"Let's go and have coffee somewhere."

"Let's precede it with *Vada*."

"And make it like old times."

"Yes, let's bring back the old times."

"Minus *Ma*?"

"We have to find her Sitara."

"Where could she have gone?"

"She is not in Delhi. I have tried all her contacts."

"Lucknow?"

She has nothing, no one there."

"Then could she have...."

"Yes she was talking about going to Indore. That is where she must have gone."

"These artistes…why do all their decisions have to be emotional ones?"

"She had gone to you."

"So she had and to you."

"She was relying on your support."

"And on yours. Though I had told her that you wouldn't give it. Seems like I was right."

They both glowered at each other. Sitara was the first to lower her eyes. "You are right."

"You are not alone in your shame. All of us who have kept quiet over this should feel ashamed of ourselves."

"Oh, Amrita Aunty. I have been such a fool."

"So have I. But it is never late to make amends."

"It isn't?"

"No it isn't. It cannot be. Awakening would be useless if it was to come when all is lost. Surely something can be salvaged."

"We have to look for her."

"Yes. That is the first thing we have to do. But where?"

"Surely she would have informed someone, taken information about Shah Bano's whereabouts."

"You are right. Who would be the best person to give her this information?"

"Shah Bano's lawyer."

"Let's call Danial Latifi."

III

"It is really beyond me. How could she just leave without even the address of this woman?"

"Well, she did try to contact Danial Latifi."

"For Pete's sake, since when has leaving a message on the answering machine become a form of contacting. Why didn't she stay the night?"

"Where?"

Amrita opened her mouth to reply and then shut it.

"You didn't reply Amrita Aunty. Where could she have stayed? With her daughter who let her husband turn her out of her own house or with her friend who at the eve of life reminded her that they belonged to different communities and could not share a common cause. She was not left with much choice."

"Don't Sitara. Open self-criticism is a form of self-pity. Let us not indulge in it. Not yet."

"Amrita Aunty, it is four days now. Will we find her?"

"We'll stop somewhere for lunch and by evening we shall be in Indore."

"It was good of you to come."

"No, it would have been good if I had gone with her. But there are always the forerunners and the followers. I guess for all my pretensions, I never had the makings of a leader, never could see things to the end. There were others who did it for me and I believed them to be my achievements. There is a difference between a leader and a capable manager. One is not the other. I was always meant to be a follower. Now that I know, I shall be a good one."

IV

"Try to understand my position Mrs Govind Ram. You must admit that the issue is extremely delicate and as in charge of the district, I can't afford to have a hand in any disharmony."

"But Mr DC, I am not asking you to take any steps about the matter. We are not even asking you to help us in our endeavours. Why are we not allowed to meet Shah Bano? Even if she observes the purdah, which she does not, we are both women. So what is the objection of her family? She seems to be virtually under house arrest."

"Madam, I do think that you are being rather drastic in your observations. Any man has a right to the privacy of his house. We cannot intrude. After all, they are not criminals."

"But it is not any man's house. It is Shah Bano's house. Why is her son turning us away? We would not have objected if she herself had come out and asked us to get lost."

"Maybe she is the one who instructed him to tell you this. Suppose we were to help you to barge in and Shah Bano was to say that it was she who had instructed her family to keep outsiders away. Then where would I be? My position would be that of an ordinary gatecrasher. Do try to understand my position. Ah! Tea at last. So you see Madam, things move slowly in Government offices but they do move." He gave a saccharine smile that remained frozen for five seconds in expectation of the laughter that an IAS officer's joke always manages to generate. After all, it was the joke of the most powerful man in the district.

"Nothing would make him move his arse, so we do understand his position of no change," Amrita whispered over the rim of the tea cup.

Sitara smiled and racked her brain, willing it to throw some move that would help squeeze some result. They had been in Indore for the last twenty-four hours but it still seemed like a dead end. In the first place, nobody seemed to know who Shah Bano was. When queries persisted, they admitted to having read about her in the papers but feigned ignorance about her whereabouts. Sitara was not in favour of contacting the police. She did not want the whole administration nor the fundamentalists alerted. However, she had to yield her stand when no results were forthcoming in the first twelve hours. The DC was found to be out of station and his office did not seem to have a clue about what they were enquiring, the SP, a Syed Muslim, was welcoming enough but had clammed up the moment he heard their enquiry.

They hit dirt only after Amrita decided to go to the local RSS office. Her logic—this was a Muslim issue and the RSS would be keeping tabs on it. The RSS volunteer had even offered to provide them a guide, which they had hurriedly refused. Armed with the address they made for the poorest neighborhood of Indore. They had located the small house but the two-roomed structure had been turned into an impregnable fortress. They had tried four times. Each time a male member had come and literally shooed them away. The fifth time round, their car had been surrounded by a group of mullahs and rowdy youths. A smashed front screen and Amrita thought that this was a good enough reason to contact the DC. Though he sympathized with the damage to the car, he was very definite about not changing his position. Gulping down his tea, he coughed and pointedly picked up a file. "You could of course register the case with the police. Then it might be labeled as an effort of one community to downgrade the other. And because there would be no eyewitnesses, it could mean flaying of tempers in both communities and that I couldn't…"

"For the love of God, are there only communities left in this country? Whatever happened to the humans?"

Sitara put a restraining hand on Amrita's arm. "Please Sir, we are not here to create any tension between the two communities. We also do not want to create any problems for you. We are looking for a woman in her sixties, suffering from acute heart ailment. In her last communication, she had mentioned that she wanted to come here to meet Shah Bano and give her moral support. We only want your help to find this woman. Name as we said earlier is Safia Abbas Jafri. She might have changed it, so here is her photograph."

The DC took the photograph and gave it a long look. "She looks familiar, even her name seems familiar."

"She is a well known Urdu writer. She recently received the Nehru Award for literature."

"Of course! That is what it is. Then how come she is behaving like this. Is she mentally....?" He stopped and looked meaningfully at Sitara.

"Just what do you mean? Of all the obnoxious.....'"

"Please Amrita Aunty. I think we are unnecessarily going round in a rigmarole. Yes, she was depressed and when in one of those moods she often did things, which...er...a normal person would not do. That is why we are here. No sense in hiding facts."

"I wish you had said so right at the beginning," the DC accused her, looking at her in a way that tried to convey to her that accepting a deranged parent was the duty of every offspring and that she should have carried a placard saying 'I have a depressed parent.'

"Now that you know, can you help us?" The DC began to feel trapped and started wriggling to escape. "Well, it is all right for you to say this, but in my position...."

"We are not interested in Shah Bano, either as a person or as a case. She has cropped up because my mother had mentioned coming to see her. Now can you help us?"

"Madam, the communal tension in this case is tremendous. In my position, one can never be sure. If you were to meet Shah Bano, without court orders...."

"Is the woman in jail?" bristled Amrita.

"But we needn't meet her." Sitara made another detour to by-pass the red tape. "Can't someone from your office go to Shah Bano's house and make enquiries whether someone of this name or face had come to meet her in the last four days?"

"Well I think...."

"Please Sir, you are my last hope."

"Don't madam, don't weep please. I will do whatever I can. Hey you, call the SP and ask him to be here in five minutes."

Amrita was grim and snatched away her hand when Sitara tentatively reached for it.

"I know you are angry with me."

"You do? Well how very observant of you. Fancy calling your mother mad."

"I didn't do anything like that. We had come to a dead end. I had to get things moving. All I said was that she was not herself because she was depressed."

"Well, she wasn't. She could not have been. Not now. Not then when she had turned up at my doorstep with you on her hip. She was worried then, a little lost and maybe even desperate. But she was not depressed. That is what made me keep her. I knew she had that 'never say die' quality. She would always see things to the end."

"I know. That is why I am here. If she had decided to stand by Shah Bano, she would do just that. To her last breath. But do believe, I am desperate. Why can't we find any trace of her? At the moment, it is more important for me to locate her. Shah Bano, both as an individual and as *Ma*'s cause has to take a back seat."

"You are really worried and honestly unhappy. I thought your tears at the DC's office were good acting."

"They were but these aren't."

"How is one to know the difference child?"

"Past experience, I guess."

"The past, both yours and mine, has not been a very forth right one, has it? You must admit that once you entered your teens, you made a concerted and I might say, a very successful effort to distance yourself from Safia."

Sitara wiped her face. "Yes, an effort that *Ma* accepted without any protest. The gaps that I created, she never made any effort to bridge. She never thought that I might be creating the gaps just to see if she would cross them."

"Maybe she understood it as an effort to be free yourself of her influence and being a true democrat, let you keep those gaps in the hope that they would help you develop as a person."

"I always had this feeling that I was so much of a responsibility on her. That she would have been so much better off if I had not been there. Maybe she would have married again and lived—really lived."

"Oh no! She would not. She loved your father too much and you were his extension. In a way, she always had your father with her because of your presence. You were never a responsibility—you were her life. As for living it, do you think we—you and me have lived a better one? Women like Safia and Shah Bano live a life because they fight for it. True, they lose and often but then they are only battles that are lost. The war goes on."

"Is it too late to join it?"

"I don't know. I hope not. People like you and me are always late or battles would not be lost. Let's pray that we are not too late.... for our sake."

The hotel manager was standing on the steps when Amrita's car turned into the gate. Watching his podgy figure bouncing down the path, the driver stopped the car and Amrita rolled down the glass. "Message from the DC's office. Kind of urgent. Says you should reach there at once."

* * * * *

THIRTY-THREE

I

"I think this is another wild goose chase. Nobody really saw her there."

"But this beggar seemed fairly certain."

"Anyone would be after they had been shown a photograph ten times."

"He said he saw her going with a Sikh man to *Bada Saheb*."

"Which is really very helpful because we don't know who *Bada Saheb* is. We have talked to the signal man, the head coolie, the head waiter, the parcel in-charge, the ticket checker, the waiting room caretaker, even the head sweeper."

"Except the station master."

"Who is very conveniently on leave."

"But he must have a house in the railway colony."

"We shall check of course, but I still think we are simply chasing our tails. After all, why hasn't anybody else seen her?"

"You forget it was half past one in the morning. I can understand that you are tired and want to rest. Why don't I proceed with this constable and you go back to the hotel and rest."

"Are you giving a broad hint that I am getting old?"

"Well...not quite."

"But almost. Well, you do not. Finding Safia is as important for me as for you. Stop listening to our bickering. Servants these days have no manners. Drive on."

"Where to Madam?"

"What were you listening for then?"

"Calm down, Amrita Aunty. Driver, ask someone the entrance to the railway staff colony."

II

A middle-aged man with a salt and pepper beard and jet black—very obviously dyed—hair opened the door. He looked at Amrita enquiringly and then his glance moved to Sitara and the enquiry was replaced by an unnerving expression of recognition followed by a twitching of the upper lip and flaring of nostrils—that lent a cynicism to the look of recognition. He seemed to be holding a debate within himself that neither Amrita nor Sitara dared to interrupt. Then he nodded his head and gave his narrow shoulders a shake—like a famished mongrel deciding to swallow the stinking garbage.

"Please come in. You are no doubt relatives of Begum Safia Abbas Jafri."

The unquestioning definiteness of his statement was unnerving and they merely nodded.

He motioned to a pair of easy chairs, "Sit down please. You are her...?"

"This is her daughter. I am her life long friend."

"Married?" His deep-set sharp eyes scanned Sitara's face.

"Look Mister...."

"Imtiaz Ali," he obliged rather grudgingly.

"Yes, Mr Imtiaz Ali, I would be grateful if you would tell us where Safia is. We have been worried sick trying to get a clue of her whereabouts."

"Yes. I should tell you that, shouldn't I?" He stopped and concentrated on his hand, studying it as if he had just discovered that he possessed one and getting to know its each detail was the most important work in his life. Amrita glanced at Sitara and raised her tired eyes to the ceiling.

"Yes, I should do that. But I wonder?" He got up purposefully and walked to a chipped, ink blotched, wooden desk. Opening the single drawer, he brought out an exercise book and flipped through the pages, stopping at some and murmuring a few lines. Amrita was opening her mouth to impatiently question him again when he looked up and catching her off guard, smiled his slow knowing smile.

"You know if I was a Hindi film director, I could create some very dramatic moments from this kind of a situation. I could not recognize you, though you look so much like her, wait for you to introduce yourself, jump up and embrace you and holding you to my breast, I would cry, 'Oh my daughter, where were you etc.' Then I could begin a long detail of how she came here, alone, without a reserved seat, sitting for more than twenty two hours in a cramped second class compartment. How her train, which was supposed to be an express, was more than seven hours late, the way she thanked me for the first cup of proper tea she had since she left home—your home or was it hers and you still managed to throw her out. I could do all that and then saying that she was staying with friends, I could take your car across Indore and outside it, guide you through the gates flanked with slim white minarets, nodding sagely at your surprise because you were being led through lines of graves. I would then lead you to a new grave covered with snow-white jasmine flowers and breaking down, cry out, 'This is your mother child, this is where she is.' But I am not a film director and for a stationmaster, life and death are as simple as one train coming and another one leaving. I shall tell you in the coarse way left open to me—your mother died five days ago, on the night that she reached here.

She suffered two attacks and succumbed to the second one. No one was with her. I had left her alone in the hope that she would be able to sleep, which she did. She knew that she was very close to making an exit and took the few hours left to write a few pages, make a few scribbling on this notebook. I found her sitting on my table, her head on this exercise book, with notes on how the *Shariat* has to be reformed. Being a Muslim, I was able to claim that she was a distant cousin, who had no one left in the immediate family. The police still insisted on keeping her body in the mortuary. I managed to get it only yesterday afternoon when the police was satisfied that no one would come for it. The mortuary is supposed to be air conditioned, but it never works. The body was in a bad shape. The burial was a quiet one and took place in the poorest side of the graveyard with only three people present—the *Maulvi*, the gravedigger and me. I burnt a solitary oil lamp on the grave, but as I turned back after a few steps to see the grave for the last time, I saw a ragamuffin boy run to it and snatching it quickly, take it to his mother who was standing behind a tree. I wanted to go back and scold them but the way the mother was stroking the boy's head and the joy lit on their faces made me stop. It would probably go into their evening meal and give it some flavour or maybe their tumble down hut would have a light after many days. I came away with the nagging feeling of guilt that I had somehow not done enough for your mother. However, after reading this copybook, I know that I did the right thing. It is the living who matter. The dead are trains gone by.

She had been writing as I said. I had taken the copy, hoping that some day I would be able to use it to get a better deal for Muslim women. I suppose it is yours and it is my moral duty to hand over what is yours by legal rights. I wonder, really wonder, why she came alone? Why she died alone? No! Do not answer me. Who am I to question you? It is your conscience that would question and you shall be cornered into answering it. You would probably placate it with many reasons. The most logical one would be that after all, you did not want her to die, did not know that she would die. And you would be right. You did not want her to die but you did not give her chance to live. She would have lived if she had had support for her cause, support in the shape of a single female individual. She would have lived, not physically maybe, but as the only educated, well-placed Muslim woman who had the guts to call a wrong, a wrong.

Therefore, madam, this is the notebook and I will bring her bedding and hand bag. I gave away the sari that she had been wearing to the woman who came to wash the corpse. I must tell you that something very interesting happened then. The corpse was in such a rotten state that this woman refused to touch it. I then decided to put your mother's theory to test—you shall find it explained in detail in the exercise book. I took this woman aside and told her the reason and circumstances of your mother dying at the station. The woman heard it all and asked to be shown the place where the washing had to be done. When she had completed everything, I extended fifty-one rupees, the fee for the burial bath, towards her. She shook her head and picked up her *abaya*, preparing to leave. When I insisted, she said, "I am not a professional. I am the first wife of a man who has three. My three children and I have to eat. This was the only job, with maximum compensation and least competition for an illiterate Muslim woman. Your sister had also come for me. God rest her soul."

* * * * *

INTERLUDE

A visit to the grave was paid, presumably. Some candles lighted, some incense burnt, some flowers laid, some tears shed. The one called Amrita pledged to continue the work that Safia had not been able to initiate. The one named Sitara promised to be the guiding star of the movement for gender equality, irrespective of religious perimeters. The air in the graveyard brings out the best in people and vows are made at a grave or beside a pyre—solemn, sincere, quickly forgotten. Most graveyards and cremation grounds have eateries near their gates. Food, to revive the primary link with life, good food to help people make an effort to work towards improving it and delicious food to make it worth living.

What the Sitaras or Amritas did or did not do came to mean nothing in the future. What did make a difference was that the Shah Bano case and the Supreme Court's decisions was over ridden by an agitated, nervous Parliament which was more afraid of losing their vote banks and more interested in appeasing the Muslim clergy than in seeing justice prevail. The fall out of this was that the Muslim fundamentalists, in an organized manner, took over the leadership from the liberal, progressive Muslims. It is they whose faces began to appear on the television screens, speaking on behalf of all Muslims, they who decided and ordered Muslims to vote for or against a party, they who now tell women to switch husbands, sleep with the rapist father-in-law and treat the husband and father of her children as her son, they who issue fatwa at the drop of a hat and they who see that it is carried out. Exactly four decades before the Shah Bano case, fearing intense communal riots, the country's leadership and the colonial rulers had agreed to divide it. The riots still happened, families were torn, property destroyed, hundreds and thousands were killed. The defining of new borders drew deep furrows between the two communities. The next generation of Hindus and Muslims was just the beginning to get a hold of itself and find its feet in the independent, democratic India when the country's leadership struck again. In its urge to preserve the democratic freedom of an individual to practice any religion, it took away—from a large section of the population—the right to live with dignity. All Muslims were now accepted as backward looking, retrogressive, fundamentalists. The clergy became more aggressive and offensive and the liberals were on the defensive. More Muslim women took to wearing *burqa*, more men sported beards and skull-caps. The will to be one with all humanity—as creatures involved in the same struggle of improving life—vanished. Sects, divisions, units, compartments, clans, castes and groups, took its place. The once homogeneous mixture turned tepid and decantation was the natural outcome where the particles named Muslims are seen to be moving only in one direction—downwards.

FROM SAFIA'S JOURNAL

Freedom is a faith, just as equality, peace or friendship. Like all faiths, it has to continuously keep redefining and reinventing itself to survive. The believers of this faith, as of any other, have to be contributors in this process because it is their perception of it which would reinvent or redefine it. Perhaps that is why men cannot even begin to understand what freedom is to a woman or what is the meaning of gender equality. The whole perplexity of freedom for women is that men have taken the responsibility of denying or granting it. Women have let men usurp the very fundamental—the definition of freedom as it is to be gained, as it is to be lived.

How am I to write immortal works when I am not free?
How am I to answer when I am not asked?
Why should I waste time in writing verses?
If Time itself loses those verses?
I write in a durable kind of language.
It shall be long until they are implemented.
To achieve the fundamentals, great changes are needed.
Little changes are the enemies of great changes.
My thoughts have enemies, therefore, I must be free.

For something to define itself, the primary factor is the belief that redefinition is required. For this to come about, there has to be an acceptance of the fact that life out of a faith in its present form is dwindling, movement has stopped and stagnation has begun. With stagnation naturally comes rot that increases with time.

Separate religious systems have their own definitions of freedom. In the early civilizations, the concept of freedom was very different from that of the large empires, which differed from the feudal system and which again was vastly different to the capitalist world. In the last few decades, largely because of the two world wars and several communist revolutions, Europe and the nations influenced by it initiated a process of continuous analysis of freedom, sovereignty and its absorption for the betterment of individuals as well as the society as a whole. This process opened up further debates on freedom to be, to love, speak, believe and govern. Man learnt to know man, not because of the community, race or nation, but as individuals.

While all this was going on for men, the woman was left out in the cold. In major socio-political decisions, the women were not even consulted. No one asked the Jew women whether they needed an Israel for safety, nobody asked the Muslim women whether they needed a Pakistan because they could not live under a democratic government with a larger representation of the majority community, nobody asked them if they wanted so many wars of various kinds or for that matter so many communist revolutions that professed the equality of mankind.

In the case of the European women, a large number of men had gone to the two wars. For years, women controlled the production and the economy. The wars ate into the male population and those who did come back were happy enough to let the women keep at least some of the control. Women, with the discovery of their latent capabilities aggressively refused to give up their newfound freedom. Thus was initiated a process of the society as a whole undergoing a continuous process of reinvention, from the revival of Buddhism in Europe and Scientology becoming a religion to gay marriages and nudism.

However, what of the countries that had been reformed, their boundaries remarked, nations newly created? Amongst these were the countries of the Arab world, India, Pakistan and almost the entire Africa. The dominant religions of this region are Islam and Hinduism. Democracy in India, with its distorted and marred face, still manages to hold out. Various acts have seen to it that at least legally the Hindu women get a better deal. Strangely enough, the same democrats become a cringing, frightened lot when it comes to touching the *Shariat*.

The Arab world with its huge oil reserves and newly found power, set about at once to destroying—with a little help from the two super powers—whatever democracy had seeped into its autocratic systems. Progressive nations were as a policy weakened or destroyed—Lebanon, Turkey, Jordan, and Syria. Christians and Muslims, who had so far lived more or less peacefully, were thrown into civil wars. Continuation of these wars destroyed the faith in peaceful co-existence and mutual tolerance. The last effort of forming a progressive alliance within the Arab world—often also called the Muslim world—the UAR was wiped out and with that the effects of Turkey under the Kamal Ataturk's regime that had abolished the *burqa* for women and given them rights to educate themselves and participate in politics. *Shariat* staged a come back, did away with all the reforms and began wrecking vengeance on the liberal forces within Islam. Its foremost targets were women. They were denied education and knowledge. Those still hanging around institutions of learning were carefully weeded out. Women now could not vote, could not hold separate bank accounts, could not move around without a male companion, could not say no to a marriage fixed by their father or other elders. In short, woman was back to being a commodity, created for the pleasure of man and since he was incapable of deriving any other pleasure from her than the physical one, she was confined to the areas where she would be most available for it—his home. The black head-to-foot cover was back in full force. So much so that even the public execution of a princess who had made an attempt to escape the isolation of the harem had to be carried out with her covered in a black *burqa*. And she? Having failed in her one and only attempt for freedom and so near death when tons of earth would hide her face forever, she did not dare to make a bid to uncover her face and face the circle of the jeering males, egging on the executioner with the naked sword. The greed for the kill, the lust for the woman, the self-righteousness of having shown the woman her place was stark naked—their faces were not covered.

The *Shariat* says that a woman has to be kept happy, so happy that she would not desire anything beyond the boundaries of the *zenana* and gold is said to make a woman happy. The *Shariat* did not say so but the man knew it. To make up for the weakness of the female body and its incapacity to wear more than a certain amount of gold jewellery, mirror frames, make-up cases, tables chairs, beds, bath tubs and even commodes of gold were ordered for the *zenana*. No one asked the dying princess why she had risked her life for freedom. No one asked the women in the *zenana* if they were happy shitting in gold lavatories. Nobody tried to find out if she would have preferred a harp or a book. Music is banned by the Qur'an and books.....well, the best book is the Holy Qur'an isn't it? When the most superior book is available to her, why need she read inferior ones?

All that is the past. Let us not lose our bearings and begin by asking a few questions. These are not my questions; they have been asked time and again and shall be continuously raised until satisfactory answers are found.

The Supreme Court pronounced its judgement on the Shah Bano Case and upheld the decision of the Bhopal High Court, that of granting her Rs 179.20 per month as maintenance from her husband. The simple decision whether a woman is entitled to a paltry sum of Rs 500 as maintenance under section 125 of the Criminal Procedure Code or as a Muslim woman she gets nothing, has emerged as 'Muslim vs the Rest' issue.

Why should a judgment—which brings about some social reform, one that gives a better deal to the woman or addresses her need as a woman, not as a woman of a particular community—produce a hostile reaction from the men of the community? Why do educated, well-placed women of the community side with their men to crush their more unfortunate sisters? Najma Heptullah stated on the floor of the Parliament, "Islam was not made by the Parliament or the Supreme Court. They have no right to interfere." Why does not anyone point out to her that neither was Hinduism, Christianity, Buddhism or any other religion? Why then are changes possible in them through Acts and Legislation? Why is a bill for the protection of the Muslim women introduced and passed in the two houses of the Parliament without consulting even one woman from the Muslim community, whom it professes to protect?

The law is a means for protecting those who are virtuous and weak and for punishing those who are strong, immoral and bullies. For a person who would not touch another's property, it does not matter whether the punishment is imprisonment for a period or the cutting of the hands. The law is meant to deter those who would take advantage of the weak and having flexed their muscles are on the look out for loopholes within the law to escape punishment. So adept are they at finding the loopholes that it is necessary to keep revising and updating these laws to suit the changes in the existing social order.

It cannot be said that the Muslims all over the world are living in the same social set-up as existed in the Arab world centered round the Mecca. The Bedouin tribes had given up their nomadic habits only a few generations before Prophet Mohammad. The laws were meant to give them a code of civilization to co-exist peacefully. The Muslim Personal Law centered more on the women because the Prophet realized that they were the most exploited and mistreated. He wanted them to get respect and love and not just a right to exist.

Allama Iqbal, the great poet and philosopher had said after the formation of Pakistan, "The question which is likely to confront Muslim countries in the near future, is whether the laws of Islam, the *Shariat* is capable of evolution? A question which is sure to be answered in the affirmative."

Since Iqbal's question, nine countries that call themselves 'Islamic States' have made the necessary changes to provide for "...a large number of middle aged women who are being divorced without any means of sustaining themselves and their children." However, the Indian Government, under the pressure of the Muslim male has successfully put a stop to any sort of evolution in the Islamic Law. Not only do they not allow any sort of evolution, they even question the Supreme Court's right to interpret the Muslim Personal Law and term it as interference.

Islam accepts marriage as a contract and not something that heavens arrange. It is but natural that there would be instructions about the dissolving of this contract. In the *Ayat* 241 and 242 of the Qur'an, the question of maintenance is answered:

"*WA LIL MOTALLAQATAY MATA UN BIL MAAROOFAY HAQQAN ALAL MUTTAQUEENA*"

'For divorced women maintenance/provision is a reasonable scale. This is the duty on the righteous.'

"KAZALEKA YUBAIYYANULLAHO LAKUM AYATEHEE LA
ALLAKUM TAQELOON"
'Thus doth God make his sign to you, in order that you may
understand.'
From the Holy Qur'an by Yusuf Ali, Page 96

The Muslim Personal Law has in fact made a remarkable contribution by providing the concept of divorce to Hindu and Christian
Personal Laws, where it was unknown before. While these religions
have kept up with the changing circumstances, is it possible for the
Muslim laws safeguarding the rights of the Muslim women to remain
static? Once deemed highly progressive, laws get out dated and have
to be adapted to contemporary standards of justice of any society.

The Muslim fundamentalists claim that a pittance given to an
old woman would endanger the future of their religion in this country. According to them, no judge is qualified to interpret the Holy
Book, only a *Maulvi*, often little more than literate has the right to
interpret the Qur'an.

Shah Bano gave her thumb impression on a typed statement written by the *Maulvis* of Deobandh and Barelwi Schools withdrawing
her petition and refusing to accept the judgment of the Supreme
Court. The cyclostyled bit of paper was titled *"Zameer Ki Awaaz"*.
Before this, she appealed first to the local administration, then the
state administration and finally to the prime minister himself to
provide her adequate protection. The government was too busy
bringing in the Bill for the Protection of Muslim Women. A Bill
that not only quashed the Supreme Court's decision in Shah Bano's
case, it thrust the responsibility of looking after a divorcee on her
family, her siblings, her well-to-do children and if all of them are not
forthcoming, then on the Wakf Board. In other words, it gives the
divorced woman a choice between prostitution if she is young and
beggary if she is old. Shah Bano was neither a political leader nor a
film star. Her appeal for protection went unanswered.

In his speech in Parliament, in defense of the Bill for the Protection of Muslim Women and condemning the Supreme Court's
judgment, ZR Ansari, Minister for Environment had said, "In case
no amendment or change is brought in the provision of maintenance
to Muslim women, then in that case, we will prefer to give poison to

our wives than give them divorce." Was Shah Bano facing a similar kind of threat? Did she fear for her life and was it this fear that made her put her thumb impression on a statement and appeal to the courts to review their judgment?

The Chief Justice, not supposed to speak about his judgment said, "This is the first time I have heard of a successful party ask for a review of a judgment that went in her favour. Why would a successful appellant want to disown her success?"

Where can a seventy-five year old woman turn to for support? As a poor Muslim woman, Zakia Khatoon remarked on hearing about the Bill, "Mullahs should be there to talk about religion. Who are they to tell us to sell our bodies or to beg for food?"

The benefits of a more progressive, liberal and rightful law shall be for all sections of the society. The plight is of the poor women. That is why it is they who need to be addressed. Since they are the biggest losers, they shall become the soldiers realizing that the battle if lost would not cost them anything but if won would give them a life of dignity. Do not think that they shall be cowed down by the clergy, do not believe that they have no voice or strength. Help them to rise up and see them change the world.

It has been said that the end of every century sees a rise of social, cultural and religious clashes. The beginning of the new century witnesses the redefinition of fundamentalism, which within a decade or so formulates a pattern of intolerance. Come the second and the third decade and a tussle begins between the fundamentalists and the liberals, which progresses to become an open war in the fourth decade. The middle of the century sees the rise of liberal and progressive ideas, leading to changes in social setups, redefining of the cultural fabric, a brighter and fuller life that begins to degenerate as the century again crawls to its end.

Perhaps. The century has ended and a new one is enfolding. All that they predict could happen. It might be advisable to wait for the closed fist of the new century to open and release what it holds. It just might have a better deal for women. Or would it be better for the women to step forward, wrench the tightly closed fingers open and fling to dust whatever it holds for them. Then draw their own lines of fate and fortune on the new century's palm, set out to build a world to suit the destiny they have forged for themselves—a world in which they shall be one with the earth, the only paradise that exists, living the life as the only one they shall have, being the God they were always meant to be.

* * * * *

GLOSSARY

Aapa	Sister
Aasha	Rajasthani wine
Abaya	An overgarment worn by some women in muslim-majority countries. The *abaya* should cover the whole body save face, feet, and hands.
Abba	Father
Alaap	Wordless elaboration in classical music
Ameerzade	Rich man's son
Aqueek	Precious stone
Arya Samaaj	The reformist section of Hindus
Asharfi	Gold coin
Attar	Indian perfume
Azaan	Call for *namaaz*
Bahu	Daughter-in law
Balaposh/Dulai	Light coverlet of cotton wool
Bania	Shopkeeper/small businessman
Baraat	Bridegroom's party
Baul songs	Folk form of bengal
Bhabhi	Elder brother's wife
Bhadralok	Gentleman
Bhaiya/Bhai	Brother
Bhudaan	Donating surplus land, propagated by Vinobha Bhave
Bua	Aunt
Burqa	Black head to foot covering for Muslim women

Chaman	Garden; a city in Afghanistan
Champa/Bela/ Raat ki rani/ Mogra	Indian flowers
Champa kiran	Net gold border
Chhaila	Beau
Chhota Laat	Lt Governor
Chhoti Bahu	Younger daughter-in law
Chikan sari	Hand embroidered cotton sari
Chulha	Fireplace
Dal-ki-mandi	Upper-class area of courtesans
Dar-ul-ulum	School for Islamic clergical training
Darvesh	Minstrel
Dessehri	A kind of mango
Dholki	Small percussion instrument
Didi	Sister
Dupalli topi	Cap of fine muslin
Dupatta	A long scarf that is essential to many South Asian women's suits
Dushala	Shawl
Ektara	Single stringed instrument
Fatmahi meher	Negligible amount fixed by Prophet for his daughter; it shows mutual trust
Firangi	White foreigner
Ganapathy	Lord Ganesha
Ganga jamni	Gold and silver
Garam masala	A mixture of spices
Haleem	Mughlai dish with five grains and meat
Haveli	Large square house with at least two inner courtyards
Huzoor	Sir

Iblis	Satan
Iddat	Period between the pronouncement and formalization of *talaaq*
Ikkas	One-seater
Imam	A male spiritual and temporal leader regarded by Shiites as a descendant of Muhammad divinely appointed to guide humans.
Jagatdhatri	The peaceful form of Durga, earth
Jatak Tales	Refer to a voluminous body of folklore-like literature concerning the previous births (*jati*) of the Buddha.
Jhanjhar	Ornaments for feet
Kaaba	The holy shrine at Mecca
Kalaam Paak	The Qur'an
Kalakand	Milk sweetmeat
Kalidar gharara	A dress with a long train
Kamasutra	A sanskrit treatise on lovemaking
Kandiel	Small, globe chandelier
Karanphool/ Jhumka	Ear ornaments
Kardhani	Ornament for the waist
Katha Mandals	Group of storytellers, usually from the Puranas
Kathakali	Classical theatre form of Kerela
Kayastha	Upper class business community
Kewra	Edible fragrance
Khaddar	Handspun and woven cotton
Khan Bahadur	Honourary title given by the British to Indians
Khansama	Chief chef
Khas	Popular fragrance used as coolant
Khas/Gulab/ Motia/Shama- ma-tul-ambar	Indian perfumes

Khilafat Movement	One of the nationalist movements for Independence
Khuda Hafiz	God protect you
Kofta/Korma/Paye/Nehari	Meat dishes of the Mughal cuisine
Kufr	Blasphemy
Laddoo	Sweetmeat
Lahaul-e-vila-koovat	A common abuse of Arabic also used in Urdu
Lota kambal	Water vessel and blanket
Ma	Mother
Majlis	Gathering
Malaich	Dirty, usually used for Muslims
Malkin/Memsahib	Madam
Mamujan maternal	Uncle
Manu Shastra	A work of Hindu law and ancient Indian society; contains codes of conduct pertaining to the caste system
Marsiya/Nohakhani	Narration of Hussein's (Prophet's grandson) martyrdom
Maulana/Maulvi	Muslim clergy
Meher	Woman's security fixed at the time of marriage
Mirasin	Professional singers handling the marriage rituals
Mushairas	Collective reading of poetry
Nagra	Handmade shoes
Najeeb-ur-tara-fain Syed	A pure bred Syed with no mixture in the last seven generations
Nakkhas	A locality in old Lucknow

Nanbai	Muslim cook/baker
Naushe	Best men
Navarasa	Nine moods coded in Bharat Muni's *Natyashastra*
Nikaah	Muslim marriage
Paandaan	A multi-potted container used to keep betel leaves and betel nuts
Paigham	Formal proposal
Pakora	Fritters
Palki	Palanquin
Panchsheel	Five Buddhist principals for disarmament
Phagun	Spring
Qur'an Khani	Group reading of the Qur'an
Ramleela/Krishnaleela	Theatrical presentation of the stories of Rama and Krishna
Salaam	Muslim greeting
Saleem shahi	Hand embroidered shoes
Salwar/churidar	Pyjamas worn by women
Sanatam Dharma Pravachan	Hindu religious elaboration
Saraswati putra	Sons of goddess Saraswati—musicians, dancers
Sargam	Octave
Sarkar	A salutation; used here for Justice Saheb
Satyagrahis	Non-violent protesters
Sawan	Monsoon
Shahi-tukra	Mughlai dessert
Shariat	Muslim law
Sheermal/Abi roti	Kind of bread
Shervani	Long coat usually worn by Muslim men
Shraadha	Death rites

Shukria	Thank you
Spasiba	Russian for 'thank you'
Sua-e-yasin	A chapter from Qur'an
Suhagan	Married woman
Swaraj	Self-governance
Taal/Samn	Rhythmic cycle and its beginning
Tabla	Two piece percussion instrument
Talaaq	Divorce
Tamasha	A traditional folk play form, often with singing and dancing.
Tanpura	Four string musical instrument
Tasha	A percussion instrument
Tehri	Spicy rice dish
Thumri/Dadra	Forms of semi-classical music
Toda/Khandi	Rhythmic pieces of Kathak and Odissi dance
Trishanku	The demon who hangs between heaven and earth
Vazu	Ritual of washing before offering *namaaz*
Vilayati teem-taam	Foreign showoff
Yakhni	Mughlai soup
Zamurad	Emerald
Zauq	Well-known urdu poet in the last Moghal emperor's court
Zenana	Women's quarters

WHO'S WHO

Pandit Jawaharlal Nehru—A Freedom fighter and the first prime minister of India. He was the co-founder of the Non aligned movement, propagator of the Buddhist Panchsheel principles for peace. He wrote the *Discovery of India*.

Shah Bano—a Muslim divorced woman from Indore, who after more than three decades of divorce demanded maintenance from her husband, which was granted to her by the lower court and the high court. Her husband appealed in the Supreme Court on the plea that the Muslim Law Shariat does not make any provision for alimony or maintenance. The apex court upheld the decision of the High court, leading to an uproar in the Muslim community. The decision of the Supreme Court was over-ruled by the Parliament.

Hussein—Grandson of Prophet Mohammad, he refused to compromise on the issue of inherited caliphhood, ruling that there should be a general vote to elect one. Yazid, the self proclaimed Caliph invited him over to the city Shaam for talks. Stopping him at Karbala, near the river, Yazid insisted that he vote in his favour or die. When Hussein refused to give in, Yazid had him and seventy-two male members of his family, among them a baby boy of six months, massacred in Karbala.

Yazid—Self proclaimed Caliph, he declared himself the Caliph after the death of his father Muaviya. He was the person responsible for the martyrdom of Hussein.

Shirin Farhad—a popular love tale of Arabia. Shirin, the girl and Farhad the boy belonged to two warring tribes. It has been adapted in a ballad form in both Hindi and Urdu and is performed in the

Nautanki folk style. It is extremely popular and sung on all occasions to show how war destroys true love.

Maulana Abul Kalam Azad—Freedom fighter and Minister in Nehru's first cabinet. One of the most secular leaders, he opposed the formation of Pakistan, maintaining that nations are not formed on the basis of religion. He gave the concept of cultural academies and the Indian Council for Cultural Relations. He is considered one of the founders of Modern Indian Culture.

Danial Latifi—Shah Bano's lawyer, veteran Leftist and trade union leader. He stood by Shah Bano till the end.

Mohammad Iqbal—popular Urdu poet, a nationalist in his early years, he was amongst the first in the Muslims to conceptualize the 'Two Nation Theory' that led to the partition of India.